Diary of a
South Beach
PARTY GIRL

Diary of a South Beach

PARTY GIRL

A NOVEL

GWEN COOPER

S|S|E

SIMON SPOTLIGHT ENTERTAINMENT
New York London Toronto Sydney

SSE

SIMON SPOTLIGHT ENTERTAINMENT

An imprint of Simon & Schuster

1230 Avenue of the Americas, New York, New York 10020

Copyright © 2007 by Gwen Cooper

All rights reserved, including the right of reproduction in whole or in part in any form.

SIMON SPOTLIGHT ENTERTAINMENT and related logo are trademarks of Simon & Schuster, Inc.

Designed by Yaffa Jaskoll

Manufactured in the United States of America

10 9 8 7 6 5 4 3 2

Library of Congress Cataloging-in-Publication Data

Cooper, Gwen.

Diary of a South Beach party girl : a novel / Gwen Cooper. — 1st ed.

p.   cm.

ISBN-13: 978-1-4169-4089-0

ISBN-10: 1-4169-4089-8

1. Miami Beach (Fla.)—Fiction. I. Title

PS3603.O58263D53 2007

813'.6—dc22

2006026460

AUTHOR'S NOTE

This is a work of fiction. The characters, conversations, and events in the novel are the products of my imagination, and no resemblance to the actual conduct of real-life persons, or to actual events, is intended. Although, for the sake of verisimilitude, certain real people do make incidental appearances or are briefly referred to in the novel; their interactions with the characters I have invented are wholly my creation and are not intended to be understood as descriptions of real or actual events, or to reflect in any way upon the actual conduct or character of these real people.

To my parents, Barbara and David, and my sister, Dawn, with inexpressible pride and gratitude.

To Laurence Lerman—it is miraculous to me every day of my life that the greatest man I've ever known loves me too.

And, in loving memory, to my grandfather David Berkowitz and my grandmother Claire Moskowitz Berkowitz, one in a long line of women in our family who never lost their "witz."

Here's how you make a vicious circle: You take any plain circle and caress it until it shows its vices.

—Eugene Ionesco

PROLOGUE
South Beach: A Sunny Town for Shady People

There used to be a joke about the typical table setting at a South Beach dinner party: fork for the tongue, spoon for the nose, knife for the back.

Sounding jaded is, of course, the main business of life when you're living in a town known the world over for its sheer, over-the-top debauchery. But for those of us who were the true locals—not the celebrities, trust-funders, and royals who came to party with us, but the ones who made the party worth coming to—world-weariness was more than an obligatory show we put on for the press and for each other. It was our right.

The truth is, most of us couldn't believe our gee-whiz good luck at ending up in a place like South Beach. We'd crawled out of banal suburbs and listless small towns where we'd always been considered too *something*—too funny, too flashy, too pretty, too gay, too imaginative, or simply too loud. Our mothers didn't approve of us. Social pundits reviled us. But deep down, we knew that everybody wanted to be us—secretly wanting to club-hop till daylight, air-kiss in the VIP lounge, or walk down a red carpet with flashbulbs popping at least once in their workaday lives. So getting to sound blasé and over it all? That was a privilege, by God, that we'd earned.

Not that there wasn't any truth behind the table-setting witticism. In South Beach there was a lot of double-talking and a lot of ambition. A lot of intrigue—both sexual and political. More blatant social climbing than you could find in a Jane Austen novel. And, naturally, a lot of drugs.

It was kind of a crazy place for a nice Jewish girl from the suburbs like me to find herself. At the age of twenty-five, having just ended a four-year relationship with a stable professional-type guy, I moved out of my boyfriend's house in the burbs and into my friend Amy's house on the Beach. Amy was a demimonde jet-setter of uncertain origins—someone who lived everywhere and nowhere, and whose finances were as mysterious as her moods. Her mother was a Brazilian fashion model and her father hadn't been heard from in at least a decade, and Amy—with the twice-blessed inheritance of Mom's jaw-dropping good looks and Dad's irresponsibility—had settled into a ramshackle two-bedroom guest cottage on one of the older estates on Pine Tree Drive.

I couldn't have known then what I was getting myself into. The life of a straight girl living and dating on South Beach was like nothing I've ever experienced before or since. No place else can you find yourself flying on a billionaire's private jet one day and driving your boyfriend to a crack house the next—all while maintaining a nine-to-five job. In fact, just getting through the typical day-to-day (or, more accurately, night-to-night) was a challenge that often required a crack team of specialists and more than a little pharmaceutically induced courage. But to understand the life I lived—or the seemingly insane decisions that a relatively normal girl like me ended up making—you'd have to understand what South Beach was like at the time. And what a time it was. . . .

When I was younger, my father would always point to the downtown Miami skyline as we drove past and say, "There it is: the city that cocaine built." This was in the '80s, the days of *Scarface*, *Miami Vice*, and the "cocaine cowboys." Miami wasn't the glamour-set hot spot it had once been, but television and movies were reminding the general population of our beaches-and-corruption brand of éclat. You could fire a gun down Ocean Drive and not hit anyone. I attended high school in North Miami Beach and graduated without so much as hearing the phrase "South Beach." Coconut Grove was where the party was, where my friends and I sneaked out on Saturday nights hoping to talk susceptible bartenders into looking the other way.

While I was away at college, the southern edge of Miami Beach was being rediscovered. Calvin Klein shot one of his famous Obsession campaigns on the Beach, using only locals as models. Gianni Versace built an extravagant, opium dream of a mansion on Ocean Drive. A prescient slickster by the name of John Hood promoted a club night called Fat Black Pussycat, transforming the once-quiet streets into a carnival of the gorgeous and bizarre. Madonna and entourage were spotted at various inner sanctums. Artists, fashion designers, and gay men headed north from Coconut Grove and east from the mainland to populate the Beach's aging Art Deco apartments and shops.

Following in their wake came the everybody-else who would make up the mélange I embraced as family: bikers and bankers; drag queens and club kids; actors and models; publicists, waiters, and real-estate moguls; socialites and suburbanites desperate for a good time and some identity reinvention; and a somewhat more dubious crowd who were there simply because they'd had to leave someplace else and wanted to needle in a sunny haystack for a while. Celebrities came out to spend under-the-radar time with the newly beautiful crowd. Jerry Powers and Jason Binn launched *Ocean Drive* magazine. A club scene emerged, different from the gore-and-whore excess that had marked the peak of New York nightlife decadence, but directly descended from it by virtue of its refugees who came to heal themselves in the balmy climes of the South.

To a native like me—who left for college when the Beach was a wasteland and came back four years later to find it an official *scene*—it seemed to happen overnight.

When you grow up living in Miami, your sense of distance tends to be skewed. You're closer to Cuba, at a mere 228 miles, than you are to your state capital of Tallahassee. You're apt to feel you have more in common with people in L.A. than with those in Orlando and Jacksonville. South America is your spiritual cousin in ways that Tampa will never be. And while the drive over the causeway separating the Beach from the mainland may have only been about fifteen minutes, the two places had a physical and social landscape so different from each other as to be virtually unknowable to their respective residents. You could visit and spend your time and think you had a fix on it, only to discover that there was an entire life to the place as closed off to you as the Forbidden City.

Some of the differences were so obvious, they were almost unnoticeable. Miami, like L.A., is a huge system of highways and boulevards, where everybody drives everywhere. But South Beach, like Monaco, was small in area and short of parking, and people walked or took cabs at least as often as they drove. In fact, it was possible to live and work on South Beach and not have a car at all. The pedestrian-friendly lifestyle felt more cosmopolitan—and more like a real community—than the mainland. It was certainly much more insular. And while the rest of South Florida was a sunny suburban sprawl dominated by air-conditioned malls, office parks, and chain restaurants, those landmarks were nonexistent on South Beach in the earlier days. That's all changed, of course, but where Lincoln Road (South Beach's Art Deco/Mediterranean Revival pedestrian mall) now features Pottery Barn, Victoria's Secret, and a Regal Cinemas multiplex, it used to be home for local artists, drag bars, and illegal after-hours clubs hidden behind opaquely windowed storefronts.

I've heard a lot about the alleged snobbery of South Beach: its blatant caste systems, its pitiless doormen, its shallow obsession with fame and wealth and beauty. But when I think back now on the years I lived there, it's the feeling of acceptance that I always come back to—because South Beach was absolutely the most accepting community I've ever lived in. There were a few simple rules—most of them tacit—that you had to live by, but if you did, the island was yours. You were invited to all the parties, guest-listed at all the doors, and you could even get your picture in all the local papers and magazines. You could live like a millionaire, *with* millionaires, and never pay a cent for anything.

And people would love you. For all of the posing and preening that life on the Beach encompassed, we all genuinely loved each other, the Beach, and ourselves for being there—possibly in that order (wait . . . strike that, reverse it). The defining question that separated the ins from the outs in the South Beach world wasn't, *Who do you know? What do you do?* or even, *How much do you have?* The one important question—the question that nobody would ever come out and ask, but the only question that ultimately mattered—was, *Are you, or are you not, one of us?*

The most important part of being one of us—or "people like us," as we liked to put it—was being completely nonjudgmental. The cardinal rule of the social scene was never to judge anybody for their personal choices: not what drugs they did, or the bathhouses they frequented, or which or how many people they slept with; nothing that could fall under the ambiguous umbrella of "lifestyle."

You were free, if not encouraged, to judge people for things like lackluster fashion choices (anathema in a body-conscious party town) or any appearance of mainstream conformity (which we avoided as if a single instance might turn us into pillars of salt). Gossiping about each other's nighttime pursuits was the activity of choice for whiling away those pesky daylight hours. But nobody was ever looked down on and nobody ever printed anything negative about what we did. South Beach operated in much the same way as the old Hollywood studio system, except our studio made parties instead of movies. The glamour of the constant party was our business, and protecting our homegrown stars from their own excess was our mutual responsibility. Private lives were kept private as long as everything looked good for the cameras. The press, police, and local politicians knew not to go looking for too much trouble and so, for a long time, they almost never found any. We encouraged each other to be as outrageous as our imaginations could conceive, and helped each other bury any real damage the outrage caused. Otherwise, we wouldn't be able to live the way that we did—and it was the lifestyle that mattered most.

It goes without saying that an environment like that can pull the magnet right out of your moral compass. For years, I lived a sort of double life where I spent my days building a career and my nights building a reputation. I was a working girl who wore business attire every day and a femme fatale who wore gowns and boas every night, and it's only now, with the 20/20 of hindsight, that I can see the contradiction—or the inevitable expiration date that comes stamped on all such packages. When the in-crowd is that seductive, and all you have to do to be one of them is be willing to do anything at all, you stop asking yourself things like, *Is this right?* and start asking yourself things like, *How much will this hurt tomorrow?* That is, until you stop asking in the first place.

Not that I thought about things in such clear terms back then. I was too busy discovering the joys of cocaine and men with sketchy backgrounds (the one inevitably leading to the other) to think about much of anything. But the important thing to remember is that it wasn't all real and it wasn't all fake. My transformation from good girl to party diva happened in one night and it took years to happen, and never really happened in the first place. One step takes you over the edge, but the fall . . . the fall you could write a book about. . . .

Diary of a South Beach

PARTY GIRL

BOOK 1

February 1997–January 1998

ONE

I first met Amy Saragosi during what I now refer to as my *Bell Jar* phase. That is, for roughly twenty-five years I'd been busily fulfilling my destiny as achiever of good grades, winner of awards, and attainer of a respectable, middle-class lifestyle. I was closing in fast on the brass ring and I was exhausted.

Growing up in an upper-middle-class Miami suburb, I had been raised to expect everything and nothing. Everything in the sense that I would have—as a matter of course—a good education, a successful career, an equally successful husband, the exact right number of children, a big house with the requisite Florida swimming pool, and a healthy retirement fund. Nothing in the sense that there were no other acceptable options for me to pursue.

Overachievement was the philosophy I'd been bred into, and it was a philosophy I'd taken to heart. A volunteer and part-time political activist since my high school days, I'd selected a career in nonprofit administration because it seemed like the best way to do good (something that mattered a lot to me) while earning a name for myself in Miami's professional/political community (something that mattered just as much). I'd worked my way up through the ranks, assisted in part by active memberships in groups like the Greater Miami Chamber of Commerce, Leadership Miami, the United Way of Miami-Dade's Young Leaders, and the Hannah Kahn Poetry Foundation. I even had a picture-perfect, up-and-coming Cuban boyfriend of nearly four years to whom, as was assumed by everybody—myself included—I would get engaged any second now. We had settled into a snug "starter" house on the outskirts of Coral Gables—a neighborhood so old-money placid it could've been underwritten by Valium—and everything was falling neatly into its designated place.

More and more, though, I'd begun feeling as if I didn't have one more promotion, Chamber of Commerce award, or evening of being charming to my fiancé-to-be's high school friends left in me. I don't remember exactly when or why the persistent feeling of boredom I'd been living with for months became simply a dull emptiness. I just know that, eventually, I took to overeating, spontaneous crying jags, and an utterly prosaic sexual affair with a coworker. We'd drive to the cheap motels along Calle Ocho, patronized by prostitutes and porn addicts, where twenty-one dollars got you a room for two hours, free condoms, and no questions asked.

Every day I was being hollowed out bit by bit. I knew, somehow, that it was only a matter of time before the whole structure collapsed on itself and exposed me to everyone as a fraud who'd never been as bright or well-adjusted as she'd led them to believe. Most of my waking energy was spent in giving careful attention to the integrity of the facade, so that the failure lurking beneath the surface of the success-story-to-be would never see the light of day. I was tired all the time, taking lengthy naps after work that still didn't keep me from falling asleep most nights before ten o'clock.

Those of you who've ever taken Psych 101 or watched *Oprah* are probably saying to yourselves, *Ah! She was depressed! Burnout . . . fear of failure . . . fear of success . . . classic case, really.* And you're at least partially right. But, for me, it wasn't as abstract as all that. I wasn't self-destructive or suffering from a generalized fear of success.

I was afraid of succeeding because I was pretty sure that I hated every-thing I was supposed to succeed at.

An inveterate bookworm from as far back as I could remember, my imagination was always full of alternative lives I could be living in Paris among poets, or in L.A. among movie moguls, or in South American jungles among revolutionaries. I'd fantasize about tragic relationships with artistic men, or sophisticated parties where conversations had gleefully sharp edges. I wanted those things so badly, sometimes my very teeth hurt from the wanting. It was the business of attaining them that was beyond the power of my imagination.

Because I'd always read a lot, I'd always gotten good grades and succeeded at work-related projects without trying particularly hard. But I had no idea how to make my life more exciting within the rigid confines of the suburban straight-and-narrow—or how to step out of the straight-and-narrow altogether. I'd always known how to achieve things, but I didn't know how to *do* things. By default, I'd ended up doing what everybody else expected me to do and feeling, at the ripe old age of twenty-five, like life was passing me by.

So, when I thought about my life, I pictured it as a riderless horse galloping at full-pace in a straight line, dragging me along behind it with one foot trapped in the stirrup toward a bland, colorless future.

In the midst of this, Amy dropped into my life like the moment of Revelation that all true believers wait for.

I was working for the Miami-Dade affiliate of Unified Charities of America, running their direct service volunteer program. Amy was doing freelance translation work of some kind for one of the big downtown law firms that had offices in the same building. We were two of a handful of smokers at a time when cigarettes were becoming the catch-all bogeyman of the politically correct set and we constantly ran into each other downstairs, cigarettes in hand. We began to know each other by sight, then began to talk, and quickly became friends.

Like most hard-core book nerds, I'd always secretly suspected that I was much cooler than people gave me credit for. Amy's singling me out for friendship seemed like independent proof. It wasn't just that she was one of the most beautiful women I'd ever seen, with dark red hair, enormous Brazilian-brown eyes, and the kind of perfect body you were supposed to have but probably didn't. But—at my own age of twenty-five—Amy already had the irreverent, fuck-'em-all self-confidence that only comes one of two ways: staggering good looks or years of hard living.

Amy had them both in spades.

When two women who hardly know each other decide to become best friends, a lengthy period of exposition usually ensues. It's almost like the first few months with a new lover—you want to tell each other all your stories and hear all theirs: where and how you grew up, what your family was like, the men you've loved, the things you've done.

Amy's stories were well worth the price of admission, although you never really knew how much was true and how much had been exaggerated for the sake of good storytelling. I believed every word she said as if it were gospel truth, mostly because I absolutely wanted to believe it all, but the timelines got a little wobbly around the edges if you looked at them too closely.

As near as I could piece together, Amy was a Brazilian native whose father had eventually fled back to his homeland of Turkey. Amy's mother had gone after him with the questionable intention of dragging him back, and a fourteen-year-old Amy had ended up in Manhattan, sharing a SoHo apartment with a nineteen-year-old model. By seventeen, Amy was a full-fledged drug addict, working as a stripper to support her habit. In and out of rehab by eighteen, she'd pursued degrees in linguistics and anthropology through various universities in Berlin, Paris, and Seattle. She'd been engaged in Paris to a famous-in-art-circles sculptor, and in Seattle to a small-time real-estate magnate who was, allegedly, stump-stupid but obscenely gorgeous. Now single, Amy had settled in South Beach so she could be closer to her brother, who also lived on the Beach. She traveled extensively when she wasn't working, killing time overseas with artist friends and shadowy million-aires, and celebrities from Bob Dylan and Courtney Love to Michael Douglas and Brad Pitt. She'd even once been an invited guest to a party at Madonna's home.

I was never to know where Amy got the money for these trips, as I was also never to know how she paid for her reckless shopping binges or the bursts of extravagance she would sometimes treat us both to. That she couldn't finance her lifestyle through her freelance work was almost certain. I suspected that she might still be in touch with her parents and that they sent her money, but the one time I'd asked about them, Amy had answered with a curt, "I haven't heard from either of my parents in years."

I told my own stories in turn. Not that they were much in comparison with Amy's—suddenly, my hijinks at out-of-town high school debate tournaments or college fraternity parties seemed like the most humdrum forms of naughtiness. The daughter of a lawyer and a medical office manager, my family dynamic was nowhere near as complex as Amy's—which is not to say that my family and I were close. I knew without question that my parents loved me, but there was always an undercurrent of discomfort—of unspoken tensions, or brawls waiting to erupt—that had kept us from forming the friendly-grownup interaction most of my friends had developed with their own parents post-college.

A childhood lived through books had made me the kid who'd always done well on standardized tests (sexy, right?), and I therefore went the way of the chess club when the smart kids and the cool kids inevitably separated in high school. I told Amy how my two favorite extracurricular activities had been writing and the debate team, and how teachers had assured me that both of these skills would take me far. I'd brought home a more or less constant stream of trophies and awards. Other parents had thought I'd probably be a "good influence" and encouraged their kids to hang out with me.

I'd majored in creative writing in college and spent four years eating, breathing, and sleeping poetry. I told Amy about Lara Jacobs, my best friend in the world dating back to our college days when we'd run wild through local bars and practiced the fine art of driving boys crazy. Under Lara's tutelage, I'd learned to embrace my inner extrovert and had, I felt, blossomed from high school brainiac into sociable, semi-sophisticated college heartbreaker. Amy actually reminded me of Lara—now living in California—who was also smart, beautiful, and unflinchingly confident, although her Scarsdale upbringing was a far cry from Amy's "little girl lost" years. It was with Lara that I'd smoked pot for the first time, the only drug I'd ever attempted, and it had made me feel pretty rebellious until I met Amy.

Amy and I were friends for many months before I first saw her with cocaine, and I think now it was a deliberate choice on her part—something she was holding back because she sensed (correctly) that I wouldn't be able to handle it yet. I remember asking her, gently and not wanting to sound judgmental, if maybe it wasn't a bad idea for her to use drugs. "You know," I said, "because of the whole rehab thing."

"Rehab doesn't get you off drugs," she told me matter-of-factly. "Rehab teaches you how to *manage* your drugs."

One thing about Amy: She had an undeniable gift for subtle irony.

It's true that I liked being around her for the world-wise witticisms and glimpses at a life of adventure and celebrity. Amy had a way of assuming you were listening to her not as an audience, but as an equal—somebody who was as much of an insider to that world as she was. You knew it wasn't true, but you believed it because she believed it and what, at the end of the dog day, was there that Amy didn't know?

But there was also a universe of sympathy buried beneath the been-there-seen-that facade. You could dredge up the ugliest secrets you'd never shared with anybody and feel that you'd only been holding back until you could finally offer them up to her, and be absolved without ever having been judged.

Soon we were taking all of our cigarette breaks together. She'd buzz me from her office, saying, "Let's go down for a smoke, and, hey, can you bring an extra cigarette for me? Oh wait, forget it, you smoke those Lights. I always feel like my fontanels are caving in trying to suck enough nicotine out of those things." I'd been accustomed to eating a takeout lunch at my desk over a pile of work, but now Amy and I were going out every day for proper, sit-down lunches. Occasionally she would even treat us to one of Downtown Miami's pricier lunch spots overlooking Biscayne Bay, where bankers and suspiciously cash-rich customs officials basked in sun-soaked opulence.

And back and forth the conversation would go, sometimes pausing but never ceasing, like a frenetic game of tetherball.

Looking back on it all, I think the most pivotal decision I ever made was when, in college, I decided to take up smoking. It seems like everywhere I look these days, somebody's trying to make me feel all sackcloth-and-ashes about this nasty little addiction, and I wish I could muster the appropriate remorse. But, if not for smoking, Amy and I would never have become friends. And becoming friends with Amy was one of those events that took my life in an entirely different direction, to the point that I can't imagine now where I would be or what my life would look like if it had never happened.

Not that the changes happened right away. I was, without a doubt, drawn to Amy and intrigued—although somewhat scared—by the South Beach lifestyle. But I was still firmly rooted in my Coral Gables existence, trying to find a way to dabble in Amy's life while maintaining the ground I already knew.

As you've undoubtedly guessed, a big part of that ground was my boyfriend, Eduard (his name at birth had been Eduardo, but he'd eventually dropped the *o*). I'd met him when I was twenty-two—ironically, at a fundraising party for an independent film held in a South Beach club named Van Dome.

Eduard was brilliant: He had a master's degree in comparative literature, spoke five languages fluently, and could do calculus in his head. His typical demeanor was one of quiet reserve, although he was given to rare bursts of temper and even rarer moments of sweet, unselfconscious goofiness that always went straight to my heart. Tall, slender, and fair-skinned, he spoke English without a trace of an accent. I was short and (ahem) buxom, with wavy-curly black hair, dark eyes, olive skin, and a far more outgoing disposition; people meeting us for the first time tended to think I was the "ethnic" one.

Eduard was a PhD candidate and adjunct professor of literature and film studies at the University of Miami. He was working on his doctoral thesis and writing a screenplay (film was a booming business among industry types eager to take advantage of Miami's year-round sunshine while abusing their expense accounts). Although he wasn't Jewish, he was so hyper-educated and success-bound that my parents eventually reconciled themselves. We dated for a while and, after a respectable period of time, moved in together.

It seemed as if I were right on track for the happily-ever-after goodness I'd prepped for my whole life. Eduard and I had discussed honeymoon options, picked out names for our children, and earnestly debated the merits of public versus private schools. Most of my own friends had moved to other cities after high school, so Eduard's friends had become my friends—although not without a certain amount of friction. Their wives and girlfriends were all very proper, respectful Cuban girls. I was most definitely not. After one too many political arguments (Miami's Cuban community is a tough place to be a left-leaning Democrat—especially if you're as opinionated as I was), I found myself known among Eduard's friends as *la brujita*. Literally translated, it means "the little witch." *La bruja* ("the witch") was a way in Spanish of referring to a particularly difficult or irksome woman—and while the "-ita" suffix was meant to indicate affection, I think Eduard's friends saw me as this mouthy interloper who they liked and all, but who they couldn't help wondering when they'd finally see the last of.

Eduard and I were aware of South Beach—as you really couldn't help being if you lived in South Florida—but were far from being part of the scene. Two or three times a year, we'd trek over the causeway and toss way too much money into parking, club entries, and drinks. For the most part, we were content to remain on the mainland, having regular dinners with his family and impromptu get-togethers at the homes of his friends to play dominoes.

As his thesis and his script both advanced, Eduard started spending countless hours in the library or his office on campus. For months at a time, he would work late nights and weekends, leaving before I got up in the morning and coming home after I'd already gone to bed. Given my lack of a social life outside of his, this inevitably meant more and more time alone in an empty house.

Although technically not a suburban wife yet, I tried filling my time in the ways lonely suburban wives do—with civic groups and volunteer activities. Plastering on my cheeriest smile, I helped raise money for battered women's shelters, spent time in soup kitchens, and started a literacy program at an elementary school in Little Haiti. And, after a couple of years, I fell into the aforementioned affair. An action-packed inner life coupled with entirely too much time by oneself is almost always a dangerous combination.

Eduard never found out about my extracurricular activities, but we did find ourselves fighting more frequently. The arguments would start over stupid things—a wet umbrella left on a hardwood floor, let's say—and work their way up to grand theatrics involving clenched fists, loud threats, and airborne appliances. I think we both knew the relationship was ultimately doomed, but we were also both people who loathed the idea of failing at anything. Besides, I knew I was supposed to marry somebody someday, and I couldn't imagine who I would ever marry if it wasn't Eduard.

And, for a long time, we truly did love each other. Sometimes I would look up at him washing dishes, or reading a book, or debating whether to wear his glasses or his contact lenses, and I'd think . . . well, nothing coherent, really. Just a feeling of wholeness, of contentment. I'd seem to hear a voice in my head saying, *Ah, yes . . . yes, yes, yes . . .*

Amy and Eduard tried to like each other at first, for my sake, but even I could tell their attempts smacked of insincerity—they were working at complete cross-purposes. Amy had just gone through a best-girlfriend breakup and was looking for a new partner in crime/sidekick to do the South Beach nightlife crawl with her. For his part, Eduard certainly didn't want me running around South Beach till all hours, especially in the company of somebody like Amy. "How come you're not spending as much time with that girl Tammy from your office?" Eduard asked one day, a world of unspoken disapproval inflected in his voice.

I didn't want to tell him that Tammy—a preppy, well-meaning Midwestern girl—had hated Amy practically on sight, and vice versa. I'd tried a three-way lunch once and the experience had been so profoundly uncomfortable, I'd found myself nostalgic for the time my high school boyfriend's mother caught us in her bed. Tammy had let me know—not with an outright demand, but in the subtle, social language universally understood by women—that a choice needed to be made, and there really was no choice.

"Tammy's okay," I replied, "but all we really have in common is bitching about how her husband and my boyfriend are never around."

That ended the discussion.

Amy and I progressed from workday lunches to leisure-time excursions. She invited me to her house a few times, which was filled with exotic carved wood and stone pieces that were an equal mix of Far Eastern and Native American. She would prepare mysterious meals with recipes she'd learned in Tibet or Peru. I went shopping with her once but shied away from future shopping expeditions after she tried repeatedly to talk me into clothes that were tight, low-cut, or otherwise attention-drawing. My own taste leaned toward the neutral and loose-fitting, and I was always careful to cover up my chest as much as possible.

"Come on! You have such a great little body—let people see it," Amy said.

"No, *you* have a great body," I corrected her. "You're just in serious denial about mine because we're friends."

In my best attention-deflecting attire, I started following Amy through South Beach's clubs and dive bars. I'd usually abandon her sometime around eleven o'clock to make sure that I was home and in bed by eleven thirty. Amy invariably stayed out and partied far into the night, taking pains each time to let me know that absolutely *nothing* worth drinking for ever happened before midnight.

One of Amy's friends was a club promoter named Mykel, who had a Thursday night party at a South Beach club called Liquid. The opening of Liquid had been attended by such luminaries as Madonna, Naomi Campbell, and Calvin Klein. Robert De Niro was said to be a regular. It was the kind of place I'd never even contemplated having the nerve to try to enter on my own.

Mykel's party at Liquid was called Back Door Bamby, and it became a regular stop for us. This might sound insanely naive now, but it was news to me that clubs had weekly parties with names, thrown by people called "promoters" whose job it was to keep the party semi-private yet filled to capacity with the right crowd. I had thought that clubs simply opened their doors at night, set up a velvet rope and a cash box, and waited for the people to come.

Back Door Bamby was my first experience with what I came to realize was the *real* South Beach, and I started to understand the differences between visiting occasionally and spending time as a "local." Amy and I would bypass the velvet ropes without a thought of cracking our wallets for the cover charge. We'd stand at the bar with our comped drinks—sometimes with a small crew of Amy's friends and sometimes with Mykel, when he wasn't attending to party-related business. I'd crane my neck to see everything, absorbed in the ruthlessly chic decor and the quasi-porn images of women in various states of bondage, which were projected in flickering rotation on one of the walls. Occasionally, I would be alone at the bar while Amy hit the VIP section for a quick bump of her nose candy du jour or danced with any number of men and women both— never the best dancer on the floor, but always the least inhibited.

The Beautiful People were everywhere, a dazzling visual confection of flesh and glitter, churning constantly like a human testament to perpetual motion. I didn't—couldn't—fully comprehend it yet, but I felt an intense craving to let go and join them—and a smaller, quieter fear that it might never happen.

One evening, Amy invited Eduard and me to join her for dinner with her brother Marcio and his wife. We met them at Nemo's, a restaurant at the southern tip of South Beach. It was a great night for me, one that made me feel as if our friendship was truly becoming solidified. I was, after all, meeting what constituted Amy's family—a major step forward in any relationship.

Afterward, Amy made a point of telling me how much they'd liked me, making an equal point of letting me know they hadn't cared for Eduard. "They thought he was a little . . . supercilious," she said.

I knew what she was actually trying to tell me. Amy and Eduard were more or less undeclared enemies at this point, and Amy had chosen to read Eduard's natural reserve as an air of superiority—a superiority, she implied, that was wholly out of line in the presence of someone like Amy, who'd spent so much time among the wealthy and famous. *What will your life be like*, she seemed to be asking, *saddled with a man who offends others so easily?*

"He's not," I told her, not sure which one of us I was trying to convince with my denial. "He's really, really not. He's just quiet with people he doesn't know very well."

She left for Greece the next morning, going off to spend a couple of weeks on a friend's yacht. Amy traveled frequently, and I'd come to hate the time she spent out of town, to feel that her presence was the only thing making my life bearable from day to day.

I don't remember anymore what started the fight that became The Fight—the one that broke Eduard and me up. It was a hot Sunday afternoon in early June, and we'd just driven back from our usual Sunday lunch with his parents. We started quibbling about this and that, and then—in what was now predictable fashion for us—the quibbling escalated to fighting, then screaming. Eventually, I slammed out of the house and took off in my car, driving no place in particular, alternating between raw, painful sobs and pure, blind rage.

It was hours before I finally came back home. It was night already, and I realized I'd been driving around in the dark without even turning my headlights on. I walked into the house and sat down heavily on the couch, and Eduard came in and sat down next to me. He took my hand in his and we sat like that, side by side without looking at each other, for a long, long time.

I finally cleared my throat, and Eduard turned toward me. I'm not sure if he was looking at my face or if, like me, his head was turned down and away, unable to do what we both knew needed to be done if we looked at each other directly.

"I don't think I'm in love with you anymore," he said. Each word came slowly, the pauses between them painful and deliberate. "I don't think we're in love with each other anymore."

I opened my mouth to say something, to fight for this man—this relationship—that was supposed to be my forever. Instead, I heard myself quietly saying, "Okay." I brought my eyes up, looking him full in the face this time, and said it again. "Okay."

Neither of us was the type who cried easily or often; that night, though, Eduard and I held each other and cried for what seemed like hours. I kept thinking about my best friend growing up, Lisa Lauer, who'd moved away in the seventh grade. We'd planned how we would stay in touch and talk all the time and still be each other's best friends. And yet, the day the moving van pulled up, we'd cried and cried, knowing with complete finality that we would never be best friends—would probably never even see each other—again.

Finally I stood up, and Eduard offered to sleep on the couch that night. "That's okay." I attempted a smile. "I'll take the couch. I'm a lot shorter than you are, anyway."

The next day was one of the worst of my life, because it was the day when I knew how much worse things would feel before they started to feel better. I called in sick to work and pulled out the paper to look at apartment listings. The house was Eduard's; I'd made a few small financial contributions, but, on my nonprofit salary, they were nominal at best. Eduard had discreetly left first thing in the morning, and I spent most of the day alone, trying to figure out what I was going to do.

Amy called that night from Greece, and I shakily told her what had happened. "You have to move to South Beach," she said immediately, sounding like a little girl who'd just gotten exactly what she wanted for Christmas. I couldn't help but smile and mentally bless her as she added, "I would be *so happy* if you lived on the Beach!"

When a man you've spent four years with has just told you he doesn't love you anymore, nothing feels better than hearing how much somebody else *does* want you around. For a second I pictured how much fun it could be, living on South Beach and hanging out with Amy all the time.

Then I remembered my situation. South Beach was definitely too expensive for the likes of me.

"I don't think I can afford it," I told her. "And I don't even have enough time to save up for it. Eduard is being cool and everything, but I really need to be out of here as soon as possible."

"Get your stuff and come to my place," she said. "I'll call Miguel right now and tell him to give you my keys." Miguel was a friend who took care of things at Amy's house when she was out of town. "You can stay in the extra bedroom."

"Thanks." I tried not to break down for the umpteenth time that day. "I don't know what I'd be doing right now if it weren't for you."

"Stop it," Amy said. "Anyway, you know how much I hate living alone. Just go there and stock up on food—we'll figure it out when I get back at the end of the week."

And that's what I did.

TWO

July nights in Miami are a grab bag of humidity-induced misery—producing heat-swollen fingers, wildly frizzy hair, and a general damp stickiness that can make your own skin feel like a dirty garment you'd love to pull off. But there are usually one or two nights in the month that are temperate and gentle instead of sweltering and oppressive. Clusters of people materialize out of doors and seem to hold their breath expectantly, like a theater audience in the moments just before the curtain goes up.

It was on such a night that I landed in a club called Spin, a guest at their closing party. It was said that the owner had lost a large inheritance on the venture, and was hoping to avoid homelessness by inviting his two hundred nearest-and-dearest and charging five dollars apiece for admission. It seemed like an agreeably low-key way for me to make my first official appearance on the scene since I'd moved in with Amy.

Although I'd been living on South Beach for almost a month, I'd shied away from anything more adventurous than having a few people over to the house or throwing on jeans and nursing a glass of vodka at one of the local dives. Amy assumed my reluctance to go out was the result of post-breakup emotional fallout, and she was partly right. Just that morning, in fact, I'd gone over to Eduard's to pick up the rest of my things—mostly the remnants of an enormous book collection that I'd put off moving until the very last minute. Eduard and I had talked in a friendly, restrained way. I was fine until I got back to Amy's house, at which point I'd broken down completely. "It's over," I'd sobbed as Amy hugged me. "It's really over."

My boxed-up possessions, removed from the home they'd been pain-stakingly culled to complement, looked naked and sad in Amy's sparse extra bedroom; I'd had a profound feeling of my own sudden rootlessness. I'd gone from having a secure place in the world to being, I told myself somewhat theatrically, a stranger in a strange land. South Beach seemed far more socially carnivorous than the "young professionals" mixers I customarily attended. From what I'd read, it seemed as though you needed at least one of three things to get by on the Beach: money, connections, or model good looks. Being zero for three, I could feel myself reverting to the chubby, bookwormy tenth-grader I'd been before puberty and self-confidence had set in.

But Amy had stood in my room that day and announced portentously that enough was enough: There was a party that night and we were going.

The dress code for the evening, as she informed me, was "casual chic." I didn't know exactly what that was, but I was almost positive it didn't live in my closet. Amy solved the problem by digging around in her own copious closet and coming out with a dress she claimed would be perfect for me.

I took one look at the short black number with its plunging neck and spaghetti straps and said, "I can't wear that."

"Why not? This'll look great on you."

"Well, for starters, I won't be able to wear a bra with it."

Amy looked at me as if I were a little slow of learning. "So . . . don't wear a bra."

"But, um . . ." I felt like she had told me to spontaneously grow ten inches, or some other obvious physical impossibility. "My boobs are kind of big. I can't *not* wear a bra."

"It's because your boobs are big that you should *never* wear a bra at night," Amy said briskly. She burrowed through her shoe collection and pulled out a pair of black, five-inch platform stilettos.

"Okay, but I still don't have the body for a dress like that. I need to be able to, you know, do something to hide my problem areas."

"What problem areas?"

"Pretty much the whole area between my neck and my calves."

Amy was exasperated. "Would you please just trust me?" She stood me in front of the mirror. "Look at yourself. Your waist is tiny, your boobs are huge, and you have no cellulite on your thighs. I'm telling you, you have a *great* body."

I'd always thought of myself as the kind of girl who could've been really pretty if only she'd lay off the Entenmann's chocolate-frosted donuts, so it was hard for me to see what Amy saw. Nevertheless, when eleven o'clock rolled around I fixed my hair, applied light makeup, and dutifully climbed into the dress she'd picked out. I didn't have a full-length mirror, so I headed into Amy's room, announcing myself by saying, "Okay. Get ready to laugh your ass off."

Amy was putting the finishing touches on her own ensemble: black leather pants and a red-and-black bustier with an embroidered silver snake that twisted its way up the front, which was left over from a snake-themed party she'd thrown a few months earlier. In lieu of jewelry, she'd lightly dusted silver body glitter over her chest and shoulders. She looked coolly naughty and typically stunning. "I'm having issues with my mascara wand," she said in irritation as I entered. Then she looked up and her face broke into a huge smile. "Wow," she said. "I told you!"

I looked in the mirror but couldn't quite believe what I saw. I looked the way I sometimes did in my daydreams—the kind of daydreams where I was a much sexier version of me, with a better body and wardrobe than I'd ever get to have in real life. Looking at myself now in Amy's dress, I realized that wearing baggy clothes had created the illusion that I was about twenty pounds heavier than my actual weight. Amy had been right. The scooped neck of the dress gave me honest-to-God cleavage, in proportion to which my waist did look small. My legs beneath the short skirt of the dress were lean, and, in combination with Amy's sky-high heels, I looked almost leggy—something I'd given up all hope of attaining the day I'd realized I would never grow past five foot two. I had a sudden, ridiculous urge to touch the glass à la Natalie Wood in *Gypsy* and exclaim, "Mama! I'm a pretty girl!"

Amy crossed the room to her jewelry chest and pulled out an enormous collar necklace made from turquoise, garnets, and silver, like something Cleopatra might have worn (although in fact it was, as Amy informed me, a "Nepalese ceremonial piece"). It must have weighed at least a pound. "With your coloring, you'll look totally exotic in this," she said. "But be careful with it; it's museum quality and I'm not going back to Kathmandu anytime soon." She looked at me thoughtfully. "Let's make your eye makeup a little more dramatic. And we need to find you a handbag."

Like a reverse Cinderella, I piled into a cab with Amy shortly after midnight. The air blowing through the open window tugged languidly at the hem of my dress. "Are you sure it's not too short?" I asked. "I feel like I'm operating on a very slim margin of error."

"Rachel, you're five inches shorter than I am. If it's not too short for me, it's definitely not too short for you." She rolled down her window and smiled at me. "You look great. We're going to have a great time."

The core of the party was in the garden behind the club. A DJ was stationed outside, spinning an eclectic mix of tunes ranging from '70s funk to disco, cocktail party standards, and a few pop hits from the '80s. It wasn't very crowded yet; small groups of people had gathered beneath unhealthy-looking trees or were poised self-consciously on the overturned cinderblocks strewn at irregular intervals throughout the unkempt grass. There was an odd contrast between the space—neglected, overgrown, slovenly—and the people inhabiting it, who were as glossy and restless as caged predators.

I noticed a slender Hispanic man in his early twenties, holding a rectangular parcel partially wrapped in brown paper. He was circulating through the garden like a waiter with a tray of hors d'oeuvres, politely offering guests portions of something from the package. As we got closer, I could see that it was a brick of cocaine. "Do you know him?" I asked Amy.

"That's Juan," she replied. "I *think* his name is Juan."

"Is it okay for him to be doing that out in the open?"

"It's a private party."

I watched Juan as he held a miniature silver spoon up to the noses of various partiers. No money seemed to be changing hands. "So is he just, like, giving it away for free?"

Amy shrugged. "It's a good place for him to find new business."

"Oh!" I said in my best "I get it" voice. "Like when they give you free samples of cheese at the grocery store." Amy looked at me with a vaguely horrified expression, and I tried to maintain a straight face as I added, "You know you have to put these things into a context I can understand."

Amy laughed and linked her arm through mine. "Let's find the bar. We're way too sober."

We'd taken only a couple of steps when we were accosted by Raja and Genghis, friends of Amy's who'd been spending significant time at her house during the past month. Having seen so much of them, I had tentatively come to consider them my own friends as well.

Genghis was a darkly handsome Greek portrait artist, notorious on the Beach for his charm, his philandering, and his occasional moments of devastating social cruelty. He was equally well known for his startling and heavily stylized paintings of women and drag queens, which hung in many of the hipper galleries all over town. He was gay, but overwhelmingly masculine—enough to make it sting a bit if you were a straight woman.

Raja was a sloe-eyed drag queen, originally from England, and a frequent subject of Genghis's paintings. She (because, as Amy put it, "even when he's not in drag, he's always a she to me") performed at Lucky Cheng's, a drag revue on Lincoln Road. Raja had a compact, graceful build and—unlike a lot of drag queens, who went screechingly over the top—her style was always delicate and incredibly feminine. Tonight, for example, she was wearing a simple, black-sequined cocktail dress that fell to just below her knees. Her voice was pleasantly pitched in an octave that could have been either male or female. Raja always enunciated each word clearly and carefully, making even her most simple declarations seem full of stagy significance. After five or six drinks, she would usually claim to be thirteenth in line to the British throne.

"*Darling*," she said to me. "You look *fabulous!*"

"Tell her how good she looks," Amy instructed. "She fought me on the dress every step of the way here."

"Oh my God, you look like Marilyn Monroe with those curves," Genghis said. "I had no idea you were hiding a body like that."

"That's because she usually looks like something out of *Frumpier Homes and Gardens*," Raja said. "But tonight she's a *goddess*. Here, wait a second." She reached down the front of my dress and adjusted my breasts slightly, lifting them up higher against the material.

I didn't want to show that this minor invasion of my personal space had made me uncomfortable, so I backed away slightly as I said, "Do I really look okay? I don't look like one of those deluded tourists with horrible thighs who wear the short-shorts anyway?"

"Sweetie, you look *hot*," Genghis said. He slid an arm around me and nuzzled my ear. "I think you're giving me straight issues."

It should be noted that Genghis loved to flirt with women as well as men, and would probably flirt with a brick wall if he had enough liquor in him. Still, I was pleased. "Really?" I said. "Because, you know, I haven't been with a man in a very long time. So what you're doing is like teasing a puppy in a pet store window— unless you're planning on taking me home with you, it's just kinda mean."

"Who says I'm not planning on taking you home with me?" He waggled his eyebrows suggestively and I had to laugh. "I'm never attracted to women, but I'm *very* attracted to *you* right now."

"So you're saying I look like a guy in this dress."

"I'm saying you look exactly the way a woman should look. You have to let me paint you someday." With a smile that turned a shade evil, he added, "I'd love to get you in just the necklace."

"Well, I'll tell you what I'm planning on telling every man who uses that line on me tonight: Buy me a drink and we'll talk."

I looked over to Amy and Raja, to see if they wanted to join us at the bar, but they had their attention focused on a muscle-bound guy at the other end of the garden. "He looks straight," Amy was saying.

"Straight to my bed, honey," Raja replied in a sly, conspiratorial way. And, with that, the two of them were off.

Genghis and I stayed at the bar for a while, jostled every so often by partiers angling for the magically reappearing lines of coke laid out on the bartop. It was fun being taken under his wing as he entertained me with gossipy stories and pseudo-flirtatious come-ons. I had a few drinks—two, maybe, or three. Genghis introduced me to people, mostly gay men, one hand resting possessively on my shoulder or the small of my back as he repeated his litany: *This is my friend Rachel. Isn't she beautiful?* And, one after another, the well-dressed, well-toned young men would murmur an admiring assent. *She's gorgeous*, they'd say. *Sexy. She has such great energy.*

I couldn't remember ever having received so much positive attention at one time. Maybe it shouldn't have meant that much coming from gay men, but, in a way, it almost seemed more genuine than the compliments I'd received at bars from straight men over the years. After all, it wasn't like any of these guys was hitting on me. In my partially inebriated mind, it seemed as though their compliments must be completely sincere, because what other agenda could they have?

I didn't know South Beach well enough yet to understand that beauty was as much about location as it was about physical attributes. To be in the right place and among the right people was to be presumed beautiful; as a point of pride, nobody on South Beach ever associated with anybody who was less than extraordinary.

Nevertheless, the combination of the flattery I wasn't used to and the alcohol I'd never had much tolerance for left me feeling warmer and more accepted than I ever had—more than I'd felt in the entire last year of my relationship with Eduard. I drunkenly decided that I belonged here in this place, among these people who made me feel so attractive and included. I started to believe I was the girl the people around me were describing—the dazzling party girl to whom this all came as naturally as it did to Amy.

Emboldened as I was, the next step in my progression seemed perfectly clear. So when I eventually lost Genghis to an aspiring model named Kevin, who he'd been eyeing for weeks, I went back outside to look for Amy, spotting her—as I'd hoped—standing with Juan.

That night wasn't the first time I'd seen cocaine up close and personal. Since I'd moved in with Amy, it seemed I was constantly around it one way or another. I'd witnessed the lines being chopped up on the coffee table and the frequent bathroom trips when we were out at bars, hands pressed together in clandestine fashion as small plastic bags found their way from person to person. I had witnessed without judging, but also without participating. I was, after all, the veteran volunteer of any number of outreach programs aimed at keeping drugs out of schools and off the streets.

At that moment, however, I was tired of weighing every decision I made as if it were some unbreakable link in a chain that was building toward the rest of my life. I was sick of being the socially conscious girl, the girl who always got good grades and could always be counted on to do the right thing. Suddenly, all I wanted was to be young and sexy and as cool as the people around me were—as Amy herself was. It occurred to me that I'd trawled through cheap motels behind Eduard's back at least as much for the illicit thrill of the thing as for the male attention that was supposed to compensate for my loneliness. I wanted to go further now. I wanted to see what it would be like to do something that was, unquestionably, *bad*.

I walked over to Amy. "Rachel, meet Juan," she said, as she lightly rubbed her nose.

Juan smiled and inclined his head at a friendly angle, holding his diminutive spoon close to my face.

"I think your friend's trying to nasally violate me," I said to Amy.

Amy laughed. "He's just offering you a bump."

"Well, in that case . . ." I raised an eyebrow mischievously and reached around to pull my hair back.

Amy's face registered the smallest glimmer of happy surprise, but she didn't say anything. Instead, she merely helped me to position one nostril over the spoon. I pressed the other nostril closed with my finger and inhaled in a noisy, theatrical way. It burned like hell and I winced visibly.

"Now do the other one." Amy seemed entertained by my discomfort. "And don't hold your other nostril shut this time—it actually makes it harder to get a good inhale."

The second bump burned as badly as the first one had, but I was prepared for it and didn't recoil quite so hard. I noticed a thick, bitter taste in the back of my throat. "How's it feel?" Amy asked.

"Fine," I said, surprised that it was true. "I don't think I feel any different."

I was used to drugs like alcohol or pot, where you feel a sort of progressive buzz that eventually culminates in an *Oh my God I'm so stoned* moment. Cocaine isn't like that. Cocaine just makes you . . . happy. It comes on you immediately like a flash of sheer exhilaration that you somehow feel isn't even related to the drug. You think to yourself that you simply didn't realize a minute ago how good you felt, how sexy and confident and how much you liked talking and laughing and dancing. You also feel deceptively in control—not as if the drug is taking away your inhibitions, but as if you're making a well-thought-out decision to let them go.

That's at first and if the stuff you've gotten is good. Later on can be a much different story, but *later on*, fortunately, is never *now*.

I found myself trying to expound upon this at great length to Amy, about how I didn't feel any different, really, although I *did* suddenly feel happier than I had at any point in the weeks since I'd broken up with Eduard and how I'd expected I didn't know what but some kind of a major difference or to feel out of control or not aware of what was happening around me and instead it was just this really really *good* feeling of being happy to be at the party and happy to be making friends and so happy I'd met Amy and did I mention that I totally appreciated her letting me borrow this dress that everybody agreed looked so great on me?

When I finally paused, Amy said, not unkindly, "Slow down, Chatty Cathy. And don't keep clenching your jaw like that—it'll make you look tweaky."

I realized that I'd been unconsciously shifting my jaw back and forth. "What's that about?"

"It just does that to you. You'll get used to it eventually and be able to control it better."

I was suddenly dying for a cigarette and pulled one from my bag. The first drag was another small moment of bliss. I exhaled and looked around, noting that the party had filled up considerably. One tall, lanky man in particular caught my attention; he was standing under a tree in the middle of a small group of people. In a party fully inhabited by the pretty and intriguing, he stood out as forcefully as if he'd been on a stage with a spotlight trained on him. Touching Amy lightly on the arm, I nodded in his direction. "Who's that guy?"

"What guy?" Amy followed my gaze, then subtly squared her shoulders and straightened her back in a way that made her seem two inches taller. "That's John Hood."

· · ·

I can't say that I'd never seen anybody like him before, because I had—anybody who'd seen Humphrey Bogart in *The Maltese Falcon* had seen somebody who looked like this guy. My guess put his age somewhere around thirty. His outfit was a cool noir gangster getup, straight off the Warner Bros. lot: a dark blue pinstriped suit, underneath which he wore a light blue shirt and a dark blue, red, and white tie. There was a neatly folded white handkerchief peeking from his breast pocket. On his head he wore a cream-colored fedora, underneath which his dark blond hair formed a widow's peak at his forehead.

His face wasn't conventionally good-looking, but it was compelling. It was a face constantly in motion; from moment to moment, his expression would change with such subtle fluidity that you didn't want to look away. His slightly crooked nose and lean, wiry build hinted slyly at criminal mischief and back-alley brawls. His manner was both casually elegant and studiously tough.

I watched him as he accepted a hit from Juan and talked with his companions. When he spoke, he could become intensely animated—swooping arms, large gestures, sudden giant steps backward. But when he was listening, his movements were small and controlled. Even the way he smoked his cigarette seemed like an homage to black-and-white mobster movies. His thumb and forefinger maintained a death-like grip on the filter, and, in between long drags, he would jab the smoke out impatiently—as if, now that he was done with it, he was annoyed to find it still hanging around.

"What's his story?" I asked Amy.

"How much do you want to know?"

"Just the basics, I guess."

When dealing with John Hood, even secondhand, nothing was ever basic. The first thing you should probably know is that "Hood" was not, in fact, his real last name. Nobody knew his real last name, or even knew of anybody who knew it. It was as if he'd sprung up fully formed one day, complete with a hardboiled persona and cartoon alias like an implausible story he was gonna stick to. Amy told me that not even the cops knew Hood's real name—this despite the fact that he allegedly had a rap sheet longer than *War and Peace*.

Like any place inventing a history for itself, South Beach already had its legends and tall tales and epic heroes. John Hood was one of them. He was the man behind Fat Black Pussycat, the famed Monday-night party at a club called Risk that was credited as one of the original prime movers of the SoBe scene. Even I had heard of Risk, a club co-owned by Chris Paciello—and allegedly financed by the Gambino crime family—that had burned down two years earlier under suspicious circumstances. It was at Fat Black where Chris had met Ingrid Casares; the two had gone on to open Liquid, and a nightlife empire was born. It was sort of like being at a party in Vegas and having somebody casually point out Bugsy Siegel to you. And even knowing what Bugsy Siegel was—thief, murderer, gangster—chances are you'd still want to meet the guy.

Hood may have been all or none of those things; nobody could say for sure. It was hard to pinpoint exactly what he was. His reputation as one of the local drug trade's more conspicuous consumers was already well cemented, and the stories of petty thefts and con jobs to support his habit were legion. And, in addition to being a drug devotee, lounge lizard, and former club doorman, Amy told me he'd written book and music reviews for places like *Spin*, *Paper*, the *Village Voice*, and even *Rolling Stone*. Hood had been educated at Yale, and the one thing nobody ever disputed was that he was one of the smartest guys you'd ever meet.

There were, on the other hand, rumors that he was a pimp—rumors spawned by his appearance on an edition of *The Geraldo Rivera Show* about "pimps with degrees, or something like that." Although, Amy assured me, it would be just like Hood to scam his way onto *Geraldo*—to pretend to be a pimp and make a quick buck off America's gullibility, while mocking what the rest of the country thought they knew about South Beach.

Either way, he'd unquestionably been connected with a bank robbery two years back, earning his photo (sans name, naturally) a temporary spot on the "Ten Most Wanted" list hanging in the Miami Beach post office. After this little escapade, he'd made a hasty departure for parts unknown. Some said he'd gone to New York, others to Havana. His photo having finally come down from the post office wall, Hood had recently returned to reclaim his spot in the South Beach pantheon and look for new projects to occupy his considerable talents.

"You should definitely meet him," Amy said as he looked up and spotted her. "He's really high-profile on the Beach."

Hood strolled over and the two of them embraced lightly, kissing each other on the cheek. "Hood, I want you to meet my new roommate. This is Rachel Baum."

"Hood, John Hood." His handshake was brief and emphatic. His voice had a smoky, whiskey-and-cigarettes quality, like someone who'd just come off a six-day bender. "Nice to meet you."

When I talk about Hood now, it's tempting to slip into the '40s gangster, B-movie parlance he always spoke in. His knowledge of all things pop and pulpy— movies, music, fiction—was vast and spanned the last forty or fifty years, and this sensibility found its way into his everyday speech. He told us about an after-hours club that had just opened ("These cats have a groovy new spot on Lincoln Road"); a book he was reading ("This dame's writing is like silk cuffs on battered fists"); and, after some prompting, gave us the thumbnail of his latest stint as a guest of the State of Florida ("I crocked a couple of Canadians with a blackjack after I found 'em holed up with a dame I was seeing").

"Dame"? I found myself thinking. *Who does this guy think he's kidding?* Although I had to admit that listening to him was great good fun. He never laughed out loud—he hardly even smiled—but there was laughter in his voice. It was as if everything he said was an in-joke, and he was covertly inviting you to be hip enough to get it.

The genius of it was that the comic-book dialogue made it difficult to take his rep as a thug seriously. It was as if he were playing a character, merely acting the part of the ne'er-do-well tough guy. Even the one crime I'd heard him cop to so far seemed almost chivalrous, after a fashion. Most women will tell you they don't want a boyfriend who'd pummel some guy they caught her with, but most of us are secretly prepared to forgive—and be flattered by—the boyfriends who do.

Raja soon pulled Amy into a conference with another drag queen. Left alone with Hood, I realized how far I was from the Chamber of Commerce parties I was used to, where people could be summed up as simply as, *This is Stan. He works for Merrill Lynch.*

We mostly talked about books at first. Or, rather, Hood mostly talked and

I mostly listened. The way Hood talked about books was obsessive almost to the point of being sexual, like a poet with a gift for describing his fetish. As a fellow book junkie, listening to him rant on the written word was like its own kind of drug—something pure and needle-sharp that mixed with the other chemicals already in my system, leaving me as close to giddy as I'd been in months. He talked to me about Hemingway and Borges and Jacques Derrida, and other writers I'd never heard of at the time, like Donald Goines and Iceberg Slim.

"If we're strictly talking fun with words," I finally jumped in, "my first love is Dorothy Parker. My personal favorite is, *Ducking for apples—change one letter and it's the story of my life.*"

Hood cocked an appreciative eye in my direction and pulled a heartfelt drag off his cigarette. "So you're a lit chick. Most people around here can't spell 'literature.'"

"That's okay. I just spent four years with a guy who never did anything but read and work—I'm thinking there's a whole world outside of books."

I hadn't meant to talk about Eduard, and the thought of him—a thought I'd been studiously avoiding—had me reaching into my bag for another cigarette, rooting around for a light. Hood reached into his pocket and, in one continuous and single-handed motion, produced a book of matches, bent the cover back and a single match forward, and struck it with his thumb against the sandpaper, holding the lit match in front of me. It was a gesture so quick, it seemed like a magic trick—I'd never seen anybody make the simple act of lighting a match look so cool.

And, as I caught myself in that schoolgirl-with-a-crush thought, I realized I might be getting into trouble.

"You can't blame the cat for wanting to keep you under wraps," Hood said. "If you were my chick, I'd probably lock you up somewhere and guard your door to stop anybody suspicious. Like anybody with lips. *Where are you going with those lips?* I'd say."

"So I take it you don't buy into the whole *if you love something, set it free* concept."

"I think 'love' is just another way of saying 'greed.' And greed is wanting to keep what you love all to yourself."

"Wow, that's . . . I was going to say 'deep,' but I think I'll have to go with 'frighteningly fucked up.'"

"Cheese and crackers!" Hood exclaimed, taking a giant step backward and clutching his hat with both hands in apparent horror. A few nearby partiers looked up from oversized martini glasses to see what the commotion was, smiling faintly at Hood's antics. "What kind of language is that from a dame like you?"

I couldn't help but laugh out loud at the thought that *I* might be shocking *him.* "You're supposed to be a *pimp* and you're giving me a hard time 'cause I said a bad word? You're telling me you never curse?"

"A bad man needn't have bad manners," Hood responded. "I never swear in front of a dame."

"Well feel free to let loose." I tried to match his tough-guy tone. "*I* swear like a sailor on shore leave and I have no intention of stopping now."

He looked at me disapprovingly. "It's a lazy way of making your point. People who curse a lot only do it because their vocabularies aren't as big as their ambitions."

"I don't know. Don't you sometimes feel, as a writer, that the expletive is the exact right word to use?"

"As a writer, I try to find the exact right word to use without resorting to tricks that any slack-jawed high school kid could master."

"What about something like the first line of Philip Larkin's 'This Be the Verse'?" I argued. "*They fuck you up, your mum and dad / They may not mean to, but they do.* I think 'fuck you up' has an impact that 'screw you up' would completely lack."

"Haven't read it," Hood said dismissively. "There hasn't been any poetry worth reading since the 1920s. Maybe even earlier. Nobody reads it anymore except the people who write it—it's completely irrelevant."

I was appalled. "How can you just dismiss an entire art form that way?"

"Because it has almost no redeeming value. All this no-reason-no-rhyme, 'let's talk about our feelings' stuff is the biggest undone deal ever to waste white space."

"I *write* poetry," I told him heatedly. "And all that 'no rhyme stuff' just means that, as an artist, you have to be even more self-disciplined because you don't have a set of rules telling you what to do."

"And is that what you are?" He seemed amused, almost mocking. "An artist?"

I was abruptly embarrassed at having been startled into an expression of genuine feeling, and my neck grew warm. "Don't ask me hard questions." I sighed, fluffing up my hair. "It's taking all of my brainpower right now just trying to look as good as everyone else here."

Hood's barbed eyes tripped over me with something like approval, but he didn't bite, choosing instead to light a fresh cigarette. I brought one out too, hoping to see a repeat performance of his match-lighting gimmick. I wasn't disappointed.

"Have you ever thought about quitting?" I asked him as I exhaled, not really meaning to imply that it was a good idea, but wanting to change the subject.

"Nah. Quitters never win and winners never quit."

I laughed again and he almost, almost, smiled. "Do you mind if I borrow that the next time somebody tells me I should quit?"

"Well it's true! I think in an era where everybody waxes tears-and-drama about 'commitment issues,' addicts are completely underappreciated. Being addicted to something takes real commitment."

"So, as long as we're talking about addiction and other taboo subjects," I ventured, "is it okay if I ask you a question?"

"Sure."

I hesitated, knowing that I probably shouldn't bring it up but unable to resist. "Are you *really* a pimp? Because—and I hope you won't take this the wrong way—but you don't talk the way I'd think somebody who was a pimp would talk."

"Is it *really* such an interesting subject?"

"Hey, I'm just trying to figure out if you're flirting with me or sizing up potential merchandise."

Hood's eyebrows went up. "Who says I'm flirting with you?"

I tilted my head to one side. "Isn't that what you were doing?"

"I've been accused of a lot of things, but never anything as middle-of-the-road mainstream as 'flirting.' I'd go so far as to say 'swingin' banter,' maybe, but—"

"You know what?" I casually stubbed out my cigarette and smiled. "Let's forget I brought it up."

Hood pulled his own cigarette from between his lips and threw it down into the dirt of the garden, grinding it beneath the toe of his shoe. Then he picked up my hand and held it with the palm facing up. He leaned in closer so that the brim of his hat grazed my forehead—close enough to kiss me, if he'd wanted to.

"Here's a village," he said, lightly touching a spot at the top of my palm. "And here's another village." He touched a spot farther down, closer to the base of my wrist. "And here," his finger gently traced a line down the center, "there's a river separating them. It's too deep to wade across and the current's too fast to swim or sail across and there's no bridge. So how do the people from one village get to the other?"

It's amazing the things your body knows before you do. Because I still hadn't made up my mind what to think about this alleged robber of banks and possible pimp, who loved books and hated poetry—but my body knew what I thought as soon as he touched me. I can't say that my knees went weak or my breathing became faster. But it was as if my hand was the only part of my body still connected to nerve endings, and I was hyper-aware of every ridge and crevice in the skin holding mine. I felt as if I could have visually identified his fingerprints just from the physical memory of what the tips of his fingers felt like.

"Hmmm . . ." I tried to think. "Airplanes? Helicopters?"

"Nope. No airplanes, no helicopters."

I concentrated, feeling somehow that it was very important to score well on this impromptu IQ test. I wasn't sure if he was trying to gauge my intelligence or the extent to which his touch could rattle me; either way, I was determined not to give an inch.

After a moment, Hood said, "Just say you don't know."

"Hey, give me a minute; I can get this."

"No, you won't."

"A little credit, please." I affected a slightly offended air as I pondered. "Is it one of those *they don't bury the survivors* kind of things?"

Now he was impatient. "Look, just say *I don't know*."

I rolled my eyes. "All right, fine. I don't know."

"I don't know either." He grinned like a man who'd gotten away with the entire cookie jar. "But it's been nice holding your hand."

With that, Hood lightly tipped his hat and walked away.

THREE

Genghis arrived at our house the day after the Spin party for the afternoon brunch Amy and I had fallen into the habit of throwing together on Sundays. We'd drive over to Epicure and pick up small tidbits of things like salads, pastas, cheeses, and various breads and cookies. Sometimes it would just be us; other times people would float in and out of the house throughout the day, bringing bottles of vodka and old movies like *Auntie Mame* and *Sunset Boulevard*.

That particular Sunday, we were already hosting Amy's brother Marcio and his wife, Maria. Despite Marcio's married-with-children status, we'd been questioning his sexuality ever since Amy's Oscar-night party. Marcio had gone to the bathroom and come bursting through the door a few minutes later in a series of twirls and high kicks, singing, *WHEEEEEN you're a Jet you're a Jet all the way . . .* We'd all laughed, but I'd turned to Amy and whispered, "Not for nothing, but do straight guys do that?"

We'd made our usual Epicure run that Sunday, but the effort of it had almost killed me, and I secretly hoped people wouldn't show. I'd awoken with a hangover so bad it felt like the Apocalypse had set up a staging area in my head, my nose so stuffy I could hardly breathe. Amy was a little green around the gills herself—although, by the time Marcio and Maria and then Genghis showed up around three o'clock, she was decidedly perkier than I was. I was lying listlessly on the couch, convinced I'd never be able to get off it again.

"Do a couple of bumps," she kept urging me. "You'll feel better."

"I don't want to feel better," I'd protested with sour melodrama, pulling a sofa cushion over my head. "I just want to die right here."

"Oh, for the love of God, you're such a drama queen. At least have a Bloody Mary."

"I'd rather swim naked through an open sewer than touch a drop of alcohol right now."

"Believe me," Amy said, "right now you look like you *did* go swimming in an open sewer—have the Bloody Mary."

By the time Genghis arrived, I'd rallied enough to get out of my pajamas and tidy my hair a bit. "So," Genghis threw over his shoulder, after he'd kissed my cheek and headed for the kitchen, "I hear John Hood has a crush on you."

I struggled to sit up. "Did he tell you that?"

"Heard it from somebody else. People noticed you two talking last night." Genghis returned with a martini and looked around in confusion for a place to set his glass. "Didn't there use to be a coffee table here?"

"I replaced it with the drum," Amy said. And, sure enough, there was an enormous, tribal-looking drum—easily big enough for five people to sit around—where the coffee table had been only a week before. "It'll give us something to play with when we're bored."

"We're always bored," Genghis replied. He put his cocktail down on an end table, where one of Amy's three cats immediately jumped up to inspect it.

"Getting back to John Hood," I interjected. "I believe you used the word 'crush'?"

"Why? You interested?"

"Right," I scoffed. "Like I could bring a guy with a criminal record home to meet my parents." I paused. "Why is everybody looking at me?"

Seduction has always been one of my favorite words. There's the obvious sexual connotation and, I must admit, that's always been part of the appeal. But also implicit in the idea of seduction is the idea of being taken, of letting something, or someone, stronger than you are take you over. It's an idea that's enormously compelling to a control freak like me. To be seduced means you're not entirely responsible for your actions—certainly not the one to blame if things go wrong.

A crucial part of the seduction process is the obligatory initial protest. (*"No, no!" she protested, her creamy bosom heaving against her tight bodice. "I must not."*) Accordingly, on most nights, I would insist to Amy that I was staying in with a book and going to sleep early. This was token resistance and we both knew it. Amy's responses would range anywhere from telling me how disappointed everybody would be not to see me, to advising me to stop wallowing in my "depression," or, when all else failed, assuring me that I was the laziest person she knew. Sufficiently flattered and guilted by turns, it was easy enough to follow where I was led and postpone important critical thinking to some hazy future date.

I was being seduced: by Amy, by her friends, by her lifestyle, and by South Beach itself. South Beach was a town in the business of seduction; it was the local industry, like cars in Detroit or steel in Pittsburgh. It was sensual in the strictest meaning of the word. Everything about it was designed to overload the senses—the clubs with their chaotic music, lithe bodies, and flashing strobe lights; the ocean and beaches peeking coyly around the sunny pastels of the Deco buildings; the amber and red-roofed Spanish-style structures, fronted by palm trees and kaleidoscopes of tropical flowers. Sometimes the sheer, overwhelming beauty of the place and its inhabitants was so sharp, it was almost painful. My heart would race in a coke-tinged way and I would think, *If I could just hold on to it for a second . . .* and then the thought would break off, because there never was an ending to that sentence—not one I could put into words, anyway. But I began to understand why men fall desperately in love with beautiful women no matter how self-destructive, or how pointless, the affair.

And, like a beautiful woman, South Beach was able to incorporate even tragedy into its charm, painting itself with a patina of depth and glamour without ever revealing a single, visible scar.

Three days after that fateful party at Spin, Gianni Versace was murdered on the front steps of his Ocean Drive mansion. If *Where were you when Kennedy was shot?* was the defining question of America in the early '60s, then *Where were you when Versace was shot?* was absolutely the defining question of South Beach in the late '90s. Having the ability to answer it—even knowing that it was a question worth asking—made me feel a part of South Beach for the first time, gave me the right to speak about it in the first person, hesitantly using words like "we" and "us."

All the talk around town in the subsequent days was about Andrew Cunanan—the manhunt underway to determine his whereabouts, theories as to motives (*I heard Versace and his lover picked him up for a three-way,* was the most common speculation), and grave discussions from people who claimed to have spoken, sat, drunk, danced, or otherwise interacted with him in the days leading up to the shooting. Had Cunanan been running for political office, it seemed unlikely that he could have found the time to press more flesh than he allegedly had in the days right before the murder.

But, gripping and ubiquitous as the story was, it was hard for me to pay attention.

Andrew Cunanan wasn't the criminal uppermost in my thoughts.

Amy and I spent a lot of time out in the weeks that followed, pushed by a shared, restless impulse that had us out at bars late into the night, even though it was during the typically dead summer months. We weren't the only ones feeling restless; most of the year-round residents were out on those summer nights, lured by a pick-the-scab compulsion to discuss the details of Versace's shooting over and over again.

It was partly the drugs that had us out so frequently. At first we clung to the pretense that we used cocaine solely to enhance our going-out experience. I couldn't help but notice, though, how we never even thought of leaving the house until the drug dealer had arrived; if he was two hours late getting to us, we were two hours late getting to wherever we were going.

We'd usually decide to make the buy early in the day, talking to each other on the phone from our respective offices. "I want to party with Connie tonight," one of us would say cryptically, or we'd smoke a cigarette outside and make some passing reference to "our crazy friend Connie, who keeps us up all night." Any phone or semipublic conversation about buying, sharing, or using drugs had to be carried out in code. "Connie" was our word for cocaine, and it was "Tina" when we talked about crystal meth (a drug I still hadn't experimented with). If we wanted a larger quantity than usual, Amy would call the dealer and tell him she felt like shooting pool (translation: "Bring us an eight-ball").

If South Beach was my seducer, then cocaine was its willing accomplice, whispering that I could have more fun and be more charming than I'd ever believed possible. Despite the catastrophic hangovers and increasingly painful workdays, I came to associate the way cocaine made me feel with the way being around Hood felt—that headlong feeling of being simultaneously on top of my game and dizzyingly, euphorically, out of control.

I was usually out with at least the partial hope of running into John Hood. He was a hard man to pin down, an elusive cipher seemingly above the mundane conventions of prearranged plans and phone confirmations. I never knew when or where he'd show up. I'd be standing at a bar someplace with a cigarette in my hand, and suddenly he'd be at my elbow with a light and a wolfish grin. "Hey hey, baby doll," he'd say as he brushed his cheek against mine. "What's the what? Whatcha reading these days? I just picked up the latest Harold Bloom—now *there's* a cat who's read everything." He was always sharply dressed in a vintage suit and his trademark fedora, always energetic and full of conversation about nightlife and books, or wild stories (true? untrue? who could say?) about guns and fights and treks into the dodgy recesses of Miami's inner cities, where one could partake of superior—or at least more colorfully obtained—drugs.

How could I even keep up with conversations like that? Talking to Hood was exciting, but he almost always made me feel shy and illiterate by comparison. What would have read as pure, shuck 'n' jive phony on anybody else was fascinating in him—he was just so *smart*, so authentically . . . well, whatever the hell he was.

One night, Amy noticed me scanning the crowd and asked if I was looking for him. "What'd be the point?" I quipped. "Hood's like a cop: always around when you don't want him, never around when you do."

Nevertheless, I was looking.

A typical evening began at around eleven thirty at Lucky Cheng's, where Amy and I would catch one of Raja's sets—invariably consisting of high-energy lip-synching to CeCe Peniston's "Finally." We'd enjoy free cocktails at the bar with Donna Marie, a gorgeous young bartender/model, and the random odds-and-ends friends Amy loved to collect. We also eventually became friendly with the claque of drag queens who waited tables and milled around the front when they weren't performing.

I found their presence exhilarating, discovering in myself a love of color and spectacle—of outrageous costumes and heightened dialogue—that I'd never felt comfortable owning up to before. Even their names rolled around in my imagination like bright, iridescent beads: names like Sexcilia, Adora, Kitty Meow, Taffy Lynn, Chyna Girl, and Connie Casserole.

Lucky Cheng's was mostly a tourist destination, a sideshow put on for out-of-towners or mainlanders looking for an "adventurous" take on the traditional bachelor and birthday parties. There wasn't a lot of action to be found, but Amy and I and her small group of disciples were always guaranteed ample bar space, while the gawkers clustered in groups of five or more around tables in the dining area. That, coupled with the free liquor, made it an easy place to start our nights.

Eventually, after Raja got off work, we'd end up at the Deuce, one of our favorite hangouts in those days and unquestionably the diviest dive bar on the Beach. In an era of blink-and-you'll-miss-'em clubs and restaurants, Mac's Club Deuce—which had been around at least forever and possibly longer—had all the authority of a grizzled patriarch.

Sandwiched on a side street near a tattoo parlor and a pizza joint, the Deuce was small and dimly lit, painted entirely black on the inside, with a mirrored wall that kept it from feeling claustrophobic. The other walls were adorned with neon girlie sculptures abandoned after a *Miami Vice* shoot, as well as framed photos of everything from snapshots of locals to a large, life-sized black-and-white of Humphrey Bogart. There was a listing pool table and a jukebox containing tunes of what Amy called the "Stairway to Freebird" variety. The stools around the curving bar were rickety and cracked, the bartenders were tough and salty, and on any given night the place could erupt into fights, brawls, or brouhahas of all description. Every subculture was reflected, so you would frequently come across tattoo artists and trannies rubbing shoulders with millionaire playboys or even the occasional celebrity. "It's like the cantina in *Star Wars*," was how I described it to Lara during one of our usual twice-weekly phone calls. "The one where Alec Guinness says, *You will never find a more wretched hive of scum and villainy.*"

The drinks were mercifully cheap, and the Deuce was open seven days a week from eight a.m. until six a.m.—making it a popular retreat for partiers either just heading out or looking for a place to kill time before heading to an after-hours. The best thing about the Deuce, however, was that it was strictly locals only; if you found yourself at the Deuce, it was a pretty sure bet that you either lived on the Beach or had been brought there by someone who did.

Given the setting, any attempt to create our own drama seemed almost superfluous—but we were pretty good at doing so just the same. One night somebody slipped GHB into Raja's drink, and Amy and I had to take her back to our house, dragging a nearly inert drag queen between us through the streets of South Beach at three a.m. as we tried desperately to hail a cab. Another time, a friend of Amy's named Consuela—a post-op trannie—had, over the bartenders' objections, climbed onto the bar to dance in drunken ecstasy ("For quarters, daaaaaaahling!"). She'd promptly fallen off, fracturing her collarbone. Once, Amy and Marcio's wife, Maria, got into a cataclysmic argument. Maria liked to get drunk and make out with Amy, who was occasionally willing to accommodate her—mostly in the hopes of enticing a tattoo artist named Curly who worked across the street. Maria, however, had come to take it for granted that any night at the Deuce would culminate in some sort of girl-on-girl interplay. As Amy angrily told me over lines in the Deuce's bathroom, it was one thing to do *that* once in a while for kicks, and quite another to be expected to do it *all the time*.

But, of all the nights we spent in the Deuce that summer, it's the night of Genghis's birthday party that stands out the most.

It was a swampy late-August night, and the streets were so hot and sticky that it felt as if the asphalt was oozing up around the soles of my shoes. I was wearing a dress I'd bought that afternoon on Amy and Raja's advice—a long black tube that fell all the way to my ankles and was slit dangerously up one side. The material sucked me in so tightly around the middle that it was like wearing a corset, one that produced exaggerated curves above and below. Sashaying around on my new, ultrahigh heels, I felt like somebody doing a Jessica Rabbit impression. I wavered between thinking I looked great and thinking I looked ridiculous, but I caught more than a few appreciative glances as we made our way down Washington Avenue—enough to convince me that getting attention justified whatever pangs of insecurity I felt.

We walked in at about two a.m. with a fairly large group—maybe ten people—having just come from dinner and drinks at Lucky Cheng's. The typical Deuce Saturday-night chaos reigned. Our favorite bartender, Krystal, a voluptuous black lesbian with a platinum buzz cut, gave us free rounds in honor of the occasion. Hood had met up with us at the bar, and I was going through my usual routine of pretending I barely noticed him while taking a careful, surreptitious survey of every person he spoke with.

The fact that we were celebrating a birthday meant the distribution of "party favors" had started before we'd even left the house, and had continued unabated in various bathrooms and backseats of cabs; by two a.m., I was well on my way to achieving coked-out nirvana. Eventually, though, my liquor buzz started to override my cocaine high, and I headed for the bathroom with a small Baggie to even things out.

I had just finished putting key to nose when the door flew open and an extremely large and obviously drunk man staggered in. I was somewhat discomfited—but, hey, it was the Deuce—and I helpfully informed him that the men's room was next door.

His eyes were unfocused as he lurched forward. *"Bonita,"* he slurred. He reached for me and attempted to grab my chest. *"Bonita."*

"Dude, get *off* me!" I protested, and, when it became clear that things were about to escalate into an out-and-out wrestling match, I brought my heel up hard into his shin (thank God for stilettos), pushing past him back into the bar.

I was fairly shaken up when I rejoined my group (things like this almost never happened at Leadership Miami cocktail parties); but, not wanting to seem like a baby—because, hey, it was the Deuce—I attempted to play the incident off as bar-story humor. "Oh my God, you guys! You won't believe what just happened!" I recounted the tale and told it funny, mimicking the slurring and eye rolls like a champ. Everybody cracked up, but nobody seemed more entertained than Hood, whose eyes and mouth rounded into almost perfect *o*'s of amusement. His hands flew to the top of his hat as he laughingly asked, "Which guy was it?"

I looked around and spotted my perp near the pool table. "That guy." I pointed him out. "The one in the white shirt."

Hood took my hand and I forgot all about drunken bathroom predators. "Come with me," he said. "I want to introduce you to a friend of mine." He led me to the opposite end of the bar and seated me on a stool with my back to the entrance, next to a nondescript guy who was drinking alone and chatting with Krystal. "Robert, this is Rachel. Rachel, this is my friend Robert." Robert smiled and greeted me as Hood put a twenty-dollar bill on the bar. "Robert's going to buy you a drink," he told me, "and keep you company for a little while. I'll be back in a minute." I could see Hood, duskily reflected in the mirrored wall, as he stood behind me and winked over my shoulder. "Keep an eye on her, man," he added to Robert, and then he was gone.

I was aware only of a sense of drunken disappointment—clearly, I thought miserably, Hood was trying to set me up with one of his friends. In my own defense, it wasn't at all unusual for Hood to make an introduction and then disappear; he had a way of being everywhere and nowhere at once, like a game of Whac-A-Mole. I wished I were on the other side of the room with my own friends, instead of enduring the humiliation of a guy I unofficially liked playing matchmaker between me and his drinking buddy. On the other hand, Robert was friendly and complimentary and I decided I had nothing to lose by enjoying one cocktail—maybe I'd even make Hood a little jealous.

I noticed that, attentive as he was, Robert's eyes kept darting over my shoulder. I finally asked him what was going on and he replied, "I think I was supposed to distract you, but you might want to see what your boy is doing for you."

I turned around and saw Hood manhandling my bathroom assailant to the bar entrance—no small feat, considering he must have had at least eighty pounds on Hood. It looked as if he was attempting to struggle, but so efficiently did Hood have him gripped, he couldn't even turn around, much less land a punch.

People were watching in a sort of tranquil amusement. Not the tense, absolute silence of a bar anticipating a fight, but more like a group of people pausing briefly to observe the entertaining—and predictable—antics of a family member.

Hood pushed the man roughly through the front door, which swung open wildly and struck the Deuce's outer wall with a loud, reverberating clang. "Get the fuck out," Hood said, his tone so calm it was almost conversational. Lighting a cigarette, he added, "I see you in here again, something you care about gets broken."

The man swayed for a moment on the concrete just outside the door, clearly considering his options. Then he muttered something unintelligible, spat on the sidewalk, and weaved unsteadily away.

I didn't even realize I'd been holding my breath until I heard the air escape my mouth in a long, whistling rush. I'd never seen anything approaching a bar fight, had never—now that I was thinking about it—witnessed violence of any kind outside of movies and TV shows, or the occasional schoolyard shoving match.

But it was clear that I was alone with my shock. Everybody was already back to their drinking, talking, and pool playing, as if nothing at all unusual had occurred.

Hood loped over to Robert and me and ordered a drink from Krystal. Then he produced a vial from his pocket and deftly poured two small white lines onto the bar, pressing a cut-up straw into my hand and motioning me to take the first one.

I cupped a hand surreptitiously around my nose and bent my head briefly over the bar. Then I brought it quickly back, looking up into Hood's face with what I knew was, for the first time, a completely serious expression.

Hood's eyes met mine. For a split second, they were as earnest as my own.

"Thank you," I said softly. And I allowed my hand to rest lightly on his.

FOUR

"It was crazy," I told Lara over the phone a few days later. "But in this totally fucked-up way, it was the most chivalrous thing anybody's ever done for me."

"So you're into this guy." It was a statement, not a question.

"I don't know." I lit a cigarette. "Although he's so smart, he makes me feel like Cletus the Slack-Jawed Yokel. Seriously, it would freak you out."

"Oh boy," Lara said wryly.

"What?"

"He's the supersmart guy who does all the drugs you like doing these days and who beat up some pervert in a bar for you."

"He didn't really beat him up," I replied, willfully missing the point. "It was more like he shoved some pervert around."

"Whatever. You're into him, is all I'm saying."

I hesitated. "Do you think it's the worst idea ever?"

"I think it's what you want right now. If it gets to be a bad idea, you'll stop wanting it."

What Lara was really saying was, *I think a relationship with this guy is a horrible idea that couldn't possibly end well. But you and I have always known that there are two kinds of girlfriends: the ones you worry about when it comes to guys and the ones you don't—and you and I have never had to worry about each other that way. So have your fun, but don't take any of this too seriously.*

"That goes without saying," I responded.

"I know," Lara said. "Just don't forget who you really are."

It was unnecessary advice; it's impossible to forget something you can't remember anymore.

. . .

45

It was a conversation that I couldn't repeat to Amy, but I did hesitantly ask if it seemed to her that I'd been changing lately.

"People don't change," was Amy's reply. "They only become more of what they are."

I wondered about it, lying in bed and trying to come down in the three hours I typically had between when I'd gotten in and when I'd have to get up again. Everything in my life was radically different, but was I changing or simply becoming more of what I was? Which was the real me—the person with the nine-to-five cubicle job, or the curvy bombshell I sometimes caught a glimpse of in the mirror at night?

Sometimes it felt like I was becoming the person I'd always known I was, the person I was meant to be. It was like finding out that the strange woman you passed at the newsstand every day but never paid attention to was actually your real mother—that the people who'd raised you were the ones who were strangers. And you'd realize that you'd always known it somehow; always noticed that her nose and the shape of her eyes were exactly like yours, and that she drank her coffee with her pinkie finger held straight out, just the way you did. She was you and not you and familiar and foreign all at once, and the only thing you were abruptly sure of was that you'd spent years ignoring a tiny voice in the back of your head at Thanksgiving dinners and family gatherings that had whispered, *This isn't where you belong.*

More and more, it seemed like the day job was the part of the equation that didn't add up—the X variable that couldn't be solved for. It was starting to feel a little surreal to put on crazy ensembles and chase after drugs and felons and party people until four in the morning, and then find myself a few hours later, exhausted and red-eyed, sitting in a cubicle under fluorescent lights while poring over budget reports.

Making everything harder was the growing realization that, now that I was single, it would be many more years—if ever—before I'd eke out anything like a decent living in the world of nonprofit administration. There was no way, for example, that I'd be able to afford my own apartment on my current salary; as it was, I could barely afford to pay for my car and insurance, and my share of the rent at Amy's. I was tired of burning the candle at both ends and still being broke when I tallied everything up at the end of the month. Mostly, I was tired of feeling guilty for being so tired of things all the time.

Every day started to feel like rubbing a cheese grater over raw nerve endings. I found myself waking up with free-floating anxiety, what Amy called "sword of Damocles feeling." One morning I woke up completely covered in hives, every last inch of my skin red and swollen. *Too much stress,* the doctor said.

I talked to Amy about it late one night as we split a slice of pizza we'd impulsively grabbed on the way home (we had, as usual, neglected to eat dinner before going out). "I'm burnt out," I said, "from the breakup and struggling so hard for years to get ahead and the pressure at work—everything."

Amy listened without interrupting. Finally she said, "You've gone through a lot of stressful stuff in the last few months—some of the most stressful things a person can go through: a major breakup, a move, a complete lifestyle change." Then she hit me with the money question: "So what do you want to do instead?"

"You mean where else would I want to work?"

"I mean what else would you theoretically want to do besides nonprofit?"

"I'm not sure." I paused for a moment—mostly to avoid acknowledging that I'd already considered this and thought of an answer. "What I like most about my job now is producing our fundraising events or dealing with the press—like when I have to try to get them to report on a project we're doing or something. I guess maybe I'd like to work in PR." I frowned. "Of course, I have practically zero experience and no way of getting any while I'm doing what I do now."

Amy finished the last of the crust and dabbed at her mouth with a paper napkin. "Quit your job," she said, as if it were the only obvious solution.

"Sure. Then I can pay my bills with that whole 'making-it-on-my-looks' career that the day job was holding me back from."

She rolled her eyes. "Look, you were just saying how what you wanted right now was the kind of job you don't have to stress about, right?"

"Right . . ."

"So get one of those jobs. Be a bartender or a waitress at nights and spend your days doing intern or freelance work or whatever. Then you get the best of both worlds." She threw the empty pizza bag in the general direction of the trash can. "Plus, I'll bet bartending or waiting tables pays more than what you're making. And it'd be fun! You'd meet tons of people, and I could hang out at your bar and you'd give me free cocktails."

There was no denying that she had a point. And the idea of stopping for a while, of putting down all the responsibility and walking away from it, made me feel like a kid who'd found out he was getting an extra month of summer vacation.

The next day, I got the name of a bartending school from the Yellow Pages and enrolled in a three-week course. For three hundred and fifty dollars, a team of "expert mixologists" in a South Miami strip mall promised to teach me the basics of slinging drinks and behind-the-bar protocol, and would even help me put together a bartending résumé. Later, Amy helped me embellish this résumé because "it's not like any of these places are going to check your references."

Quitting my job was surprisingly easy. I didn't want to tell them that I was giving up the important task of saving the world in order to work behind a bar and cheat the IRS out of a percentage of my cash tips. I mumbled something about "a great opportunity" in "marketing and communications," gave my notice, and that was that. I said essentially the same thing when I resigned from my various volunteer groups, explaining that I would have to dedicate most of my time to pursuing my new goals.

Telling my family, on the other hand, was a far greater ordeal. No matter how much I tried to assure my parents that this was a temporary, and strategic, move on the path to better things, the conversation quickly disintegrated into a scene from *Long Day's Journey into Night*. I was subjected to three hours of painful histrionics, which finally boiled down to two pieces of unshakable wisdom from my mother: "Your father and I didn't spend eighty thousand dollars on your college education so you could be a bartender!" (which was, actually, a fair point) and, "What normal, professional man is going to want to marry you now?"

"Right," I'd snorted to Amy when I was retelling the story. "Because there's nothing guys hate more than a busty woman who serves them."

Within a very short period of time, I'd landed a bartending job at the

Sands, a conspicuously elegant renovated hotel on Ocean Drive that played host to rockers, movie stars, and jaded celebutantes. Sometimes I'd look up from mixing a martini and see George Clooney or Bianca Jagger standing in front of me. My shift was from eight p.m. to two a.m., four nights a week, and I told myself that this left me with more than enough time during the day to pursue my longer-term goals.

Perhaps inevitably, though, once I was freed from the commitment of the nine-to-five grind, I quickly fell into a pattern that revolved around self-indulgence. I was, for the first time in my professional experience, working a scant twenty-four hours a week—practically a part-time job. And I was making more money than I ever had, often as much as three hundred dollars a night (my previous salary had been five hundred dollars a week). And not paycheck-every-two-weeks-with-taxes-deducted money, but immediate money, cash-in-the-hand money.

Needless to say, there was plenty to spend it on. And spend I did, on drinks, drugs, new clothes to knock 'em dead in when I went out at night. It was a thrill to walk into SoBe's boutiques with a wad of money I'd earned the night before and spend it on the fantastical concoctions that—under Amy and Raja's coaching—I was learning to deck myself out in.

On a typical evening, I'd race home after my shift ended, do a quick change and a couple of bumps to get started, and be out and ready to party by three a.m. When you don't start partying until three in the morning, you don't always want to go home at five o'clock, the time at which the clubs were legally required to close. For this purpose, there were after-hours clubs. The ones that served alcohol were technically illegal, but generally tolerated, and usually housed in an empty storefront or warehouse. The after-hours allowed you to party until noon the next day—or later, if you felt like it.

Our favorite after-hours spot occupied an empty retail space on Lincoln Road, conveniently located across from a small, Spanish-style church. We'd spill out of the club early on Sunday afternoons—recoiling like vampires from the agonizing sunlight—just as families were exiting from their weekly devotions. Rather than giving us pause or making us consider the wickedness of our ways, we lived for this contrast; it always reaffirmed how much more glamorous and decadent our lives were than "regular" people's. Donning the sunglasses we learned to carry with us, Amy and I would usually cast amused looks at each other until one of us would wail theatrically, "*Why? Why* does this wretched ball of light in the sky torment me?" at which point we'd erupt into outright laughter.

It was a matter of strictest dogma in the cult of nightlife that daylight was evil, an unfortunate interruption of all things after-dark, something to be reluctantly tolerated but never embraced wholeheartedly—unless, of course, one was working on one's tan, the only reason for which daylight could justify its existence.

Sometimes Amy and I would forgo the after-hours scene altogether, preferring to stay home with Raja and Genghis and have the kinds of late-night conversations that always seem especially intense when you're high. We'd talk about everything—from parties and local gossip to more serious conversations about families, friends growing up, first loves, and youthful traumas. I was always particularly amused by Raja's habit of referring to everyone—male or female—as "she." "Don't worry about *her*," Raja said one night in reference to Genghis, after some particularly acerbic comment he'd just made about my makeup—which Raja had applied for me that night. "She gets cranky when her painting isn't going well—don't you, baby?" Amy made sporadic attempts to turn the conversation to John Hood and our edgy banter that never seemed to materialize into anything. In the absence, however, of any declarations or first moves on Hood's part, I was unwilling to open the subject of him and our hypothetical interest in each other to public debate.

Once, Amy and I talked about the early days of our friendship and our initial impressions of each other. Amy said wistfully, "I had to make sure you didn't want anything from me. Everybody always wants something from me, but I could tell you just wanted to be my friend."

It was a moment of vulnerability that was rare in Amy. It made me aware of the price you paid, I guessed, for always being the person at the party who everybody wanted to talk to. And, the truth was, I *had* wanted something from her; I'd wanted everything from her, actually. We all did.

Despite our hectic after-hours schedule, Amy still had her day job to contend with. She'd usually get up at around nine o'clock in the morning (having been out until at least four a.m. the previous night), go to the office, work out with her trainer, and then "disco nap" during the earlier part of my bartending shift, making a cameo appearance at my bar sometime around eleven. She generally came alone and stayed for a single cocktail, as the Sands was a little too upscale—and a little too touristy—to make it a comfortable hangout. As the weeks went on, Amy began to compensate for the weekly sleep debt by downing a roofie on Sundays and passing out all afternoon. "I'm going to become one with my mattress," she would announce, closing her bedroom door. "I'll see you tonight."

For my own part, I made sure that I was in bed by ten a.m. on the days I had to work. In theory, I'd sleep until six p.m., although it was usually a twitchy, jittery sleep at best. Amy suggested roofies a few times but I always resisted, rationalizing that it was one thing to do blow every night, but taking more drugs to come down would mean that I had a *problem*.

The lack of sleep took its toll, but I was far too self-medicated by then to be overly concerned. Lara asked once if I wasn't worried about the damage I might be inflicting, and I demurred by cheerfully replying, "I've killed so many brain cells that the remaining few are erecting monuments and holding candlelight vigils."

I knew on some level that the way I was living would inevitably catch up to me, but I tried not to think about it much. There's a saying bandied about in Victorian novels that would come to mind: *Sufficient unto the day is the evil thereof.* Which is basically a fancy way of saying: *Buy now, pay later.*

John Hood was still around, and I ran into him as often as I ever had—probably even more often, actually. He was always edgy and erudite and just the least bit flirtatious, but that's all there was. Eventually, I heard rumors that he'd moved in with an ex-girlfriend, or maybe it was a current girlfriend. Since nobody knew exactly where—or how—Hood lived, anything was possible.

In the meantime, it had been over three months since I'd broken up with Eduard and even longer since I'd had any close encounters of the best kind. I made my first tentative forays into the South Beach hookup scene, and soon there were plenty of mornings when either Amy or I would wake up to find a strange male invader in our kitchen. Amy's taste ran to men who she described as "dirty," and Curly the tattoo artist was soon playing frequently in her rotation. There was also a somewhat older stockbroker named Ron in the picture, and he was surprisingly considerate about stocking the fridge or treating us to breakfast on the mornings he was there.

I, on the other hand, met with less than resounding success. Not because guys weren't interested, but because I seemed to have a remarkable talent for selecting men who—and there's no polite way of saying this—were criminally insane.

There were, for example, the charming actor/model who'd been committed to the state mental hospital after trying to burn down his parents' house; the real-estate developer whose assets had been frozen and who called me from jail at five in the morning to come bail him out (I'd declined); the handsome barfly who'd been arrested on the rooftop of an elementary school with what had appeared from a distance to be a high-powered rifle but, upon closer inspection, was actually a long-handled broom (begging the obvious question: What was he doing on the rooftop of an elementary school with a *broom*, of all things?).

Amy tried to console me by offering up stories from her own colorful dating history. "I had this stalker in Seattle who would break into my apartment and steal my underwear and things," she told me. "Then one day he doused himself in gasoline and lit a match—right on my doorstep." She paused to fasten an errant sandal strap. "His mother had the nerve to call and say I should raise the money to pay for his skin grafts."

"That's *totally* unreasonable," I sympathized, somewhat uncertainly.

Regardless, it became a running gag that the Rorschach inkblot test could be replaced by simply showing men a picture of me; if their response was, "She's hot," you could cart them straight off to a rubber room. I'd decided to move on and try to forget about Hood, but there didn't seem to be any clear contenders to take his place.

Late one Saturday night—or, rather, early one Sunday morning—Amy and I were at our favorite Lincoln Road after-hours, drinking near the makeshift plywood bar that ran the length of the room. The place was packed, but over the crowd, I could see Hood's telltale hat clearing a path. Amy went to greet him while I waited sedately with my drink in hand, refusing to stir an inch and have it said that I'd sought him out. I saw Hood glance in my direction as he huddled with Amy and a couple of other people, and then Amy was headed back toward me while Hood beat a trail to the front door.

"We have to go," she said, her voice low and urgent, when she reached me. "Dump your stash on the floor and go to the back exit. The cops are coming."

I took in the scene before me: party boys and drag queens chopping up lines on the bar or licking the coke off each other while the driving staccato of techno music thumped around us. "What are you talking about? The cops never bust these things up."

"Well, they're coming now. Do you want to stand around having a philosophical discussion and end up calling your parents from jail, or do you want to get out of here?"

I had a flashing, sobering vision of what that phone call might sound like. "Right," I said. "Back door." I pawed through my evening bag, regretfully chucking the better part of an eight-ball, as we briskly made our way to the alley entrance. I noticed a few other people, friends of the ones Hood had spoken to, doing the same.

By the time Amy and I were safely a couple of blocks away, a herd instinct seemed to have taken over the crowd to warn of impending danger. We could faintly hear the blare of police sirens over a din of surprised, panicked voices that spilled out into the otherwise silent streets. The clackety-clack of high heels on pavement halted momentarily as Amy and I paused to contemplate our close call.

The sun was coming up. It hurt like a Band-Aid ripped off too quickly, spilling blood into the Atlantic Ocean as it rose.

"Come on," Amy finally said. "Let's get some breakfast at the 11th Street Diner." We turned and slowly made our way south.

FIVE

Summer had become fall almost before anybody noticed. The change of seasons is subtle in Miami, and it's easy to miss the signs if you're not paying attention. The most obvious giveaway is the sudden influx of tourists multiplying swiftly in stores, restaurants, and nightclubs, like piles of autumn leaves in the streets of northern towns.

While the rest of the country's calendar runs from January to January, the South Beach calendar runs from October to October, measured by the rise and fall of what's simply called Season: the annual October-to-May pilgrimage of partiers fleeing colder climes. Season is when event planners and club promoters spend seven months striving to outdazzle each other with a giddy array of see-and-be-scenes. Velvet ropes and red carpets come out of storage like the party dresses of young girls preparing for spring formals.

While most people spend the month of December figuring out what their New Year's resolutions are going to be, South Beach locals spent a good part of August and September setting their personal goals for the upcoming Season. We'd sat around discussing it at Amy's house one day—Amy, Raja, Genghis, and me. Raja was finally going to get her much dreamed-about hair salon off the ground. Genghis was finally going to get a portrait commission worth at least twenty thousand dollars.

"What are you going to do this Season?" I'd asked Amy.

"I'm never going to be seen twice in the same outfit," she'd replied.

The approach of my twenty-sixth birthday, coupled with the advent of Season, had me thinking about my own personal goals: I wanted a viable career in public relations and marketing; I wanted to have fun; I wouldn't say no to finding the love of my life; most of all, I wanted the minor disagreements that seemed to be cropping up between Amy and me to disappear once and for all.

Recently there'd been some tension between us. Nothing major, but little things—the kinds of things, I assured myself, that occurred all the time between roommates.

When I had first moved in with Amy, the understanding was that I'd pay for a third of the rent plus half the utilities—an arrangement that had seemed more than generous on Amy's part. Once I'd started bartending, I'd taken to the mutual convenience of paying Amy in cash rather than writing checks. Lately, though, Amy would come to me two or three days after I'd handed my money over, crossly demanding payment. My confusion, having already paid her, only irritated her further.

I never doubted that Amy had genuinely forgotten the money I'd given her, but it bothered me that she thought I was attempting to mooch. I already believed that I'd never be able to repay her for all she'd done, and I was jabbed by a kind of sharp remorse whenever I gave it much thought. A couple of times I'd simply paid her twice, figuring that, even at double the price, I was still getting a pretty good deal, overall.

In the meantime, I started keeping a careful written account of our financial transactions, including the amount, date, time, and location of each payment I made. I didn't think I'd ever quite have the nerve to confront her with it (*See?* I would say, *I did so pay you two hundred thirty-eight dollars right here in the living room at five forty-seven p.m. on October first*). But I wrote it all down just the same.

Fortunately, these episodes were few and far between, and it was Amy herself who'd insisted on making all the preparations for my birthday celebration. Since it fell on a Thursday, we decided to make an appearance at Back Door Bamby. Amy's friend Mykel had taken on Genghis and John Hood as partners in the venture, and they'd moved the party from Liquid to a club farther south on Washington Avenue called KGB. The night of my birthday was, coincidentally, Bamby's debut in her new home.

Everybody was in high spirits that night—Amy included. We were joined by all the usual suspects in our party pack: Raja, Consuela the trannie, Marcio and Maria, Tim (a young trust-funder who owned a fledgling modeling agency), and Ned and Jack (who were brothers and friends of Raja's from prep school).

Genghis was the only one who couldn't attend, since he had to be at Bamby early for opening night. Amy treated us to dinner at Pacific Time on Lincoln Road. By the time we reached KGB shortly after midnight, we were in the kind of good mood that can be purchased only by blithely discarding the better part of a thousand-dollar dinner while imbibing enough coke to clothe half the Colombian army.

The door at KGB that night was manned by Gilbert Stafford, a six-foot-five black bear of a man who was, Amy later told me, one of New York and South Beach's legendary club doormen. Upon seeing Amy and Raja, he herded an overanxious group of causeway crawlers (the SoBe equivalent of New York's bridge-and-tunnel crowd) to the no-man's-land side of the velvet rope. "Hello, daaaaahlings!" he boomed in a deep, powerful bass. He kissed Amy and Raja on both cheeks and officiously ushered our group inside.

We bypassed the empty ground level of the club, pausing to check for any bars or bathrooms that might come in handy later, and climbed the stairs to the VIP area. *Get up! Get up, y'all!* the music cajoled, as we entered a space that managed to feel cavernous and intimate at the same time. Most of the newer clubs on the Beach were taking the form of impossibly sleek, stylized interiors; KGB was one of the few that still felt a little bohemian around the edges.

Ornate, red velvet couches with gold-leaf frames were clustered around low tables throughout the room. They looked especially dramatic against the black walls, which were hung at sporadic intervals with some of Genghis's paintings—arresting portraits of women wearing boots and bustiers or brandishing riding crops. The women in Genghis's portraits always struck me as both enticing and faintly violent, and their presence lent the room a witchy air. Most of the lighting appeared to come from numerous red votive candles, although I assumed there was some additional lighting source cleverly tucked from view. In any event, the room was so dimly lit that it took a minute for our eyes to adjust.

A large balcony—possibly larger than the inside space and featuring its own bar—opened to our right. A few intrepid souls had already found their way out there. The room itself was about two-thirds full, a good sign for the promoters, considering it was still early. And it was a good crowd, too; my barely educated eyes picked out faces recognizable from the numerous local gossip columns. It had scandalized Amy when I'd first admitted that I never read them, so I'd started doing so. "Doesn't it seem weird to you," I'd asked her a few days ago, "that nobody printed anything about that raid we almost got caught in?"

Amy had looked at me oddly, saying, "Nobody would publish that kind of negativity."

Now Amy subtly pointed out Isabella Shulov sitting with friends on one of the couches closest to us. I had actually been aware of Isabella's existence since well before I'd moved to South Beach. She wrote the "Queen of the Night" nightlife column for the *Miami Journal*, and was one of the more acclaimed South Beach pioneers—that first wave of late-'80s settlers and party people who'd initially put the town on the map. She was also the most socially sought-after woman on the Beach—possibly the most sought-after *person* on the Beach. Of indeterminate age, Isabella had a regal, catlike beauty and a flawless hourglass figure. I watched her gift several admirers with high-voltage smiles as they hovered over her couch, waiting for an audience.

Isabella was notoriously selective about when and where she bestowed her favors. Genghis had been talking about her all week, boasting of her expected presence in a way that told me he was secretly anxious she might not show. Amy seemed to think he had reason to be anxious. "Right," she'd remarked several times. "Because Isabella Shulov is such a good friend of Genghis's." But here she was in all her glory, and her presence would be considered quite a coup.

"Hey, baby." Genghis himself was suddenly at my side, rubbing my shoulder and arm distractedly as he kissed me, Amy, and Raja in succession and waved hello to the rest of our group. His eyes roamed the room as he greeted us, but they came back to rest momentarily on me. "Happy birthday—you look so pretty!" He smiled and indicated an area with three couches arranged around a small table. "I've been holding that table for you guys."

We'd barely seated ourselves when a mile-high waitress was beside our table, her sharp collarbones gleaming like a row of medals above her sleeveless top as she efficiently produced a bottle of Absolut in an ice bucket. She also provided lime wedges, several decanters filled with cranberry and orange juice, tonic water, and an assortment of glasses. "Compliments of the house." She tossed me a sullen, indifferent look that was about as unpracticed as an actor's audition monologue. "For your birthday."

I turned to Amy. "Did you tell them to do this?"

"Nope."

"Genghis?" I guessed.

Amy shook her head again. Her smile was teasing. "You must have an admirer."

We knew there was only one person it could be.

The evening wore on and my alleged admirer had yet to reveal his presence. Growing restless, I told Amy that I was going to the bathroom for a bump and elbowed my way through the thickening crowd. I was passing the bar when I heard a man's voice say, "Now *that* is a *fabulous* top."

I was wearing a form-fitting red Chinese top with gold embroidery and a mandarin collar, which I'd paired with a long, tight black skirt. It had the demurest of slits on one side, coming up to just below my knee. I thought the whole ensemble *was*, if I might say so myself, pretty fabulous.

I turned to locate the speaker and found myself facing a somewhat short—maybe about five foot six—black-haired man, with a slim mustache and goatee that made him look distinctly devilish. He was wearing a tight, red, open-necked top (just a hint of curly black chest hair peeking out) underneath a black suit. He looked like he was a few years older than I was; probably no more than thirty, I guessed. He was holding a martini glass in one hand and a cigarette in the other, and the broad smile on his face carried all the way up to his black eyes.

"Thank you," I said.

"You can't possibly be here alone, are you, darling?" he asked.

"Actually, I'm here with some friends. How about you?"

He sighed. "I *was* here with a date, but I seem to have lost him. Somebody must have distracted him with a shiny object."

"It must have been *very* shiny if it distracted him from *you*." I was becoming well versed in the mutual-admiration-society tone of South Beach social chitchat, but I found myself meaning it in this case. I already liked this guy. I could tell.

"Well, you know how men are."

"Please!" I said. "Don't tell *me* about men. Lately, I seem to be dating exclusively among the clinically insane."

"Oh, we all have stories, honey."

"Not like mine."

"Intriguing," he said, except it sounded like "in-*tree*-guing." He sipped his martini and commanded, "Do tell."

I knew that it was a challenge, that he was hoping I had some real horror stories ready for him. Accordingly, I gave him the more colorful highlights from my recent dating escapades and was treated to progressively enthusiastic laughter as I went on. I brought it home with the tale of my arsonist: "So I couldn't for the life of me figure out why he'd stopped calling. And then one day I ran into his roommate, who told me that he'd been committed to the state mental hospital—*for trying to burn his parents' house down!* And I was like: 'What, they don't have *phones* in the state mental hospital?'"

Breathlessly, between peals of laughter, he asked, "Have you ever thought about doing stand-up comedy?"

"No, although I *have* considered signing up for some sort of dating twelve-step program. Like, I admit that I have a problem and I'm powerless to control my own love life, and I'm ready to submit myself to my higher power. I'm not sure what the other steps are, but I figure somebody'll fill me in as I go along."

He pretended to consider this. "I think one of the steps is apologizing to people."

"Screw that." I pulled out a cigarette and accepted his offer of a light. "What do I have to apologize for?"

He lit a fresh cigarette for himself. "I'm Ricky, by the way. Ricky Pascal."

"I'm Rachel Baum. It's absolutely lovely to meet you." We formally air-kissed on both cheeks.

The music was so loud that we were almost shouting. People pushed in on us, occasionally spilling liquor from overfilled martini glasses or coming perilously close to our arms with lit cigarettes. We edged away from the bar toward some less-congested real estate a few feet away.

Just then, Isabella Shulov walked by. "Hello, Miss Bella," Ricky called out to her.

"Hello, my darling Ricky!" Her voice was full of lilting, happy affection as they kissed hello. "And who is *this* gorgeous diva you've discovered?" She smiled in my general direction.

"Isabella Shulov, meet Rachel Baum. Rachel, this is Isabella Shulov, one of my very best friends."

"It's a pleasure to meet you." I pressed my cheek against her cool, satiny one.

"I *must* leave; I'm on such a tight deadline," she was saying to Ricky. "But we'll talk tomorrow?" It was a question whose answer she was already sure of, and she was gone before another word was said. Ricky turned his attention back to me.

"So what do you do?" he asked.

"Right now I'm bartending at the Sands. Long-term, though, I'm trying to get into events and PR." I paused. "What do you do?"

He pulled out his wallet and handed me a business card. RICARDO PASCAL, it read. ACCOUNT EXECUTIVE, DORFMAN STONE RODRIGUEZ.

Dorfman Stone Rodriguez was one of the most prestigious public relations firms in South Florida. Miguel Rodriguez was a state senator and pulled in all the high-profile political accounts. Keith Dorfman had numerous connections among the largest real-estate development projects—malls, hotels, that kind of thing—and was usually able to secure their business. This, however, was not why he was notorious. About fifteen years earlier, his first wife had been murdered, and Keith Dorfman had been the primary suspect. Although he was never formally charged, no other suspects were ever identified. The rumor mill consensus was that he'd done it—and gotten away with it.

Not that these stories had hampered his professional progress, of course. This was, after all, Miami.

"Very impressive," I said.

Ricky produced another business card. This one read RICKY PASCAL, SOUTH BEACH CELEBRITY. I laughed.

"When I first moved here," he said, "I didn't know a single person. So I'd read *Ocean Drive* and memorize people's names and pictures. Then I'd go up to them at parties and pretend I'd already met them. I'd say, *Hello, Lewis, it's Ricky Pascal. So good to see you again! We met at so-and-so's party.* Most people are too embarrassed to admit they have no idea who you are. Then I'd give them this card." He smiled. "They never forgot me after that!"

I looked at him admiringly. "The word *chutzpah* seems insufficient."

"So you want to work in PR." All laughter was momentarily gone from his voice.

"Yes," I replied.

His expression was appraising. "I'm going to help you."

I was waiting impatiently in the bathroom line, where I'd been deposited by Ricky. He'd said he was leaving and asked if I wanted to share a cab with him. I'd looked at him blankly. "But it's early." It was only two thirty.

"You know, darling," he'd replied in an instructive manner, "it's good to be out there and let people see you, but it almost never pays to be the last person at the party."

It was the first time since I'd moved to South Beach that anybody had suggested going home early. "I'm sure you're right," I'd answered. "But I'm here with a group. I'll leave with them."

He'd kissed me on the cheek. "I'll call you tomorrow, then."

Now I was starting to wish that I'd bailed. It had been far too long since my last pharmaceutical pick-me-up, and, by the looks of this line, relief might be hours away. Then I remembered the downstairs bathroom we'd spotted on the way in.

The house lights were on in the empty lower portion of the club. The silence was almost total, broken only by the muted sounds of disco wafting from upstairs; it made for an unnerving contrast. I was crossing the room when someone said, "Hey." Despite—or possibly because of—the fact that I recognized the voice as John Hood's, I jumped visibly.

He was standing in the doorway of a miniscule room that appeared to be the club office. Behind him I saw harsh fluorescent lighting, a rickety-looking desk, and a metal filing cabinet. "Kind of late on a school night for a dame to be wandering around alone."

"Didn't you hear?" I approached him with what I hoped was a discreetly seductive sway. "I dropped out of school."

"Well, all major milestones and lifestyle choices deserve acknowledgment. As do birthdays." He gestured me into the office, where I saw several expert lines laid out on the desk. He closed the door behind us and handed me a ten-dollar bill rolled into a cylinder.

It was the first time we'd ever been alone together; Hood seemed to fill the entire space. My breathing sounded preternaturally loud in my own ears, and it made me acutely self-conscious.

"I was thinking about you the other day," he said as I bent over a line. "I was reading this article in the *New Yorker* waxing rhapsodic about some famous poet or other."

I stood up and raised a hand to my nose. I knew there was a ridiculous grin on my face, and I inwardly cursed one too many vodka cranberries for my inability to control it.

He caught it and smiled faintly. "What are you smiling at?"

I blushed and turned my face down. "Nothing." Then, almost reluctantly, I looked back up and my eyes caught his. I took a breath. "Just that you think about me sometimes."

I was never sure exactly how it happened—who was the first one to incline their head, or close their eyes, or take an infinitesimal step forward. I only knew that I was suddenly pressed up against the filing cabinet, caught in a buttery melting of lips and tongues. I was aware of steel handles digging into my back. I sensed somehow that it was deliberate on his part—that maybe he wanted it to hurt, just a little.

Maybe we both did.

Donna Summer was playing upstairs. *Ooooh . . . it's so good it's so good it's so good it's so good it's sooooooooo good.* I couldn't help it: I laughed against his mouth.

"What's so funny?" he asked in a low voice.

"I know it's a cliché," I said, "but did you ever feel like your life was a movie with a soundtrack?" He smiled again, a man indulging a talkative child, and brought his hand up to the side of my face.

There was a brief, respectful rap at the door. "John, are you in there?" a muffled female voice said.

"In a second," Hood said, and I turned my head. "It's not—," he started.

"That's okay." I gently pressed past him, resting my hand on the doorknob. "Amy and those guys are probably wondering where I am, anyway."

I felt deflated all of a sudden. I didn't know if Hood did or didn't have a girlfriend, or if this was or wasn't her at the door. Most likely, I thought, it was one of the club's bartenders. But it came upon me in an abrupt flash that, for however much *I* thought about *him*, Hood had an entire life that had nothing at all to do with me—one that was undoubtedly filled with women who wanted him, or who he wanted, or who actually got him on some kind of regular basis. *There has to be a reason why he's never even called you.* Wondering if he *really* liked me, or if he'd simply seized upon the opportunity presented when I'd wandered by, made my head hurt. It was easier just to leave.

My hand turned on the doorknob. "Thanks for the bottle service and the . . ." I motioned to the table that still had a few lines laid out. *The scene of the crime,* I thought. "Everything," I finished. I opened the door, with barely a sidelong glance at the willowy girl waiting just outside, and walked quickly up the stairs.

I found Amy and Raja still ensconced at our table, happily enjoying all the benefit of the buzz I'd just lost. They were deep in conversation with Cubby, the nightlife reporter for a weekly South Beach paper called the *Wire*. "Hey," I said to Amy. "I'm taking off. Wanna come with?"

"Don't be ridiculous! It's your birthday!"

"I'm kind of beat. I think I'll call it an early night." In my peripheral vision, I could see Hood circling the room. I wanted to let him find me, wanted to watch and see if it was even me he was looking for.

Cut your losses, said the voice in my head. *What were you going to do, marry this guy? Rent movies and cuddle on the couch? Fight over whose turn it is to do the dishes?* I kissed Amy and Raja good-bye and made a beeline for the door.

On my way out, I saw that Ricky was, miraculously, still there. I touched his arm. "That offer to split a cab still good?"

"Of course, darling." He was obviously pleased to be escorting me out after all. "But I thought you were staying till the bitter end."

"Changed my mind." I attempted a careless smile. "Isn't that a woman's prerogative?"

After the comfortable darkness of the club, the sickly tangerine glow of streetlights felt hostile—jeering at my tousled hair and the lipstick I was sure was everywhere but my lips. The traffic on Washington Avenue was bumper-to-bumper, and we had to walk for blocks before we finally found an available cab. The driver was tired and unfriendly; clearly, he'd seen enough disheveled partiers like me for one evening. He barely acknowledged us, seemingly focused on the horizon, as he whisked us efficiently through the chaotic South Beach streets.

SIX

Ricky was as good as his word. He called the next day, and then the next, and then the next after that, and soon we were talking all day, every day. Within only a few weeks, I found myself unable to remember what life had been like before we were friends.

I'm the kind of person who doesn't make close friends easily. Outgoing as I am, I've always been shy at the core, hesitant about trespassing too far on other people's inner lives or giving them too much leeway into my own. So my closest friends have always been the ones who don't have any concept of the word "boundaries." They just kind of show up on my doorstep one day and then move right in—sitting on the couch, putting their feet up, and announcing casually, *By the way, we're best friends now.*

Ricky not only didn't have a concept of the term "boundaries," he probably wouldn't have recognized the idea if he'd heard it. "We need to fix your hair," he told me during one of our first cocktail excursions. "It's not working."

My hand went involuntarily to the top of my head. My hair had been long, curly, and wild for as long as I could remember. "What's wrong with it?"

"It's too short in the front and too long in the back, and the whole thing looks like the eighties exploded on your head." He sipped his martini, his eyes twinkling above the glass. *You know I adore you*, his eyes said. *You can handle hearing this.*

I suddenly realized how much long hair was a part of my self-image. "I think men like women with long hair."

"Gay men like women with *good* hair, and it's the gay men you have to impress if you want to make it in this town." I couldn't help laughing when he added, "Straight men like big tits; as long as you've got those things sticking out of your chest, the boys'll find their way to you."

It was logic that couldn't be argued with; I made an appointment at

65

one of the more exclusive salons on South Beach ("all the models use him, darling"), and my long, loose curls were clipped to just below my chin and tamed into waves. "You look like Elizabeth Taylor in *Butterfield 8*," Ricky pronounced.

Ricky never did have much in the way of tact. The eldest child of an Afro-Cuban woman and a French father who hadn't been heard from in twenty years, what Ricky had was passion, and lots of it. It was obvious in everything about him—the irrepressible laughter, the utterly shameless pursuit of the things he wanted, the temper that was lightning quick to flare up and even quicker to recede. Mainly, though, it was obvious in his big heart; Ricky, beneath all the carefully affected gloss of South Beach superiority, had one of the biggest hearts of anyone I've ever known.

He'd arrived on the Beach perhaps two or three years earlier, fleeing New York and an uninspired existence waiting tables. After a variety of jobs—including massage therapist and go-go dancer—he'd briefly been Isabella Shulov's assistant. The two were still fast friends. Ricky had also dated one of the town's more high-profile PR moguls—one of those guys who knew everybody, went everywhere, and, for a time, had always had Ricky at his side. Neither of these relationships, however, accounted for all of Ricky's eventual nightlife notoriety. It's always been my belief that character is destiny and so, in my eyes, Ricky's rise through the ranks of aspiring SoBe socialites had all of destiny's inevitability—his personality would allow for nothing less.

If you'd asked Ricky what his favorite word was, he probably would've told you that it was "me" (followed closely by "I" and "myself"), because if there was one thing Ricky dearly loved, it was attention. But Ricky's real favorite word was "glamour." It was his religion, the organizing principle around which he'd built his life. He was in love with the golden age of Hollywood studios— the days when Joan Crawford and Clark Gable had ruled the lots—and, as far as he was concerned, South Beach was where its last vestiges could be found. It was a place where men and women still put on suits and gowns when they went out in the evenings; where "drinks" were eschewed in favor of the more elegant "cocktails"; where VIP sections were private and plush and always served champagne. Ricky wasn't much of a philosopher, but I think he saw South Beach as an expression of our better selves, a sort of last-ditch salvation. As long as such a place was possible, he might have said, there was hope for humanity.

I thought at first that Ricky had all the answers. I bought into the image of himself he presented—the guy who had the town wired. I wondered why he'd taken me on as a project, why he even bothered with somebody so off-the-radar and tried to turn her into a star.

I had to know him for a while before I figured out the truth: Ricky was lost—almost as lost as I was. His work at the PR firm was low-level and low paying, and he hated—absolutely hated—having a day job in the first place. What Ricky wanted more than anything was to be the South Beach Celebrity he'd already anointed himself. He knew everybody and was invited to all the parties, but there was something missing, some crucial yet hard-to-pinpoint element that would elevate him from random party personality to nightlife immortal. He needed a gimmick.

Enter one busty sidekick.

Ricky took me to all the parties he was invited to—and, now that it was Season, that could be as many as four or five in a single night. "Do your spiel!" he'd demand imperiously, whenever he felt that a conversation at a cocktail party had lagged. This was my cue to hit the highlights from my *Rachel Dates Crazy Losers* routine, and he laughed as hard the twentieth time he heard it as he had the first. Once, I'd varied it by adding, "Seriously? I've made more men insane than syphilis." He'd laughed so hard that people had turned to stare, smiling to themselves as they watched him. After that, he made me repeat that line all the time.

He also stuck by his offer of helping me to gain PR experience. He did freelance work for some of the smaller, newer venues in town, whose getting-off-the-ground budgets couldn't accommodate the fees of the pricey PR power players—or the exorbitant retainers charged by corporate outfits like Ricky's own Dorfman Stone Rodriguez. He brought me in on a few of these accounts, introducing me as a "fabulous new publicist" who'd just moved to the Beach and who was looking for projects. I got my first small gigs, writing press releases and sending out alerts about upcoming events or the additions of new chefs and hostesses. The work wasn't sexy and it paid next to nothing, but I was finally able to add a "PR Experience" subhead to my résumé, with genuine creds to back it up.

Partying with Ricky was an entirely different experience than partying with Amy. Amy prided herself on hanging out in places or going to parties that never drew tourists, because the only people who knew about them were locals. Ricky's world was about exclusion—he liked to go places that everybody in the free world knew about, but that only a select handful could get into. If the line in front of the club wasn't at least a block long, then it almost wasn't worth Ricky's time to bother going in—what was the point of breezing past the velvet rope if there wasn't a clamoring pack of the less fortunate to witness our arrival? And wasn't that what those people waiting in line *wanted*? Ricky would always argue. Didn't they wait just to see the chosen few traipse down the red carpet, so that when *they* finally got in—and paid through the nose for door fees and overpriced cocktails and bottles of liquor that had been marked up as much as 500 percent—they'd feel like they'd gotten their money's worth?

"You've spent too much time hiding in that dive bar," he said once, referring to my nights at the Deuce. The Deuce, with its come-one-come-all brand of egalitarianism, was the very antithesis of everything Ricky stood for.

The clubs that Ricky took me to were worlds away from the Deuce. We'd walk into Bash or Groove Jet or the Living Room and head straight to VIP, joining friends of Ricky's at reserved tables where complimentary bottles of champagne were standard equipage. Occasionally, we even found ourselves drinking with the club's owners. At Liquid one night, Ricky introduced me to Chris Paciello and his partner Ingrid Casares. Ingrid was aloof and standoffish, with a cool, elfin beauty. But Chris was charming and soft-spoken, and I noticed how he always personally arranged a VIP table for Ricky whenever we made an appearance.

One evening in early November, Isabella passed along two tickets to see Chaka Khan perform at Glam Slam, Prince's club on Washington Avenue. Glam Slam was an enormous, multilevel throwback to an era when a nightclub could be big enough to contain an entire South American village. We entered with our complimentary passes, were led to a complimentary table in the highest tier of the VIP section, and were presented with a complimentary bottle of champagne.

Whitney Houston and Bobby Brown were seated with a small group at the table next to ours. When Chaka performed "I'm Every Woman," Whitney was coaxed to join her onstage, and the two of them nearly brought the house down. Spotlights remained lovingly trained on Whitney as she performed, and they followed her obediently back from the stage to her table. She lingered for a moment before taking her seat, standing right behind me as she basked in the lights and the ecstatic ovation. In a moment of spontaneous exuberance, she squeezed my shoulders in a brief hug-from-behind before the spotlight finally, reluctantly, left her to her privacy.

"See?" Ricky exclaimed in delight. "This is why we never settle for the cheap seats."

Lara always said that adult relationships are nothing more than a continual playing-out of our social issues from high school. As much as I would hate to think that's true (could there be a worse hell than perpetual high school?), I've found that she's almost never wrong when it comes to her basic assessments of human nature. As the underlying tension that had been brewing between Amy and me became more conspicuous, I didn't initially connect it to my growing friendship with Ricky. But Lara's take on it was: "There's no such thing as the perfect threesome; eventually, you get to that two-seater car on Space Mountain and somebody has to ride alone."

Amy seemed to take to Ricky initially and made an effort to incorporate him into our regular going-out group. Ricky resisted, however—the first person I'd ever seen enter Amy's orbit without being pulled all the way in. He was always charming and funny when he hung out with us, but I could tell he was ill at ease.

"Do you not like Amy?" I asked him directly one day.

"It's not that I don't *like* her . . ." He paused. "But have you ever noticed that all your little group does is sit around that house getting high, or plant yourselves in that dive bar and take turns telling Amy how wonderful she is?"

The conversation was bordering on the treasonous. "I don't know if that's an entirely accurate assessment," I said carefully.

"Look, darling, I don't mean to be disrespectful. But I don't think Amy wants friends. She wants subjects who worship her; she wants an *entourage*. And I'll occasionally be part of an entourage for Isabella Shulov because she's . . . well, she's *Isabella*, but I'm not doing it for anybody else."

His perception may have been based on what I'd told him of the financial disagreements Amy and I were having. I'd impulsively confided in him one day after one of our more recent scuffles. Ricky listened carefully but seemed confused. "I don't understand," he said. "Why can't you just tell her that you already gave her the money, or why can't you set up a system for keeping track?"

"I feel guilty," I admitted. "She's done so much for me. Isn't she entitled to more than what she's getting?"

"You two made an arrangement. If she doesn't like the arrangement, she can change it, but you shouldn't feel bad about sticking to your end of it." His expression softened. "Besides, 'what she's getting' from all this is a fabulous friend like you. And a truly generous friend would never make you feel like you were taking so much from her, because *she* wouldn't see it that way. That's what generosity is."

I smiled. "Does that go for you, too? You've also been doing a lot for me."

"What are you talking about?" But I could tell he was pleased. "Girl, not that many people can put up with as much of my craziness as you do. I know you probably find that hard to believe, but it's true."

I spent a lot of time trying to figure it all out, both then and much, much later. Why did my relationship with Amy go so quickly downhill? When did it start? What was it that I did wrong? I've always felt that I must have done something wrong, because people who are your friends don't just wake up one day and decide they don't love you anymore, do they?

I've never arrived at any completely satisfying answer. I think, to some extent, that friendships between unequals are always ultimately doomed—the very inequality does you in. At some point, you find yourself wanting to say things that you'd normally have no problem saying to a friend, like, *No, I don't feel like Chinese food tonight*, or, *No, you can't borrow my new dress that I haven't worn yet*. You can't say it, because how can you quibble over such things with somebody who's done so much for you? And yet, some nights you really don't want the damn Chinese food, and you really don't want the damn dress to leave your closet.

Eventually, the person on the other side starts to wonder; she can tell you're thinking things that you're not saying, and she wonders what else you might be thinking and not saying. Maybe you never really liked her as much as you both thought you did. Maybe you two wouldn't have become such close friends if she hadn't had the spare room you needed to live in or all the friends you needed to make. Why do we end up loving the people we choose to love, anyway? When all is said and done, is there ever such a thing as purity of intentions?

I wish I had the answers to these questions, but I don't. I guess the short answer is that I'd simply needed too much when I'd met Amy, and Amy'd had too much to give. *The endings are always contained in the beginnings*, one of my college lit professors used to say. Maybe that's true—not just in novels, but also in life.

Lara thought Amy resented all the time I was spending with Ricky, and there's probably some truth in that. I certainly wasn't on my previous 24/7 beck-and-call schedule. I also found myself using less cocaine when I was with Ricky; he never touched the stuff, and it isn't really a fun drug to do alone. And the parties that Ricky took me to started earlier. On the nights I wasn't working, we'd make our first appearance around eight thirty at some seven-to-nine affair and return home at a relatively reasonable two a.m. or so.

In any case, a certain mean-spiritedness found its way into Amy's and my everyday conversations. The first time I caught a glimpse of it was when I finally told her about my encounter with Hood at KGB. "So what you're telling me," Amy said, "is that you knew he might have a girlfriend, but you made out with him anyway?"

"It's not like it was a plan." Amy knew how I felt about Hood; how could she not understand? "It just sort of happened."

"Whatever." She got up from my bed, which is where we'd been having this little heart-to-heart. "But when some guy cheats on you someday, don't wonder why you have such bad karma."

After that, I noticed a whole new tenor in our group dynamic. We'd always poked gentle fun at each other—light teasing that was meant to be more funny than hurtful—but the tone of Amy's jokes directed at me started to feel a little aggressive, as if she wanted people to laugh *at* me rather than with me. It was like it was sleepaway camp and I was the chubby kid in the bunk who everybody picked on.

Most of these incidents were too minor to justify recounting them in great detail. Still, it's worth giving one representative example.

We were all at Amy's house one night—Raja, Genghis, Marcio, Maria, Amy, and I—and we'd made a potluck dinner. Everybody had contributed at least one dish, and, with eight or more dishes to sample and compliment, a copious amount of food had been consumed. As we sat around relaxing afterward, I could feel the waistband of my jeans digging into the flesh of my stomach, which I was very much afraid might be protruding visibly through the tight T-shirt I was wearing. I shifted around in my seat, trying to get more comfortable.

Amy looked over at me. "That's right, Rachel," she said. "Suck in that gut."

Everyone tittered, and I smiled gamely; my only recourse was either to do so or to respond in kind—and there was no payoff for me on any level to start playing that game with Amy.

Still, we all know that when one woman makes a disparaging comment about another woman's weight—no matter how minor it might be—she means to draw blood.

One morning, Amy came into my bedroom at around seven thirty. She was already fully dressed, a circumstance in itself unusual enough to have me fully awake before my head left the pillow. "What's going on?"

"Marcio got arrested last night. They picked him up for urinating outside a bathhouse." Bathhouses were where gay men congregated if and when they wanted to engage in drug-fueled, multipartner, anonymous sex free-for-alls. "I have to go to the bail bondsman to get him out."

"But—" I was clearly missing something, and I struggled to understand. "Why doesn't Maria go get him out? Is it a money issue?"

"I don't think he wants Maria to know about it yet, and I can't blame him—all things considered."

"Is it really such a big deal?" I was still a little slow on the uptake. "I mean, public urination isn't exactly classy, but all guys do it at some point, don't they?"

"Rachel," she said, and, by her exasperated tone, I could tell my ignorance was wearing out her patience. "It's *Marcio*, outside of a bathhouse, out of his pants. Do you really think he was 'urinating'? Are you that naive?"

"Oh." And then, a split second later, the dots connected in my mind. "*Oh!*" I said. "Yeah. It's probably better if you're the one who deals with it."

I never found out what explanations Marcio made to Maria when he got home. When Amy finally picked him up, he was insisting that he'd simply been caught relieving himself in an inappropriate place. Nevertheless, the five of us (including Raja) decided to go to a house party that night on one of the small, residential islands surrounding South Beach—feeling a need to defuse any tension that might be brewing between Marcio and Maria.

Ricky had been duly called and invited and had duly rejected the invitation. "There's a fabulous party at Groove Jet," he told me, "and Greg and Nicole have specifically requested your presence." Greg and Nicole Brier were the owners of Groove Jet, as well as Groove Jet in New York and Jet East in the Hamptons.

"I'm kind of locked into this," I said ruefully. "But I'll talk to you tomorrow."

"Call me tomorrow, love," he echoed, and hung up.

The soiree was standard house-party fare: semicasual outfits, lots of blow and mid-priced vodka, and deafening music pouring from the stereo speakers. There were also a fair number of straight men, and, in my ongoing quest to erase all thoughts of John Hood, I found a cute prospect almost immediately. It's true that his hair had an unfortunate tendency to feather a bit on the sides, but, as a fellow sufferer of unruly curls, I was prepared to concentrate on his winning smile and sharp wit.

Eventually, I brought him over to my friends. They talked to him briefly, in a don't-get-too-friendly-with-us way, and he left to go find me a fresh cocktail. Amy and Raja started in almost immediately, pronouncing him a "loser" with "wretched" hair, which was to be expected because I was a "loser magnet." "What are you thinking, Rachel?" Amy summed up, with an expression of both humor and contempt. "He looks like Andy Gibb!"

Marcio hadn't said a word during this entire exchange. But when Amy said "Andy Gibb," it prompted Marcio to begin singing, *Love is—higher than a mountain* . . . Everybody laughed and took up the tune, loudly singing in unison, *Love is—thicker than water!*

I felt a quick, hot-and-cold flush of anger—so overwhelming that I knew, even as I was conscious of it, that I couldn't contain it; the closest I'd come to control would be in deciding where I directed it.

It was, of course, Amy who I was really angry with, Amy who had been hurting my feelings day after day for weeks. But I couldn't say anything to Amy—not in the heat of the moment, not later in a moment of calmness. How could I lash out at somebody who'd done so much for me?

And, in a way that I couldn't quite admit but was nevertheless aware of, I was afraid of Amy—Amy who would unfailingly know where every one of my deepest insecurities lived. What I secretly feared the most was that I was, in truth, average and forgettable, that somebody like me had only succeeded so far on South Beach because Amy had picked me out—and that, with a word, she could send me back to mediocrity and separate me from Raja and Genghis and almost all of the friends I'd made so far.

So, instead, I turned on Marcio. "Yeah?" I spat, and there wasn't a shred of playful humor in my voice. "Well, at least I didn't get arrested for jerking off outside a bathhouse."

They all looked at me, stunned and speechless. Marcio's face paled as if I'd kicked him in the crotch.

The remorse came even more quickly than the anger had, and it was about ten times worse. "Marcio, I'm sorry," I said immediately. "I'm so, so sorry." *What's happening here?* I wondered. I felt sick and sweaty, almost dirty; random acts of meanness hadn't been a part of my repertoire since my earliest swing-set days.

"It's okay." He tried to smile. "Forget it."

I was persona non grata for the rest of the night. Nobody spoke to me during the remainder of the party, and Amy bid me a curt "Good night" as soon as we got home. It was the longest she'd gone without talking to me since I'd moved in with her, and, somewhere beneath the fear and embarrassment, I was grateful for the quiet.

SEVEN

All the talk around town in the following days was about White Party Week, an annual fundraiser for various AIDS charities that kicked off the Wednesday night before Thanksgiving and culminated the following Sunday. People flew in from all over the world to attend, and Ricky was abuzz with news of parties like White Knights, the Snow Ball, and Muscle Beach. Unfortunately, my work schedule didn't permit me to attend any of the events, although I did get to bartend at one officially sanctioned White Party Week cocktail reception at the Sands.

Hood, who I hadn't seen since that night at KGB, was in the crowd—talking to George Plimpton, of all people. Hood brought him over to my bar station to make the introduction, for which I was floored and grateful. As was Hood's wont, he quickly disappeared again, leaving me in the awkward—but exhilarating—position of trying desperately to think of something unforgettably witty to say to *George Plimpton* that would express my poets' solidarity and profound respect.

Nothing had come to me in the thirty seconds that he'd remained in my vicinity, but, as we watched Hood get swallowed up by the crowd, Plimpton remarked, in a voice I'd heard so often in recordings that it thrilled me to hear it in person, "There goes a brilliant young man."

It was three o'clock in the morning by the time I got home, and I'd been on my feet for nearly twelve straight hours. I groaned inwardly when I heard Amy's voice summoning me into her bedroom—at that particular moment, any in-depth altercation was way at the bottom of my wish list. But Amy and I hadn't had a real conversation since the incident with Marcio. I figured I was about to receive my long-overdue comeuppance.

I entered Amy's room and found her in bed wearing a silk bathrobe, propped up against a mountain of pillows. The only light in the room came from the television set across from her bed. "I think it's time you moved out," she said without preamble. "Right after the New Year would be best." When I didn't immediately respond, she added, "It's not that it hasn't been great having you here, and I don't want you to think we're not friends anymore or that we won't still see each other all the time. It's just that Raja needs a place to live, and I think it needs to be her turn now."

I fleetingly thought of what Ricky had said about Amy and her subjects. She looked for all the world like a queen deciding amongst the competing interests of various underlings as she absentmindedly glanced around me to get a better view of the TV.

"Understood," I said. "I'll start looking tomorrow."

A sense of relief at having gotten off so easily was mingled with a deeper sense of loss; despite what Amy said, I knew I'd just been informed that I was being fired from the position of best friend and replaced with a more suitable candidate.

Although I'd already been thinking of getting my own place (coming home to a tense house every day was difficult), I was a little scared. I'd never lived on my own before. Money was good at the bar right now, but what if it stopped coming in? Living by myself, I wouldn't have any kind of a fallback plan if worse came to worst.

"We all have to grow up sometime," was Ricky's response to this fresh crop of worries. "You'll figure it out as you go along; that's what we all do."

"True." I was silent for a moment. "I don't even have any furniture or anything. And I don't have as much money saved up as I should for first and last. You don't know anybody looking to sublet, do you?"

"Let's ask around. I'm sure we can come up with something."

Our break came through Kojo, a friend of Ricky's and another long-time SoBe denizen. Kojo knew somebody in Forte Towers on West Avenue who planned to move to Italy at the end of the year. His lease ran through July, and he was looking for somebody to take it over until then, at which point it would probably be easy enough to renew.

The apartment was a spacious one-bedroom overlooking Biscayne Bay. Ricky and I spent about five minutes looking into the walk-in closets and the balcony shimmering with watery reflections from the Bay before I announced, "I'll take it!"

"Just think of all the boys you'll have sex with here!" Ricky exclaimed.

"Let's not get ahead of ourselves," I said drily. "I don't even own a bed yet."

As you've undoubtedly guessed, political discussions of any kind were a rarity on South Beach. There were a small handful of local issues that would occasionally flare up and capture people's interest—sometimes, for example, the older homeowners would band together and demand that the clubs be required to close earlier (we were against that), or the city council would debate whether or not to add gay protection language to Miami's antidiscrimination laws (we were for that). But most of what I heard at the bar, from tourists and locals alike, was the usual chatter about sun, soirees, and celebs. So it was out of the ordinary, to say the least, when the first customers I had one night, just two days after White Party, were a couple of locals dressed in grown-up suits and ties, discussing a story that had recently been in the national news.

The story was pretty simple: A young boy had been molested by his soccer coach or Cub Scout leader or something like that. The man had been caught and tried but was released on a technicality, and the boy's mother had shot the molester to death in front of the courthouse. Now she was being tried for first-degree murder. It was a case that had been discussed at Amy's house, and, in a moment of atypical accord these days, we'd agreed that we would have done exactly the same thing.

"I wouldn't like your chances with a Miami jury," one of the men was saying to the other. "You're honestly telling me you'd prosecute it as first degree?"

"Of course I would," the second man said. "And I'd get the conviction."

"There's no way you'd get it," the first guy said. "Ask anybody around here. Ask her," and he motioned to me as I approached to get their drink orders. "See what she thinks."

It wasn't the first time somebody had tried to pull me into a debate at the bar. "I have no opinions, gentlemen," I said, with my best how-may-I-help-you cheerfulness. "I'm just here to provide service with a smile."

The second guy turned to face me. He was in his early thirties; tall and broad-shouldered, he had coarse dark hair in full retreat from his forehead, dark eyes, and darkly tanned skin. His features were too strong to be considered handsome, but his face was intelligent and he had a manner that reminded me of Hood in a way—an air of being a man in a town full of boys.

"Two Heinekens," he said. "And then I'd like to know what you think. Honestly." He placed a business card on the bar and slid it toward me. It informed me that he was Peter Santos, a division chief with the State Attorney's Office.

"What division?" I asked.

"Homicide," he said. "So you can see my interest in your opinion is more than bar banter."

"Well—and this is just what *I* think . . ." I knew that the first rule of good bartending was not being too opinionated, but sometimes (and by "sometimes" I mean "almost always") I couldn't help myself. "The guy got what he deserved, and the last thing that boy should have to deal with is having his mother taken away from him. I'd never convict the mother under those circumstances."

"The law is the law," Peter said firmly. "You can't let people take it upon themselves to create exceptions for this or exceptions for that just because things don't go their way." I must have made a face, because he said, "Go ahead—say what you want to say."

"I was just thinking that it *seemed* like you wanted my opinion, but maybe what you really wanted was the chance to soapbox your own."

"I did want your opinion," he replied with a kind of rakish humor. "Now that I know it's the wrong opinion, I'm hoping to change your mind."

"Personally, I think justice demands that exceptions be made for exceptional cases. *A society in which justice for the individual takes a backseat is a society in which the front seat is not worth sharing.*" I popped the caps off the beers. "I didn't make that up," I added. "It's from—"

"*American Jurisprudence,*" he finished. "You read *American Jurisprudence*?"

I blushed slightly and turned to discard the bottle caps. "I read a lot of things."

He looked at me more closely. "You don't look like someone who spends a lot of time reading."

I raised an eyebrow. "Did they teach you how to make those kinds of snap judgments in law school, or are you just naturally gifted?"

He grinned. "I see you're also a smart-ass."

"Oh, it's not just my ass, darlin'." I returned the grin and headed for the other end of the bar, where a group of patrons were waving anxiously for my attention. "There isn't a single inch of me that's not smart."

Things got busy after that, and I didn't catch up with Peter again until he asked for his check. He and his friend settled up, dropped some extra cash on the bar, and left. I was a little disappointed; I'd been sure that I'd sensed sparkage. *Maybe I went too far*, I thought.

I noticed Peter lingering by the door and conferring with his friend. Then he came back to the bar alone and stood in front of me. "Look," he said. "It normally takes me three or four months to hate a girl as much as I hate you right now. I think maybe we've got something here."

I smiled and reached behind the cash register for a pen.

"A prosecutor?" Ricky was aghast. "A *prosecutor*?" He made a big show of edging his chair away from mine.

"What are you doing?"

"I'm waiting for you to get struck by lightning or something."

"Oy, would you *stop* it?" We were sitting on Ricky's balcony overlooking Alton Road as we shared a pitcher of Cosmos I'd just made. "I thought you'd be happy for me. I know how much you hate the idea of me and Hood."

It was true: As far as Ricky was concerned, Hood's full name was John "that-juvenile-delinquent-he's-a-menace!" Hood. Ricky was actually friendly with Hood and had nothing against him in general—unless we were talking about him as a possible romantic interest of mine.

"Yes, but do you have to go to such extremes?" I could tell he was working himself up into quite a tizzy. "First a felon and now a *prosecutor*? Have you thought about what's going to happen when your boyfriend the prosecutor finds out how you like to party?"

I sighed heavily. "First of all, we've been out on exactly one date. Second of all, you know the kind of guys I've been with lately—the fire starters and the embezzlers and the nut jobs. Maybe what I need is a little law and order in my life. Maybe I'll give up all that 'partying' stuff." Off of Ricky's skeptical look, I added, "Or, you know, cut back on it a little."

"Well, keep him away from me. This has disaster written all over it."

"Look at it this way," I argued. "Maybe he'll get elected to political office someday, and then I'll be like Eva Peron! You can come over to the Casa Rosada and play dress-up with me."

"Ooh! That would be fabulous!" He brightened momentarily, but the frown soon returned. "I don't understand why you can't find some nice, *normal* guy who's smart and fun and has a real job, and who can go twenty-four hours without having to talk to the police."

I snorted. "Tell you what: *You* find me that guy on South Beach and *I'll* date him."

"Sometimes I think you like driving me crazy," Ricky muttered, and I laughed; driving him crazy really was a lot of fun.

Peter was my first real dating experience since I'd moved to South Beach—the kind where the man picks you up, takes you out for a meal, and ends the night with a kiss. Except for the being-picked-up part, that is—you never knew what would be going on at Amy's house, and, as long as I was still there, it seemed unwise to bring the long arm of the law right into her living room.

Our relationship progressed nicely, in good-old-fashioned dating format, from light good-night kisses on the first few dates, to under-the-shirt-over-the-bra action sometime around date four, and, finally, to overnight stays in his apartment. Located on Meridian Avenue, Peter's place was a comfortable two-bedroom decorated in typical bachelor fashion, crammed from floor to ceiling with untidy piles of law books, old newspapers, and football memorabilia.

Although South Beach was a small town, and Peter and I had several acquaintances who overlapped, he wasn't part of the club-scene crowd that Ricky and I were usually with. Nevertheless, I was trying to stay away from cocaine altogether—you never knew who'd see you where, and I didn't think the best publicist in the world could give Peter the positive spin on my drug use.

I came home from dinner with him one night to find Amy waiting for me in the living room. Before I could even say hello, she greeted me with, "Did you see Juan tonight?" Juan was our drug dealer.

"I don't think so," I answered.

"But you were on Lincoln Road."

"You know I was," I said slowly. "I told you that Peter and I were going to the Van Dyke."

Amy was sitting on the couch with her knees raised in front of her, picking angrily at one of her toenails. "Juan says he saw you and you said something to him about me wanting to buy a lot of drugs."

"Amy . . . ," I started. *Where to begin?* I thought. "I didn't see Juan tonight. And even if I did, does that sound like something I'd really say? *Hey, Juan, how are you? Amy wants to buy a lot of drugs.*"

"Well, Juan's English isn't that good."

"Not to mention," I continued, "I was on a date tonight *with a prosecutor.* Believe me, the last thing I was doing was talking about drug buys—for anybody."

"All I know is I've been hearing from people that you've been saying things behind my back."

"This is ridiculous." I paused, unsure how to proceed. "I don't know who these 'people' are," I finally said. "But tell them they can say whatever they have to say directly to my face."

Incidents like these popped up more and more often. Amy would accuse me of secretly talking about her to an anonymous group of "people," whose names she would never disclose. True, I'd gone to Ricky for advice on how to handle the arguments Amy and I had, as I knew Amy confided everything in Raja, but I'd never been the type to spread malicious gossip about a friend. I didn't understand how someone as close to me as Amy had once been couldn't figure that out.

"I can't drop her as a friend," I told Lara during one of our frequent phone conversations. "I'd be nowhere right now if it weren't for Amy—or, even worse, hanging out on my parents' couch in the suburbs."

"Sometimes," Lara said, "people can cancel out your obligations to them by how they treat you afterwards."

With everything that was going on—Amy, the move, my fledgling PR work—Peter was a welcome counterpoint of the stable and familiar. Here, finally, was something that I could comfortably settle into: a boyfriend with a day job and professional aspirations, who liked to eat pizza on the couch, watch movies and Dolphins games, and talk about the people we dealt with at work. It was always a toss-up whose stories were better—his criminals and derelicts or my celebrities and drunks.

It was four or five days before Christmas. I was leaving work, and, even at two thirty in the morning, Ocean Drive was a mob scene of tourists, roiling sidewalk cafés, and cars idling in the stop-and-go traffic. Amid all the visual clutter, it took me a second to realize that John Hood was standing on the sidewalk, smoking a cigarette and waiting for me.

When I was in high school, my favorite song was "Talk Dirty to Me" by Poison. I have vivid memories of zipping around Miami, in the secondhand red Mustang my parents had bought for me, and becoming wildly excited whenever I'd hear it on the radio. I'd roll down the window, crank up the volume, and sing along at the top of my lungs. Eventually I went out and bought the tape. I played it maybe five or six times before it was relegated to a neglected corner of the glove compartment, buried beneath the owner's manual and some discarded school notebooks. Playing it whenever I wanted wasn't any fun—it was the thrill of hearing it on the radio when I least expected it that had me hooked.

I had no more control over when or how I saw Hood than I did over what songs the radio stations aired. I didn't know his phone number or where he lived or how he spent his days or when or where he'd show up at night. Maybe if he'd been the tune I could pop into my tape deck whenever I felt like it, the effect his appearance always had on me wouldn't have been so powerful. Or maybe I'm just making excuses. All I can tell you is that as soon as I saw him—in his retro black suit, cream-colored dress shirt, and customary beige hat—I couldn't have picked Peter out of a lineup.

"Hey," I said, as I accepted a light kiss on the cheek. "What're you doing here?"

"Haven't seen you around much lately, and when I do you've usually got an attack dog with you." I knew he meant Ricky. He dropped his cigarette to the pavement and I watched it spark briefly, then blacken beneath the toe of his immaculate suede saddle shoe. "I've got a new place and all my books out of storage. You're the only dame I know in this burg who might appreciate both, so I thought I'd buy you a cocktail and take you back to see them."

"I don't know if that's a good idea," I hedged. "It's pretty late and I have a job interview tomorrow."

"Give me a lift and we can negotiate on the way. Is your car around here?"

I already had my car keys out, and it seemed silly to refuse him a ride home. "It's in the garage on Twelfth." *Besides*, I told myself, *it's always safer to have a man walk you to your car at night.*

Following Hood's instructions, I drove down Collins Avenue and pulled into a half-empty parking lot behind a dilapidated residential hotel at the southern end of Ocean Drive. All but one of the streetlights were extinguished, and we could hear merengue music and occasional shrieks of laughter drifting from various dark corners of the Beach. "This was only about nine blocks," I told him. "You probably could've walked."

Hood gave me a look that implied I was wasting his time by saying stupid things. "Turn it off for a minute," he said, and pulled a vial out of his coat pocket. He took the car keys out of the ignition and, with a fluid, practiced motion, loaded powder from the vial onto one of the keys, holding it to my nose.

That first bump was so goddamn good that it felt like somebody had replaced the blood in my veins with liquid sunbeams. I was suddenly feverish with the realization that I'd been on the verge of giving it up altogether. *Oh, baby*, I thought. *How did I ever let you get away?*

We sat in the car and talked for a while. Hood was rereading some of his favorite books, ones that detailed at great length how to rob banks and build bombs and commit untraceable murders. In fact, it was one of these books that had inspired him to participate in that bank robbery a couple of years back—the one that had forced him to "lam it" to New York. He'd mainly been responsible for the planning, he told me, and hadn't even taken a share of the money.

"If you didn't want the money, then why'd you do it?" I asked.

"For the drama." He pulled a face and I laughed.

"And how's Bamby doing? You guys still getting a good crowd?"

"You know how it is. We should all be raking in the greenbacks, but these cats can't stop claptrapping about 'better' ways to promote and run it." He smiled ruefully. *I'm John Hood*, the smile said. *Are they really telling me how to promote a party?* He looked at me from the corner of his eye. "It'd be superswell to see you there again sometime."

There was silence for a moment, thick with cigarette smoke and broken only by the sound of Hood chopping up lines on the dash as I leaned across him to get to them.

"Hey," I finally said, "what's your real last name?"

"Ask me no questions and I'll tell you no lies."

"Oh, come on. I really want to know."

"Quit asking." His irritated tone made me briefly afraid that I'd gone too far. He took a last hit off his cigarette and flicked it out the car window, smiling almost imperceptibly. Then he said, "You're the only person I know who makes me nervous."

I threw back my head and laughed again at that one, laughed until the tears came to my eyes. "*Me?* I couldn't hurt a fly if I wanted to."

The coke was almost gone and the sky was bruised with approaching sunrise. "Maybe we should call it a night," I said. Hood got out of the car and slammed the door shut, then leaned against it and lit a cigarette. *Stay in the car and yell good night through the window*, I told myself, even as I grabbed the keys and followed suit.

The smell of the ocean was so intense, it was almost a taste. *The air is redolent of salt*, I thought. "Redolent" was a word that my college poetry professor had tried hard to purge from my writing. *It isn't a word you'd ever use in real life*, he'd insisted. But I couldn't help using it now in my head: The air was redolent of salt and the cars in the distance sounded like comets, and Hood's face in the half-light was as inscrutable as a letter written in a foreign language.

"It was good seeing you, Hood," I offered. I moved forward to kiss him on the cheek.

In a move so quick it nearly made me fall down, Hood brusquely pulled me to him and then used the weight of his body to push both of us up against the side of the car. We were kissing, frantic as only five months of party lust and a gram of coke can make you.

My thoughts were fragmented—single words I may or may not have said out loud. *John.* I took one of his hands and slid it under my skirt. I kept my hand on his as his fingers moved and I moved with them, and then the movement of his hand under mine was the only thing I cared about. *There*, I thought. *Please.* The keys in my other hand were biting into skin and Hood's voice was against my ear and he was saying, *Let me hear you. . . . I want to hear you. . . .*

Afterward, I leaned heavily against him, sweaty, trying to catch my breath. We were still kissing and I smiled against his mouth. Then I pulled back and almost whispered, "I should go."

"Come inside with me."

"I can't." It was too much to consider on the spur of the moment. I knew that I couldn't sleep with Hood and then go back to life as usual. And I didn't want to be someone he slept with once and forgot about. I didn't know what it even made sense to want from a man like John Hood, but I knew I wanted more than that.

I turned back to the car and opened the door. Hood grabbed my wrist. "I don't know if I'm ready to say good night yet."

"I don't know either," I responded, torn for a moment. Then I couldn't resist. I kissed him on the cheek, pressed my lips to his ear, and murmured, "But it's been nice holding your hand."

He laughed out loud, possibly the first time I'd ever heard him do so. He hugged me tightly for a second, then released me. "I'll call you tomorrow," he said.

"Tomorrow." I got into my car and drove away.

EIGHT

Tomorrow, and tomorrow, and tomorrow / Creeps in this petty pace from day to day . . . In my moments of greatest internal melodrama, it always helped to put my sufferings into Shakespearean terms. It made it all seem nobler somehow; more like the stuff of real tragedy.

And suffer I did over the next few days—at night when I tended bar, and in the mornings when I showered and dressed, and basically every second of every hour when I wasn't actually unconscious.

The phone stubbornly, spitefully, refused to ring. I joined the ranks of tens of thousands of phone-scorned women everywhere, bumbling around with variations on a single theme playing in my head: *Why? Why hasn't he called? Did he lose my number? Did something happen to him? Did I do something wrong?* And, of course, there were no answers—the one person who could've made sense of it all had clearly dislocated his dialing finger.

Fortunately, I had other things on my mind to help keep my Hood obsession at bay. The job interview I'd told him about hadn't been something I'd made up to get out of going home with him—I had been contacted by a small nonprofit organization that was looking for an in-house public relations manager. I was excited about the possibility of a full-time PR job, but wasn't sure how I felt about returning to nonprofit.

"Well, at least it's a PR job and not an administrative job," Ricky said when I told him about it. "What's the organization called, anyway?"

"Drug-Free Kids of America."

Ricky choked, literally choked, on his martini. I pounded him on the back but was sorry I'd helped him catch his breath once he opened his mouth again. "Well, darling, I'm glad to see you're planning on keeping hypocrisy alive and well into the new year."

"I told you, I'm quitting all that," I protested. "And it's not like I think high school *kids* should do drugs just because *I* used to. There are lots of perfectly legal things I do all the time that kids shouldn't do—like drinking and smoking and having sex."

Ricky tried to contain his laughter, but he was done for by the time I got to the end of my little speech. I was laughing too. "Shut up!" I sputtered. "I'm at least eighty-five percent sincere about this, and if I crack up during the interview they definitely won't hire me."

This, of course, all happened before the night in my car with Hood. I'd tossed and turned when I'd finally gotten to bed, strung out from coke and the memory of Hood's lips and hands. It was eight in the morning before I'd fallen asleep, and my interview was at noon. I'd managed to pull it together but was positive I'd been less than coherent, babbling on about photo ops, school-based initiatives, and press-friendly community service projects. Nobody was more surprised than I was when they called the next day and offered me the job. I gave notice at the Sands, letting them know that I'd be leaving as of December 29, and that was that.

"Oh, boy," Ricky said when I gave him the news. "Most people end up in hell by accident, but you've really got it all planned out, don't you?"

"What are you, Jiminy Cricket? Can't you just be supportive and happy for me now that I've finally gotten a real PR job?"

"Oh, honey, you know I always support you no matter what you do—God help us all." In a more sober tone he added, "And you know what else? I think you'll be fabulous."

Christmas came and went, and New Year's Eve was looming. New Year's, I learned, was considered a bad night to be out and about by many of the South Beach locals (*The whole town is overrun with amateurs*, Ricky said disdainfully). Most of the people I knew were planning to stay as far from the main drags as possible. Peter called to invite me to a friend's party, but I told him that I was spending New Year's Eve in Boca Raton with Lara, where she and her three siblings came down annually to visit their parents during the holidays.

"Don't drink too much," Peter told me. "You don't want to have to move with a hangover." Peter was coming by on New Year's Day to help me move from Amy's house to my new apartment.

"It should be pretty tame," I said. "Just the two of us catching up."

"Well, have a happy New Year. I can't wait to see you." I heard the unspoken ending of his sentence: *since you've been avoiding me all week.* I hadn't been able to face him since I'd seen Hood. I was hoping that things would be clearer in my mind once I spoke with Hood, but Hood never called.

In the meantime, I couldn't wait to see Lara. "Look at your new hair!" she exclaimed as soon as I got out of my car and we hugged.

"I know. It's short, isn't it?"

"Yeah, but you look awesome."

It was great seeing Lara and her family again, as I'd done at least once a year since college. Seeing them now, along with Lara's preschool-aged nieces and nephews, was like being in somebody else's vision of what congenial, upper-middle-class life was supposed to look like. *Snapshots of the normal,* I thought. I realized that it hadn't been long since everything I'd aspired to could be summed up by what was here—talk of jobs and weddings and new homes and college funds for the kids. It was only a year ago that Eduard had been the one to drive me up here to see Lara. We'd taken her to a New Year's Eve house party in Little Havana, where Eduard's friends taught Lara (a naturally gifted dancer) how to salsa, and it had never occurred to me to question whether the following New Year's Eve would pass in exactly the same way. I hadn't even met Amy yet, and the craziest things I'd ever done were the times in college when I'd gone to parties and, drunk on grain alcohol, danced a little too suggestively with fraternity guys.

Lara and I went out to lunch and caught up. She was working in the promotions department at Sony Music and was on the fast track to a vice presidency. She was also planning to move in with her boyfriend in a few months. It was the first time I'd ever heard Lara utter the phrase, "I could end up marrying him."

She listened as I laid out my tale of Hood-related woe. "So how was the fooling-around part?" she asked.

"Amazing. Intense." I tried to keep my grin dialed down to appropriate levels. "Of course, now that he hasn't called since, the letdown is also amazing and intense. I wish I knew what was up."

"I can't tell you anything you don't already know," Lara said. "Except that you can't keep avoiding Peter. You're sleeping with the guy, which means you owe him the face-to-face breakup, if that's what you want to do."

"But I don't necessarily want to break up with Peter. I have no idea what I want." I paused. "Except, obviously, I'd like Hood to pick up a phone at some point."

New Year's Eve was comfortable and mellow. We had dinner with Lara's family and then went to a small lounge not far from their house, where we listened to live jazz and toasted the New Year with champagne. I was on the road home fairly early on New Year's Day. Peter was coming by at three o'clock to help me move and, in true procrastinator fashion, I hadn't even started packing yet.

"Call me tonight from the new place," Lara said, and I hugged her hard, wishing she didn't have to go back to California so soon.

Amy's house was silent when I let myself in. New Year's Eve flotsam and jetsam floated around the living room; empty liquor bottles, cups, Baggies, and noisemakers greeted me balefully, like a pack of guard dogs ready to pounce at an unwelcome intruder.

The door to my bedroom was slightly ajar. I pushed it open and saw that the room was completely bare: the mattress had been stripped, the desk cleaned of papers, the closet emptied. Several unsealed cardboard boxes were scattered throughout the room, and I could see that each one had been filled hastily—in a disorganized, willy-nilly fashion—as if by a burglar who'd been interrupted before he could finish the job.

I must have woken Amy up when I came in. She wandered down the hall, lightly rubbing her temples. "Hey," she murmured hoarsely when she saw me. "Did you have a good New Year's Eve?"

"Um, yeah," I replied. "What happened to my stuff?"

"Oh." She looked around. "Well you hadn't started packing yet, and I was afraid you might be trying to put off moving out, and Raja really needs to move in tonight. So we all packed up your things for you."

It was hard to say what the worst part was. Was it that the need to have me out was apparently this overwhelming? Was it the violation of having other people go through all my things in my absence, putting their hands on everything from my underwear to my writing journals? Or was it the indignity of having everything I owned tossed randomly into boxes like so much trash to be discarded? And was it *possible* that Amy didn't understand how egregious a violation of the laws of common decency this was?

I knew—I thought I knew—that she had done it to hurt me, and I was angry. In a way, though, I was grateful for my anger. It had liberated me. I finally had a good reason to do what I'd wanted to do for weeks.

So I turned to Amy, smiled a big smile, and said, "Thanks! This is such a big help! You guys saved me hours of work."

I knew I would never voluntarily speak to her again.

"Where do you want the books?" Peter called. I was in the bedroom, putting sheets on my new bed (which, along with a small TV, was the only piece of furniture in my apartment so far). Peter was in the living room, trying to make order out of chaos.

"Just leave it for now," I called back. "I'll take care of them myself."

"Then give me something else to do."

I'd decided that I would be honest with Peter about what had happened with Hood. *Look*, I'd say. *I ran into this guy one night who I knew before I even met you. Nothing major happened and I haven't spoken with him since then, but we did kiss and I thought you should know.* I didn't think it was necessary to go into more detail than that. I was prepared to accept questions, recriminations, and a certain amount of anger. My guess was that he probably wouldn't want to keep seeing me after that, but, given my own inability to make any decisions, at least somebody would be deciding something.

"By the way," he called in to me now, "do you know a guy who calls himself John Hood?"

I froze. The question caught me completely off guard, and I was glad that I was in another room. Had somebody seen us together? Did Peter know something? Was he trying to trick me into a confession before I got to make one voluntarily? My self-protection instinct kicked into overdrive. *He's a prosecutor*, it reminded me. *Just give him "yes" and "no" answers.*

"Yes," I said.

"I thought you might. He's pretty big in that party crowd you hang around with, isn't he?"

"Yes."

"Did you hear he got arrested?"

"No!" I came in from the other room as quickly as I could while still appearing nonchalant. Peter was now in the kitchen, struggling with the coffeemaker he'd brought as a housewarming gift. "What happened?"

"They picked him up a few days before Christmas. He skipped out on his probation a while back and went to New York. Guess they finally caught up with him."

"So—" My voice sounded tight and unnatural. I cleared my throat and started over. "So how much longer are they going to hold him? A couple of days?"

"Oh, he'll be gone for a while—six months to a year, at least." Peter hunted through a box for a couple of coffee mugs. "They'll make him serve out the original sentence."

I wandered into the living room and started pulling books from one of the boxes, sorting them into piles. Titles blurred and kaleidoscoped in front of me: fiction, poetry, drama. *For the drama.* I pressed my fingers to the corners of my eyes.

"Here," I said, as Peter came in with the coffee. "We might as well start stacking these against the far wall."

BOOK II
January 1998–August 1998

NINE

In most parts of the free world, New Year's Day is the hard barrier beyond which parties and revelries dare not go. But South Beach was always a town that prided itself on following no rules except its own. As long as the rest of civilization (north of the equator, that is) was gripped in the icy throes of winter, South Beach would continue to gather the frozen, huddled masses into a warm and vodka-soaked embrace.

The parties were raging stronger than ever, and it seemed as if Ricky and I were at every one of them when we weren't working. I had worked out a schedule with Drug-Free Kids that had me in their offices thirty hours/four days a week. I'd also picked up a part-time bartending gig at the South Beach Bistro on Lincoln Road, from seven to eleven p.m. on Mondays and Tuesdays.

Working two jobs to make ends meet often meant that managing my finances was a struggle, and Ricky's salary barely let him break even once he'd made the mortgage payment on his small condo. Our strapped-for-cash status, however, was never an impediment to our good time. We went to everything, paid for nothing, and enjoyed a lifestyle similar to the rich-kid crowd we were rubbing elbows with. Money was never an object because it was never a consideration. Usually, I'd leave my apartment for the evening with ten dollars for cab fare in my bag and come home with five dollars still remaining.

To my friends, like Lara, who lived in other parts of the country, I had become their number-one authority on all things South Beach, and they were full of questions. *Where are the best places to go?* they'd ask. *How much does it cost to get into a club? How expensive is it to get a VIP table?*

I hadn't the faintest idea. To this day, I couldn't tell you if the going cover charge for a typical hipper-than-thou club was five dollars or fifty. The notion of exchanging money for entrance seemed almost quaint and very far removed from me—like the things that people in books did. I was reminded of something

I'd read once about French noblewomen before the Revolution, who'd had no idea what their own kitchens looked like simply because they never visited them. As far as which clubs I preferred, I had no preference whatsoever; I went wherever Ricky said the place to be that night was, and the name on the door or the distinguishing decorating touches inside meant about as much to me as Chinese algebra.

It was all a blur of color and music and heartbreakingly beautiful people that Season. Ricky and I went to club nights, restaurant openings, art galleries, and black-tie charity galas where we sat at tables paid for by benefactors we hardly knew or corporations we couldn't have named. Sometimes our seats were comped by the charities themselves, which—much like the clubs that courted us—were trying to get the right crowd and create the right atmosphere so as to tempt money from the pockets of the people who had it.

We went to fashion shows and magazine parties and private soirees at the mansions of the millionaires and celebrities who lived on Star Island. We went to Bash, which was owned by Sean Penn, and danced on tables with titled Europeans and Brazilian movie stars, or schmoozed with models at Sylvester Stallone's Bar None. We went to 821 on Lincoln Road—a relentlessly sleek, teeny-tiny space and a favorite among the locals—for Taffy Lynn's "Studio Filthy Whore" party. ("The first club I ever went to was Studio 54 when I was a kid," Ricky would proudly inform me.) 821 also hosted Mary Dee's infamous lesbian Thursdays, which were attended by everybody—straight, gay, and bi alike. We went to Lua on Española Way and visited hallowed halls like the Liquid Lounge, the Living Room at the Strand, Glam Slam, KGB, and, of course, Groove Jet. We went to tea dances on Sunday afternoons and then, perhaps, to Jazid for live jazz and cocktails on Sunday evenings. We tended to stay home on Saturday nights, when causeway crawlers would inundate the Beach and generously pay enough in a single night to underwrite the freebies the locals got during the rest of the week. One fine Friday night in January, Ricky even managed to score invitations to the *Ocean Drive* fifth anniversary party, whose guest list was the ultimate arbiter of who was hot and who was not on the SoBe social scene. We mingled with the likes of Niki Taylor and Alonzo Mourning of the Miami Heat, and were very impressed with ourselves.

It had traditionally been Ricky who received the invitations in the mail and then wrote everything down in his calendar, telling me that day where we'd be that night. But, as people began to recognize me, they asked for my mailing address and soon my own mailbox was overflowing with party invites. Some were elegant and calligraphied while others were slick and brash, festooned with four-color photos that bordered on the obscene. I began pasting them into a scrapbook that I'd flip through from time to time. *Lee Brian Schrager cordially invites you to a black-tie benefit for . . . Mykel Stevens presents Bad Ass Bitch . . . Special Guest Sexcilia at . . . DJ Jo-Jo Odyssey spinning . . .*

Going through my scrapbook in my private hours always made me smile. *The story of a life*, I would think as I looked at it all.

I was still seeing Peter and Ricky had found a boyfriend of his own—a guy named Julian who worked as a catering manager for one of the larger hotels. Neither Peter nor Julian were much for the local jet-set scene, so Ricky and I reserved at least two nights a week for the exclusive use of our respective significant others. I would swing by Peter's apartment after-hours on the nights I went out with Ricky, crawling into bed with him at two thirty a.m. or so. "Hey, kid," he'd say sleepily, as I undressed and got under the covers. "You realize some murderer might walk tomorrow 'cause I won't be in any shape to beat a confession out of him." Waking up a little, he'd throw an arm around me and pull me closer. I would briefly think of Hood as I whispered back, "Just doing what I can to support the criminal element—they're what keeps this town interesting."

Peter and Julian were quite vocal in expressing their objections to Ricky's and my nightlife exploits. I wasn't sure exactly what Julian's issues with Ricky were; from what Ricky told me, I sensed that it was about control—that Julian didn't want his boyfriend gallivanting around town without the appropriate protection, but also didn't want to accompany him and provide an escort. Julian was about ten years older than Ricky, and his taste ran toward quiet, civilized dinners with other couples, as opposed to all-night clubland bacchanals.

Peter's reservations were far easier to figure out: He mistrusted the clubs and the night crawlers and everything that went along with them. "I work closely with the drug task forces," he would tell me. "There's a lot of bad stuff going on in some of these clubs."

You don't know the half of it, I would think. But I'd confine myself to saying dismissively, "I don't do drugs," which was, technically, true. Ricky and I were almost always drinking to excess these days, but there was certainly nothing illegal about that. I was sticking to the letter of the law, even if I was violating the hell out of its spirit.

Peter was still concerned that even the appearance of impropriety would interfere with my work on behalf of the antidrug crusaders. I think he was hammering that old chestnut about how you can't serve God and Mammon at the same time, but I was convinced that I'd be the first person in recorded history who was smart enough to get away with it. I would feel a deep satisfaction as I looked at my closet, divided by halves into conservative business suits on the one side, with an assemblage worthy of a Vegas showgirl on the other. I would think to myself that it looked like the closet of a spy or a secret agent, somebody living a double life. After so many years of toeing the line, it secretly thrilled me to think in some nonspecific way that I was getting away with something.

These conversations between Peter and me occurred more regularly as the weeks rolled by, and I began to devise clever strategies to get out of them. I'd learned early on that Peter (like a ridiculously large percentage of the male population) was a sucker for the occasionally affected Southern accent. So, when he'd start blah-blah-blahing about the recklessness of my nighttime pursuits, I would open wide, innocent eyes and, in my best Scarlett O'Hara impersonation, I'd say, "Well, Ah *trah* very hard to be good, Mr. Prosecutor. . . ." Then I'd drop my voice by an octave and snuggle close to him. "But you make me do such *bad* things." This usually earned me a roar of laughter and a one-way ticket to the bedroom, where all such conversations (among other things) were temporarily tabled.

As time went by, I began to be amazed that I'd ever been so intimidated by the scenesters I now partied with on a daily basis. There was surprisingly little attitude in South Beach's VIP rooms. Getting past the velvet ropes could be a Herculean task if you didn't have the right look or know the right people, but, once you'd made your way into the inner sanctum, you were accepted without question. It seemed to me that the social ladder in South Beach had just one rung—the only real trick was finding the ladder in the first place.

One of the best examples of how class order melted away under the night-lights involved Ryan Pfeiffer, co-owner of the South Beach Bistro and my boss. Ryan was very cute in a dead-ringer-for-Sean-Penn sort of way, and was notoriously surly with his employees—he'd once dressed me down in front of the entire staff for throwing away a half-eaten roll he'd left on the bar. When he saw me at parties, however, he would always approach me in a drunkenly desultory fashion, slinging one arm around my shoulders and trying to inconspicuously graze the top of my cleavage with his fingers. He always gave me the faintly slurred greeting of, "Hey . . . you."

"I work for that man," I said to Ricky one night, "and he has no idea what my name is. And even worse, he doesn't know my name and he thinks I might actually go home with him."

"We all forget names sometimes," Ricky replied. This was true. Ricky and I had, in fact, worked out a code to circumvent the name-forgetting problem we occasionally ran into. If we greeted someone by saying, "Hello, sweetie-darling," this was our way of saying to the other one, "Please, for God's sake, introduce yourself because I can't remember this person's name to save my life." If it was just "sweetie" or just "darling," all was well, but "sweetie-darling" meant that a potentially devastating faux pas was right around the corner.

"This is different," I said. "It's one thing to forget somebody's name and it's another thing to *try to have sex with somebody* whose name you don't remember. Especially since I work at his restaurant."

In any other place and at any other time, I would never have had the nerve to do what I ended up doing to get Ryan to remember—once and for all— who I was. But I was becoming increasingly daring, both from the permissive ambiance that permeated South Beach and from my burgeoning acceptance within its social schema.

I was standing at the bar at KGB one night when I felt a pair of arms encircle me from behind and pull me back against a man's chest. Craning my neck around, I looked up into Ryan's face. I turned and wound my own arms about his neck, pressing my body as close as possible to his—so close that I could see my reflection in his half-closed eyes.

"Ryan," I said. I lowered my voice, enunciating my words slowly and carefully. "I will take you home right now," I told him, "and give you a full half-hour of the most unbelievable head you've had in your entire life." I paused for a beat and ran one of my hands from his shoulder to his chest. "If you can tell me what my name is."

Ricky was standing behind Ryan, making a horrified face and gesturing furiously while trying not to spill his cocktail. It was a toss-up who looked funnier: scandalized Ricky, or Ryan as he stepped back and made an almost physical effort to focus on the question before him. "How about ten minutes if I get the first initial?" he suggested hopefully, and I laughed.

"I'm not haggling," I told him. "This is your standard take-it-or-leave-it type deal."

He tried hard to maintain a serious expression as he continued to bargain downward. "I really only need about three minutes."

"I wouldn't brag about that if I were you, and I might remind you that the clock is ticking on my offer."

I could almost see the alcohol-drenched wheels struggling to turn in his mind. Finally, he said, "I don't know. I'm sorry, I know I should, but I don't."

"It's Rachel," I said. "Rachel Baum. And it's definitely a name you should know, considering you sign my paychecks every week."

"Oh, yeah! I thought I recognized you from somewhere. Besides parties, I mean." He took a swig off the glass of scotch he was holding. "So I guess if I push my luck, I'm running into a sexual harassment suit."

"Pretty much."

"Unless you want to dance with me?" He smiled in a winning way that had undoubtedly succeeded with legions of girls in the past—and it almost succeeded with me, so charmed was I to see him playing neither the drunken groper nor the tyrannical boss.

"I'd love to some other time," I said, somewhat regretfully, "but right now I should get back to Ricky." Ryan grinned good-naturedly and shrugged. Then he kissed me on the cheek and ambled off.

"Are you *insane*?" Ricky demanded as soon as Ryan was gone. "What would you have done if he'd remembered your name?"

I couldn't stop myself anymore and gave in, laughing harder than I had in weeks. "Trust me, I was one hundred percent positive that he wouldn't have known my name if he'd picked it out of a hat." Sipping my cocktail, I added, "Besides, that was totally worth it. You should've seen your face."

"You're trying to give me a heart attack, is what you're trying to do," Ricky said, and I could tell that he was attempting to control his own laughter.

For the rest of the time that I lived on South Beach—even several years later—every time I saw Ryan Pfeiffer, he'd make a big point of saying, "Hello, *Rachel*. How are you, *Rachel*?" Until finally I had to roll my eyes and say, "That ship sailed a long time ago, Ryan. Let it go."

As much as Ricky had pretended to be appalled, he loved that story and told it everywhere; Ryan was always "poor Ryan Pfeiffer" whenever Ricky referred to him after that. I think Ricky knew that it was an exercise in one of the first lessons he himself had taught me: No matter what you do on South Beach, never let them forget your name.

Part of never letting them forget your name was dressing the part, and Ricky and I had hours of fun putting together ensembles for my public appearances. "Push those tits out, honey!" Ricky would say whenever we went shopping. "They're what's getting us past the doormen."

I took all the money I wasn't spending when I went out and put it into my wardrobe—and soon I had a collection to make any Hollywood starlet jealous. I had gowns and cocktail dresses of all descriptions—ones with sequins and straps and ones that were matte and strapless; dresses made of little more than mesh and netting; gowns that were backless and ones that were high necked; knee-length and floor-length and oh-my-God-it's-a-Band-Aid length; gowns with ostrich feathers or rhinestones; solids and leopard prints, embroidered and patterned; evening dresses in black and red and gold, or featuring wild Pucci prints in shocking pinks, yellows, and electric blues; dresses that showed cleavage and dresses that showed leg and more than a few that showed some of both. And I bought wild, extravagant jewelry to go with them—huge necklaces, bracelets, and earrings made from beads, rhinestones, and silver; or tribal-looking pieces made from shells and savage, rough-hewn, semiprecious stones. Sometimes I eschewed jewelry altogether and covered every inch of exposed skin in shimmering bronzers or body glitters. I would wear boas like a romantic '30s movie queen or huge faux-fur wraps like a modern-day drag queen or—on rare occasions—black leather pants with black silk tank tops, like a high-glam biker chick. "Never forget," Ricky would tell me, "you're competing with models and drag queens for the attention of gay men."

The ultimate goal of attracting all this attention was to get your name and photo in the nightlife columns that graced our numerous local magazines and newspapers—or, possibly, featured on the local TV shows that covered nightlife, like *The Scoop with Connie Cabral* or *Live Wire* or *Steph Sez* or *Deco Drive* (which was the most prestigious, since the other three were cable access, whereas *Deco Drive* ran on the Fox affiliate).

All the news in South Beach was good news, with our local press operating on that mom-popular dictum: *If you don't have anything nice to say, don't say anything at all.* Naturally, nothing was ever printed about individual arrests, or stints in rehab, or who was spotted doing what in which bathhouse. But the rule extended beyond that and included a strict, unspoken prohibition against criticizing any club, promoter, party, or person by name. The closest anybody would come would be to politely refrain from mentioning anything (so that, if a party was truly awful, you wouldn't read an unflattering write-up of it in the papers—you simply wouldn't read about it at all).

It was, therefore, crucial to receive even the sporadic validation of seeing your photo in the papers. Occasionally Ricky and I would find his name or picture somewhere after a week of parties. Mine, however, had yet to show up.

The press turned out in droves toward the end of January for the Groove Jet anniversary bash. Groove Jet was always a scene, but it seemed as if every last resident in the 33139 zip code was there that night. In the crowd I saw the people I was starting to know by sight and, in some cases, by introduction: pioneers like Isabella Shulov, Louis Canales, and Andrew Delaplaine; club promoters like Tommy Pooch, Tony Guerra, and Michael Capponi; Glenn Albin of *Ocean Drive*; renowned publicist Charlie Cinnamon; high-profile partiers like

Lydia Birdsong, Adrina Balistreri and Adam Kohley, and Merle and Danny Weiss (the acknowledged "First Couple" of South Beach). The lights from the cameras were hot, the champagne was cold, and I found myself occasionally blinded by the reflection of flashbulbs off of sequins and glitter.

Ricky and I spent most of the evening beating a slow trail back and forth between the interior of the club and the outdoor VIP courtyard. Since getting to the bar was such a nightmare, we'd made the unusual move of each stocking up on two cocktails at once, and I concentrated carefully on not spattering vodka cranberry all over my champagne silk dress.

As we were leaving the bar, I saw Amy out of the corner of my eye, walking past us in the opposite direction. She looked breathtaking as usual, and my stomach jumped. *Just pretend you didn't see her,* I told myself, and quickly averted my eyes. Ricky was behind me, and I heard her greet him as he paused briefly to kiss her hello. She detained him by the arm for a moment and whispered something in his ear. I continued walking toward our table.

"Didn't you see Amy?" Ricky asked when he finally reached me.

"Oh." I carelessly tapped my cigarette against the ashtray. "Is Amy here?"

"Yeah, she's here. And she saw you." The night was musky, the air around us heavy with sweat and smoke and perfume. Ricky took his jacket off. "She's pretty pissed that you walked right by without saying hello."

"Here's the thing: If I said anything to Amy, it would turn into a fight. And I have a theory that it never pays to fight with anyone who's crazier than you are."

Ricky chuckled. We both knew that I was still leery of tangling with Amy directly, but we also knew that the one wound I could inflict—more than anything I could say or do, because Amy's beauty and entire mode of living made her impervious to such injuries—would be to ignore her altogether.

"Well, congratulations, darling," Ricky said. "You have your first enemy on South Beach."

"Funny." I picked up my cocktail and toyed with the straw. "Having Amy as an enemy doesn't feel any different than having her as a friend."

I was in my office the following Friday. It was one of those hectic days—the kind where the phone won't stop ringing, the coffeemaker won't work, and your coworkers seem to grow extra mouths just so they can ask you twice as many questions. My mother and Peter had both called that morning, and I'd asked the receptionist to tell them I'd call back. When Ricky called, however, saying it was urgent, I told her to put him through.

"Darling," Ricky said immediately. "Have you looked at today's paper yet?"

"Not even. I'm so crazed." I picked up my unopened *Journal*. "Give me a hint and tell me what section I'm looking for."

"The weekend section, obviously. Isabella's column."

Other than a spot in *Ocean Drive*, Isabella Shulov's "Queen of the Night" column was arguably the most coveted photo op on the Beach—not just because she was *Isabella*, but also because the *Miami Journal* was a bona fide, mainstream newspaper, and everybody in South Florida read it. It was Ricky's habit to page through her nightlife highlights first thing every Friday morning.

I extracted the weekend section and flipped through it until I spotted Isabella's familiar photo adorning the top of the page. And there it was, big as life: a picture of Ricky and me. *Nightlife celebrity* **Ricky Pascal** *and newest diva-in-residence* **Rachel Baum**, the caption ran. *Seen at Groove Jet's anniversary fête.*

I realized that Peter and my mother had probably already seen this. Peter might be calling to congratulate me or to lecture me on the perils of nightlife decadence—it was hard to know for sure. My mother would, presumably, be pleased but curious as to what I'd done to earn myself a photo in the paper.

"Wow," I said. "This is pretty major." I tried to keep from feeling too gratified. *What does it really mean, after all?* I asked myself. Nevertheless, I was delighted.

"Well, my darling," Ricky said. "You have Amy Saragosi for a nemesis and a photo in Isabella's column. I'd say you've officially arrived."

TEN

After years of growing up in one of Miami's many far-flung, anonymous suburbs, small-town living came as a bit of a culture shock to me. South Beach—measuring only about one square mile—was a small town. It was like Peyton Place with Art Deco and movie stars. The only way that I could ultimately make sense of it was to put it into a context I already knew, so I always thought of South Beach as something similar to my college's fraternity and sorority system. Going to a club at night, I would have the same sense I'd had of walking into a fraternity house party, knowing that I would already know almost everybody there. I would compare Lincoln Road to the student union—the place where everybody gathered between classes.

Considering the social structure, I decided that there was one general übergroup of three or four hundred people who threw all the parties, ran all the papers, controlled the local government, always made the scene, and had at least a first-name awareness of everybody else. As in college, this general group broke down into dozens of subcliques—groups of twos, threes, or fours who everybody recognized as being inseparable. Wherever you saw club promoter Kevin Crawford, for example, you were sure to see his leggy sidekick Desiree Reyes. Andrew Delaplaine, who published *Wire*, could always be found in the afternoons warming a corner of the bar at 821, usually in the company of Crispy the bartender and *Live Wire* correspondents Janet Jorgulesco and Scott Hankes. The writers and editors of *Ocean Drive* ran in a get-thee-behind-me pack. And the drag queens were an entire clique unto themselves.

When I'd lived with Amy, I'd been a part of her clique. Nobody from that group was speaking to me anymore, but, before I could get too nostalgic, I found myself with a new codependency cadre to take their place.

It's hard to remember anymore exactly how or when or why our little group gelled. I know I met Kojo Goldstein early on, Ricky's friend who'd helped me find my apartment. But that wasn't when we became close. In fact, for a time, Kojo always had trouble remembering me—not just my name, you understand, but my entire existence. For months, whenever Ricky and I ran into him, he would introduce himself to me as if for the first time. I'd remind him that we'd already met, and he would always say the same thing: "You're so beautiful, I really should remember you."

"I know it ought to bother me," I'd say to Ricky, "but he totally sells that 'you're so beautiful' line. I can't stay mad at him."

Even before I got to know Kojo well, I sensed a sweetness in him—albeit a reluctant one. He struck me as a guy who wore his heart on his sleeve but who'd rather go sleeveless, if only he knew how. I remember wondering how he'd lasted so long in the social rough-and-tumble of South Beach—a town that was fun and friendly, but not always gentle.

Of medium height and build, Kojo had blue eyes and the kind of rough, darkish-blondish hair that you could tell would instantly grow into Jew-fro if left to its own devices. His name at birth had been Joseph, but he'd legally changed it to Konnor when he was of age. Kojo was the combination of the two names he'd used back when he was a DJ, and, as with John Hood, it was an identity that stuck.

Kojo's parents had divorced when he was in his teens, and his father had died about ten years later. Kojo's mother still lived in L.A., where Kojo had grown up before moving to Chicago. In addition to DJing, he'd worked variously in advertising, retail, restaurant management, club promotions, party planning, and, occasionally, drug dealing. He and his older brother had been friends with Andy Warhol, and Kojo had an original Warhol portrait of his brother (who'd died of an overdose) hanging on the wall of his enormous Lincoln Road loft.

He'd eventually moved to South Beach, where he speedily established himself as a public figure. He was a member of the White Party Week and Winter Party Week committees, and served on committees for the South Beach Business Guild and South Beach After Dark. He'd also started *SoBe Style* magazine, a strictly local glossy that came out weekly and provided ample coverage of everything hot and hype-worthy on the SoBe scene. In another ain't-it-a-small-world coincidence, it was Kojo who'd used the remainder of his trust fund to open the ill-fated nightclub Spin.

"That closing party was one of the seminal nights in my life!" I'd exclaimed when I first learned this. "That was where I—" *That was where I met John Hood*, I'd been about to finish. *That was where I did coke for the first time.* But these were things I had resolved to put behind me, so I'd settled for concluding, "It was one of the first real parties I went to on South Beach."

"So glad you could be there." He gestured around his apartment. "Your five dollars helped me keep a roof over my head." Indeed, Spin had sucked what was left of Kojo's bank accounts dry, having never received the kind of support he'd undoubtedly hoped to garner with all of his community service. After months of struggle (during which he'd fruitlessly invested his last fifty thousand dollars in *SoBe Style*—which had gone on with his partners, but without him), Kojo had gotten work as a salesclerk at an Eastern-themed furniture and jewelry store on Lincoln Road called Moondance.

Mike Becker was a reporter on the news show *The Times*, which was going to premiere on the soon-to-be-launched WAMI in Miami (Barry Diller's grand experiment in local television programming). Our mutual friend Joe had introduced Mike to me at a dinner party as his "hide-the-body friend," his theory being that everybody needed at least one friend you could call at three in the morning and ask to show up at your door ten minutes later with a shovel and a car—no questions asked.

Mike had been raised in the farmlands of Nebraska, although he'd subsequently toiled away at small local stations in Cleveland and Minneapolis before moving to South Beach with Seth, his lover of ten years. Seth was HIV-positive and, about two years earlier, the HIV had mushroomed into full-blown AIDS. Believing that Seth was dying, Mike had quit his job and gone deeply into hock in order to finance an extended trip for them through Europe, wanting to make the most of whatever time Seth had left. Except that Seth had, perplexingly, refused to die, and the end result of all this alone time together was that the two of them could no longer stand each other. They'd recently broken up, and Mike was alone for the first time in over a decade.

Mike was the straightest gay man I'd ever met; although he was always funny, he was often tactless and crude, collected comic books, and had decorated the living room of his apartment with a pinball machine and a fire hydrant. Regarding his off-camera wardrobe . . . well, perhaps the most telling description of Mike's fashion aesthetic came from his dad; when Mike had finally come out to his parents, his father had been momentarily nonplussed before saying, "Aren't you guys supposed to dress a lot better?"

Mike and I had done a gay man/straight girl insta-bond the night we met, and he, like Ricky before him, had gotten my phone number and didn't stop dialing it for the next three years. We went to a movie the next day and had dinner the night after that, and a few days later he took Kojo—one of his closest friends—and me to a staff party for WAMI's news division. That was the night Kojo finally learned how to remember me; thus, the nucleus of a group dynamic was born.

So I guess, as I follow the genealogy back to its earliest roots, it was Mike who was the glue—the genus, genius, and cock-eyed visionary behind our somewhat improbable and occasionally dysfunctional subgroup on the ever-bustling Island of Misfit Toys. It was Mike who kept track of all our birthdays, planned all our group outings, and whose philosophy it was that there was no point in doing anything singly or in pairs when we could just as easily do those same things in a group of three or more. And it was fitting that it was Mike, the most generous of us all—the one who'd give you five dollars out of his pocket even if he was down to his last ten.

I often observed to Ricky that the only accurate way to measure South Beach relationships was in dog years, that a year of friendship on South Beach was equal to seven years of friendship anyplace else. All three of them—Ricky, Kojo, and Mike—were loud and raucous and hilarious, and they lived and loved to such excess that I didn't always know how to keep up with them. But despite (or probably because of) all that, they very quickly became my family away from family. I still can't imagine how I would have lived my life on the Beach without them.

And I don't want to.

Of course, as Lara had pointed out once, the course of true group love never does run smooth. Ricky was initially a little reluctant to sign on for a foursome. He genuinely liked Kojo and Mike, but as far as he was concerned, he and I were going places and the lighter the load, the easier the climb. A couple is a marketable commodity; you can always seat two extra people at a dinner party or breeze them inside the club, even when the line's around the block. Groups, though, are cumbersome, and Ricky liked leaving his options open.

Kojo, on the other hand, was usually in a state of quasi-hibernation. I think he blamed the South Beach social elite for the downfall of his club—for imbibing all his free liquor while never giving him the kind of press that would've drawn the causeway crawlers who made things profitable. Every couple of months or so, he would re-emerge at some splashy, high-profile event and be semiresentful when people expressed surprise at seeing him again (for the record, it was always happy surprise—people persisted in loving Kojo far more than he gave them credit for). "It's not like I was *dead*, darling," he would say.

Mike didn't care where we went or what we did as long as we were all together and there were plenty of Latin boys for him to ogle. He had a preference for South Americans bordering on the fetishistic, and he loved when they called him "*papi*" or told him his wheat-blond hair and slate-blue eyes were "*muy bonito*." He didn't understand why Ricky resisted too much togetherness, or why Kojo resisted going out all the time.

And me—what did I want? I just wanted to have friends to love who loved me back, to build a support system after the two-in-one blow of having my relationships with Eduard and Amy fall apart within a six-month period.

Naturally, I was anxious that any potential rough edges between Peter and my new friends be smoothed over. It was Kojo, sensing my concerns, who offered to host a round of "getting to know you" cocktails for the five of us in his loft one February night. Kojo had once been known for throwing legendary parties in that loft—fundraisers, for example, on behalf of groups like Save Dade, a local civil rights organization that championed various LGBT (Lesbian, Gay, Bisexual, Transgendered) causes. He would invite everybody of note on the Beach, from drag queens, club kids, and party promoters to Mayor Kasdin, city council members, and some of the town's wealthiest (and shadiest) real-estate developers. "Fags, freaks, and felons," he would say, quoting Truman Capote's philosophy of how a party ought to be composed.

Kojo's loft was painted white and accented in primary colors—a bright blue cubicle couch with red throw pillows, a coffee table made from cheerful yellow plastic. He had etageres loaded with kitschy toys and pop-culture memorabilia, mostly from the '70s. Ricky and Mike arrived early the night that I brought Peter over, and the three of them worked to create a "lighting concept" by covering Kojo's track lighting with colored gels, tingeing the space with a warm, mysterious glow. They also stocked Kojo's bar with beer and wine and munchies, while carefully concealing any contraband that might be unwise to display in front of my officer of the court.

Despite all the preparation, it was disastrous from the get-go. When Peter and I got to the downstairs door and rang the buzzer, Kojo leaned over the balcony and shouted, "*Where* have you been—we called for a fag-hag over two hours ago!"

I turned and smiled at Peter. *Aren't my friends funny?* my smile said.

Not really, Peter's eyes answered.

God bless them, they did try. Mike, the news producer, helpfully informed Peter that everybody in his business appreciated a good homicide. Ricky, with a certain mock-naïveté he could assume when he chose, wondered aloud if Peter's job was as glamorous as *Miami Vice*. Kojo, who could never sit still for more than five minutes at a time, manned the turntables that were always set up in the far corner of his living room, taking breaks from playing DJ to try to engage Peter in conversation. "We love her boobs," he told Peter, and I think he thought he was congratulating Peter on having such a busty and fabulous girlfriend. "If you two break up, we get custody of the boobs. It's in the pre-nup."

"Tell you what," Peter replied. "If we break up, you can keep them. But while I'm here, maybe we should find a more appropriate topic of conversation."

The truth is, I don't think anybody could have said or done anything to make that evening go down well. Part of Peter's job was to size people up on a first meeting, matching them to the list of profiles he'd accumulated in his head over the years. So I think he knew there were drugs on the premises as surely as if they'd been in plain sight.

More than that, though, there was a competition taking place that night, and the trophy was my attention. Straight or gay, they were all men—and men who can't share a woman will fight off the others until somebody's out of the running. Peter knew these guys would have been just as happy to see the last of him—happier, even—and he, in turn, had no desire to see them gain any more influence over me.

As I put it to Ricky when we discussed the fiasco the next day, "Somebody should've just peed in a circle around me. Then at least everybody would've known who'd marked what territory."

As February wore into March, Kojo and Mike gave me my first exposure to the more overtly gay subculture of South Beach—at clubs like Twist, Paragon, Salvation, and Loading Zone. These were strictly boys' clubs, and I was often the only girl there; just me and acre after acre of shirtless, sweaty, hard-bodied boys, dancing ecstatically to whatever techno music was the moment's latest-and-greatest.

Then there was the Warsaw Ballroom on Collins Avenue, the legendary pleasure dome that was one of South Beach's first and best monuments to hedonism. In its heyday, everybody from Susanne Bartsch to Gianni Versace threw parties at Warsaw. The crowd was more mixed, and more glamorous, than the other boy clubs and was therefore the only one Ricky cared to frequent on a regular basis, although he was known to make late-night appearances at Twist and Salvation once the evening's chicer events had culminated.

Large enough to encompass a stage, Warsaw had been the site of some truly over-the-top spectacles. Among the most notorious were evenings of "performance art," wherein simulations of various left-of-center sexual acts had somehow devolved into the real thing. Had the owners received a nickel along with every fine and citation they were served with, Warsaw might still be open today.

It was at Warsaw where I tried Ecstasy for the first time. It was pleasant enough, the way that it sent warm currents shooting through my limbs, but it almost felt like it was slowing me down. It didn't lift me up and out of myself or give me the rush that cocaine did.

It was also at Warsaw where I saw my first go-go boys, muscular young men in neon green thongs and mod-ish white go-go boots who danced on the bar for tips and more. I was standing with Ricky and Mike one night, taking it all in, as I told them that Peter and I had been having problems lately. "Maybe you shouldn't drink so much before you go over there," Ricky said. He nodded meaningfully at the empty martini glass in my hand that represented the fourth cocktail I'd consumed since my arrival.

"There are two things I know in life," I responded. "Number one, money does buy happiness, and number two, liquor does solve problems."

I'd just finished imparting this bit of tongue-in-chic wisdom when one of the thonged dancers jumped down from the bar and approached us, wrapping his arms around me and planting a wet kiss on my cheek. "You're gorgeous," he shouted over the music, pressing his mouth to my ear. "Do you have a boy-friend?"

I felt unaccountably shy all of a sudden. "Um, I think the question is, do *you* have a boyfriend?"

He beamed. "Actually, the right question is, do I have a *girlfriend*? And the answer is no." He tightened his arms around my waist and rubbed his hands along my back. "I get off work at five. We could go back to your place."

I was used to more flirtatious foreplay (or, y'know, name introductions) before apartment go-sees were scheduled, and didn't know how to handle this very direct request from this very almost-naked guy. So I shrugged and smiled and waved my hands around to indicate that I couldn't hear him over the music. Then I put a dollar bill in his thong and sent him on his way.

"What was that about?" Ricky asked as the go-go boy left.

"He wanted to come home with me."

"And you turned him down? Look at him! You could crack a walnut on that ass!"

I rolled my eyes. "I'm a straight girl, remember? Straight girls don't go right from eye contact to sex."

"You should treat yourself, honey! You never treat yourself!" He said it as if we were discussing whether or not I should cheat on a diet with a hot fudge sundae.

That was the night when Mike explained to me the concept of a "trick"—gay shorthand for a commitment-free, one-night stand. It was a word that could be used as both verb and noun: For example, one could say, "I tricked with a totally hot muscle-boy last night." It was also equally correct to say, "I took this trick home last week and then, two days later, I see the trick on Lincoln Road wearing my new Gucci belt!"

Tricking was the raison d'être of clubs like Warsaw and Twist. It was the consensus of Ricky and Mike that I'd passed up a prime tricking opportunity by letting my go-go boy disappear. "But I didn't even know his *name*," I protested, to no avail. Nor did arguing that I was already involved with somebody get me anywhere.

The lights in the club flashed around me in brilliant, multicolored beams, as if I were trapped in the heart of a prism. The music poured so hard through the speakers that the glass I was holding vibrated. It was an incongruous place to ponder the future of a relationship. But I was starting to think that staying with Peter might be more trouble than it was worth. After all, I got all the male attention I could ask for from Ricky and Kojo and Mike, and the countless other men—gay and straight—who brought me cocktails and lit my cigarettes and told me (as they dutifully told all the regular female scenesters) how beautiful I was. And it wasn't like sex was hard to come by either. It was offered everywhere, mine for the taking, even when I was flanked by gay men in one of the gayest clubs on the Beach.

Warsaw at four a.m. was hardly the appropriate locale for deep thinking. I told myself that it didn't make sense to try to figure out my future with Peter right then and there.

Nevertheless, I could read the writing on the wall. I was becoming an expert in downward trajectories.

My office at Drug-Free Kids wasn't really an office, per se. What I actually had ownership of was one desk in the middle of a fair-sized office suite. There were only five of us who worked there: me, two school coordinators—who took the programs to the "streets"—an executive director, and an all-around girl Friday who served as receptionist and office assistant. Only the executive director had his own private office; the rest of us clustered in the larger public area.

Needless to say, there wasn't much in the way of privacy for phone calls.

So when Peter called me a few days after the Warsaw incident to discuss our relationship, I knew I was in trouble.

"You were supposed to come over last night," he was saying. "You didn't even call to cancel."

I tried to remember. Was I supposed to be there last night? It was getting so hard to differentiate one night from another, except for the two nights a week I tended bar. Ricky had taken me to a very important party at Bash for something or other. I'd had a vague, nagging feeling that I was forgetting something, but hadn't been able to pinpoint it.

"Hold on a second," I said, catching the receptionist's signal that I had another call holding. I pressed the button for my second line and said crisply, "This is Rachel."

"I wrote a poem last night," said a voice I recognized as Kojo's. "Actually it was an epic poem except really it's an interpretive dance and it's all about your boobs."

"Oy, Kojo." I was laughing even as I tried to sound exasperated. "Now's not a good time. Let me call you back." I clicked back over to Peter. "Still there?"

"Yeah, I'm still here." His voice was terse. "Did you forget or did I just never make it onto your social calendar?"

"Look, I'm sorry, okay? I'm in the middle of this charity golf tournament we're planning, plus it's the height of Season. . . ." The red light on my phone was flashing again. "Sorry. I have another call holding. Give me two seconds." I pressed the blinking red button. "This is Rachel."

It was Mike. Mike was having problems with Adonis, his on-again, off-again boyfriend. The two of them had an arrangement whereby they were allowed to trick with outsiders as long as they did it together in the context of a three-way. Apparently, Adonis wasn't living up to his end of the bargain, as Mike had come home the other night and found Adonis and a trick on the couch. I didn't even know how to begin to advise Mike; the whole idea of a monogamous relationship that sometimes included third parties was something I couldn't quite get my head around.

". . . so I told him, *I didn't give you keys to my apartment so you'd have a more convenient place to trick behind my back*, and then *he* was like . . ."

"Mike," I interrupted, "Peter's on the other line and he's not in a good mood. I'll call you later." I pressed the button. "Peter?"

"This is bullshit, Rachel. I hardly ever see you or talk to you anymore, and when I do, it's always like this—with you being distracted or forgetful or drunk."

"So now I'm a giant lush because a couple of nights a week I have a couple of drinks?" He started to respond, but I cut him off as the receptionist signaled me yet again. "Hold on, Peter." Pause. "This is Rachel."

"Hi, girlie," said Ricky. "I just called to tell you that Merle and Danny Weiss loved meeting you last night. I talked to Merle this morning and she couldn't stop raving about how fabulous you are."

"That's great," I said. "But right now I've got a pissed-off boyfriend holding on line two."

"Oh boy. Call me when you're done with that little drama." He hung up.

"Let me ask you a question," Peter said when I'd clicked back over. "Did they not have a pay phone where you were? Was it out of order? Did you forget to bring change?"

"Jesus Christ," I muttered under my breath.

"What did you say?"

"I *said*, 'Jesus Christ.' I was *thinking*, 'Arguing with this guy feels like arguing with my father.' Got any more questions you're not going to let me answer? Or maybe I should go and you can have this conversation by yourself."

"Maybe I'm asking and answering my own questions because you go out every night and come back too drunk to carry on a real conversation."

I was so tired. Like most days, I was also slightly hungover from the night before. My head was throbbing. *Why can't he just leave me alone?* "Well, with as much fun as you've been lately, it's not like I can stand being around you when I'm *sober*."

Ouch, I thought, even as I heard it coming out of my mouth. I looked around to see if any of my drug-free coworkers had heard me. They all busily pretended to have no idea what was going on. Peter was silent, and I took a deep breath to steady myself. "Look," I said in a gentler tone, "now really isn't a good time for this conversation."

"I'll call you tonight." He hung up without saying good-bye.

I stayed in that night, waiting up until daybreak for Peter to call. I even tried calling him a couple of times, although I didn't leave any messages. But the phone never rang. Not even once.

I watched through my window as the morning sky turned a pale pink. I thought drowsily that I'd love to have a dress—one perfect party dress—in exactly that shimmering, delicate, shell-pink color.

It occurred to me that it was the first time since I'd moved to South Beach that I'd watched the sunrise from my own bed.

ELEVEN

The mail I received in those days consisted mostly of mundane bills and the party invitations that outnumbered them nearly four to one. So I was unprepared, and more than a little surprised, when I came home from work one afternoon in late March to find a letter bearing Amy's return address.

Before moving out of Amy's house at the end of December, I'd given her a check for the last of my share of the phone and utilities. I may as well admit up front that bookkeeping has never been among my talents, which, coupled with the fact that Amy had waited almost three months to cash the check, had led to a most unfortunate mix-up. In short: The check bounced.

I skimmed over the two-page, single-spaced letter that Amy had sent along with the returned check. . . . *why you feel you don't have to pay your bills like other people. . . . all the times I paid for your "party favors" . . . perhaps you should move away from South Beach, a town that surely holds no place for you. . . .* There, I knew, Amy had deliberately slung the most hurtful arrow in her arsenal. I imagined her and Raja as they'd sat together at the computer while Amy composed this. *Oh, darling,* Raja would have said, chuckling gleefully. *You're so mean.*

I was about to crumple the letter into a little ball and throw it away when I noticed something written under Amy's signature. I smoothed out the page and took a closer look.

Amy had CC'd the letter to my parents.

"No!" Ricky gasped. His eyes widened. "No, she *didn't.*"

"Oh, yes," I replied. "Yes, she did."

"What a cunt!" Mike said.

We were all at Ricky's apartment. I had brought over the letter, along with copies of *Saturday Night Fever* and *Hairspray*. Mike had called Ricky when he

117

hadn't found me at home and, upon learning I was there, had shown up twenty minutes later bearing a bag of pot, a bag of chips, and Kojo.

Everybody looked at me to see my reaction to Mike's use of the ever-dreaded C-word. "Oh, I don't care," I said. "It's totally cunty. I believe in calling things what they are."

"Exactly," said Kojo. "A cunt by any other name would smell just as—"

"Do *not* finish that sentence," I interrupted. I was laughing. "That is *repulsive*."

"I couldn't agree more," said Ricky. He went into the kitchen and added more vodka to our martini glasses. "That's why I stopped dating women."

Now everybody's eyes swung over to Ricky as he walked back into the room. "*You* used to date *women*?" I asked.

"Of course I did. Back in high school."

If Mike was the straightest gay man I knew, Ricky was definitely the gayest. While he wasn't exactly what you would call effeminate, it was hard to imagine anybody mistaking him for a heterosexual. "Were these women deaf-blind mutes?" I teased.

"Oh, shut up!" Ricky handed me my glass and flung himself onto the couch. "We're not here to discuss my sex life. So what did your parents say when they saw the letter?"

"Fortunately for me, they have no idea what 'party favors' are and didn't even ask. As far as the rest of it goes . . ." I shrugged. "Whatever. My mom raised a daughter, so she's seen this kind of schoolyard stuff before. She just said I should mail Amy a cashier's check and move on with my life."

"What did Lara say?" Mike asked.

"Pretty much the same thing you did. Except she used the word 'loser.'"

"Let's play Mad Libs with it!" Kojo exclaimed. He grabbed the letter from my hand and located a pen on the coffee table. "I need the name of a person in the room."

"Don't use me," Ricky protested. "I hate those things."

"*Ricky P.*," Kojo said. He wrote it down.

Ricky sighed mournfully. From my position on the floor, I squeezed his leg in a sympathetic hug, and he leaned over and kissed my forehead. "Don't pay any attention to her, darling," he said in a low tone, so that only I could hear. "You're fabulous, and we all love you."

The next day, I went to the bank for a cashier's check and sent it to Amy with a letter of my own. *Dear Amy*, it said. *Thanks for your interest in my future plans. Enclosed please find a cashier's check for the remaining balance owed. I apologize for the mix-up. Best, Rachel.*

Ask anybody on South Beach and they'll tell you that nobody is a native. Even among the pioneers, they'll say, nobody was *originally* from Miami Beach, and almost nobody was even originally from Miami.

As with most South Beach stories, that wasn't strictly true. I, for example, was a true-blue native; my family connections on the Beach went all the way back to my great-grandparents on my mother's side, who'd opened the first grocery store on Miami Beach. My great-aunt Elaine—my grandmother's sister and an almost unreasonably beautiful woman in her day—had been a nightclub dancer when World War II army officers and naval gunners were trained on the Beach, and family legend claimed that she'd had a brief fling with Clark Gable. My great-uncle Morty and his crazy wife, Rita, passed their Saturday nights at the Club Tropigala in the Fontainebleau Hotel, where Uncle Morty would tip everybody—down to the bathroom attendants—a hundred dollars a pop if they remembered to call him "Mr. Gould." My mother grew up on Jefferson Avenue and graduated from Miami Beach High. After she and my father were married, they spent evenings at The Forge, a plush steakhouse on 41st Street, which was then a favorite mobster and movie-star hangout.

Like all those whose unalienable right to snobbery is based on long-standing ties to a place, my parents were practically allergic to the changes on the Beach. They hated how "flashy" and "crowded" Miami Beach had become, and were slightly resentful of the way the "new people" had pushed them out. It was amusing to hear my mother's reaction one Wednesday afternoon, a few days after I received Amy's letter, when she called to ask where I was going that night.

"The Forge," I told her, and the nostalgia on the other end of the line was almost audible.

"Really?" she said. "Does Alvin Malnik still own it?" South Beach might not be a complete write-off if Alvin Malnik still owned The Forge.

"Actually, I think his son Shareef owns it now."

"Shareef?" She considered this. "You mean his boy *Mark*?"

"I guess," I replied. "I think he changed his name to Shareef because his second wife was an Arab princess or something."

My mother snorted very expressively. The snort meant: *There's no part of that sentence that didn't offend me.* "You'll have to tell me what it looks like now. You know, Meyer Lansky used to eat there all the time—it was a big hangout for Mafia hoods."

I was amused. "I don't think there's a Mafia on South Beach anymore, Mom." *Except the velvet mafia*, I thought. "But I'll tell you how it looks."

The Forge was the place to see and be seen on Wednesday nights, thanks to promoter Tommy Pooch's Wednesday-night party. The bar scene was atypical of South Beach—it was, as Ricky often observed, where pneumatic blondes gathered to separate middle-aged businessmen from their money. The restaurant itself, however, was a veritable galaxy of SoBe's glitterati.

Ricky and I, accompanied by his boyfriend, Julian, had ten o'clock dinner reservations with Isabella Shulov and her new boyfriend, Finn. I'd opted for simplicity in my appearance and wore a long, black, spaghetti-strapped gown that revealed discreet vistas of cleavage and back. "Don't you look pretty, Miss Rachel!" Isabella enthused when she saw me. I was fairly happy with how I'd turned out, but still felt almost invisible next to Isabella. She was wearing the palest possible sea-foam green dress, which showed her blue-green eyes and fair skin to great advantage. She had tossed a scrumptious white fur stole about her shoulders, against which her light brown hair gleamed like jewels in a shop window.

We arrived a little after ten thirty, and uniformed valets helped us from our cabs as a steady stream of Bentleys and Ferraris rolled behind us. The exterior of The Forge was kitted out in a mutedly gaudy, faux neoclassical style, with the obligatory palm trees flanking its facade. The interior was roomy and opulent, featuring a wide expanse of dark wood and brick, brass fixtures, velvet chairs and banquettes, crystal chandeliers, extravagant Tiffany stained glass, and antique oil paintings. Because we were with Isabella, our banquette was conspicuously front-and-center. Our obsequiously attentive waiter assured us that our entire meal was complimentary.

We picked distractedly at caviar and steak and sipped champagne while the hobnobbers and table-hoppers, one by one, paid their respects to Isabella. Shareef Malnik himself stopped by, with his current wife—an MTV Latino veejay—in tow. Chris Paciello, making an appearance outside one of his own restaurants, graced us with a few minutes of polite small talk. Tommy Pooch came over, of course, and other nightlife notables including Tito Puente Jr. and Iran (pronounced "eh-*rahn*") Issa-Khan, the renowned photographer who'd shot Paloma Picasso's ad campaign back in the '70s. Iran had since accumulated hundreds of photo portraits of celebrities and royals. She came by to inspect Isabella's date, a young man in his mid-twenties and a relative newcomer to the scene. "Make sure he is good to her, dahling," Iran said to Ricky in her husky, heavily accented voice. She stroked Ricky's face. "Her heart is so soft, you know."

In between visitors, we were discussing Ricky's latest enterprise. He'd decided to write a nightlife column for *Palm*, which was striving to become Miami's city magazine along the lines of *New York* magazine. Ricky had written a sample column on spec and forwarded it to his friend Dave, who was an editor there. Dave had loved the idea—convinced by Ricky's pitch that *Palm*'s lack of nightlife coverage was a glaring hole in their editorial. The column would appear monthly under the title "Beyond the Velvet Rope."

I was thrilled for Ricky; even though a monthly column wouldn't pay him enough to quit his much-hated day job, he was on the road to the higher profile he craved. Isabella was also proud of her protégé. The only one at the table who didn't greet this as good news was Julian, who looked positively jaundiced at the thought of Ricky spending even more time out at parties.

"You need a handle," Isabella was saying. "Something like 'Queen of the Night'"—she smiled modestly—"so people will remember you." Her brow furrowed delicately. "I've got it!" she finally exclaimed. "We'll call you 'Mr. Nightclub.'"

"'Beyond the Velvet Rope with Mr. Nightclub,'" Ricky mused. His face broke into a broad grin. "It's *fabulous!*"

"To Mr. Nightclub," Isabella said. She raised her champagne flute, and the rest of us followed suit. "To Mr. Nightclub," we chorused.

Good news like Ricky's was impossible to contain at one table: The important next step in establishing himself as a newly minted force to be reckoned with was to spread the word as far and as quickly as possible. So after we finished eating, we got up to do some table-hopping of our own. *Kisses, my darling! . . . Look how gorgeous you are! . . . Have you heard? . . .* Palm *. . . Mr. Nightclub . . . Isn't it fabulous? . . . Of course, you'll see your name in the column. . . .*

We eventually found ourselves at the table of Mindy Lipschitz, an enormously wealthy and distinctly middle-aged woman who was frequent on the nightlife circuit. She applied her eye makeup with such a heavy hand that, as Kojo noted, Liza Minnelli would've said, "Girlfriend needs to go easy on the spackle." Mindy was dining with a distinguished, Middle Eastern-looking gentleman in his late forties. He was wearing a silk tie and light gray suit that, I guessed, cost roughly the equivalent of four months of my rent. She introduced him as Yusuf. "My name is Rachel," I said politely, and held my hand out to him.

Yusuf stared—conspicuously—as he took my hand and raised it to his lips. "You are beautiful," he said in a heavy, exotic accent.

Having told you how often people said I was beautiful, it might sound disingenuous to claim now that Yusuf's comment made me blush down to my toes. But people on South Beach would say you were beautiful in the same perfunctory fashion that people in other places say, *How are you? How's work?* On those rare occasions when somebody said it as if they actually meant it, it never failed to throw me.

"Thank you," I murmured. I angled slightly closer to Ricky, who was chatting with Mindy.

"And what do you do, Rachel?" he asked.

"I work in public relations."

"Ah." He smiled self-deprecatingly. "I have many business ventures that sometimes require public relations services. Perhaps you have a business card?"

"I think so." I dug around in my beaded black evening bag until I finally unearthed one of the cards I'd had made up in my aspiring freelancer days, before I went to work for Drug-Free Kids. Somehow, it never seemed cool or glamorous to give my Drug-Free Kids cards out. This card bore the legend: RACHEL BAUM, PR/MARKETING COMMUNICATIONS, as well as my home phone number. "Here you go," I said, and handed it to him.

Ricky squeezed my elbow in a gesture that meant it was time to move on to the next table. "It was nice meeting you," I said.

"It was a pleasure to meet you," Yusuf replied. "I will call you someday and we will discuss business."

The rest of the night was a whirl of free champagne and liberal air-kisses. It was three a.m. when I finally got home, and I could hear the phone ringing as I opened the door. I ran for it, assuming it was Ricky, and nearly tripped over the phone cord in the dark as I breathlessly said, "Hello?"

"Yes, is this Rachel?" a man's accented voice queried. "This is Yusuf. We met earlier tonight at The Forge. I thought you might like to join me for dinner tomorrow night. We can discuss some marketing assistance I might need."

Although I had blushed like a schoolgirl when Yusuf told me I was beautiful, I wasn't actually simple enough to believe that a man would call at three in the morning and invite me to dinner in order to talk marketing strategy. Nevertheless, he'd made an impression, and I was intrigued. "Okay," I responded after a moment's hesitation. "That sounds great."

"Wonderful. I will pick you up at nine o'clock. Do you have any preference as to a restaurant?"

"No." And then, trying to get a little of my own back, I injected a flirtatious note in my voice. "Surprise me."

Yusuf took me to Tantra, an aphrodisiac-themed, restaurant-cum-nightclub on Pennsylvania Avenue. It featured the *de rigueur* decor of curtains, candles, and a vaguely Asian flair. There was also a separate room known as the sod lounge; it had real grass growing from the floor, a black ceiling full of fiber-optic stars, and several tented tables and couches at ground level with enormous red-and-gold cushions and hookah pipes. I had been to their opening party a few months earlier but had yet to dine there. "Let's eat in here." I tugged on Yusuf's sleeve and indicated the sod lounge.

"Of course," Yusuf replied, and he spoke, sotto voce, to the whippet-thin hostess.

"I'm sorry, sir," she said, "but those tables are all reserved."

Yusuf took out his wallet and was about to settle things the old-fashioned way when the manager, Thom, approached. Thom had also been my manager at the Sands, once upon a time. "Hello, Miss Rachel!" he cried warmly when he saw me.

"Hello, Thom." We kissed on both cheeks. "Thom darling, I know it's awfully inconvenient on such short notice, but I was wondering if we could have a table in the sod lounge."

Thom's eyes flickered over to Yusuf and they said, *Money*. Then they flicked back to me, in a floor-length gown slit up to my—*Youth*, his eyes said. "It's not inconvenient at all, sweetie. Right this way."

I glanced over at Yusuf to see whether he was irritated or amused at my handling of things. I was relieved to see amusement. "I think you are cut out for public relations," he said.

I got more of Yusuf's backstory over dinner. He was forty-seven, Lebanese, had never been married, and lived all over the world. His family was in banking, he told me. Among other business enterprises, they also owned a trucking/transportation network in the Middle East. This gave me some pause. *Drugs?* I wondered. *Arms trading?* But I quickly dismissed those thoughts as ridiculous.

After dinner, we went back to Yusuf's home on Fisher Island. Accessible only by air or via a private ferry—which, much to my delight, Yusuf drove his Mercedes right onto—Fisher Island was where Oprah Winfrey and Jeb Bush kept lavish, villa-style homes. We cruised swiftly down the tiny streets, past deserted golf courses, pools, and a gemlike gourmet shop. They were as precisely picturesque in the dark as a toy village constructed for a model train. Eventually Yusuf turned onto an even smaller side street and drove up a short ramp into a gated parking garage.

He led me into a softly lit living room. The room was a good two thousand square feet and the vaulted ceiling went up two stories. There was a caramel-colored suede couch that seemed to go on for miles. On the walls were canvases by Kandinsky, de Kooning, Rauschenberg, and others I felt I should recognize. I also noted framed photographs of Yusuf with various international dignitaries, including President Bush.

In the middle of the room was an enormous coffee table. Yusuf crossed over to it and opened a large, carved wooden box in its center. Inside the box were dozens of plastic vials filled with white powder.

It had been a while since I'd partied with Connie—not since before I'd gone to work at Drug-Free Kids—and I'd thought I was pretty much over it. Seeing it now, though, I found myself almost shaking in my desire for it.

Yusuf noticed my reaction, but misinterpreted. "Is everything all right?" he inquired. "If you don't like it, I can put all this away."

"No, no," I said hurriedly. "It's just . . ." I paused. "I just don't think I've ever seen this much in somebody's home before."

Yusuf grimaced disdainfully. "Unless you buy in quantity, what you get is garbage."

We seated ourselves on the couch, and Yusuf produced a small mirror, straws, and a razor blade. He offered me the first line and it was, possibly, the best coke I'd ever done. It tasted pure; maybe it even was. I was suddenly so happy, so giddy, so *high*, that I almost wept.

Soon we were kissing furiously—kissing and doing lines until the two actions were virtually indistinguishable. Yusuf slid the strap of my dress down over my shoulder and held up one of the vials, poised to spill its contents over the tip of my exposed breast.

"May I?" he asked, with all the formality of a man asking if he might pin on a corsage.

I thought fleetingly of Amy. Amy must have done things like this before she'd even finished high school. *A town that surely holds no place for you. . . .*

"Yes," I said softly. I watched as Yusuf's head lowered, and then I closed my eyes.

TWELVE

For our second date, Yusuf took me to his house in Barbados for a long weekend.

He'd dropped me off at home Thursday night at around four a.m. (I'd refused to spend the night), and I was a little surprised when he called on Friday afternoon to ask what I was doing that weekend.

"Nursing my hangover, I think." The downside of doing drugs of the superior quality of Yusuf's is that the coming down is that much harder. "Hangover" was, perhaps, the wrong word. "Depression" was probably closer to the mark—the kind of depression that could be fixed only one way. I was at my desk, trying to persuade potential donors of the importance of expanding our antidrug programs in Miami's public schools, and I was working on a serious jones. Which should have been, if not my first clue then certainly the most obvious, that there was something gravely wrong with this picture.

"I was wondering if you would like to come to Barbados," Yusuf said. "I have a home there, and it would be wonderful if you could join me. We could leave tonight and return Monday afternoon."

I was silent for a moment as I considered this turn of events. "I'd love to see you this weekend," I finally said, "but I don't know if I can go away." I rattled off a checklist of everything I'd need to do between now and then—trying to stall while I figured out if I wanted to commit to three days out of the country with a man I'd met thirty-six hours earlier. "I'd have to pack; I don't know if I have any clothes to take with me that don't have to be dry-cleaned. I'm not even sure I'd have time to get organized between when I leave work and when we'd have to be at the airport. What's the absolute latest I can give you an answer before we need to buy the tickets?"

There was a pause on the other end of the line. "You misunderstand," Yusuf finally said, and there was restrained, but affectionate, humor in his voice. "I have my own jet, which will fly us anytime tonight that we wish. I have to meet briefly with some bankers tomorrow morning, but after that we can have a nice, relaxing weekend." When I didn't immediately respond, he added, "Besides, Sunday is my birthday, and I would very much like to spend it with you."

Why? I thought, but obviously I couldn't say that. Naturally, I said yes. I'd be less than honest if I didn't admit to being sold as soon as a private jet was mentioned. I called Ricky to fill him in on my plans, knowing that he, along with Kojo and Mike, would panic if they were unable to locate me for an entire weekend. "How glamorous!" Ricky said when I told him. "What should I tell Mike and Kojo?"

"It's not a secret or anything—I just don't feel like making the decision by committee." I sighed. "Now I have to figure out what to pack."

"I'll come over after work and we'll pick out outfits. You've got more than enough in that closet of yours to look fabulous for three days."

The whole trip was absolutely ridiculous, in the sense of being crazy, extreme, and completely over the top. The jet was small and luxuriously appointed, with a flight attendant to bring us champagne and finger foods and anything else we may have wanted. We didn't see much of her during the three-and-a-half-hour flight. I'm not sure where exactly she retired to when she wasn't waiting on us; truth be told, I was so high and buzzed even before takeoff that there isn't much about the flight that I can remember anymore.

Yusuf's house was a sprawling, West Indian plantation-style home on the western coast of the island. There were eight bedroom suites, each larger than my entire apartment, with immense dressing areas, marble bathrooms, and sunken tubs. One side of the house faced a lagoon, where a yacht and several smaller boats bobbed sedately in private slips. The other side faced the ocean and featured a swimming pool and Jacuzzi. From a certain angle they seemed to merge with the ocean, forming a widening crystal rainbow in perfect hues of turquoise. A walkway descended through a hibiscus-strewn garden directly to the pinkish-white sands of the private beach.

Yusuf employed a small staff to keep the house running, even in his absence. There were a chef, a maid who immediately unpacked my bag and pressed all my clothes, and a butler who served us high tea on the patio in the British tradition. I wondered what they thought of me, how many other girls like me they'd seen come and go over the years. But we never made any real conversation, and their sangfroid faces betrayed nothing.

I wanted to play it cool, to seem as unimpressed as if I'd grown up seeing houses like this every day of my life, but I couldn't. That first night saw me scampering through the house like an overexcited two-year-old. Yusuf followed behind, laughingly refusing my suggestion that we rotate bedrooms every night. "I think that would make things too difficult for the staff," he said, and I lowered my eyes in mock contrition at having taken the staff for granted.

Soon enough we ended up in the living room, where Yusuf chopped up lines on an elaborate silver tea tray. We threw off our clothes and christened the pool and hot tub before finally tumbling into bed hours later, hot and shivering at the same time. Sometime before sunrise, Yusuf placed a small tablet in my mouth. "A Quaalude," he said. "So you will sleep." I drifted off thinking that Quaaludes seemed charmingly old-fashioned—that Yusuf, underneath it all, was a charming, old-fashioned guy.

I slept late the next morning and awoke to find Yusuf gone. I heard his voice in the other room, rising and falling in a language I couldn't identify, as he conferred with his bankers. As if she'd been waiting to hear me stir, the maid knocked politely and entered with a newspaper, inquiring what I wanted for breakfast. She returned shortly with eggs, coffee, and orange juice on a tray. I ate and then showered leisurely, thinking how nice it was to be so well attended to.

Yusuf and I didn't leave the house much that weekend, except to go down to the beach. There was no need to go anywhere when we already had so much to amuse ourselves with. I found myself trying to be endlessly inventive sexually, casting my eyes about the house for props that could be brought into play. Expensive silk ties were crumpled and knotted to become impromptu cuffs and blindfolds. It was so clear that Yusuf could be with any woman he wanted; I felt a need to justify his choice of me. *Anything you want . . . ,* I whispered. *It's your birthday weekend.* That first-night ritual of applying the coke—never more than inches away from us—to my body was always repeated in differing variations. It seemed almost incomprehensible that we'd met only a few days before.

We were very late getting back on Monday night, and I missed my bartending shift without so much as a phone call. By then, though, it hardly seemed to matter. It's amazing how quickly being around that kind of money can make you feel insulated, protected—as if it were yours.

Ricky's boyfriend, Julian, threw a dinner party a few days later. I think it was Ricky's idea—he and Julian hadn't been getting along very well as of late, so a dinner party seemed like an appropriately coupley undertaking. I arrived early to help with the preparations and endure the questioning about my weekend that I knew I'd have to face sooner or later.

Julian's apartment was a standard model of a certain type of South Beach condo. The buildings had gone up in the late '60s and '70s, and the units usually consisted of a large, perfectly square living-and-dining room; a smaller, perfectly square bedroom; and an alcove kitchen. They also featured orangey-red clay tile throughout and tiny balconies with wrought-iron railings. Julian's place was very similar to Ricky's, actually. However, unlike Ricky's home (which, like mine, was furnished with the sparseness of those who forgo comfort in favor of wardrobe), Julian's place was decorated to within an inch of its life. Every place the eye could rest was cushioned, curio-ed, painted, planted, tabled, tapestried, bedecked, bedazzled, or be-rugged. And there were, inexplicably, dozens upon dozens of boxes—large wooden boxes and small ceramic boxes and steamer trunks and hollow lacquered cubes that contained sets of ever-smaller boxes, like Russian nesting dolls.

"What's with the boxes?" I whispered to Ricky as Julian went into the other room to hang up my wrap. "Are they for drugs? It'd be pretty hot if they were all for drugs."

"What do you want from me?" Ricky, who knew even less about cooking than I did, pretended to check on the chickens roasting in the oven. "The man likes boxes."

Julian returned and poured me a martini from a crystal pitcher. "So Ricky says you have a new sugar daddy."

I threw a murderous look at Ricky, who was innocently tossing a large salad and avoiding my glare. "I do *not* have a sugar daddy. I happen to have been out once or twice with a man who happens to have money."

"And a jet," Ricky piped up. "Don't be forgetting about the jet, Miss Thing. Private jets are fierce."

"Whatever," I said. "Tell me what's new and exciting in the world of Mr. Nightclub."

Now it was Ricky's turn to scowl as I smiled sweetly. It had only been a week since Ricky'd been hired to write his column for *Palm*, and already the demands on his after-dark schedule had increased threefold. He and Julian had been bickering about it for days, as Ricky knew I was well aware. Julian picked up a tray of hors d'oeuvres and carried them into the living room. "Something I said?" I asked Ricky. I sipped my cocktail.

Ricky made a face. "He'll get over it. Did I show you my new business cards?" He pulled out his wallet and produced a stack of cards bearing the *Palm* logo and pronouncing him: RICKY PASCAL, "MR. NIGHTCLUB," NIGHTLIFE COLUMNIST.

"Wow! Very nice," I said. "I'm surprised they got these for you so quickly."

"They didn't. I took the logo from a letter they sent me and had one of the graphic design guys in my office make these up."

I smiled again, a genuine one this time. "Of course you did, darling." I kissed him on the cheek. Julian re-entered the kitchen, and Ricky quickly put the cards away. "So who else is coming tonight?" I asked.

"Four other couples, friends of mine," Julian said. He grinned playfully. "You'll be the only diva—Ricky and I know how much you love the attention."

"That's true," I replied gravely. "But I think you should know that when I'm the only fag-hag to work a party, I have to charge extra."

Julian and Ricky laughed, and the tension all three of us had been feeling was put aside. For now.

My relationship with Yusuf was something that I was reluctant to discuss with anybody. I obviously couldn't get away with avoiding it altogether, but I always found ways to turn the conversation away from myself whenever his name came up. This was true even of Lara. I was calling her less frequently than I used to;

when we did speak, I was careful to get her talking about what was going on in her life—her job, the new place with her boyfriend, her possible upcoming move from San Francisco to L.A.—so as to avoid having to give too much information about my own.

"What do you think your parents would say about Yusuf?" Lara asked on one of the rare occasions when I let myself be drawn into a discussion on the subject.

"I think if I ever tried to cross the threshold of my parents' house with an Arab man who was my father's age . . ." I paused. "My father might actually buy a gun."

My South Beach scene-making schedule with Ricky, Mike, and Kojo continued on with hardly any interruption; fortunately, Yusuf wasn't in a position to monopolize much of my time. He traveled frequently and was in town only sporadically—no more than a couple of days a week. I usually got very little notice when he was in town, so I found myself dropping things— from plans with friends to bartending shifts—at the last minute whenever he was around. I'd never been the type to bail on a previous commitment in order to accommodate a guy, feeling that it was a mark of insecurity (*What if I say no and he doesn't call me again?*). But wealth has a way of creating its own irrefutable demands. One quite simply did not say no to a man like Yusuf over nitpicky details like the lack of twenty-four hours' notice.

Yusuf wasn't much of a club guy, but there were dinners at Joia (Chris Paciello and Ingrid Casares's haute cuisine Italian on the tip of Ocean Drive), the Strand, and the ferociously elegant restaurant in the Hotel Astor on Washington Avenue. We spent afternoons on his yacht or by the pool at his Fisher Island home, coked up to our eyeballs. I had no idea what he did with his time, or what other women there might be, when he wasn't with me. Truthfully, I didn't care; we didn't have that kind of relationship. It was enough for me that the times we had were good and the sex was always exciting, taking place as it did against the backdrop of multimillion-dollar homes and a seemingly limitless drug supply. After calling in sick to the South Beach Bistro a few too many times when Yusuf was in town, I found myself no longer employed there. But I didn't care about that, either.

Sometimes, though, the idea that I was living out of my depth caught up to me. One day, Yusuf and I went to the Bal Harbour Shops, Miami's most upscale shopping Mecca. We walked by the Fendi store, and, in the custom of wistful window-shopping women, I all but pressed my nose against the glass to get a better look at a wildly expensive handbag that I couldn't have afforded even if I'd been willing to go without food for a month. Lusting for things in shop windows that I'd never be able to buy was such an old habit of mine, I didn't pause long enough to remember that I was with a man for whom price was no concern. Before I knew what was happening, Yusuf was inside the store. I found him at the counter, holding the bag I'd been eyeing. "Is this the one you would like?" he asked.

I backed away, as if he were holding something alive and feral that might strike out at me. "You don't have to . . . ," I started. "I mean, it's very sweet of you and I *appreciate* it and everything, but . . ."

Nice girls don't use sex to make rich older men buy them things, was the thought that trailed through my head.

Yusuf looked amused, as I learned he always would at times like these. I sometimes wondered if this was the source of his attraction to me, in a town full of models who not only looked better than I did, but who would have been infinitely more comfortable than I was with this kind of dynamic. For a man like Yusuf, it must have been a rare find to discover someone who could keep up with him on a three-day coke bender but who was still, on some level, corruptible.

I ended up with the Fendi, but I didn't feel great about it. I told Ricky the story, looking for validation of my feelings on the subject. His response was, "Ooh! Tell him your best friend needs Gucci." I laughed, because the answer was so typically Ricky—so typically South Beach—that I didn't know why I'd expected anything else. Ricky didn't take my discomfort seriously because he didn't really understand it. I didn't fully understand it, either. On the one hand, as the girl who'd been most notable in school for doing everybody else's homework, it was fun to play out the fantasy of being someone who wealthy men showered with expensive baubles. He had money, I didn't, and what could possibly be wrong with his buying me gifts from time to time?

But it didn't feel completely right, or comfortable, and I tried to avoid additional shopping trips altogether.

The most persistent tug at my conscience, however, was the rift between my day job and my after-work adventures. There was a hypocrisy between the two that was so clear, there was no way I could miss it. But—and this is a hard thing to admit, even now—I liked the hypocrisy. I liked the feeling that I was living these two completely different lives, that the people who knew me by day wouldn't have been able to recognize me at night and vice versa. It felt . . . *sexy*. It was part of what had drawn me to Hood the night we'd met—the idea that he was a gentleman and a thug and a club guy and an intellectual, all at the same time. He was all of these contradictory things that everybody says you can't be simultaneously, except that Hood *was*.

I told myself that I'd never let things spin out of control the way Hood had. And who was I hurting, after all? I was doing good in my efforts to keep drugs out of schools and the hands of children, and what difference did it make what I did with my personal time as long as it didn't affect my work?

As you can see, I had it all figured out. I was a smart girl with a good head on her shoulders, as people told me practically every day.

The problem with being too smart is that, inevitably, you end up outsmarting yourself.

It was an early May morning, and I was at the Drug-Free Kids office, putting the finishing touches on a huge publicity event that was taking place the next day. It was the biggest event we'd held since I'd started working there, and it was crucial that it be a success. Ordinarily this would have meant a temporary moratorium on any party plans. But Yusuf had arrived in town late the previous night, and two a.m. had found me at his house—dressed to kill, although not dressed for long.

I'd made it to work on time and—miracle of miracles—sheer adrenaline kept me functioning at almost peak form, despite the fact that I was operating on only two hours of sleep. The day was hot, as May mornings in Miami tend to be, and the air-conditioning operating at full capacity barely offered relief. I took off my suit jacket, underneath which I wore a sheer, scoop-necked silk tank top. I noticed odd, sidelong glances from my coworkers; they either wouldn't look at me directly or, even worse, would smile far too brightly if I managed to catch their eyes. I wondered what was going on but was too busy to pay much attention.

Eventually, I went into the bathroom to splash cold water on my face and clip my hair back. And that was when I noticed. Either I'd managed to miss them that morning in my mad scramble to get dressed, or they'd needed a few more hours to fully form. In any case, they were painfully visible now when I looked at myself in the light.

I was covered in bruises—giant, glaring, Technicolor bruises. They started on my neck and chin and crept vividly down my upper arms, back, and chest—at least, as much of it as was visible above the neckline of my top. A quick check confirmed that they extended to my breasts and torso as well.

I tried to remember what I could have done last night that would account for my condition this morning. So much of what I did with Yusuf was hard to remember, obscured as it was by more liquor and coke than I'd ever thought my body could sustain. I remembered feeling almost numb at one point—cocaine'll do that to you, especially when applied directly to the skin. I hadn't been able to feel things enough; I'd kept pushing Yusuf to greater heights in order to get my body to respond. Yusuf had been into it with an intensity that had taken me by surprise. He'd thrown me around the room like a sumo wrestler, slamming me against walls, counters, and bed frame. I'd laughed helplessly as pillows and lamps and empty glass vials went flying every which way.

I thought it was funny. I'd had quite a time of it last night, and my bruises were testament to the achievements I was making in my nightlife career—like the badges I'd earned in Girl Scouts. I thought of what my friends would say, the jokes we'd make and how we'd all laugh about it (note to self: Remember the "Girl Scouts" bit). How glamorous, darling, Ricky would say, in a faintly sarcastic way meant to indicate that, while he didn't exactly approve, he understood the toll that our lifestyle sometimes took on our bodies. Kojo would say something witty, like, Black-and-blue: It's the new black. I didn't know what Mike's opinion would be, although I sensed he wouldn't approve, but I wasn't overly concerned with that now. My chief concern was whether I should put my coat back on immediately when I returned to the office, or attempt to play it off nonchalantly, since everyone had already seen all there was to see. *Screw it*, I thought. *Who cares what they think?*

I returned to the office and my coat stayed off. I interacted with everybody as if nothing were amiss, and, after a couple of hours, I was relieved to note that they were once again making eye contact with me. They all went out to lunch in the early afternoon, but I stayed at my desk, attending to a million last-minute details.

The only other person who stayed behind was a coworker named Jimmy Watkins. Jimmy weighed in at a massive a six-foot-four, three hundred pounds—and it was three hundred pounds of solid muscle. He'd been a defensive tackle for the Florida Gators back in college and was now one of our two school coordinators. Jimmy was on a mission in a way that I remembered having been able to relate to once, a long time ago. He was deeply committed to improving the lot of Miami's inner-city kids and believed that cleaning drugs off the streets was the best first step. There was a gentle, sweetly humorous quality to him that belied his imposing stature. He was married and had an infant daughter, and it was clear from our frequent conversations that he adored both wife and child.

When everybody else was gone, Jimmy approached and stood over my desk. He looked down at me, his eyes full of compassion and anger. "I'm not going to ask any questions," he said. His voice was quiet and firm. "I just need to know where I can find him."

My scalp tightened and prickled and I turned my eyes from his. Suddenly, it didn't seem so funny anymore. It wasn't funny at all. Nobody was going to laugh about this with me. Nothing that could put that look on Jimmy's face, that tone in his voice, could possibly be funny.

He was looking at me like a father—and he *was* a father. I knew what he was thinking: *If anybody did this to my daughter, I'd kill him.*

I had an almost overwhelming impulse to throw myself into his arms—to bury my face, sobbing, in his chest. *Forgive me*, I would say, although I didn't know for what—or by whom—I hoped to be forgiven. It was a feeling that came upon me so swiftly, the surprise of it almost made me break down. *God, I'd kill for a bump.*

I took a deep breath to steady myself, to check the tears I felt collecting behind my eyelids. The moment passed, and I smiled in a manner that tried to say, *Isn't it silly how we're making such a big deal over nothing?*

"It's not like that." I hated every word that was coming out of my mouth. "I . . . it's not what you think it is, honestly. " He hesitated, unsure if he should push the issue or let it go. So I added, "If you really want to help me, you can call the principal at Jose Marti Middle—he loves you and he's been giving me the runaround all morning." He continued to waver. In a last-ditch effort, I relented and said softly, "Look, it means a lot that you care. But, believe me, there's absolutely nothing wrong. If there were, you know I'm a pushy-enough loudmouth to look out for myself."

That convinced him—at least enough to get a laugh and send him back to his desk, clutching the phone number for Jose Marti Middle School that I'd shoved into his hand. A little while later everybody else came back from lunch, and the day continued to churn inexorably toward five o'clock.

When I knew that nobody was looking or thinking about it anymore, I shrugged my jacket back on.

THIRTEEN

There were Drug-Free Kids clubs in about fifty different schools throughout Miami-Dade, and the membership criteria were simple: Kids had to be willing to submit to a urine test proving they were drug free and to sign a pledge promising not to use illegal drugs at any point in the future.

Once a year Drug-Free Kids had a big blowout; they would gather hundreds of kids from schools all over Miami for a single-day bonanza of drug tests, food, and fun. Dozens of porta-potties were set up to facilitate the drug testing. There would also be games and activities, eating and socializing, and plenty of press photo ops for me to wrangle. In between drug testing there would be kite flying and volleyball, which everyone agreed would make a great visual for the cameras.

The event would be held this year on the 17th Street beach, and I had to be there well ahead of the eleven o'clock start time for setup and logistics. Mike had made the incredibly generous offer of joining me for a seven a.m. breakfast and had, with much arm twisting, roped Kojo into the plan. We met at the Van Dyke—eight blocks from Kojo's apartment, four blocks from where Mike worked in WAMI's Lincoln Road news studio, and five blocks from where my event would take place. I arrived punctually in my uniform for the day: jeans, sneakers, and a black T-shirt emblazoned with the Drug-Free Kids slogan: DRUG-FREE AND WILLING TO PROVE IT.

"Oh, no," Mike said as soon as they saw me. "Oh, no no no no no." He and Kojo dissolved into helpless, hysterical laughter.

I stood there for a moment and accepted it. Then I said, "All right, you guys. All *right*." I made a brisk cutting gesture with my hand across my neck and sat down. "That's enough out of you."

"I think we should all get them," Kojo said when he finally sobered. "Let's see how much money I have left in the emergency irony fund."

"Let's change the subject." I opened a menu. "Who's got an interesting story?"

"I tricked with a hot Venezuelan last night," Mike replied. "All I need is someone from Ecuador and I'll have the whole map of South America."

"Glad you're getting some use from those INS forms on your bedroom door," Kojo said. Actually it was Kojo, spoofing Mike's love of South American boys, who had mounted a plastic bin full of I-90 green card applications in Mike's apartment. Kojo now turned to watch a blond skater sail by. The skater cast a look back as he glided past. "Do you think it's possible somebody's cruising me this early in the morning?"

"You boys really live in a constant porn movie, don'cha?" I observed.

"Jealous?" Kojo responded. I smacked his arm with my menu.

"Hey—what're you doing this weekend?" Mike asked. "Is Daddy Warbucks in town?"

I'd long since given up trying to get my friends to refer to Yusuf as "Yusuf," or by any designation that didn't include the word "daddy." So I merely shook my head and said, "He's gone for the next two weeks."

"You should come over to my house," Kojo said. "Saturday night we're having one of Kojo's famous"—he assumed a Southern accent—"*oooooold*-fashioned country back-shaving parties."

Now it was my turn to laugh. "I'm sorry—you're having a what now?"

"It's fun," Mike said. "A bunch of us go over to Kojo's place and we take turns shaving his back. Then we get high and eat stuff."

"You know how much I love you, Kojo darling, but I'm not *in love* with you. . . ." I noticed Mike peering at me closely. "What's wrong? You're not implying that *I* need to be shaved, are you?"

"What happened to your neck?" Mike asked. "It's all bruised up."

"Oh." I shrugged. "I got a new night table, and I rolled into it last night while I was sleeping."

Mike looked confused. "You didn't get a new night table."

"Yes, I did," I replied evenly. "I got it last week, and I banged into it last night. Shall I draw you a diagram?"

"Let's pretend 'coffee' is the safety word," Kojo interjected. He signaled the waiter. "I think I need some."

. . .

The event went even better than I'd hoped. Close to a thousand kids turned out, the lines at the porta-potties were at least ten deep, and the press were eating it up with a spoon. The sky was a clear, hard blue, doing away with that one fear that haunts every planner of an outdoor Miami event: the threat of rain. It was perfect.

Or, at least, it was until sometime in the late afternoon. The lines at the porta-potties had, inevitably, petered off as the day progressed, but the press were still trickling in. And that's when our executive director had a truly inspired idea. Why not give them photos of the Drug-Free Kids employees putting their money where their mouths were, so to speak? In other words, *we* would all take drug tests ourselves, and the newspapers could snapshot us entering and exiting with our little plastic cups—thus proving that we had the same level of commitment as the kids we served.

"I don't think it's such a good idea," I said to him, away from the others. "The focus should really be on the kids, not on us—that's what the story is."

"We'll give them another angle," he replied. "Then they'll have something to choose from when they go to press."

"With all due respect, I think you're missing the bigger picture. And, besides, there are only five of us. It won't even last long enough to keep them here any longer."

"Something is better than nothing," he said firmly. He picked up several of the labeled plastic cups that were set up on a nearby table, signaling over the other Drug-Free Kids staffers. He wrote my name on one of the cups and turned me in the direction of the porta-potties. "You're not shy, are you?" he teased.

"Of course not," I scoffed. My mind raced, looking for a way out. My skin felt hot, and my stomach clenched so hard that I wondered if vomiting would, somehow, invalidate the test. How long did cocaine last in your system, anyway?

In any case, there didn't seem to be anything I could do about it now. I held my little cup grimly and headed for the portable toilet. *Dead girl walking.*

Ricky and I spent the following afternoon at the Delano pool. We had agreed that we were becoming shockingly pale for two people who were so naturally dark-skinned; a day of tanning was definitely in order.

Ricky's building featured a miniscule pool, but it was overshadowed during the better part of daylight hours. My own building at Forte Towers boasted a sparkling, Olympic-sized pool right on Biscayne Bay. Ricky didn't like the Forte pool scene, however—the men's bathrooms around the pool, he told me, were always occupied by party boys shooting up their drugs of choice and performing illicit acts on each other. So when Ricky proposed the Delano's pool as an alternative, it was a welcome suggestion.

The Delano was a sumptuous, beachfront, fifteen-story hotel on Collins Avenue and 17th Street. The lobby was breathtaking, flowing straight from outdoor to indoor and back out again. Upon entering the hotel, one passed through the bougainvillea-adorned front doors into the lobby area, which sprawled out two hundred and fifty feet to back doors that exited onto the Blue Door Restaurant's patio and the hotel pool. The floorboards were dark wood, and the ceiling arched up to impossible heights. On either side, diaphanous white drapes (white was the Delano's signature color) fell several stories from ceiling to floor, billowing in the soft breezes that the open-air setup encouraged. I often thought the Delano's lobby looked the way I hoped Heaven would look.

Through the back doors, wide marble steps led from the restaurant to ground level. The pool itself was oversized and rectangular and seemed to stretch all the way to the ocean (although, as you approached its farthest edge, you could distinctly see the sugary beach). The water flowed over the edges of the pool and drained into nearly invisible receptacles, which constantly recycled the water and pumped it back in. Classical music piped underwater. About a third of the pool, the portion closest to the beach, was only a few inches deep—shallow enough that a few elegant tables and chairs had been set up so that one could, technically, be in the pool and enjoying a cocktail at a table at the same time. More than a dozen coconut palms soared around the pool's perimeter; at night they glowed white under dramatic spotlights, like silent geisha pausing mid-dance. Farther back from the pool were the cabanas that were always occupied by celebrities—rock stars, movie actors, writers, royalty, and all the others who provided the nightly conflagration against which our own nightlife luminaries burned even hotter.

A poolside chaise at the Delano was almost harder to come by than a seat on the space shuttle, even if you were a paying guest at the hotel (the official minimum standard for having access to the pool at all). But Ricky's star was on the rise these days; his first column had finally appeared in *Palm* a couple of weeks earlier, and people were starting to line up to do him favors. One of them was a beautiful Colombian named Paulo, who was a pool boy at the Delano. He'd promised us a prime spot and complimentary cocktails all day, as long as we arrived no later than noon, and Saturday found us sipping Bloody Marys and basking in our good fortune. We'd already seen Marc Anthony and Antonio Sabato Jr. head toward the cabanas. Behind-hands whispers claimed that Puff Daddy had also been spotted.

"So they fired you?" Ricky asked.

"Not exactly," I replied. "They gave me the option of 'resigning voluntarily,' which means I still have a shot at getting a decent reference from them."

"That sucks, sweetie. And it's so unfair! You got so much great press for them at that event."

"No," I said slowly. "It's not unfair. I mean, it's not just a job to them—it's a cause. They take it seriously and I didn't, and you can't really blame Drug-Free Kids for not wanting a tweaky PR director."

Ricky nodded solemnly, acknowledging the truth in my remark. "How much money do you have in the bank?"

I grimaced and lit a cigarette. "I've been hemorrhaging cash since I lost my job at the Bistro. Once my rent and utilities checks clear, I'll have about fifty dollars to my name." A waiter appeared at my elbow, silently replacing my empty Bloody Mary glass with a fresh round. "I figure if I walk places instead of taking cabs," I continued, "and replace eating dinner with party hors d'oeuvres, I can make it stretch for a couple of weeks."

"Can you ask your parents for money?"

"I *really* don't want to." Just the thought of it made me feel ill. "Then I'd have to tell them (a) that I lost my job and (b) why I lost my job. I'd rather just get a new job and sell it to them as, *Hey, I've traded up!*"

"And how are things with you and Yusuf?" He looked straight out onto the pool as he asked.

The fact that he'd referred to Yusuf by name—and not as "Daddy," "Sugar

Daddy," or "Daddy Warbucks"—was, we both knew, as close as he would come to acknowledging that he'd noticed my fading bruises and made a pretty shrewd guess as to their source.

"Things with Yusuf are fine." I looked at him from the corner of my eye. "We were both really high the other night and things got a little out of hand. I don't want to additionally complicate things by asking for money." I paused for a moment and attempted to blow a smoke ring. "I got a box from him this morning—from Paris—with a crazy-expensive Dior dress inside. Meantime, I need an expensive new dress right now like I need a hole in my head."

Ricky sighed. "And the glamour continues." A group of models sauntered by, clad only in kitten-heeled sandals and bikini bottoms. Ricky looked at me apprehensively. "*You're* not going to go topless, are you?"

"Are you kidding?" I rolled over onto my stomach and adjusted my Chanel sunglasses, a gratis gift-bag item from a party I'd attended earlier in the week. I grinned at Ricky. "I'm broke and these babies may be the only collateral I have left. Why would I give it away free?"

By the time Yusuf returned to town two weeks later, my fifty dollars had dwindled down to fifteen. I had no immediate job prospects and panic was setting in.

The last time I'd seen Yusuf was the night before my luckless Drug-Free Kids event, when he'd been shocked upon seeing my bruised-up condition. The fact that he was shocked had gone a long way toward my deciding that there was no real reason to end things with him. The moment of crushing remorse in my office had been simply that—a moment. After its initial intensity passed, I'd still been left with the feeling that Yusuf was an exciting man, that wherever I was going with him was an exciting place to be. I told myself that I'd reacted as emotionally as I had only because I was coming down.

We'd gone our separate ways after dinner that night. He was leaving early the next morning and I had to be up even earlier for my event, and we both felt, perhaps, that we'd OD'd on fun for a while. We'd spoken on the phone a few times since then, and I had avoided telling him that I'd been fired; that whole forty-eight-hour stretch was sufficiently embarrassing that I had no desire to relive it. But Yusuf had attempted to reach me at the office one day, and the receptionist informed him that I no longer worked there. The rest of the story came out quickly thereafter.

Now I was standing on the balcony adjoining the master bedroom of Yusuf's Fisher Island home, looking onto the light-studded twilight of the Miami skyline and Biscayne Bay. The sky and water were a vivid, luminous indigo. *We really do live in a beautiful place,* Ricky would often remark wistfully as we looked out on views like this, and I always silently agreed.

Yusuf came out onto the balcony with two glasses of red wine, which he placed on a small table. He took my arm, gently, and led me over to the chaise lounge next to it. Then he sat down, drawing me down and back against his chest, and wrapped his arms around me. He stroked my hair. "Tell me what you dreamed last night. You seemed restless."

Without turning around I said, "Do we have that kind of relationship?"

"What do you mean?"

"You know—the kind where we talk about what we dream or what our fears are or the things our fathers said that hurt us."

He chuckled. "Why should we compartmentalize like that? We spend all this time together and I feel that I hardly know you."

The man has a point, I thought. "Well," I started reluctantly, "I have this recurring nightmare about a tornado. I'm trapped somewhere—like my house or my car—and there's this tornado coming. I can see it through the window but I can't get away. Then it comes right through the middle of wherever I am and cuts everything in half."

He was silent, and I could tell he was turning it over in his mind. "You're afraid of chaos," he finally pronounced. "But now there will be no more chaos, because I am here to take care of you."

You are the chaos, I thought. Aloud I said, "Freud says that all dreams are wish fulfillments. So maybe what I'm afraid of isn't chaos, but the fact that I sometimes *like* chaos."

I'd initially said it to be flip, chafing slightly at the *I'll take care of you* sentiment. Maybe I'd even wanted to show off a little. As I heard myself, though, it sounded like truth. I'd spent so much time with Eduard, miserable because I'd felt nothing. Blind panic might not be the most positive feeling in the world, but at least I was out there in the world feeling *something*.

"I must go to London next week," he said now, "and after that I'm returning to Beirut for a month." He sipped from his glass of wine. "Why not come with me? The Season is almost over here, and I would love to introduce you to my family."

It was a pretty big, and pretty unexpected, gesture. I wasn't sure how keen I was to visit Beirut, but either way, now was definitely not the time for an extended vacation.

"Thanks," I said. "That's an incredibly sweet, lovely offer. But I need to stick around here and find a job."

"Our bank is introducing a new line of credit cards in the fall. We'll need somebody to oversee the marketing. I see no reason why that somebody shouldn't be you."

This time I did turn around. "Are you serious?"

"Of course." He smiled broadly. "We could pay you . . ." He named an outrageous figure, one that was easily five times greater than what I'd earned at Drug-Free Kids. "We could include an extra allowance for wardrobe and buy you a car, since you will be representing our company. A BMW, perhaps?"

"Yusuf," I started, and then I stopped. I couldn't accept this, could I? "I don't know that I'm the right person for the job. I don't think my level of experience is on a par with what something like this would require."

He dismissed my concerns with a wave of his hand. "You are a very smart young woman. And we will surround you with the best people. Besides," he added with a wink, "I think people will be forgiving of any mistakes you might make since you will be, as they say, playing with the boss." He got up and disappeared inside, turning on a small lamp that rested on the desk in his bedroom. I could see that he was writing something. He returned with a check and placed it in my hand. It was made out to me in the amount of five thousand dollars.

"This is so you have walking-around money," he said.

And there it was.

It suddenly all connected in my mind—the presents, the drugs, the bruises. The offer of money was simply the purest expression of what was already going on. There were names for girls who took cash and prizes in exchange for sex. (Or, as Yusuf had so delicately put it, "playing with the boss.") Some of them were crude and some just technically accurate.

None of them were names I wanted applied to me.

When you're down to your last fifteen dollars, five thousand dollars is all the money in the world. It was hard to do what needed to be done, and my hand trembled as I held the check back out to him. "Thank you, Yusuf. I mean it. This is so great of you, and I genuinely appreciate it, but I can't accept it. Not the check or the job or any of it."

"But why not?" He looked puzzled. "Why shouldn't I help you?"

"Because I wouldn't be able to respect myself." I flashed back to the rise and fall of my friendship with Amy. *Relationships between unequals are always, ultimately, doomed. The very inequality does you in.* "And, eventually, you wouldn't be able to respect me either." I paused, realizing what had to be said next. "I think," I said gently, "you should probably take me home now."

His face registered understanding. "I see," he replied slowly. "You are saying that you no longer wish to see me."

"I don't think I should."

"I would like to change your mind."

"Believe me," I said with a wry smile, "a big part of me wants that too. But I can't."

We rode back to my apartment in silence. As we pulled up to the entrance of my building, Yusuf kissed me on the cheek and said, "Please always feel free to call if you need anything."

"Thank you," I replied. "For everything." I kissed him on the cheek as well. "Have fun in London."

A glance at the clock once I was upstairs confirmed that it was still early. I picked up the phone and called Ricky, telling him the story. When I got to the part where Yusuf had offered me the check, I heard Ricky's breath pull in sharply. "The *nerve!*" Outrage quivered in his voice.

"Well, it wasn't completely out of line," I said. "It's not like I never took anything from him before."

"No, I mean giving you a check! The man owns a bank! The least he could've done is given you cash. Why should you be bothered running all over town with checks to cash?"

"Oh, Ricky." I sighed. "You really don't understand why it's *wrong* to trade sex for money, do you?"

"Well, honey, I don't see what the big deal is. You give it away free to losers all the time."

"Thanks," I replied drily. "That observation will in no way cause me to wake up screaming at four in the morning."

"So what are you going to do?"

"Dunno. I hear they give money to women for harvesting their eggs. Do you think I've damaged mine too much with all the drugs?"

Ricky laughed. "Get some sleep, sweetie. It'll all look better in the morning."

The next night, Kojo invited me over for dinner. Mike and Ricky were already there when I arrived. It was like a déjà vu of the previous evening as Kojo handed me a check.

"This is from all of us," he said. "Just to help you out until you find a job."

I looked at the check. It wasn't enough to pay my rent, but it was enough for me to live on for a few more weeks while I looked for work.

As if reading my mind, Kojo added, "We were going to throw you a rent party, but we thought you'd want to keep it out of the papers. But there's always that option if worse comes to worst."

I might have been the poorest one at the moment, but none of us ever had two nickels to rub together. I knew the sacrifice that had gone into the making of this relief fund. "I'm overwhelmed, you guys," I said. "But I can't take this from you."

"It's only a loan," Mike said. "We should all make an 'in case of emergency, break glass' pact."

"We've all had to live on Easy Mac at some point," added Kojo. He put his hand on mine, the one that was holding the check, and pressed my own hand closed around it. "I'm buying stock in Rachel Baum, and I think it's a smart investment."

I looked over at Ricky and he was smiling at me. I tried to keep my eyes from tearing up.

"Would a group hug be incredibly cheesy?" I asked. "Because I hate cheese almost as much as I love you guys right now."

They all rose. "I call shotgun on her boobs," Kojo said.

FOURTEEN

It was only a few days later when Ricky called in hysterics. "Julian broke up with me," he announced.

"I'm coming right over," I replied.

It sounds horrible, but I was almost grateful for Ricky's problem. I was getting tired of dwelling on my own, of trying to silence the ever more persistent thoughts—louder with each passing day of unemployment—that told me over and over, *You're a loser. . . . you've ruined your life. . . .* I had never really failed at anything before, but this time I had managed to fail rather spectacularly—both in my job and in my personal life. I hoped that dealing with Ricky's breakup would take me out of my own head for a while.

I was at his door a few minutes later with the bottle of Absolut I'd been saving in my freezer for an emergency. "Do you think I'm shallow?" Ricky asked, as I put down my purse and keys in his kitchen and set about fixing us a couple of stiff drinks.

"Yes," I said cheerfully. "But your shallowness is so profound that it's like a kind of depth."

I beamed at him. He looked like he was about to cry. "Oh, sweetie." I carried the cocktails into the living room and hugged him. "I was just kidding. What happened?"

"Julian thinks I'm shallow. And he's sick of all this 'Mr. Nightclub' stuff. He's sick of all the parties I go to and all the VIP rooms and everything."

"Sick of VIP?" I affected great incredulity. "What kind of a person gets sick of VIP?"

"That's what I said! And then he said he's sick of dating Mr. Nightclub. He doesn't understand why this is all so important to me."

"Oh, whatever," I said. "All of a sudden Julian is the arbiter of who's deep and who's shallow? Do you honestly think *Julian* wakes up in the morning and

thinks, *Gee, I wonder what I can do for the orphans today*?" I lit us each a cigarette and passed one over to him. "Trust me—nobody who's spent that much
time over-decorating his apartment is thinking about how to make the world
a better place."

Ricky laughed, but he looked unconvinced. "I don't know; shouldn't there
be more than all this stuff?"

"Absolutely—there's family and friends." I took one of his hands in mine.
"And I don't know anybody who has a better, more generous heart or who loves
the people he loves more than you do. Plus you're good-looking and funny as
hell, and if Julian doesn't appreciate all that, then fuck 'im. You can do better."

This time his smile was genuine. "Who knew you gave such good advice?"

"Oh!" I said brightly. "I'm remarkably insightful for a strung-out, unemployed coke whore."

Ricky laughed again. "How are things going with the job hunt?"

"They're going. Still no luck."

"Have you sent your résumé over to the Agnew Group? They have some
fabulous PR accounts, and their offices are right on Lincoln Road."

"I haven't seen any job postings from them." I downed the last of my
vodka cranberry. "But I guess it couldn't hurt to try."

I was surprised at how quickly the Agnew Group called after I faxed them my
résumé. I should've known right then that they were desperate.

"So, let me ask you," Josh Capra—in his early thirties and one of the
vice presidents of the firm—said after I was seated across from his desk, "have
you heard anything about the lawsuit the State of Florida just settled with Big
Tobacco?"

"I think I read something about it," I replied. "It was a multibillion-dollar
settlement, wasn't it?"

"Yes, it was. And a certain amount of that money has been earmarked for
an education campaign, targeting twelve- to seventeen-year-olds, to keep them
from smoking. The brand name for the campaign is FACTS, and the slogan is:
They sell you fiction, we give you FACTS. The idea is to expose the marketing lies
perpetrated by Big Tobacco that sell the concept of smoking to kids."

I was nodding in an encouraging, interested way, but I was uneasy about where this was going.

"The campaign kickoff," he continued, "is July thirty-first. We're planning a series of events across the state over a fourteen-day period. The idea is to have a train, called the FACTS Train, that stops in fourteen cities—a different one each day—and have a press rally at each whistlestop, with concerts in seven of the larger cities. We'll also have an education component aboard the train, so we'll pick up about a hundred kids at each stop, educate them on how to start FACTS clubs in their schools, take them to the next town, then bus them back to their point of origin. I see from your résumé that you have some experience in event production and cause-related marketing."

"Yes," I said carefully. I thought about the fiasco that had been my involvement with Drug-Free Kids. "It sounds very exciting and I'd love to be a part of it, but I think I should tell you up front that I'm a smoker."

Josh smiled. "That's okay—just *never* smoke in front of the client." He shuffled papers around on his desk. "I should tell *you* up front that we're offering this as a freelance position. We'd pay you on an hourly basis—just through the course of the project—and there won't be any benefits. But it'll be really high profile. It's a major campaign launch, and Big Tobacco is a hot news item right now."

Beggars can't be choosers, I thought. Aloud, I said, "How much of it is in place so far?"

"Well, we have the concept. And we've made some initial contact with radio stations in each of the markets, to help us with promotion. That's about it. Would you be able to start tomorrow?"

Nothing's been done yet, I thought wonderingly. Tomorrow was June 2. That meant I'd have just under eight weeks to pull it off. I'd have to find seven concert venues, fourteen press rally venues. Just organizing *one* concert in that time frame would have been a challenge—not that I would know from experience, having never produced a single concert in my life. I'd have to figure out how to get a train and a system for identifying and accurately transporting fourteen hundred kids (if even one of them wasn't returned to their parents on time, it would be a nightmare). I'd have to negotiate with the venues, secure the "big name" entertainment. There'd be lighting and sound and technical issues at each venue, and each venue would, I knew, have its own quirks and idiosyncrasies that would be wholly different from any of the others. Just managing the fourteen sets of bureaucratic mazes in each city in order to get the necessary local permits would be a full-time job. And the collateral materials! Surely we'd need signage and palm cards to promote the events; pamphlets and press kits; T-shirts and tchotchkes to give away to the kids. *That* would be its own full-time job. *These people are insane*, I told myself.

I'd orchestrated volunteer activities and a few press events, but nothing on this scale. I didn't think I could do it. Frankly, I didn't think it could be done. But I was broke and I needed a job. And, even if I hadn't, it was too big to pass up—it was one of those career opportunities that comes along once and either makes you or breaks you. What did I have to lose?

"I think I'd better start tomorrow," I said. We spent a few minutes negotiating an hourly rate. Then I stood up and smiled at Josh, shaking his hand. "Thanks so much for the opportunity."

Life as I knew it changed completely after that. Even in the beginning, before things got totally out of hand, I was working between sixty and seventy hours a week on the FACTS Train. Once again, I had committed to my career and living drug free, and I found it to be surprisingly easy going. There were moments when I craved coke with an intensity that alarmed me, but the near-constant adrenaline rush of working on a stressful and all-consuming project like the FACTS Train was almost a close-enough replacement to satisfy me.

I knew it would be almost impossible for me to be around coke and turn it down, so the key was in avoidance. This was made easier by recent crackdowns in the club scene: Some of the clubs were actually getting serious about enforcing their "no drugs on the premises" policies, and usage had become almost exclusively relegated to the bathrooms. And if you were caught with drugs in the bathrooms, you might actually get kicked out. No less a personage than Raja had been ejected from Liquid, and escorted to the front door by bouncers no less, for conspicuously snorting from a bumper of K in the ladies' room. It seemed as good a time as any to pull my head out of Baggies and focus on work.

Work at the Agnew Group was grueling, but challenging, and I was amazed at how much I was actually enjoying it. And if the demanding schedule put a crimp in my nightlife calendar, it didn't seem to matter much, as hardly anything went on in South Beach during the summer anyway. About the only important social events that occurred off-Season were high-profile birthday parties, and the end of my first week on the FACTS Train brought the birthday party of Gerry Kelly. As Ricky took great pains to inform me, there was no way—no matter how crazy I was with work—that I would be allowed to miss it.

Gerry Kelly was an Irish fashion designer who had arrived in South Beach by way of Barcelona a few years earlier, and who had rapidly become one of the town's important club promoters. He also maintained a couture business on the side, which dressed some of SoBe's wealthier women and more conspicuous drag queens. He currently managed the club Shadow Lounge, formerly Van Dome, where I'd first met Eduard—in what now seemed like a different lifetime.

I knew who Gerry Kelly was, as did everybody on the Beach, but I had never been introduced to him. Nonetheless—having finally attained a temp-to-perm spot on what seemed to be South Beach's only mailing list—I'd received an invitation to his birthday party and had RSVP'd in the affirmative.

The invite specified a Studio 54 theme and requested "over-the-top attire." Trying to figure out what would be more over the top than my usual club-going wardrobe had proven something of a challenge. I finally hit upon the perfect solution by chance.

Walking down Lincoln Road one day, I passed a boutique whose front-window mannequin was wearing the most extravagant feather boa I had ever seen. Dyed an intensely bright shade of electric yellow, it was enormous—at least triple the circumference of my arm—and made up of lush, fluffy, plumy feathers. Stretched out to its full length, it was over six feet long.

It was an accessory to draw attention away from even the drag queens, and it would, I thought, take a certain amount of nerve for a girl who wasn't a drag queen to try to pull it off. As this thought passed through my head, my mind was made up. I rushed into the store and breathlessly demanded of the girl working behind the counter, "How much is that boa in the window?"

As it turned out, it was on display from the storeowner's private collection and wasn't for sale. "Everything on South Beach is for sale," I told the girl. I plunked my credit card down next to the cash register and urgently insisted that she get the storeowner on the phone; he and I spent the next ten minutes negotiating a price, finally agreeing upon an entirely reasonable fifty dollars.

"You're not just a fag-hag—you're a fag-*haggler*," Mike said, when I regaled my friends with the tale of the boa.

I wore it to Gerry Kelly's birthday, draped around my elbows and behind my back, paired with a very short black dress and strappy, needle-thin stilettos. The brevity of the dress left quite a bit of my skin bared, and I'd covered everything—down to my hair and eyelids—in a light coat of iridescent body glitter.

"Darling! You look *fierce!*" Ricky exclaimed delightedly when he came to collect me. "You look like you just got off a float at Carnaval! It's *very* Studio 54."

We arrived at Shadow Lounge precisely one half-hour late—late enough, we'd agreed, to be fashionable, but not so late as to appear disrespectful. A receiving line had formed in the immense entryway. As it crept forward we could see Gerry waiting, flanked by two enormous, suited young men. He warmly pressed the hand of each attendee. "Thank you for coming," he murmured with a smile, inserting the name of each partier as they passed. I thought of footage I'd seen of Queen Elizabeth—or other august dignitaries—ceremonially greeting the aristocracy as they filed into a formal state dinner.

"Is this going to be awkward?" I whispered to Ricky, as we got closer to the front of the line. "I've never actually met the guy. He has no idea who I am."

"Don't worry," Ricky whispered back. "Wearing that boa was genius—if it even occurs to him that he doesn't know you, he'll think he should."

Finally we reached Gerry himself. He took Ricky's hand briefly. "Thank you for coming," he said in a low, gracious tone. Then he did something completely unexpected. He stepped forward from his entourage and gathered me into an embrace, kissing each of my cheeks. When he released me, he clasped both of my hands in his. "Thank you so much for coming to my birthday."

It was the most effusive greeting we'd seen him bestow on anybody yet. It might sound silly to say that I was impressed at being thus singled out, but so I was. My astonishment continued as Gerry whispered something to the man standing to his right, who in turn escorted us over to the gorgeous model-boy standing behind the velvet rope that guarded the upstairs VIP section. Before I knew it, we were settled at a table with a bottle of champagne.

"I think this boa just paid for itself," I said to Ricky, as the waitress poured us each a glass of champagne and dropped a sliver of strawberry into mine. "Although I'm having Eliza Doolittle issues. I feel like I've either perpetrated a huge fraud or been anointed in some way."

He chuckled. "Probably a little of both."

Ricky had claimed I'd "arrived" back in January when Isabella Shulov first put my picture in her "Queen of the Night" column. But, looking back on things now, I think it was the night of Gerry Kelly's birthday party. There was a sea change that occurred that summer in the way I was regarded on the scene— subtle, perhaps, but unmistakable. And it all seemed to start that evening.

Everybody who was anybody was there, of course. Our bottle of champagne went quickly, shared with the other scenesters who stopped by our table. Once it was gone we circulated around the room ourselves, struggling to discern familiar faces in the dim smokiness of the club. *If there's a cure for this, I don't want it . . .* , Diana Ross insisted, as my boa was petted and stroked and tried on by just about everybody we saw. Shadow Lounge typically played electronica, but tonight the DJ was exclusively spinning '70s disco at such high volume, we could barely hear the people we talked to. Not that it really mattered—the trick was to watch people's faces for the cues that told you when to smile or laugh at whatever they'd just said. Ricky and I smiled and laughed like pros, posing for so many photos that I felt as if two dazzling blind spots had been permanently burned into my corneas. Glenn Albin even took our picture for *Ocean Drive*, an honor that Ricky bore in a sanguine fashion belied only by the brief, excited squeeze he gave my hand.

We ran into Finn and Isabella with Isabella's photographer, Manny, in tow. Cameras were like homing beacons on South Beach; between the people who were taking pictures of Ricky and me for their nightlife columns, and Ricky taking pictures of people for his own column, it eventually became unnecessary for us to look for people we knew—everybody came to us.

"Oh my God!" shouted Adrina Balistreri, arriving with Adam Kohley, when she spotted us. "That boa's amazing!" She grabbed it from me and flung it dramatically around her neck, prowling back and forth while sucking in her cheekbones in an impromptu supermodel send-up.

Adrina was the one girl on South Beach who I had a secret crush on, in the sense that—of all the women I'd met or seen so far—she was the one I most wanted to be friends with. Mischievous as a kitten and radiating sexual energy, Adrina was slim and lithe with long, corn-silk hair. Like Chloë Sevigny, who she resembled, you almost couldn't decide if she was pretty or not—yet, unable to look away from her, you would have insisted that she was beautiful. Adrina wrote the nightlife column for *Channel* magazine, and also cohosted the cable-access nightlife show *Channel Surfing*. A crazy all-night partier who'd allegedly once disappeared on a three-day bender with Perry Farrell, she always seemed to be at the center of a whirling centrifuge of fun. She was also one of the best dancers I'd ever seen, and she and Ricky—an outstanding dancer himself—tore it up on the disco round amidst an admiring circle of onlookers.

Adam, her best friend and *Channel Surfing* cohost, was also blond and slim, with the round-eyed, innocently pretty face of a cherub. He greeted me by embracing me from behind and rubbing against me suggestively. "I'm not a straight man," he murmured in my ear, "but I play one on TV." Then he spun me around and dipped me back, nuzzling his face between my breasts and licking his way up to my neck as I squealed and struggled in girly mock protest.

Cubby, who used to write the nightlife column for the *Wire* but now wrote for the *Sunpost*, took my picture and introduced me to Michael Tronn, the new club director at Liquid. The Beach was abuzz with talk of Michael, a recent New York transplant. It was said that he'd been one of the infamous New York "club kids" a few years ago. A former cohort of the notorious Michael Alig, he'd had his picture on the cover of *New York* magazine as one of the movement's founders.

"Hello, my angel," Michael said with a hug upon being introduced. The smile he greeted me with was so charismatic, I fleetingly wished he was straight.

He kissed me on both cheeks. "I know we hardly know each other, but you're so beautiful that I must call you 'my angel.'"

I laughed, utterly charmed. Then I pulled my face into an expression of exaggerated pity and stroked his arm in a caressing, affectionate way. "You know, other people in this town are going to be mean to you on account of how ugly you are, but *I* promise never to shun you."

Michael laughed also, and we took a moment to bask in our mutual flattery. Then he said, "I understand you're a poet."

I was surprised. "Where'd you hear that?"

"Ricky told me."

I turned to glare at Ricky, who had his back to me as he chatted with Isabella. "I write sometimes," I admitted reluctantly, although it occurred to me that I couldn't remember when I'd last dedicated any serious time to my poetry.

"I'm doing Beatnik Guido in a few weeks, and I'm looking for people to read original poems. I'll be reading one of my own." When I hesitated, he added, "Just one or two short pieces—nothing too heavy. It is a club, after all."

One of Michael's first acts at Liquid had been to promote a VIP-only party called Guido in the Liquid Lounge on Friday nights, which he'd begun to vary each week by adding different sub-themes. One week, for example, it was Sid n' Nancy Guido, and everybody was instructed to attend in '80s punk attire. Another Friday it was Out of Africa Guido, and we'd donned pith helmets and animal prints while sipping champagne in a VIP lounge that suddenly looked as if it were spun from white mosquito netting.

"I have to check and see if I have anything that would work," I said. "Can I let you know?"

"Of course, sweetie." I pulled out a cigarette and he took the matches from my hand to light it for me. He leaned in closer to half whisper conspiratorially, "I'm trying to get the right people involved."

That obviously decided the matter. I heard myself agreeing, even as I thought it was unlikely that anybody would remember such a commitment—made in a club after hours of drinking—several weeks from now.

Overall, the night was a success. A few days later, when the papers and magazines came out, I was gratified to see my name and picture featured in several of them. *Among the scenesters I saw at* **Gerry Kelly's** *birthday party,* Cubby's column in the *Sunpost* ran, *were* **Ricky Pascal, "Mr. Nightclub"** (Palm *magazine), and* **Rachel Baum** (The Agnew Group), *looking far too fabulous in a far too low-cut gown.*

"What the hell is that supposed to mean?" I asked, semi-indignantly, when I saw it. Ricky cracked up. Then I saw my photo in Isabella's column and noticed how far down the neckline of my dress had plunged. "Ah, well." I shrugged. "Fair enough."

Ricky's and my picture also appeared in Adrina's column in *Channel. Adam and I partied far into the night with Mr. Nightclub himself,* **Ricky Pascal** (Palm*), and our new best friend for life* **Rachel** (babe)*.* "Adam and I had so much fun with you!" Adrina said when I saw her and Adam at 821 the day *Channel* came out. "But we totally couldn't remember your last name." And I laughed—not wanting to tell her that I was so thrilled she'd remembered me at all, I'd never cared less about my own name.

Upon Ricky's advice, I cut out all of my press mentions and pasted them into a new scrapbook he gave me. "Someday," he said, "you'll want to be able to look back and remember all this."

As usual, Ricky turned out to be right.

FIFTEEN

Summers are generally lethargic on South Beach. The stupefying heat picks up water from the ocean and suspends it in the air, which becomes thick and almost tactile. People move as listlessly through it as if they were pushing against something heavy. Thunderstorms blow up out of nowhere and drench you down to the skin, leaving you feeling breathless—and more than a little betrayed—before they disappear with such quickness, you wonder if you imagined the whole thing. Tourists and snowbirds leave in the same anxious droves that they flock to us in during Season. South Beach was never what you would call a fast-paced town, but in the summer it became downright sleepy.

That summer was different, though. The word that came to mind was one I'd learned long ago in a mostly forgotten high school science class: entropy. It means the potential energy, or the potential for chaos, in a closed system. It was a word that seemed perfectly applied to South Beach—a closed system crackling with chaos and potential energy, if ever there was one.

Much of the energy was generated by WAMI in Miami, which had finally launched after months of delays. Its mission was to be the first television network ever to deliver all-local programming, all the time. It didn't seem possible that our local media could be more self-contained than it already was, but here was an opportunity even we hadn't dreamt of.

WAMI's glass-encased studio sparkled self-consciously from the ground-floor corner of Lincoln Road's Sony building, proudly emblazoned with the slogan: THE CITY IS OUR STUDIO. Cameras were mounted along Lincoln Road, or held in the roving hands of chirpy hipster wannabes, to record us in unguarded moments. We didn't mind; most of us on South Beach aspired to live our lives on film anyway. As Warren Beatty had shrewdly noted in our patron saint's movie *Truth or Dare*, what was the point of doing anything if it was off-camera?

Word on the street was that the guy running WAMI was only thirty-three years old and had a background in everything from theater to the newly white-hot Internet—everything except television. With a thirty-million-dollar budget to burn through, no idea was too "offbeat" to be considered. Anthony Marino, who'd had a radio show on a local pirate station, suddenly had a roundtable-style talk show called *Kenneth's Freakquency*. Among the show's eventual highlights were live liposuction and a horse defecating on camera. Somebody pitched the idea of having a pair of disembodied lips read the late-night news headlines— just floating red lips against a black background—and WAMI bought it. *Ocean Drive* had been tapped to create a lifestyle show; it was said they would give *Deco Drive* a run for their money.

Of course, WAMI's production values barely rivaled those of your typical cable-access show. And while WAMI's mission was to offer twenty-four hours of local programming, what they currently offered was closer to eight hours, the rest being filled in with old reruns of *Charlie's Angels* and *Magnum, P.I.* The ratings were dismal, or whatever's lower than dismal, and Kojo was frequently heard to opine that WAMI should change their slogan from *The city is our studio* to *WAMI: Who's watching?*

But people in South Beach had dreams of stardom—had, in fact, come to South Beach for the sake of those dreams. To us, WAMI felt like a rendezvous with destiny.

Caught up in the commotion, Ricky decided that we should write a sitcom pilot for WAMI. It was about a straitlaced young woman who breaks up with her fiancé and moves in with her gay best friend on South Beach, whose longtime lover has just left him to pursue a career as a gay country-western singer (his signature song: "Rear-Ended on the Highway of Love"). We got about halfway through the script before the project was abandoned.

I had developed a decidedly unsexy reputation as a "workaholic" in those days—mostly because, whenever Ricky went out and people asked where I was, he would say, "Working! That girl has turned into a total workaholic!" So, when Adam and Adrina decided to offer WAMI a glossier version of their cable-access *Channel Surfing*, I was deemed the natural and responsible choice to hammer out a marketing strategy. They also had Lydia Birdsong on board—a brassy, fleshy blonde from Australia, who was a freelance news producer for the

Australian *60 Minutes*. Lydia had achieved international fame a few years earlier when she'd tracked Australia's most-wanted criminal to South America—and captured him.

Ricky came in on the project as well. The five of us spent hours at 821 one night, outlining concepts and future syndication scenarios. It seemed like a surefire winner, given our group's combined notoriety and nightlife-coverage creds—except that this show idea didn't go anywhere either.

Every single one of us on South Beach felt that we had a possible series in us, staying up late into the night to formulate plots and pitches and the ways in which we'd still be gracious to our friends, once we'd made it big. Rumors were constantly swirling about so-and-so's upcoming show on WAMI, which was *this close* to getting on the air, and the rest of us would react with varying degrees of ill-concealed envy. The fact that almost none of these fledgling shows materialized did little to dispel our own hopes of hitting the big time.

Although it was normally antithetical to my nature to start something and not finish it, I couldn't beat myself up too much about failing to follow through on our WAMI plans. I was always working like a crazy person, trying to cram what should have been a year's worth of planning on the FACTS Train into two months, or running with Ricky from one party to another.

All that activity should have made me feel that time was rushing away. But, when I think about it now, that summer seems endless in my mind. It was like the kind of summer you had when you were a kid—where three months was enough time to change your whole life, and the summer days separated themselves out from the rest of the year, shimmering like heat lightning.

I was now regularly clocking upwards of eighty hours a week on the FACTS Train. I was so wired on adrenaline that I was eating constantly—everything I could get my hands on—and still losing two pounds a week. "I feel like that guy from *Thinner*," I told Ricky. "I think everyone in my office thinks I'm bulimic."

Overseeing the collective efforts and billing issues for the project was difficult at best, especially given that our client—and cash source—was the State of Florida. Immediate cash was often needed to solve problems, but the State required at least ninety days to turn a check around—that is, once they'd taken thirty days to approve the expenditure. I frequently found myself saying things like, "No, *NSYNC can*not* send you an invoice and wait to get a check. They want half in cash now and half in cash the day of the concert, or they're not signing the contract." *A bureaucratic maze,* I called it in my more frustrated moments. *A cluster-fuck* was how my boss, Josh, somewhat more bluntly, expressed it.

But, in a way that probably implies severe emotional problems on my part, the stress and drama of it all was more fun than I'd ever had in my life—and it was a good feeling that seemed destined to continue far into the future. I turned up at Kojo's one night with the news that the Agnew Group had offered to bring me on full-time, once the FACTS Train was finished. I was ecstatic. Finally, my career was falling into place.

Kojo's Lincoln Road apartment was conveniently located next door to the Agnew Group's Lincoln Road offices—so close, in fact, that they shared a common parking lot—and I would beeline over there whenever I had finished for the night. Kojo would provide snacks and pot to help me unwind after my long, overworked days. He would frequently offer more than pot—you never knew what party favors were on-hand in Kojo's recreational pharmacopoeia. But I gave Kojo strict instructions not to let me so much as see the stuff; nothing could be allowed to jeopardize my work.

Mike, whose apartment was only one block off of Lincoln Road, was always at Kojo's too—calling me at precisely two o'clock every day to make sure I was planning to show at Kojo's that night. Ricky would join us on the nights when there wasn't a more glamorous social imperative, reacting with anything from humor to exasperation when Mike called him, too, every day (at two fifteen) to remind him to stop by Kojo's. "Why do I have to be joined at the hip to those two?" he would grumble, although he ended up there more often than not.

Mike would also bring over Adonis, who was his boyfriend, or Hugo, who was his other boyfriend—sometimes he would bring the two of them over simultaneously. He always liked combining the various people in his life, with no concern as to whether or not they'd "fit." He couldn't see why the people he liked might not like each other. Ricky, on the other hand, was more cautious in introducing his new love interest, a Eurasian makeup artist named Clint. You couldn't really blame Ricky for being hesitant about bringing a boyfriend around. I knew from experience how badly that could turn out.

Other guests showed up occasionally—like Carlos Flex, a local body-builder type, or coworkers of Kojo's from Moondance. It was always chaotic. Ricky would throw some salsa music onto Kojo's turntables, teaching me the dance moves that would be an indispensable part of our strategy next Season. Mike would make off-color sexual comments directed at us and at his boyfriends. Kojo would go off on obscure, stream-of-consciousness riffs that nobody else could follow. "Somebody needs to write *Kojo for Dummies*," he'd say.

I was always the only girl, and the only token heterosexual. It meant being the focus of lots of attention, which I came to enjoy and even crave. I was petted and caressed and praised for my "diva" status. It was as if the hardworking go-getter I was during the day was an entirely different person from who I was at night—and, as such, was entitled to an entirely different standard of treatment.

Ricky usually managed to pry me out of Kojo's apartment once or twice a week for a party that simply *had* to be attended. Groove Jet, Liquid, and Shadow Lounge were our top three scenes of choice. Sometimes we varied our circuit with side trips to cocktail parties poolside at the Albion or Raleigh hotels. "Nothing gets started until midnight, which is plenty of time for you to disco nap after work and still make an appearance," Ricky would argue, when I tried to protest that I was too busy or too tired. "You don't want people to forget about you, darling, after how hard we've worked."

We went to Guido one night for the birthday party of a rising young star in the fashion world named Enrique Colon. Walking in at about twelve thirty, the first thing I saw was a slender little boy—a child no taller than my chin. "Since when are kids allowed in Liquid?" I asked Ricky.

"That's Enrique," he said. "It's his birthday party—he just turned thirteen."

I nearly dropped the lit cigarette I was holding. "You're kidding me."

Ricky seemed surprised at my surprise. "He's a fashion prodigy, darling. Todd Oldham discovered him a year ago."

Naomi Campbell, Niki Taylor, Todd Oldham, and Chris Paciello were clustered at one of the VIP tables not far from our own. Enrique greeted them rapturously, receiving an equally enthusiastic greeting in return. Chris Ciccone—Madonna's brother—was following Enrique around with a camera crew ("For the documentary they're making about Enrique," Ricky informed me). There were paparazzi everywhere, snapping flash photos indiscriminately until Liquid looked like a sparklers factory.

"The emperor has no clothes," I observed.

Enrique himself came over eventually to thank us for attending his birthday party, hugging us in the spastic way peculiar to overexcited children. He seemed so genuinely, gosh-darned thrilled about the whole spectacle that I couldn't help but hug him back warmly. "This party is *fierce*, Miss Thing!" he exclaimed in a youthful, high-pitched voice, snapping his fingers once in the air for emphasis. Then he turned and scurried off.

"Oh my," I said meaningfully to Ricky, and the two of us cracked up. "We are *so* going to hell for contributing to the delinquency of a minor."

"That's okay," Ricky replied, with an amusing lack of concern. "That's where all our friends will be, and I'm sure the parties in hell are much better, anyway."

Naturally. Heaven or hell, it didn't matter—as long as our names were on the right list.

I wanted not to care about things like which parties I was invited to, or if or where my picture appeared. They seemed like such silly things to be concerned with. But then I'd see my photo in the local magazines, or get the VIP treatment at some club where there was an actual red carpet with all the South Beach paparazzi lined up on either side—and how crazy was *that*? I was just some nobody from nowhere, who'd had only one picture in her entire high school yearbook. Now I got to dress up and play at being a celebrity the way, as a child, I'd dressed up and played at being a doctor or a ballerina—and it was *fun*.

I talked to Lara from my office almost every day, filling her in on the details of my life as she filled me in on the details of hers. She understood how caught up I was in my job, naturally, being something of an overachiever herself. But I didn't know how to make her understand how caught up I was in the circus that my party life had become. She thought it sounded like an entertaining way to kill time, but it was more than that for me. I think I truly believed that if I could just keep living fast enough—as long as my job was demanding, my friends were attentive, and my picture kept turning up in the papers—I could keep things exactly the way they were now, staying young and pretty forever and ever.

As for Lara, she was moving in with her boyfriend, planning an engagement, and starting to buy what she called "grown-up" furniture for her home. I had hardly a stick of furniture in my own apartment—almost nothing beyond a bed and a TV. And I didn't want any, I told myself, grown-up or otherwise. Not in my apartment and not in my life.

It was early July when I went to Groove Jet for the wrap party of an Oliver Stone film that had just finished shooting in Miami. Stone was there, along with Cameron Diaz and Jamie Foxx. The three of them, with a group of some thirty hangers-on, had claimed the two prime tables in the VIP section.

I had arrived late, even by South Beach standards. A minor calamity involving a missing contract for the band headlining our Tampa and Jacksonville shows had kept me at the office until nearly midnight. By the time I made it home, ditched my business suit, showered, and slipped into a backless red satin gown—adding the requisite looks-to-kill makeup—it was two a.m. before a cab finally deposited me at the entrance. The line was unreal, and I caught the full gamut of dirty looks as I headed straight for the front, affectionately kissed the doorman, and was whisked inside.

The DJ in the regular portion of the club was spinning a mix of that techno/house variety that always sounded the same to me, and DJ Shannon—one of my favorites—was spinning in the VIP garden. I could hear both of them simultaneously as I located Ricky, seated with Groove Jet owners Greg and Nicole Brier one table over from the feeding frenzy that swirled around Oliver Stone et al. I identified "Cherchez La Femme" as the tune Shannon was playing and sang snatches of it to myself as I headed for Ricky. *They'll tell you a lie with a Colgate smile* . . . I hummed. *Love you one second and hate you the next one* . . .

Groove Jet's outdoor VIP section was always warm in the summer, but the place was so packed that night that the heat was almost unbearable. It took me nearly twenty minutes to work my way over to Ricky—during which time I greeted acquaintances and posed for the obligatory paparazzi pics—and I hoped that the thin film of sweat I was covered in when I finally reached him made me look dewy rather than dilapidated.

I greeted Nicole and Greg, who were, as always, uniformly cheerful, charming, and clean-scrubbed beautiful. Nicole, especially, had a way of beaming brightly when she was talking to you that made you feel as though *you* were the person she'd most wanted to see that night. I was always happy that summer— even more so on the nights when a catastrophe kept me at the office late—but my mood was still slightly elevated by Nicole as I seated myself next to Ricky.

I was filling Ricky in on the disastrous details of my day when Nicole called over to introduce us to a man who'd materialized at her side. He looked very familiar, although I couldn't quite place him. "Do you two know Andrew Lowestoffe?" she asked.

Andrew Lowestoffe was a young British architect who had occasionally entertained clients at the Sands' bar while I was working there. Although I'd never spoken to him, I'd always thought him unreasonably cute. It took me only a few seconds to make the connection after Nicole introduced us and he seated himself across from me.

Tall and slender, Andrew had the sort of tapering build and hands that seem to predestine a future in the arts. His dark blue eyes were unusually liquid, and they gleamed keenly in the subdued candlelight glowing from the center of our table. He recognized me, too, and we spent a few minutes playing *Don't I Know You From . . .* before finally agreeing that the only place we could possibly know each other from was the Sands.

Everybody seemed to sense that they should leave us to tête-à-tête for a while. We spent an unbroken half-hour discussing architecture (mainly him), literature (mainly me), and contemporary art (both of us). Each time I picked up the cool champagne glass, I was aware of how flushed my skin was becoming; each time Andrew's arm brushed against mine was static electricity in the humid night. *Entropy*, I thought dreamily. *Potential energy.*

Eventually, we came back to pondering why we'd never talked to each other when our paths had crossed at the Sands. "Of course I noticed you," Andrew said with playful gravity. "But you seemed so unapproachable."

"Who's *more* approachable than a bartender?" I wondered aloud. "That's why guys hit on bartenders all the time."

"Exactly!" he responded. "You were this very pretty girl who clearly had dozens of men vying for her attention. I was afraid you would break my heart quite ruthlessly."

I rolled my eyes and grinned at the same time, to indicate that I was duly flattered, but not 100 percent buying into his revisionist history. "That's me." I put on a French accent. *"La belle dame sans merci."*

"Ah!" he exclaimed delightedly. "You speak French, do you?"

"No, I don't speak French," I replied, and lowered my eyes. Then I looked up innocently and added, "But I'm *fluent* in Pretentious." I sipped my champagne and smiled as Andrew threw back his head and laughed out loud.

At that moment, an intense white light, attached to a WAMI news camera, shone blindingly into my face. Beyond the camera, I could see Mike whispering to a cameraman and grinning at me over his shoulder. Then Mike bent over me, microphone in hand, and raised his voice to be heard over Fatboy Slim's "Praise You," which pulsed around us. "Our viewers are wondering whether this guy's gotten your phone number yet."

I smiled sweetly into the camera. "I have no comment at this time." Then I looked around the cameraman to Mike. "Mike, could I have a word?"

Mike made an *uh-oh* face as I led him a few feet away. "Look," I said, "I'm about to close the deal with one of the five dateable straight guys on South Beach. Could you try very hard not to wreck it for me?"

"Please!" Mike scoffed. "He's gay!"

It's been my experience that most gay men believe the average straight guy is never more than a six-pack away from a bi-curious experience. But I had neither the time nor the energy at the moment to debate the issue with Mike. "He's really not," I said. "And if you don't get that camera out of our faces, you're going to need a proctologist to separate *you* from *it*—understood?"

"All right, all right," Mike said good-naturedly. "Don't get your panties in a knot, assuming you're wearing any." My expression must have indicated that I was dangerously close to the boiling point, because Mike called over to the cameraman, "Come on, Joe—we're done here. Let's go get a quote from Cameron."

"What was that all about?" Ricky shouted over the music from his station next to Greg and Nicole—and also Adam and Adrina, who had joined our group—when I returned. "Why did you chase the camera away?"

I pulled out a cigarette and accepted Andrew's offer of a light. "I was just saying hello to Mike. He said to tell you 'hi,' by the way."

"I see," Ricky said in knowing amusement. "Mike has great timing, doesn't he?"

"The *best*," I agreed. I turned back to Andrew. "Would you mind pouring me another glass of champagne?"

"You know," Andrew said, as he obligingly pulled the bottle from its ice bucket, "your friend has made things a little awkward for me."

"Really?" I took a sip of champagne. "How so?"

"Well, I was just about to ask for your phone number, but if I do it after he told me to, I'm afraid you'll think I'm less of a man."

"Ah," I commiserated with great seriousness. "You definitely shouldn't ask for it, then."

"I suppose." He managed to look both mournful and devilish at the same time. "The problem with that, you see, is that I really *would* like your phone number."

I made a sympathetic clucking sound. "It sounds like quite a dilemma."

"You could—and this is just a suggestion—make things easier by offering it to me."

"Oh, I couldn't do *that*," I protested sedately. "You'd probably assume I go around giving out my phone number to drunken sailors like it was candy."

"That's a good point." He stroked his chin ruefully, and I laughed. "I suppose there's nothing for me then, except to say masculinity be damned and ask you for it."

"Tell you what." I drained the last of the champagne from my flute and stood up. Andrew rose too. "I'll give you my phone number, and you can prove your manliness by putting me in a cab."

I kissed everybody at our table good-bye, and then Andrew and I squeezed a single-file path to the outside. I studied Andrew's back as he walked in front of me. My attempts at relationships on South Beach hadn't been very successful thus far, but I already knew that I wanted this. This was good. *Please*, I thought fervently, and it was almost like a prayer. *Please let this one work out.*

We found a cab almost immediately, and I slipped a business card into Andrew's hand as he held the door open for me. "I'll call you," he said through the open window of the cab. "Maybe we could have dinner this week."

"Maybe." I smiled at him one last time as the cab pitched forward to merge with the rushing swirl of traffic, which all but blocked the entrance to the club.

SIXTEEN

As fate would have it, Andrew's architectural firm (Lowestoffe Architects) was located in one of the office spaces on Lincoln Road. He was up on the 1100 block and I worked with the Agnew Group down on Lincoln Road's 400 block. So when he called a few days after the Groove Jet party, it seemed only logical for us to meet for cocktails somewhere in the middle.

Perhaps no single street better defined South Beach, aesthetically or philosophically, than Lincoln Road. If you ask people who know about such things, they might describe Lincoln Road's architecture as Mediterranean Revival, Nautical Deco, or Nautical Moderne. But if you go simply as a visitor to take it all in, your first and lasting impression will be one of visual profusion—of amber and rainbow; flowers and buildings; sun and shade; the endless motion of walkers and skaters wearing little more than Speedos or halter tops; and the calm, casual elegance of well-dressed patrons seated at outdoor cafés. Parrots fly overhead, either singly or in small groups, as if a reckless socialite had scattered an emerald necklace high into the air. People in South Florida were always buying parrots to keep as house pets, and they often escaped to congregate on the Beach, building chattering, communal nests in Lincoln Road's palmetto trees.

There were art galleries on Lincoln Road, and indoor/outdoor cafés; clothing boutiques and mom-and-pop shops that sold jewelry and curios from South America or the Far East. Lincoln Road was home to the ArtCenter, two performance theaters, neighborhood bar-cum-nightclubs like 821 and Score, and small cigar shops where South Beach's last few elderly Cuban men would smoke, eat *medianoche* sandwiches, and play dominoes. You could browse at Books & Books—owned by South Florida's most vocal literary advocate, Mitch Kaplan—and then cross the road to sip *café con leche* under a gaily striped umbrella at Balans. Lincoln Road is a pedestrian mall, always closed to traffic, and so there is nothing to stop you from strolling it as long or aimlessly as you please—other than South Beach's vibrant heat, which will always get you in the end.

After our first rendezvous, Andrew and I fell into a daily cocktails-after-work routine. We would typically meet for a quick happy hour at 821 or possibly the Van Dyke, where we'd eschew the sceney downstairs tables and head upstairs for live jazz and a slightly more sedate bar. "You have to let me take you out for dinner," Andrew would say, and I would sigh wistfully—there was truly nothing I wanted more. But my work schedule was so unpredictable, and would be until the FACTS Train was finished.

Proper date or no, there was no denying that I was well and truly infatuated. Thinking about Andrew felt like my body was producing some really good drug all the time. As in any early-stage infatuation scenario, we marveled at the coincidences of the things we had in common and reveled in the differences that made us so interesting to each other. We both agreed, for example, that we loved driving our cars too fast over bumpy roads and secretly delighted in airplane turbulence. We were both passionate about cheap Spanish red wine and food so spicy it made your eyes tear up, and we both felt that Tom Waits was the most underappreciated singer-songwriter who'd ever lived. "*I'll tell you all my secrets, but I lie about my past,*" Andrew quoted, and was inordinately pleased when I identified it as a line from the song "Tango Till They're Sore."

I had never been to England, but Andrew's descriptions were better than anything I'd read in books, relayed as they were through the subtle interplay of glimmering eyes and expressive hands. He talked about London and his parents and the small village in the English countryside where he'd grown up. "We'll have to go there one day," he said, and I thrilled to his casual use of the word *we*. "Everyone'll say, *Look at that bird Lowestoffe's brought back with him!*"

I wrinkled up my nose. "Will they really call me a *bird*?" I asked. When Andrew laughed, I continued, "And then will they say things like *bloody hell, sodding, lifts and lorries, bangers and mash*?"

"I think only the village idiot talks that way," Andrew replied, and I playfully stuck my tongue out at him.

My descriptions of growing up in Miami provided quite a contrast. The huge public schools I'd attended were bigger than his hometown. I told him about my glory days on the high school debate team and volunteering for the Democratic National Committee, and how as a child I'd taken pillows and blankets and made a nest for myself in my bedroom closet, where I could hide and read and nobody would find me. "What are your parents like?" he asked once, to which I responded, "Please—family is my gateway drug."

"I could end up marrying this guy, I mean it," I told Lara. "He's smart, he's sexy, he's successful. He won't try to make me give up the party scene. He could be the one."

"That's great," Lara responded enthusiastically. I could tell she was relieved that the days of felons and sketchy billionaires were firmly behind us.

As was I.

I never knew if it was by accident or by design when Andrew showed up at Beatnik Guido a couple of weeks into our still-undefined flirtation. It's *possible* that I mentioned to him in passing that I would probably be in the Liquid Lounge with Ricky that Friday night at, say, midnight or so. And I suppose it's *possible* that, when midnight rolled around and he didn't have anything better to do, Liquid seemed as good a place as any to kill time. Whatever the cause of the effect, I wasn't about to question an opportunity that the gods of good timing had seen fit to throw my way.

The only fly in the ointment was that Michael Tronn had actually remembered the promise I'd made at Gerry Kelly's birthday party, to "share a poem" at Beatnik Guido. As with so many things, it had seemed like a good idea while I was half-drunk in a club and a good-looking boy was stroking my ego. Now I wasn't so sure.

"Ooh—how fabulous!" Ricky exclaimed. I'd called him right after Michael called me. "You shouldn't worry so much, darling; Michael knows what he's doing."

"Michael was on the cover of *New York* magazine," I replied. "Michael can do whatever he wants. *I*, on the other hand, have nothing to gain from this besides looking like an idiot."

I finally decided on a sex-and-drugs poem I'd written—thinking that, if any poem I had was likely to hold attention in a club, this would probably be it. But here was another problem, because it couldn't exactly be advisable (could it?) to read a sex-and-drugs poem in front of a guy I dug, but hadn't so much as kissed yet.

This was the fresh source of concern I brought up to Ricky at Liquid when I spied Andrew at the velvet rope. "I want him to think I'm sexy and all," I said, "but I'd rather have him think I'm sexy in an elusive sort of way."

"What are you talking about, 'elusive'? He's already seen you in those dresses you wear with your tits hanging out all over the place."

"What are *you* talking about?" I protested. "*You* helped me pick out most of my dresses!"

"I know, darling." Ricky was maddeningly unflappable. "Why do you think people like Michael Tronn are suddenly so interested in your mind?"

As part of his reinvention of the Liquid Lounge, Michael had suspended an enormous swing from the center of the ceiling. It was comprised of a large wooden seat—perhaps two feet wide and four feet long—that hung from several strong ropes, glisteningly garnished with shimmering silver-and-pastel materials: silk, crepe paper, tinsel. It could be raised or lowered from ground level all the way up to the two-story-high ceiling and was a favorite spot for drag queens and the intrepidly inclined, who would swing high above our heads in dizzy abandonment and bestow their blessings on the gyrating masses below.

It was here that Michael led me when the moment he'd deemed poetry-perfect arrived. He handed me a wireless microphone and indicated that I should stand on the swing's seat, which had been considerably lowered. I hesitated. "I thought you were reading first," I said, but found myself speaking to the shrinking back of his head as he walked away. Before I knew it, two attendants were slowly jerking the swing up and up. I was so close to the ceiling that I could have reached up and touched it with my hand.

The house music was suddenly cut off. The absolute silence of a nightclub when all the music has been killed is eerie, and the novelty of it had people halting their conversations and looking up at me in a curious, expectant fashion. I felt slightly ridiculous, just standing there like that (and also petrified—every time I moved, the swing wobbled slightly, so I stood as stiffly as possible). But things got worse when all the lights went out except for a single spotlight trained directly on me. It made the silver drapery on the ropes beam with a preternatural brightness, throwing merry, sparkling patterns on the far walls of the room.

"Attention, please!" Michael's voice cut through the silence with the clarity of a silver bell. He clapped his hands together briskly and continued, "We have a special treat tonight—our very own poetry chanteuse, Rachel Baum, has agreed to read one of her poems for us."

The combination of the dark room and the painfully bright spotlight kept me from being able to see anybody. But I could *feel* everybody looking at me as I clutched the microphone tighter.

"Hi," I said, in what I hoped was a confident, comfortable tone. "This is a poem I wrote a couple of years ago; I wanted to write an erotic poem around the verb 'to roll.'" *Nobody here cares about verbs, Rachel!* I chided myself. "Anyway," I continued, "here it is." I cleared my throat and opened up the piece of paper in my hand:

Roll

> me like a joint
> spread my
> papers and finger
> my leaves
> tongue me
> up
> seal me
> turn me in your
> mouth
> wet my tip
> on your lips then
> light me suck
> me down
> take me in
> breathe
> out what's left
> I rise and surround you
> leave my scent on you
> touch parts of you I
> can't see frenzied I
> fill the air
> make it thick
> and fall
> down
> on you
>
> Until,
> full of me,
> your head rolls back,
> slack-eyed
> and still.

There was silence for a moment—and then, miraculously, there was *applause*! I clutched the ropes on the sides of the swing as it was lowered slowly from the ceiling back to the floor, the spotlight following me the whole way. Then the music came back on, the strobe lights resumed their spinning, and a small press of people knotted around me as I shakily placed my feet on the stable club floor.

It was a few minutes before Andrew was able to reach me. At the sight of him, the agitation still pulsing in my system turned to pure adrenaline. "Hey," I said, a little shyly.

"Why, Miss Baum." He smiled down at me. "Who knew?"

I blushed slightly. "I guess I may as well confess that I've smoked pot on occasion," I said, mock-sheepishly. "Um, and also I'm not a virgin."

"My, my," he drawled. "How *will* South Beach survive such vice?" We both laughed.

All I wanted was to be alone with him, but Ricky and I had a table and a bottle of champagne, and privacy was momentarily impossible. I shouted to be heard over the music until my throat was sore, and air-kissed partiers until my facial muscles were pained from puckering. I also posed for numerous photos shot by the local photo claque, flashing them the downward-looking half smile (no teeth) that Ricky had coached me on. Andrew stayed by my side the whole time. It was three in the morning when I finally turned to him and said, "I'm awfully tired. I think I need to take off."

"Let me put you in a cab," Andrew replied.

We walked for a block or so in no particular direction, the heat from the pavement rising in the July night like an evil genie. I stopped eventually, raising a hand into the air even though I didn't see any available cabs. Andrew took my other hand loosely in his, his thumb brushing back and forth against the tips of my fingers. "You have such small hands," he said, and squeezed my fingers a little tighter.

I lowered my arm. I was afraid that anything I said might spoil the moment, so I simply replied softly, "Thank you for walking me out."

Andrew's response was to pull me closer. *He's going to kiss me right here on Washington Avenue*, I thought, but I didn't care.

I've always believed that the best kissers are the ones who kiss exactly the way you do. That's what makes it feel so right. Andrew kissed exactly the way I did. His mouth felt as natural against mine as if the two were made for each other. My skin was hot and damp in the sticky summer air, but Andrew's lips were cool and sweet as fruit taken from the refrigerator.

Like grapes after all day, I thought. And then, for the first time in months, I stopped thinking.

The summer-months cycle of birthday parties continued to spin forward. Ricky's own mid-August birthday was looming on the horizon, and a great deal of thought had gone into the appropriate way of marking the (age withheld) birthday of Mr. Nightclub. Ricky had finally decided on a free-for-all blowout at Groove Jet, to be followed the next night by a more intimate dinner party—for about fifty people or so—at Joia. "That way," he'd remarked, "Greg and Nicole can't be mad at me for giving my birthday to Chris, and Chris can't be mad at me for giving my birthday to Greg and Nicole."

No birthday, however, was greeted with greater anticipation, fanfare, or good old-fashioned hoopla than Isabella Shulov's, whose party was scheduled to take place only a few days before I went to Pensacola for the first leg of the FACTS Train tour. I had precious little time for anything in those final, hectic days, but Ricky and I nonetheless spent a Saturday afternoon in Isabella's spacious duplex apartment, helping her stuff envelopes and mail out the hundreds of invitations. The invitations were pink and featured a pen-and-ink sketch of her, drawn by Genghis especially for the occasion. It dawned on me that I was likely to see Genghis for the first time since my falling out with Amy, and I anxiously scanned the guest list for other names I might be less than thrilled to see. I was relieved to note that Amy's and Raja's weren't there.

Andrew hadn't been invited either—he wasn't a diehard scenemaker and was relatively unknown in Isabella's circle. "Come anyway," I told him. "I'll ask her to put your name on the list."

"Should we go together?" It had been a week since that first kiss, and we still hadn't found a single workable night for a dinner date. It looked like it wouldn't happen until after I got back from the FACTS Train.

"I can't—I promised Ricky I'd go early with him and Isabella and Finn." Then I smiled. "I'm *going* with Ricky," I said. "But I can *leave* with you."

He smiled too and kissed me. "Sounds like I'm getting the better end of the deal."

We weren't the only pair to be split up by the vagaries of the guest list. Kojo had been invited, but Mike had not. "That's okay—I wouldn't have been able to go anyway," Mike said, seeming genuinely unconcerned. "I'm too busy at WAMI helping to build a news station out of duct tape and a Fisher-Price 'My First Satellite Dish.'"

It was a rare social event that drew Kojo out of the safety of his own apartment, but Isabella's birthday was considered sufficient occasion. He was, however, upset that we weren't all going together. I knew Kojo hated going anywhere by himself, feeling shy and vulnerable when he had to fend off SoBe's social slings and arrows on his own. "Ricky's got his nose buried so far up Isabella Shulov's ass," he complained. "He's so busy being Mr. Nightclub all the time."

"They're best friends," I said gently. "He's going early because she asked him to, not because he doesn't want to go with you."

"Why can't *you* go with me?"

"Because I already told Ricky I'd go with him—and if I change that plan to go with anybody else, it'll be Andrew."

Ricky and I made one of our infrequent trips over the causeway to Books & Books in quest of giftage. There was also a Books & Books on Lincoln Road, but it was the Antiquarian Room in their Coral Gables store that I wanted. I had seen the rather impressive bookshelves in Isabella's apartment, and was hoping to find her an appropriate something-or-other of the vintage variety. I finally located a second edition of Emily Post's *Etiquette*, dating from the 1920s, that I thought she'd get a kick out of. "It's fabulous, darling!" Ricky enthused when I showed it to him. "Isabella'll love it."

In terms of wardrobe, I settled on a shimmering, 1950s-era, pale turquoise gown—floor-length, plunging neckline, spaghetti straps—that I'd bought at a vintage store called Fly Boutique. I paired it with silver sandals and an authentic Whiting & Davis silver sequined-mesh handbag, along with their matching necklace that tapered down from my neck in a thick V and came to a point right between my breasts.

When you spend as much time as I did planning every detail of an evening, you feel like you're ready for anything. But, as it turned out, I was still unprepared for that night.

Isabella's party was being hosted by Red Square, a Russian-themed restaurant/ vodka bar on Washington Avenue. There would be hors d'oeuvres and an open bar and exclusive use of the upstairs VIP room, all compliments of the house. And Red Square was grateful for the privilege—the campaigning among various establishments to throw the Queen of the Night a birthday party had been fierce.

Isabella, Finn, Ricky, and I arrived early as per our plan and set ourselves up in the front banquette of the upstairs VIP area. We figured that people would probably throng around Isabella when they first arrived, so Ricky and I had decided to remove ourselves from the flow of traffic once the rush started.

It didn't end up working out quite that way. For one thing, people were unexpectedly prompt for a South Beach party. The invitation said nine o'clock, and at exactly nine a line had already formed as people waited their turn to wish Isabella a happy birthday. Part of the reason that Isabella had seated herself in a banquette was to escape the formality of a receiving line, but one had formed anyway. It was three abreast and snaked all the way down the stairs, through the first-floor restaurant area, and out the door into the street. Word spread that the cops had been called, as the line was causing traffic jams outside. But the cops knew who Isabella was— *everybody* knew who Isabella was—and were eager to be of assistance. They did their best to keep the partiers and pedestrian passersby safely on the sidewalk.

Glaciers cross continents more quickly than that line crept forward. People were not content, as they had been with Gerry Kelly, simply to say hello and keep moving. Part of the secret to Isabella's perennial charm was that she made each individual feel as if they had a close and unique friendship with her. She knew down to the smallest detail who each of these people were—their history on South Beach, what they were currently working on, and what they hoped to gain from it. This being the case, everybody clustered around our table as long as possible, trying to engage Isabella in conversation about their projects and plans, and receive her blessings and advice. The glittering mountain of gifts next to our table was growing at an astonishing rate, until the gift area monopolized a full quarter of the room. Almost before Ricky and I realized what was happening, we found ourselves trapped, physically unable to stand up and blend into the crowd.

I had never seen anything like it in my life.

I met new people that night and further solidified casual relationships with many more as they circled past. The benefit of having a seat at Isabella's table wasn't lost on either Ricky or me, and we used the opportunity to our best advantage. I cringed a bit when I saw Kojo working his way forward through the line. Isabella was starting to give people less of her attention, in an attempt to move things along more quickly and circulate people in from the outside. It was nothing personal—purely a logistical question, really—but I knew that it wouldn't sit well with Kojo. I noted his fleetingly hurt look when Isabella turned her head to greet someone else while Kojo was still mid-sentence. Then his face became calm and determined. "I brought you a gift," I heard him say to Isabella with unwonted firmness. "The least you could do is politely acknowledge me and say 'thank you.'"

Isabella's face was incredulous. "Are you telling me off *at my own party?*"

I stifled a smile and turned as I felt a hand on my shoulder, looking up into Genghis's face. He smiled widely and bent down to give me a warm hug. "Hi, baby!" he said. "You look so beautiful!"

Clearly, despite the months of silence after Amy and I had parted ways, Genghis and I were friends again. So I hugged him back just as affectionately. "And you, my darling, are as gorgeous as ever."

"No, but you *really* look beautiful." He refilled my martini glass from the bottle of vodka in the middle of our table. "Amy wanted to keep you as her chubby sidekick forever—it's so great to see you've gotten away from all that and come into your own."

My first impulse was to repay Genghis's "chubby sidekick" observation with one equally disparaging. But I sensed that, in his own way, Genghis was making a sincere attempt to be complimentary. What was more, he and Amy were obviously no longer on good terms, and I definitely wanted scoop. "Do you still spend a lot of time with her?" I asked casually.

Genghis made a face. "That was such an unhealthy little group," he said. "It was all about Amy being the center of everything. I think the only ones she hangs out with still are Raja and her brother. They never leave the Deuce." A handsome, tightly clad young man put his hand in Genghis's and pulled on his arm. "I have to go," he said. "But call me and let's have dinner."

"Absolutely." We kissed each other's cheeks and then he was gone.

I scanned the crowd anxiously for signs of Andrew, worried that he wouldn't be able to make it through the airtight throngs and wondering if he'd even be able to see me. I didn't spot him, but I saw something else that gave my heart a painful, quicktime swing. I set down my martini, my throat suddenly so tight that I was sure I'd choke if I attempted so much as a sip.

Standing not five feet away from me was John Hood.

I might have stared for half a second or for a full minute—it was hard to say how much time had passed. Then Hood looked up and saw me. He made a sort of happy-surprised face, clutching his hat in a comical fashion as he made his way over. In his Sam Spade suit and cream-colored fedora, he looked exactly as I remembered him. And I realized abruptly that I *had* remembered him—that I hadn't forgotten him for a single minute of a single day in the past seven months. Seeing him now, every detail of our last encounter stood out in vivid relief in my mind. My knees felt unexpectedly fluid, and I was grateful that I was seated.

He gently forced a few people aside and pulled a chair over from an adjoining table. "Hey hey, baby doll," he said. He sat down next to me and kissed my cheek. There was nothing in his tone to indicate that it had been months since we'd seen each other, or what had happened between us on that last night. "You look beautiful."

I smiled and found a socially bland voice to match his. "Says the man who just got out of prison. I'd imagine that Ricky in a cocktail dress would look pretty good to you right now."

Hood grimaced and lit the cigarette I'd pulled from my purse, then lit one for himself. I was fascinated, as I always was, by the way he smoked his cigarettes, by the way he gripped the filter between his thumb and forefinger and made the act of smoking look so *cool*. I inhaled deeply on my own cigarette, hoping it would settle me. The smoke unfurled over our heads like crepe paper and I watched it, wanting to look anywhere except directly into his face.

"I wasn't away *that* long," Hood said now. "You can't keep a good Hood down forever."

"When did you get . . . back?"

"About two weeks ago." Hood looked around restlessly, then turned to fix his dark eyes on mine. "I was hoping I'd run into you here tonight."

I felt stung. *Two weeks and no phone call.* I suddenly remembered Andrew. Andrew could be somewhere in the room right now, looking for me. I couldn't let him find me here, shaken up like this.

"So what are your plans?" I asked, changing the subject.

"The cats at Liquid want me to promote," he said. "And I'm writing a piece about life on ice for the *Miami Sentinel*."

"That sounds great." I stood up. "I should really walk around the room for a while. I haven't moved an inch from this spot all night."

He looked surprised, but didn't protest. "Let me take you out this week. I want to talk to you."

"I can't." I was surprised at the sharp jab I felt upon turning him down. "I'm leaving town on a business trip and I'll be gone for a couple of weeks."

"Then I'll call you in a couple of weeks."

"Really?" I replied tartly. "Gosh, Hood, it's news to me that you even know how to use a phone."

Hood grinned. He'd been wondering if I was giving him the brush-off because I was genuinely busy or because, maybe, I'd lost interest over the past seven months. But I had just very plainly told him that I still cared, and we both knew it. I blushed miserably, nonetheless kissing Hood on the cheek as coolly as I was able to. I noticed Ricky, who also hadn't budged from our table, looking at me curiously. I ignored him as I struggled toward the bar.

I ran into Andrew almost immediately. "Hello, lovely." He smiled and kissed me lightly on the mouth. "I thought I was never going to find you."

"Hi," I said. "Let's get out of here." Off of his puzzled look, I added, "I've been here for hours and I'm over it."

Andrew still looked slightly perplexed, but he obligingly took my hand and we elbowed our way downstairs.

Andrew lived just over the causeway on Brickell Avenue. He'd chosen to drive onto the island that night and had found a parking space not far from Red Square. We were still holding hands as we walked through the alley behind the restaurant when I stopped, forcing Andrew to stop also. I moved closer to him and looked up into his face, barely discernable in the fractured light that sifted through the rooftops above us.

"Kiss me," I said in a low voice. Andrew lowered his head to mine—softly at first and then, as I held him tighter, with more force.

I felt as if I couldn't kiss him long or hard enough. I wanted to feel his lips hard against mine and then I wanted to feel them everywhere else. I wanted him to press his body against me, to push me back roughly against the wall of the building and hold my wrists there until they chafed and bled. I wanted there to be no question in my mind. I wanted him to . . . to *take* me . . . the way that it would have been with—

I didn't allow myself to finish the thought.

Andrew finally came up for air. "I should take you home." His voice was slightly husky.

I was out of breath too. "Take me back to your place."

"Are you sure?"

"Yes." There was something abrupt and naked in my voice, and we both heard it. So I repeated, more gently, "Yes, I'm sure."

Andrew smiled and brushed his hand against my cheek. Then we turned, picking our way through the broken glass and upturned rocks in the alley.

SEVENTEEN

It was a bad sign when the phone started ringing at eleven o'clock Friday morning. I had returned a week earlier from my two utterly grueling—but highly successful—weeks on the FACTS Train, and my friends knew not to call before noon at the earliest. This wasn't much of a problem, actually, as most of the people I knew either didn't have traditional day jobs or respected the lifestyles of those who never arose until early in the afternoon. But a quick check on the caller ID showed that it was Andrew on his cell phone, and I grabbed the receiver on the second ring.

"What are you doing calling so early?" My voice was sleepy, but teasing. "It must be an ungodly hour where you are."

"Just checking in on the lady of leisure," Andrew replied. "How's your week off going?"

"Enjoying it while I can. You have no idea how good it's felt to stop moving this past week."

"Well, I'm sure the Agnew Group'll have you jumping again come Monday."

"Oh, I'm sure they will," I said. "At least they gave me the week off to recover. Two weeks straight of twenty-hour work days should be enough to earn me some downtime." I paused and stretched languidly. "How's L.A.? Did your presentation go well?"

"Really well, actually. I think Lowestoffe Architects has a decent shot at the project." There was static, and then he said, "Listen, I'm pulling into the car rental place. I just wanted to make sure we're on for seven o'clock at Joia."

"We're definitely on—I've missed you." It was a cruel fate, indeed, that had taken me on the road with the FACTS Train for two weeks and then sent Andrew to L.A. on business the night I'd gotten back. Seven o'clock tonight couldn't come quickly enough, as far as I was concerned.

"You're sure you don't mind meeting me there? It's just that I may have to come straight from the airport and—"

"Don't you worry your pretty little head about it," I interrupted. "I'll wait at the bar if I get there first."

"You're an angel." Then, in a tone that bordered on the sly, he added, "I'm looking forward to our first date."

I laughed. "Well, now that you've had your way with me, I suppose it's time you bought me a meal."

He laughed too. "Tonight, love," he said, and hung up.

I was certifiably awake now, but still reluctant to get out of bed. I rose just long enough to open the blinds onto a perfect South Beach morning. The ocean sparkled serenely and the sky was the shade of deep blue that usually means the August humidity won't be unbearable. It was dotted here and there with wispy, powder-puff clouds, and I watched them melt and merge as I lay in bed and enjoyed the luxury of thinking about nothing in particular.

By the time the clock struck noon, showering seemed like the inevitable next move. I had just turned on the water and adjusted the temperature when the phone rang again, and I scrambled back into the bedroom. The number on the caller ID was unfamiliar, but local, and I wavered before finally sighing and picking it up. "Hello?"

"Hey, it's Hood," said the voice on the other end. "Swell shindig at the Albion the other night."

I'd seen Hood once since Isabella's birthday, at the impromptu FACTS Train after-party we'd held the previous Saturday night. We'd put up *NSYNC, our headliner for the Miami show, at the Albion Hotel. As word had spread, a spur-of-the-moment soiree had sprung up in the Albion's bar and pool areas, and I'd danced with Justin Timberlake and Joey Fatone and their aptly named bodyguard House. Hood had been there and we'd chatted in an entirely casual, civilized manner. Andrew and I had talked on the phone almost every day since our night together after Isabella's party, and I told myself that I felt secure enough in my feelings for him to treat Hood as if he were no more than any of the other social friends I made polite chitchat with.

"Thanks," I replied. "Sometimes the spontaneous things turn out the best."

"Howsabout we test that theory and do something spontaneous ourselves this afternoon."

"What did you have in mind?" I asked, guardedly.

"Lunch at the 11th Street Diner and maybe a mainland adventure?"

I considered for a moment. "I'll say yes to the lunch part," I said cautiously, thinking, *What could possibly be wrong with lunch?* "But I can't sign on for anything else without more information."

"My negotiating skills are newly refined from my stint in the pokey." His voice sounded like he might be smiling. "Meet me at Liquid at one o'clock. Oh—and bring your car."

"Sounds good," I replied, and we hung up.

I knew very few car owners in those days—in fact, Kojo was the only one of my close friends who had four wheels and a motor to call his own. Ricky'd had a car a few years ago, but it had been repossessed when he fell upon hard financial times and he'd joined the great immobile masses that populated South Beach. People tended to drift into town without a penny in their pockets—having possibly sold everything they owned in order to finance the move—and found they could live quite well on SoBe relying solely on cabs, friends with cars, and their own two feet.

Still, it was patently ridiculous for me to bring my car if Hood and I were going to the 11th Street Diner, which was only about three blocks from Liquid. But there I sat in my Toyota Corolla—because Hood had asked.

As long as I had the car out of the garage, I had decided to stop at the bank, deposit my last FACTS Train paycheck, and pull out enough cash for the next week or so. I was now waiting for Hood outside Liquid, wondering what he had in mind, when the cell phone I'd acquired for the FACTS Train rang in my purse.

It was Josh from the Agnew Group. "Hey there," I said. "How's everything at the office?"

"Good. Are you recovered yet?"

I laughed. "Not quite," I replied. "But I'm looking forward to diving back in on Monday."

"That's what I called to talk to you about." Josh hesitated. "We lost one of our major accounts this week," he continued. "We really tried to figure out a way to make it work, but I'm afraid we can't bring on any additional staff right now." He paused, and I half expected that he was waiting for me to say something, but then he rushed forward with, "We'd still love to have you work with us on a freelance basis. Everybody here was really impressed with your work."

"Of course." My voice was neutral. "I appreciate the opportunity you guys gave me, and I'd love to work with you again if something comes up."

"I'm sure it will," Josh answered. "Enjoy your weekend."

"You too," I responded, but it sounded as if he'd already hung up.

It took a minute or so for the hurt to set in, but when it did, it hit hard. I'd been so proud of myself—I'd woken up one day and decided to make a complete career change, and in only a few short months I'd scored a position with one of the most prestigious PR firms in South Florida. It had meant everything to me, seeming to validate everything I'd told my parents back when I'd first announced that I was quitting nonprofit and getting a job as a bartender.

But this is what it had all come down to: a two-minute "it's not you, it's us" conversation, and I was right back where I'd started.

Such was the tenor of my thoughts when Hood suddenly appeared on the passenger side of my car. I leaned over to unlock the door and he got in, kissing me on the cheek. It was the first time I'd ever seen Hood during the day, and I was amused to note that, even in the ninety-degree weather, he was dressed exactly the way he dressed at night—in a vintage suit, dress shirt, tie, and his ever-present hat. I felt decidedly underdressed in my customary daywear consisting of a strappy tank top, shorts, and sandals.

"Listen," Hood said, as I was cruising around looking for a metered parking spot. "I was planning to treat you, but I stopped by Liquid to pick up some money they owe me and nobody was there. Do you mind springing for lunch?"

"Not at all," I answered smoothly. Hood was, after all, only a few weeks out of prison; I told myself that I hadn't expected him to be flush. I hit the brakes as a group of pale-skinned tourists in FLORIDA T-shirts crossed illegally in front of my car. "Shout if you see parking."

. . .

The 11th Street Diner was an authentic '40s diner built in 1948 by a company that manufactured dining cars for trains. It had been imported by local restaurateur Ray Schnitzer and his partners, piece by piece, from somewhere up in Pennsylvania and grafted onto the corner of 11th Street and Collins Avenue. The exterior was all shining silver and curved edges, and the interior was all low ceilings and retro Formica. The Diner was open 24/7 and was the ideal stop at four in the morning, when food became the necessary stopgap to prevent incipient alcohol poisoning. The food was good for its kind and relatively cheap and, best of all, there was a full bar.

It was to the bar where I directed my attention when Adrina—who waitressed at the Diner—approached our table with a chirpy, "Hello, beautiful people!" and bussed us each on both cheeks. I ordered an Absolut up and moodily contemplated the fate of Adrina, who was beautiful, had her own nightlife column, her own nightlife TV show, her name permanently inscribed on every guest list in town, yet still had to wait on tourists and causeway crawlers who none of us would have bothered to say "excuse me" to as we brushed past them on the red carpet. *Welcome to South Beach*, I thought, a touch bitterly, as I drained my glass in a single gulp.

Hood raised an eyebrow. "Slow down," he said, "or you won't be able to drive over the causeway later."

"I still haven't committed to driving over the causeway later." I felt slightly better after my liquor infusion and smiled brightly at him. "Are you going to elaborate on your mystery errands or do I have to play Twenty Questions?"

Hood pulled out two cigarettes, handed one to me, and lit both of them with the Zippo lighter he'd laid on the table. The smell of butane briefly filled my nostrils. "I thought dames like you liked to play games."

"*Moi?*" I made a shocked face as I exhaled smoke, laying a hand lightly on my chest. "How could you make such a base and baseless accusation?" I knew I was flirting with Hood, but I couldn't help it. I didn't even want to help it. That familiar feeling of exhilaration at Hood's mere presence was distracting me from the deeper feeling of pain over my lost job, which lay coiled like a snake ready to strike if I got too close.

Now Hood was smiling too. "I wanted to stop by the *Miami Sentinel* offices," he said. "And then there's a secondhand bookstore right over the causeway. I figured we could trawl for cheap paperbacks."

I was somewhat surprised that the "mainland adventure" in question was so mellow and actually sensible. "Okay," I replied. "I'm in." I rested my lit cigarette in the ashtray and opened a menu. "So tell me about the article you're working on for the *Sentinel*."

Hood was off and running, and I hardly got a word in throughout the rest of the meal. He described life in the "hokey pokey," as he persisted in calling it, in his typically droll fashion, although I wondered how much real ugliness lay behind the colorful anecdotes and zingy one-liners. I had to assume he'd seen things firsthand that I'd be afraid to imagine.

Nevertheless, Hood kept it light as he gave me glimpses of his life on the inside. "I took welding," he told me. "All the white guys took welding." I laughed hilariously at the thought of Hood in the equivalent of a high school shop class. He'd managed to unearth a small trove of readable books in the prison library—Dorothy Parker ("I thought of you") and Thomas Pynchon. He'd carved out a niche for himself writing love letters on behalf of other inmates who lacked the skills to "scribe smoothly" to their wives and girlfriends, in exchange for commissary items like candy bars and cigarettes. I felt a pang—I wanted to ask why he'd never written to me. But I kept silent, and he'd already moved on to telling me how his smart mouth had almost brought him to blows with other inmates on a handful of occasions.

Before I knew it, I was settling the check—leaving a healthy tip for Adrina—and we were headed back to my car. The clock on my cell phone told me it was only three o'clock, which meant I had plenty of time to drive Hood over the causeway and back and be home by six to shower, change, and meet Andrew.

"Where to?" I got into the car and Hood slid in next to me.

"Fifth Street and then the MacArthur Causeway," he replied. "I'll direct you from there."

Say what you will about Miami—and, believe me, as a native I've heard it all—it's a gorgeous city. "The Magic City" it was dubbed in a 1980s tourism campaign, and most of what you saw in brochures or from the windows of your Miami

Beach home *was* magical—sunny and shining and impossibly Technicolor, everything lightly scented with the perfume of sea salt and tropical flowers. And yet, like any big city, we had our grittier side—poorer areas and urban eyesores that gashed the Magic City like large, suppurated wounds.

I wasn't exactly sure where the *Miami Sentinel* offices were, but I had a general idea that they were somewhere on Biscayne Boulevard. Accordingly, I started to turn my car in the direction of the Biscayne Boulevard exit off the causeway. But Hood abruptly said, "Not yet—keep going."

I was confused for about a microsecond, saying to Hood, "But if we don't exit now, we're heading into Overtown." Hood didn't reply, and I looked at him briefly from the corner of my eye. I didn't say anything else either, but I realized what our approximate destination was and what our probable business there would be.

Overtown was one of the oldest black communities in Miami. It dated back to 1896—the year the city was incorporated and Henry Flagler built the railroads linking South Florida to the rest of America—and had once had a flourishing heyday of boutiques, jazz joints, and community theaters. Then it was torn up and cross-sectioned in the 1960s to build Interstate 95, and the still-beating heart of the community had been cut right out. Now it was best known as the site of the Overtown Riots of 1982, which had been followed by the Overtown Riots of 1984 and the Overtown Riots of 1989. It was where, in the early '90s, a handful of German tourists had been robbed and shot to death in their rental cars, having taken a wrong turn off the highway on their way to the Beach. Hood and I were now driving down those same streets—past boarded-up storefronts, graffiti-covered buildings, and small knots of Overtown residents who milled around the fronts of worn-looking bodegas.

I had known Overtown intimately back in my do-gooder days—at least, I'd known the Overtown comprised of places like the Miami Rescue Mission, Camillus House, and Frederick Douglass Elementary School. And I knew now that I should turn my car right around and head back the way we'd come. I also knew that I wouldn't; I don't think that I was capable of doing anything that might have made me less interesting or attractive to Hood. Besides, in a town where life was measured in cocktail party stories—and where mine, despite everything, were still remarkably tame by comparison—the prospect of intrigue and adventure at the side of John Hood had me hooked. I could already hear myself telling the story to Ricky and our friends later: *So then Hood tells me to keep going and I* knew *he was taking me into Overtown.* . . .

I followed Hood's directions as we got farther from the main thorough-fares. Eventually, he directed me into the parking lot of a one-story, window-less cement building. There was a definite compound-like feeling to the place, which was surrounded by a chain-link fence topped with razor wire. We got out of the car, and, as we walked to the steel door guarding the entrance, I noted security cameras dotting the building's perimeter.

"Is my car safe here?" I asked Hood.

"Trust me," he said. "There's no place in Miami where your car would be safer."

Hood rapped on the door briskly and it opened a crack, revealing a large black man. He looked us over briefly, seemed to recognize Hood, then nodded and stepped by so we could pass. We entered a dark hallway, where another large man appeared and efficiently patted us down, taking my purse—over my reflexive gesture of protest—and poking around inside.

I'd never been frisked in my life, and my nerve faltered a bit. I whispered to Hood, "Maybe we should just go to the *Sentinel* offices."

Hood took out a cigarette and lit it with the Zippo, the blue flame briefly lighting his face dramatically against the pitch black of the hallway. "We're already here," he replied. "You'll dig this place, I promise."

We went through another door, which swung open to reveal—a bar. That was it. I almost laughed, so prepared had I been for God only knows what. It was a completely ordinary-looking dive bar, with wood-paneled walls, a few people sitting around slightly cracked wooden tables, and a small poolroom in the back. There was a jukebox in the far corner and dim lamps hanging over the tables, and the most noteworthy thing about the place was the way the lack of windows made it feel like the middle of the night, even though it was three thirty in the afternoon.

Why had Hood dragged me all the way out here to a place like this? He led me to a small booth in the back, and, as we took our seats, a tall man wearing a bar apron approached. Hood half rose and the two of them acknowledged each other with a brief handshake. Then the man turned to look expectantly at me.

I was surprised, because this didn't seem like the kind of place that would have table service, but I said gamely, "I'd like an Absolut and cranberry, please." His expression hinted that he was waiting for something else, so I turned to Hood and added, "And the gentleman will have . . ."

The man looked at Hood and laughed, a deep laugh that came all the way from his belly. "This your woman's first time here, Wonder Bread?" he said to Hood.

Hood laughed too. Then he said good-naturedly to me, "Give him fifty dollars."

"I'm sorry?"

"Give him fifty dollars," Hood repeated. "I'll pay you back."

In for a penny, in for a pound. I counted out the cash from my purse and handed it over. "What's going on?" I asked impatiently, after the guy had left. "What are we doing here and *why* did I just give that man fifty dollars?"

Before Hood could respond, the guy was back, bearing a couple of plates, a sieve, and a large Ziploc bag filled with white powder. He set a plate down in front of each of us, then held the sieve over mine and poured some of the powder into it, sifting a small mound onto my plate. He repeated the process over Hood's plate, then deposited a couple of short straws onto our table and disappeared into a small room behind the bar.

"Holy shit," I said softly to Hood, who looked as delighted with himself and my reaction as if he had presented me with a particularly well-received gift. Then my voice turned gleeful and—even though I knew how much Hood hated it when I cursed—I repeated, "Holy *shit!* Are you *kidding* me?"

I remembered being a college student studying abroad in Europe and thinking how cool it was that there were bars in Amsterdam where you could walk in and light up a joint without anybody saying two words to you. But this was a level of underground decadence straight out of *Scarface.* I hadn't thought that such a place could even exist. A part of me knew that nothing good could come of getting coked up all afternoon when I was supposed to meet Andrew that night, but how could I leave? Even the prospect of the cops charging in at any second added an edge of danger that was more appealing than otherwise.

Besides, I rationalized, I'd lost a job today. I'd lost a *great* job today. I was entitled to a little something to make myself feel better.

And so it was that, after months of abstinence, I took the plunge again. Hood and I chopped up lines and scooped up bumps with my car keys and took turns going back and forth to the bar for the alcohol and cigarettes that were a necessary kick-start to the best kind of high. Our conversation became progressively faster and more excited, and our eyes glittered as we ordered more blow and then more and even more, until we had almost exhausted the fund of cash I'd pulled out of the bank that morning. I used my spare change to fire up the jukebox, selecting tracks by Muddy Waters and Smokey Robinson. It was crazy, I thought, to be in a place like this and going off on a mini-bender for no good reason on an otherwise ordinary Friday afternoon.

I got up at one point to go to the bar for another round of drinks. As I waited for them to be poured, a rather conservatively dressed man approached and put an arm around my shoulders. *"Oye, mami."* He gestured in the direction of the jukebox. *"¿Quieres bailar?"*

"I'm sorry, I'm with somebody." I tried to ignore the way his hand—still draped over my shoulders—was rubbing my arm.

Hood was at my side in a flash. "She's with somebody, chico." His tone was mild, but his posture exuded subtle menace.

The room tensed slightly, and it occurred to me to wonder what would happen if there was a brawl. The police would never be called—we were way too off-the-grid for regular law enforcement to be an option—and so discipline could only be maintained from within. Everybody knew that instinctively, and I could tell that each man there was already calculating at what point, and on whose side, he would get involved if involvement became necessary.

But, as with most of these kinds of things, the situation was defused almost faster than it had sprung up. The guy backed off, although not without shooting Hood a look of pure venom, and Hood and I returned to our booth.

The incident had the effect, however, of changing the nature of my high—which went from a good-all-over feeling to slight paranoia. I became convinced that the guy would lie in wait for us outside and jump us when we left. As this scenario played vividly through my imagination, it led to the thought of leaving, which reminded me that I had no idea what time it was and that Andrew was expecting me at seven o'clock at Joia. I pulled my cell phone from my purse, but I wasn't getting any reception and, thus, there was no time display. "We have to go," I said to Hood.

"Already?" He looked surprised. "We still have some left."

"Let's bag it up." I started shoveling the remainder of our most recent purchase into the plastic bags that had been thoughtfully provided, handing one to Hood and depositing the other one in my purse. "Seriously, I *have* to go—I have to be someplace tonight."

Hood started to argue, but I was already halfway to the door and he had no choice but to follow. As soon as we got outside, I took out my cell phone again. This time I was getting perfect reception, and the digital readout on the phone said 6:35.

"Shit!" I said. "Shit shit *shit!*" I flung open the car door wildly, leaned over to unlock Hood's side, and had the engine started before he'd even gotten in. It crossed my mind that I was probably far from sober enough to drive—much less to drive as aggressively as I was as I sped back toward the causeway—but I didn't see any way around it. I held the cell phone in one hand and steered with the other as I tried to reach Andrew and let him know that I was running late. I dialed and went straight into voice mail. I repeated the process three more times with the same result, before flinging the phone down in frustration and exclaiming, *"Fuck!"*

Hood, needless to say, was somewhat alarmed by this disintegration. "Everything okay?" he ventured.

I took a deep breath. "Everything's fine," I managed, somewhat more calmly. "I'm just really late for a—" I paused. "For a thing I have tonight."

"Ah." He fell silent for a moment. "I had such a great afternoon planned," he finally offered, somewhat mournfully. "I was going to treat you to lunch and maybe some books. It kind of all hit the skids."

Cocaine paranoia is an ugly thing—you can never be sure how much of it is genuine insight and how much is your own hopped-up delusion. But it occurred to me that Hood actually meant the opposite of what he was saying, that he'd woken up that morning needing drugs and a way of getting to them, and that I was simply the easiest way from point A to point B. The fact that he was now expressing regret over the unfortunate "accident" of not having had money was nothing more than a clever ploy to throw me off track, and was, in fact, *proof* that he'd been lying to me all along. My mind raced. What if Hood had never seen me as anything more than a convenience? What if the Agnew Group hadn't *really* lost an account that week, but had merely strung me along with the promise of a full-time job, always intending to let me go after the FACTS Train was over? *What if everybody was against me?*

"You're so full of it," I gritted out.

"What?" Hood looked faintly shocked.

"You got up today and you needed two things: a meal and drugs. And you probably figured, *Why not scam Rachel into buying them for me? Rachel's just a big dumb sap who's in love with me anyway.*" I shot him a quick, scathing look. "You must really think I'm stupid."

"No, I never thought you were stupid." Hood tossed the cigarette he'd been smoking out of the car and rolled up the window. "I thought you were different." He said it with the air of a man who's said something final, and didn't say another word for the rest of the ride.

It was seven o'clock and the sun was low in the sky when I pulled up to Liquid, leaving Hood on the spot where our afternoon had begun. "Hood—," I started, but he cut me off with a brusque "Forget it," slammed the car door shut, and vanished into the club.

There was nothing I could do about Hood at that point, so the imperative next step was to let Andrew know I was running late. I tried his cell phone yet again, but he still had it turned off. So I dialed Joia as I headed to my apartment.

"Thank you for calling Joia, this is Candice."

"Hey, Candice, it's Rachel Baum."

"Oh hi, Rachel!" she said. "Fun party at the Albion last week."

"Thanks," I replied. "Listen, is there an Andrew Lowestoffe there waiting for me?"

"He just walked in." She lowered her voice conspiratorially. "And he is cute!"

I smiled momentarily as I drove. "Could you tell him that something work-related came up and I'm running late, but I'll be there in a half-hour or so?"

"No problem," she said. "I'll have the bartender buy his first round while he's waiting." She lowered her voice again. "And I'd hurry if I were you—I might steal him for myself."

"Thanks, Candice." I sighed. "You're a rock star." I hung up, suddenly fraught with a new worry—because Candice, like all high-profile restaurant hostesses in South Beach, was standard-issue beautiful and would undoubtedly have zero qualms about hooking Andrew for herself, if I left him waiting alone too long.

I parked my car in my building's garage, flew around my apartment like the Tasmanian Devil as I tried to cram an hour's worth of dating prep time into twenty minutes, did a couple of bumps from the stash in my purse, and was in a cab at 7:35. I knew I was somewhat wild-eyed and wild-haired at the moment, so I spent my cab time taking deep breaths as I tried to compose myself.

I picked Andrew out almost immediately as I air-kissed Candice and entered Joia's outdoor garden area. I also spotted several other familiar faces and waved quick hellos as I headed for the table. *No time for the "Hello, darling!" routine*, I thought, as I slid into the seat across from Andrew and said, "I'm *so* sorry I'm late."

"Is everything okay?" he asked with concern, leaning over to kiss me. "You look so . . . stressed out."

"Is that the best you can do after not seeing me for three weeks?" I had meant it to sound playful, but it came out with a definite edge. Andrew's brow furrowed.

The evening progressed from there about as well as you'd expect. I couldn't, for the life of me, seem to shut up—another unfortunate side effect of coke when the person you're with isn't high and chatty like you are. I cringed inwardly but couldn't stop myself as the words poured out of me—disjointed, rambling, and almost completely nonsensical. To make things worse, I kept jumping up and running to the bathroom to dip into the cache in my bag, fearing that the only thing worse than me being high would be me coming down. I ordered cocktail after cocktail in the hopes that I could create equilibrium, but that was as futile an effort as any I'd made in the whole course of that long, misbegotten day. I watched Andrew's face become graver and graver as the night wore on.

I told myself that he couldn't possibly suspect I was high. He would undoubtedly think I was just wound up from the stressful workday I'd invented. It was a comforting thought, until I returned from what was to be my final bathroom trip of the evening. As I sat back down, I noticed Andrew looking at me in a steady, appraising manner. His attitude was that of a person to whom a great mystery has finally been revealed—and revealed to be less worthy of interest than he'd expected.

"What's wrong?" I asked.

"Your nose is bleeding," he replied flatly. He tossed his napkin at me across the table.

I took it instinctively and pressed it to my nostrils, mesmerized for a second by the sudden blush of crimson that bloomed against its whiteness. "Oh, God," I said, still thinking I could preserve an illusion of normalcy. "My allergies get so bad this time of year."

"Save it, Rachel," he said. "I don't know what's going on, but this isn't the evening I was looking forward to." He threw some money onto the table and stood up, obviously preparing to leave.

"*Andrew!*" My voice was a loud hiss that I didn't recognize. I was conscious that people around us—people I *knew*—were starting to pay attention to our table, even as they pretended to concentrate on their own meals. "*You cannot leave me like this in front of all these people!*"

Had I said anything else—something along the lines of "Please stay," or "I can explain," or even "I'm sorry"—I might have had a fighting chance. But I had said the one, exact, wrong thing. I knew it as soon as I saw Andrew's eyes harden.

"Watch me," he said, and walked away from our table and out of the restaurant.

One of the hardest things I've ever had to do was stay put at that table, finishing my cocktail and calmly smoking an entire cigarette. But that's what I did. Then I sedately made my way to the exit, stopping to greet and kiss the people I knew. I walked out alone, maintaining a serene expression, and it was only once I was inside a cab that I allowed my face to fall. *Just get home*, I kept repeating to myself. *This whole miserable day ends once you get home.*

The first thing I did when I reached my apartment was check my messages. Ricky: *Hello, darling! I wanted to talk to you about my birthday party invitations. . . .* Mike: *Hi, princess. Did you fuck him or are you saving something for the second date?* Josh from the Agnew Group, which I deleted unheard—I didn't need a bad news reprise. Tony Guerra, the promoter at Bash: *Hey, Rachel, I put you on the list for tonight and I'll hold a table in VIP. . . .*

I deleted all the messages and got into the shower, staying there for a long time. I was both tired and wired; all I wanted to do was get into bed and sleep. I hoped that if I stayed under the hot water long enough, it might soothe me into drowsiness. How was it possible, I wondered—even in South Beach—that my entire life could become so completely unraveled in a single day? In the span of just ten hours, I'd lost one job and two men—and possibly my social standing.

The phone rang as I was toweling off. It was Lara.

"Hey," she said when I answered. "How are you?"

"Strung-out and alone." I lit a cigarette. "How are you?"

"Ouch—I take it you had a bad day."

"Well," I replied, "I had the kind of day that starts with the sun shining and birds singing, and ends with a reporter saying: . . . *before turning the gun on herself.*"

Lara laughed and I laughed with her—because, really, what else was there to do?

"Do you want to talk about it?"

"Truly, no." I heaved a deep sigh. "Not now, anyway. I think I'll turn on the radio and flip through magazines until I fall asleep."

"All right. . . . I'll call you tomorrow."

I tuned the radio in to Y-100, the local Top 40 station, and flopped onto my bed with a copy of *Vogue*. The song "Everything to Everyone" by Everclear came on. *You put yourself in stupid places,* they sang. *Yes, I think you know it's true.* . . . I tried to ignore it, but couldn't anymore by the time they got to: *wonder if you will ever learn . . . yeah, why don't you ever learn?*

"Shut up, Everclear," I said aloud. I walked over to the radio and switched it off.

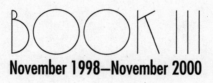

BOOK III
November 1998—November 2000

EIGHTEEN

Please don't talk about love tonight . . . please don't talk about sweet love . . . please don't talk about being true, and all the trouble we've been through. . . .

"Good afternoon!" Ricky spoke into the microphone, enunciating each word distinctly over Alicia Bridges's "I Love the Nightlife," which was playing in the background. "Welcome to this week's *The Nightlife with Mr. Nightclub*, hosted by me, Ricky Pascal, Mr. Nightclub, and cohosted by the lovely and charming Rachel Baum. Say hello, darling."

"Hello, darling," I said obediently into my own microphone.

I love the nightlife . . . I got to boogie, on the disco ro-ound, oh yeah . . .

"Today," Ricky continued, "we'll be talking to international gay porn superstar Blue Blake, who's flying into South Beach tomorrow to star in the Colony Theater's production of *Making Porn* and to serve as an honorary host of White Party. White Party Week kicks off next Wednesday, and tickets are almost sold out, so don't forget to . . ."

Season had started up again, and Ricky was as relentless in seeking out ways to raise Mr. Nightclub's profile as a debutante's mother planning her coming-out ball. So when he discovered www.WOMB.com—a local Internet station that broadcast various club DJs online and over a pirated radio frequency—it only made sense to Ricky that they should have a weekly talk show about club life itself. And who could know more about what happened on the other side of the velvet ropes than Mr. Nightclub?

This was how Ricky's pitch went, and, even though the WOMB had intended to go with all-music programming, Ricky persuaded them to give him a two-hour talk show on Thursdays from four to six p.m. He was equally successful in talking Dorfman Stone Rodriguez into bending corporate policy by allowing him to leave three hours early on Thursdays, arguing that having a bona fide radio personality on staff could only be good for business. I don't know if they really bought it, but Ricky had made his case, and *The Nightlife with Mr. Nightclub* was born.

Ricky struggled to fill the time on his initial broadcast. He'd lined up a couple of interviews with other local personalities, but something wasn't clicking for him. "I think I'm nervous," he told me. "Could I interview you first on my next show, and then you stay with me during the second interview? I think I'd be more comfortable with you there."

I couldn't imagine what Ricky would possibly "interview" me about, but I'd agreed, and the two hours had flown by with hardly a break in the action.

"We have such great chemistry—you should be my permanent cohost," Ricky said the next evening. We were at Mike's apartment, watching—upon Mike's insistence—taped episodes of *South Park*. ("Fart jokes," Ricky had deadpanned. "How very chic.") When I hesitated, he added, "Now that you're a freelancer you can make your own schedule, and it would probably help you get new clients. And just think how fabulous Mr. and Mrs. Nightclub would be on the radio every week!"

"*Mrs.* Nightclub?" I said teasingly. "Have you finally decided to propose and make an honest woman of me?"

"A hundred proposals—from *ministers*—couldn't make an honest woman out of *you*," Kojo said from his spot across the room.

I threw a sofa cushion at him. "Could we change the name of the show to *The Nightlife with Mr. and Mrs. Nightclub*?" I asked Ricky.

"I don't think we should change the name of the show, sweetie." Ricky patted my arm indulgently. "I think we should keep it on a strictly 'names above the credits' basis for now."

The three of them burst out laughing as I exclaimed, "Oh my *God*! Haven't you ever heard that you catch more flies with honey than vinegar?"

Ricky stopped laughing long enough to roll his eyes impatiently. "You and I both know you'll do it—can't we just skip the part where I pretend to talk you into it?"

"I can't believe you asked Mr. Nightclub to share attention," Mike said. He finished packing a bong and handed it to me. "Why don't you ask a school of piranhas in a feeding frenzy to share a meal?"

"I don't know what I was thinking." I lit the bong and inhaled deeply, then offered it to Ricky, who, as usual, waved it aside. I slung an arm around his shoulders, kissing his cheek noisily. "All right." I rumpled up his hair. "You've got yourself a cohostess."

I had gone into something of a depression after that catastrophic day back in August. It would be an overstatement to say that I'd been unable to eat or sleep or get out of bed—just that the color of everyday life had seemed to lose its luster, like lights being dimmed in a shadowy room. I couldn't see the point in trying for anything, when the things you wanted and worked for could disappear so quickly.

I'd moped listlessly around my apartment for a few days, and my malaise passed unremarked by my friends. The red flags went up when Ricky called to see what I was planning to wear to his birthday party, and I told him in a flat voice that I hadn't really thought about it and didn't really care. What possible difference could it make what I wore, I'd asked him, when people would undoubtedly be whispering about the huge crack-whore spectacle I'd made of myself at Joia the preceding Friday night?

Ricky was alarmed; he'd shown up at my door an hour later with Mike and Kojo in tow. "Whatsamatter, princess?" Mike asked. He folded me into a bear hug, and I was momentarily comforted by the boyish, clean-T-shirt smell of his chest. "Someone leave your cake out in the rain?"

"Let's sit down"—Kojo looked around at my conspicuous lack of furniture—"on the floor," he continued, "and we'll figure it all out."

I fixed us cocktails, and the four of us sat down cross-legged. They listened solemnly as I told my story. "That Hood!" Ricky fumed when I'd finished. "I could wring his skinny neck."

"Don't be too quick to hang it on Hood," I said. "I wasn't exactly dragged along kicking and screaming."

Ricky possessed a rare quality that marks all true friends—he could critique me relentlessly on any given subject, but couldn't bear to hear me come down on myself for even a second. "You couldn't have known what you were getting into, sweetie."

"Right." I lit a cigarette. "Because I totally thought Hood was taking me into the ghetto so we could give away lollipops and puppies to disadvantaged children." I was silent for a moment, then looked sideways at Ricky. "Do you think it'll be awful at your party?" I asked. "Do you think people will be talking about what a scene I made at Joia?"

"*Those* drama queens?" he exclaimed. "Girl, please! You'd have to dance naked on a bar someplace with your head on fire for anybody to even remember." He took my hand and squeezed it reassuringly. "You just show up on Friday looking gorgeous and act like the fabulous diva you are. And even if people do talk, at least they'll be talking about *you*. There's no such thing as bad publicity."

I had felt sufficiently cheered by our group encounter session to pick myself up and put the pieces of my life together again. Telling my parents that I'd lost yet another job was, by far, the least pleasant part. "What are you going to do?" my mother asked, and I could hear her struggling to hide full-fledged Jewish mother panic.

"I'll be fine, Mom," I told her. "I have more than enough money for now from the FACTS Train, and I'll find something else before it runs out."

Some things are easier said than done. I didn't find a new full-time job—discovering how few marketing agencies there actually were in Miami—but I picked up freelance work here and there. I coordinated small fundraising events for nonprofit organizations, wrote press releases for nightclubs, and even worked on a few side projects with the Agnew Group whenever they needed some extra help.

On the other hand, Ricky had been right when he'd said that the radio show would help me find new work, a prediction that proved downright prophetic one week in late October.

It was a few days after my birthday (which had been celebrated in low-key fashion with dinner for four at Nemo's), and our guest on the show was a famed Broadway producer by the name of Brent Carrigan. Brent had been one of the executive producers of *Les Misérables* and *Miss Saigon*, among others, and had produced albums or directed shows with luminaries including Liza

Minnelli, Bette Midler, and Barbra Streisand. He divided his time among homes in New York, L.A., and South Beach, and was producing a cabaret series at the Colony Theater on Lincoln Road called "Broadway Nights on South Beach." The series would bring celebrated Broadway stars down to South Beach for intimate cabaret performances.

We interviewed him and his business partner—a local event producer named Cindy Katz—on the eve of the series kickoff. Ricky was the one who had scheduled the interview, but he greeted it with trepidation. "Brent doesn't like me very much," Ricky told me.

"What are you talking about?" I regarded Ricky affectionately. "How could anyone know you and not love you?"

He sighed. "I used to work as Lee Schrager's assistant—you know, the guy at the InterContinental who throws the Make-A-Wish Ball?"

The Make-A-Wish Ball, held in October at the Hotel InterContinental, was one of the crown jewels of South Florida's annual social calendar. A black-tie fundraiser for the Make-A-Wish Foundation of South Florida, its committee was made up of some of the wealthiest members of the Miami community and—among various lavish accoutrements and glittering auction items—always featured performers from Broadway's A-list. Ricky and I had attended a couple of weeks earlier (with comped tickets, naturally) and had enjoyed ringside seats to a stunning performance by Bernadette Peters.

"Of course I know who Lee is," I said.

"Well, he and I weren't exactly on good terms when I left the Inter-Continental." Ricky paused, and, when it was clear that I still wasn't connecting the dots, he added, "Lee and Brent are really good friends—Brent's the one who always produces the entertainment portion of the ball."

If Brent truly didn't care for Ricky, he kept it well hidden. Mostly, he was enraptured with our secret studio lair—the location of which had to remain concealed from the general public, since we were tapping into an illegal radio signal. It was on the top floor of a cramped, wan-looking apartment building at the corner of Collins Avenue and 14th Street—only a few doors down from the Deuce. Furnished with a battered blue sofa and a chipped wooden coffee table, it was a small, square room that looked like it could have been somebody's low-rent living room. The more-shabby-than-chic decor was offset by sleek turntables and complicated sound equipment, as well as high-tech soundproofing materials that had been affixed to the walls.

"This is *wild*," Brent kept repeating, as he looked around in amazement and Ricky and I tried desperately to keep the interview on track. Brent's complexion was as dark as Ricky's and mine, and he had that trim, well-maintained appearance common to so many gay men, which made it impossible to determine if he was thirty-five or forty-five. Considering his hefty list of credits, I guessed that he had to be in his early forties. "Look at how shady and *illicit* this is." He grinned wickedly. "I'm sure the people listening want to know where we are, so I'll give you a hint and say we're at the corner of—"

"Brent, stop it—*stop it!*" Ricky and I shrieked in unison.

Brent gave us complimentary tickets to the first Broadway Nights performance—a Barbra Streisand impersonator named Steven Brinberg, who'd been imported fresh from his New York show *Simply Barbra.* We joined Steven, Brent, and Cindy afterward for cocktails at Starfish, Debbie O's salsa Mecca on Alton Road. We were all sitting at a wrought-iron table in Starfish's lush courtyard garden—with Adam, Adrina, Lydia Birdsong, and a few other friends—when Brent suddenly turned to me and said, "You seem sharp. Do you want to come work for me?"

Considering I'd done little more that evening than drink enough Mojitos to fill a swimming pool, I wasn't sure what had produced this assessment. I was, however, highly pleased by the compliment. "Doing what?" I asked.

"We could use some part-time help on Broadway Nights," he replied. "Publicity, production details, some of the grunt work. I'm out of town most of the time and Cindy has her hands full. If you're interested, I'll have her call you and set something up."

"I don't see why you think he doesn't like you," I told Ricky the next day. I was thoroughly infatuated with the idea that somebody like Brent Carrigan had deigned to take me seriously. "He couldn't have been nicer to us."

"That's because he likes *you*," Ricky corrected me. "I was just along for the ride."

"How could that even be true when he was friendly to both of us before I said two words?"

Ricky looked at me. "Gay men love you," he finally said. "Why do you think things have been so easy for you here?"

I may have effortlessly hit the mark when it came to gay men, but the affections of straight men proved more of a moving target. I had tried calling Andrew a few times back in August, but he'd never answered the phone and I never left any messages. What would I have said? It seemed better to start fresh with somebody new, and I tried to convince myself that I would eventually find someone as attractive and worthwhile as Andrew had been.

And so, a string of unremarkable prospects came and went. There was, for example, a tax attorney who'd turned to me one night after dinner with Ricky et al. and said, "Do all your friends have to be gay?"

"Well, I've never really asked them if they *have* to be, darling," I'd responded, arching an eyebrow. "But they do seem to *like* it so much better."

I even started dating a rabbi (who was also a psychologist), who I met during one of my charity fundraisers. My friends used the word "delusional" in reference to this particular attempt at a lifestyle change, but the rabbi was smart and funny and seemed pretty hip—for a rabbi. At thirty-nine, he was far younger than the rabbis I remembered from when I was growing up. "He's not a *priest*," I told my friends. "It's not like rabbis can't have sex."

At his insistence, we spent two months getting to know each other before attempting any significant physical contact. The late October night when we finally got fully frontal, we watched *Spartacus*—his favorite movie—first, but things turned out somewhat . . . er . . . disappointing. *It's not you, it's the condoms*, he told me. *They always give me trouble.*

That's okay, I said, in a line straight out of the playbook. *It happens to lots of guys. . . .*

I spent the night at his place, and he took me out for breakfast the next morning, suggesting that we go to the movies together that night. I noted that he appeared a bit detached throughout the course of the evening. "Is everything okay?" I asked when we got back to his apartment. "You seem kind of out of it."

"I think this is starting to feel too much like a relationship," he said. "I think I need a little space."

I looked around his apartment, really noticing for the first time the *Spartacus* movie poster he had hanging on the wall and the *Wizard of Oz* figurines he collected. I had a sudden epiphany. "I think you're gay," I replied. Gesturing widely, I added, "You have to admit—it's a pretty good *prima facie* case."

"What about Crazy Freddie?" Ricky suggested one evening, referring to Groove Jet's new in-house promoter who'd coordinated the launch party for our radio show. Crazy Freddie—also known as "Fast Freddie" and "Frankie Fur" because of an unusually hirsute chest—was, despite acute body-hair syndrome, rakishly handsome. "You two could be a total South Beach power couple."

"Please," I said. "I'm having enough trouble with men. I don't need to get involved with a guy who advertises the word 'crazy' right there in his name."

Then there was the handsome banker who I'd met in the VIP section of Bash. We had three spectacular dates, followed by three abrupt cancellations in a row. "This is becoming a problem," I finally said, when he called to announce his third no-show.

"Look, Rachel, you know how much I like you." He hesitated. "I don't know if I ever told you this—God, it's so hard to talk about—but my father was an alcoholic, and things were pretty rough when I was growing up." He stopped, as if he'd said all that needed to be said.

"I don't mean to sound insensitive," I replied slowly, "but I don't see what your father's drunken rampages of twenty years ago have to do with me."

"I just need you to understand that it's hard for me to get close to people. I get scared sometimes, and—"

I sighed heavily, cutting him off. "Save it for your Al-Anon meetings," I told him. "Nobody here cares."

It was after I related this incident that my friends started calling me "The Terminator," and I found that I rather liked the tough, bad-girl image it evoked. "I think I'm drama jaded," I said to Ricky. "I can't work myself up to care about all this *I need space/Daddy never hugged me* stuff."

"You're too much for most men," was Ricky's opinion. I wondered briefly if it was true—and, if so, when that transformation had taken place. "We're both too much," he added, and I knew he was thinking about Clint, who had recently announced that he and Ricky should just be friends.

None of us was very successful when it came to romance these days. Mike had had a boyfriend living with him—a young man named Carlos—who'd promised that he would eventually pay Mike back for partial rent, groceries, phone calls to South America, and the like. He'd disappeared one day—no note, no check—and turned up weeks later at a party, clinging to the arm of a wealthy, much older man we were all friendly with. And Kojo, as he'd earnestly confided to me one night, found it difficult—if not impossible—to have sex with men he liked.

Ricky had made his "we're too much" observation in a flip, humorous tone, but I knew his bravado was just a way of sidestepping the questions that sometimes kept all four of us up at night: *What if nobody ever loves me?* we secretly worried. *What if I'm unlovable?*

The one man I couldn't forget, even after Andrew was hardly more than a faint and painful memory, was John Hood. It seemed as if the day-to-day of South Beach living conspired to keep him in my thoughts—the cover story about him that appeared in the *Wire*, sporadic sightings of him at clubs and parties. I saw him everywhere but kept a reluctant, respectful distance.

Then one November day I got an envelope in the mail with two hundred and fifty dollars in cash inside—the amount I'd spent on coke that afternoon in August. There was no note and no name above the Liquid return address, but I knew exactly who'd sent it.

Ricky was unimpressed by the gesture. "That man never paid a cent he owed anybody in his entire life," he said. "If he gave money to you, I guarantee you he stole it from somebody else."

"I know he did." I smiled fondly. Ricky rolled his eyes and shook his head, but declined to say anything more.

I saw Hood a few nights later at Chaos, standing alone near the bar. Ricky and I had been dancing with abandon in the VIP section, and this was why, I told myself, I was a little breathless as I came up behind Hood and put my hand tentatively on his shoulder. I nearly jumped at how quickly he whipped around, and something in the way his face changed when he saw me kept my nerves jumping.

"I got your envelope," I said. "I wanted to thank you."

"Well, be still my crooked heart." Hood lit a cigarette and thrust his Zippo lighter back into his coat pocket. "The lady thanks me."

"Look, I'm sorry about those things I said." I toyed with the mother-of-pearl clasp on my handbag. "I was having a *profoundly* bad day."

"You're not the first to say them and you won't be the last." He made a noticeable effort to change the subject. "I caught your radio show last week. You and Ricky swung the swinging banter better than I would've expected." He pulled a palm card, the kind the clubs used to promote their parties, from his pocket. "I'm doing a cabaret act at the Bistro under the name Johnny Fortune this Monday." I took the card from him. "You should come by. My mother and my girlfriend'll be there."

My heart sank a little under the word "girlfriend"; I angrily asked myself if I had expected him to remain celibate in the three months since we'd spoken. But I smiled playfully as I queried, "Your mother?" It was hard to imagine Hood with anything as mundane as a mother. "As in, the woman who can tell me your real last name?"

"I sorta wanted you to meet her, so don't make me worry about keeping you two separated." He looked amused. "Maybe you shouldn't come."

"Oh, don't say that—I promise I'll be good."

"That's the trouble with chicks like you." Hood impatiently flicked the ash off his cigarette. "Too good for your own good."

"I'm not *that* good," I retorted, slightly nettled.

The strobe lights in the club pulsed and paused, pulsed and paused—turning Hood's dark suit and pale hat into a shifting, blinding beacon of iridescent light. The swoop and swirl of it made me light-headed as Hood raised my hand to his lips, lightly kissing my palm. "Better than you know, baby doll," he said. Then he dropped his cigarette to the floor and strolled off.

NINETEEN

The ancient feud between the Fontainebleau and Eden Roc hotels was the stuff of Miami Beach legend. The Fontainebleau opened in 1954, the brainchild of hotelier Ben Novak and architect Morris Lapidus. Lapidus created a curving, tropical fantasy on twenty acres of lush oceanfront property at Collins and 44th. The half-acre lagoon pool—complete with waterfalls, grottoes, and an island in the middle with real palm trees growing from it—was a model of decadence for its time. It was even featured briefly in the movie *Scarface*, a sort of throwaway visual reference to the casual opulence Miami Beach was capable of.

In 1956 Ben Novak's former partner in the Fontainebleau, Harry Mufson, bought up the property right next door and also commissioned Morris Lapidus to design an over-the-top megaresort. He called it the Eden Roc, and soon everybody from Elizabeth Taylor to Dean Martin was making the Eden Roc their winter playhome.

This state of affairs continued until 1962, when Novak—maddened by the dual defection of Lapidus and Mufson, and unable to bear the Eden Roc's success among the jet set—erected what would forever be known, in the legal annals and folklore of Miami Beach, as the "Spite Wall." A seventeen-story, 365-room structure on the northern edge of the Fontainebleau's property, its specific purpose was to block all sunlight from the Eden Roc's pool from noon until sunset. The Spite Wall featured no windows or balconies facing the Eden Roc save for one: one window on the Eden Roc side was installed in Ben Novak's personal apartment, from which he could gaze in unobstructed satisfaction at the Eden Roc's darkened pool and reflect upon his own shady ingenuity.

The epilogue to this tale of rival resorts is anticlimactic, as such things are wont to be. The Eden Roc eventually built a new pool on their sunny northeastern side, but as the fortunes of Miami Beach declined in the '70s and early '80s, so did the fortunes of both the Eden Roc and the Fontainebleau. The

South Beach revival of the '90s didn't initially help much, as the public's taste at that time had swung away from huge resorts to hipper boutique hotels, like the ones owned by Ian Schrager and the Rubell family.

Nevertheless, South Beach scenesters always made at least one annual appearance at the Eden Roc. The Wednesday night before Thanksgiving found us all there in our toniest glad-rags, attendees at the White Knights party that officially kicked off White Party Week.

White Party was an example of what was referred to as a "circuit party"—an ongoing series of gay-themed events held at various times in various cities around the globe. In South Beach, though, where there was essentially no distinction between the gay and straight communities, the "gay-themed" designation hardly seemed to matter, and everybody who was anybody participated. Like most circuit parties, White Party was a fundraiser for a local HIV/AIDS-related charity (Care Resource, in our case) and was complemented by a block of affiliated events that spanned a six-day period.

Kojo was still a member of the White Party Week committee, and Mike, Ricky, and I had obtained press passes that gave us carte blanche admission to all White Party Week events. The four of us attended White Knights—a cocktail reception at the Eden Roc followed by a poolside fashion show—even though Ricky and I privately agreed that fashion shows were only slightly less dull than watching paint dry. Bacardi was the official White Party Week liquor sponsor, and a seventeen-story version of their logo was projected dramatically from the Eden Roc's pool area onto the Fontainebleau's Spite Wall—which made a smooth and perfect screening surface, given its lack of windows or balconies.

The four of us covered every inch of the Beach during White Party Week, racing from daytime events like Muscle Beach to nighttime soirees like *Noche Blanca* and White Starz. Being out with Kojo was especially fun; it was easy to forget (but heartening to remember) how excited people always were to see him. Not, I decided, merely because he wasn't out that frequently, but because he had some combination of cynicism, humor, and sincerity that made people en masse genuinely happy in his presence.

We danced and "darling"-ed our way through megapromoter Jeffrey Sanker's all-night Snow Ball at the Miami Beach Convention Center, which he'd transformed into a rave-like monster club with DJs, strobe lights, ubiquitous glow-sticks, and thousands of shirtless party boys. Kojo had created a "drug flowchart" to ensure we were all supplied with our toxins of choice during the Week (except for Ricky, who drank like a fish but never touched anything else), and we dropped E in honor of Snow Ball. A good time was had by all, although I later announced to my friends that I doubted I'd attend Snow Ball the following year.

"Why not?" Ricky inquired.

"Because," I replied, "if I wanted to see that many guys blowing other guys, I'd hang out in a men's prison."

"Did anybody else just get hard at the thought of Rachel in a men's prison?" Kojo asked, and Mike sheepishly raised his hand.

"You guys are sick," I informed them, then burst out laughing as the two of them tackled me onto the bed in Kojo's apartment and proceeded to tickle me relentlessly. "Get off me, you perverts!" I shrieked, my voice muffled against Kojo's shoulder. "I'm *serious!*"

I spent an extensive amount of time expanding my wardrobe in preparation for White Party Week; fortunately, the only time when all-white garb was mandatory was at the White Party itself, held on Sunday night at Vizcaya. I found a Grecian-style white dress, nipped in at the waist with wide swaths of silver lamé rope and draping in graceful folds everywhere else. My hairstylist wove gardenias through my hair, and I thinly coated my eyelids, cheeks, arms, and chest with silver body paint. Ricky wore a long-sleeved white satin shirt and white satin pants, topped by a dazzling floor-length cape made entirely of silver sequins. A silver-sequined cowboy hat completed the ensemble.

Mike was occupied with the WAMI camera crew covering the event, and Kojo was busy with his host committee duties, so Ricky and I strolled on our own through Vizcaya's gardens. Vizcaya was a magnificent Renaissance Revival palace, built in 1916 as the winter home of industrialist James Deering and donated as a museum to the City of Miami after his death. Its breathtaking formal gardens were often rented out for private events, hosting everything from lavish weddings to official receptions for Queen Elizabeth II. I doubted, though, as Ricky and I made the rounds and posed endlessly for press pictures, that it ever saw a more spectacular spectacle than White Party. There were drag queens whose huge white wigs put them close to seven feet high and whose enormous costumes were as wildly extravagant as parade floats; heavily made-up men in white jeans and wifebeaters, wearing gigantic angel wings that stretched from their shoulders to the floor; men who simply wore the briefest possible tighty-whities with white sailor caps and go-go boots, their chiseled torsos as perfect as if they'd been carved from marble. The women's outfits ranged from plunging white cocktail dresses to feathery concoctions straight out of Hollywood's silent picture era.

We eventually ran into Blue Blake, the gay porn star we'd interviewed on our radio show the week before. Blue was resplendent in a flowing white shirt, white cowboy hat, and assless white chaps. "Hello, gorgeous!" he exclaimed, sweeping me into a hug and kissing me full on the mouth. Then he bent over and demanded, "Spank me!"

"Go ahead, sweetie," Ricky encouraged. "Spanking a gay porn star is good luck."

"Like kissing the Blarney Stone," I said, and landed a resounding clap on Blue Blake's bare backside. Then he took me in his arms again and—even though the DJ closest to us played throbbing techno music—danced me around and around in a nearly perfect approximation of a formal waltz. The thousands of white twinkle lights glittering in Vizcaya's trees and the rainbow-hued spotlights that washed over its lawns swept around me in blurred circles. "You're too much, darling," Ricky said, clearly amused. "*Too* much."

The only time I left the Beach during White Party Week was to join my family for Thanksgiving—and it is, perhaps, a telling fact that Thanksgiving dinner was the only part of the week that felt surreal. My parents and I went to the suburban ranch-style home of our oldest family friends. Their elder daughter, Melissa, who was my age, was studying for a graduate degree in psychology at Nova University—an hour north and light-years away from South Beach. Their younger daughter, Michelle, was on the verge of getting engaged to a promising young something-or-other, and he was there in ingratiating attendance. I had little to add in the way of conversation, and felt slightly uncomfortable as I discreetly knocked back glass after glass of vodka.

My mother noticed how quiet I was and sat down next to me, stroking my arm with mingled affection and concern. "What are you up to these days, pussycat?" she asked. "You hardly call anymore."

For the life of me, I couldn't think of a single appropriate response. I shrugged my shoulders and said evasively, "Oh, you know . . . the usual . . ."

Ricky, as you'll recall, had insisted on maintaining the lion's share of the credit for our radio show—but, in all fairness, he deserved more credit than I did. It was Ricky who produced the show, researching and scheduling the guests who appeared either live in our studio or via phone interviews. It was Ricky who read and responded to the e-mails we got—sometimes from places as far away as Berlin. And it was Ricky who personally went to bars and restaurants—like Score on Lincoln Road, Sushi Rock on Collins Avenue, even the Deuce—to make sure they had their radios tuned in to our show every week.

We didn't get paid, of course (although Ricky spoke rapturously of a day when we'd secure sponsors for our airtime and draw a salary), but there were perks that were almost as good as money. I received free hairstyling and skin care, for example, courtesy of White Salon, as long as I promised to mention them on the show from time to time. I was invited to events where the freebies flowed like wine—an intimate dinner party at the Museum of Contemporary Art (or MoCA, as it was called) in honor of Armani, where I received a complimentary pair of Armani sunglasses; a private gathering hosted by Prada, where all the women were given free Prada handbags. Ricky and I received even more complimentary tickets to philharmonic concerts, plays, and fundraising galas than we had the previous Season. The galas were our favorites, because we could usually count on gift bags with items donated by names like Dior, Chanel, and Dolce & Gabbana.

Everything we did was free, yet money was all around us—it was in the very air we breathed. We lived among the extremely wealthy and we lived, or so we told ourselves, as extravagantly as if we were one of them. We went to parties at their mansions on Star Island, where we were served champagne and lines on silver platters by waiters and waitresses who were completely naked, covered from head to toe in whimsical body paint. We went to the openings of five-star restaurants and were feted with free wine and exorbitant tasting menus. Our dining companion at one such dinner, casually seated next to us at an intimate table for six, was Princess Thi-Nga of Vietnam. We shared VIP rooms and dance floor space in clubs with Lenny Kravitz, Cameron Diaz, Leonardo DiCaprio, and Kate Moss. Saturday afternoons were often passed languidly on the boats or small yachts of friends. The boats would head to a particular sandbar a few miles south of Key Biscayne, just past Stiltsville (a cluster of wooden, shack-like homes built on raised platforms directly in the waters of Biscayne Bay). The water on the sandbar was only waist high, and people liked to drop anchor around it and swim or wade from boat to boat, cocktail glasses held high above their heads like the Statue of Liberty's torch.

We sighed longingly over glass cases of unbearably sumptuous jewels at a preview soiree for Bulgari's new collection. Members of Cirque du Soleil created eye-popping performance art—courtesy of Brent Carrigan—and *Ocean Drive* once again took Ricky's and my picture. One night we were even invited to a party at the Gables by the Sea manse of the French consulate, where we chitchatted with filmmakers and financiers from all over Europe.

"It's not fair," Ricky said once. "There's so much *money* floating around South Beach. How come none of it ever lands on us?"

"Fortune is a right whore," I agreed.

And there, as they say, was the rub. Money may have been in the South Beach air, but it remained as ethereal as air as far as our practical affairs were concerned. The money I'd made on the FACTS Train was going quickly, and the only thing harder than chasing down lucrative freelance work was chasing down payment for the work I'd already done. *Send us an invoice and we'll pay you in sixty days*, was the typical procedure. Inevitably, sixty days would turn into ninety days or even longer. Sometimes I'd have three months' rent in the bank and would feel as if my cash supply was almost unlimited, but there were other painful days when I'd have just paid my bills and was down to my last twenty dollars. I'd agonize over whether I could afford to order a pizza, which cost ten dollars, plus a dollar for tip. It was an excruciating way to live. Brent Carrigan and Cindy were the only ones who consistently paid me on time, and, small though the checks were, their blessed regularity was always a balm on my frayed nerves.

Ricky, Kojo, and Mike had the benefit of full-time work and steady paychecks, but none of them was making the kind of cash that allowed one to get ahead. Ricky, especially, struggled with his mortgage payments. "It's like an albatross around my neck," he'd say frequently of his condo, "but I can't get rid of it." Ricky was blissfully free from the pangs of conscience I occasionally suffered on the score of the freebies we received. "We're press and we're fabulous," he would say. "Besides, how could people expect us to live if we had to pay for all this stuff?"

Ricky's extemporaneous lectures in economic theory always amused me. "You're a communist at heart," I would tell him. "*From each according to his abilities, to each according to his needs.*"

The one thing Ricky and I invested every spare cent in was our wardrobe. It was still cheaper, we reasoned, to make sure that we looked good and were invited everywhere than it would have been to let ourselves go and have to pay for everything else.

I remember one night when Isabella Shulov, who had recently taken up trying to find eligible suitors for me as something of a hobby, suddenly exclaimed, "I know! Rachel and Manny should date!"

Manny was Isabella's photographer and was standing with us at the time. He cast an eye in my direction and noted wryly, "She looks too expensive for me."

I bristled slightly, thinking of Yusuf and everything that had come and gone since then. But I later said glibly to my friends, "Joke's on him—I'm so broke, he could've had me for the price of dinner."

It was around this time that Ricky and I started talking about our nightlife activities in terms of work. People in other places went out once or twice a week for their own amusement; for us, going out was a six-nights-a-week job.

There was a system of unspoken obligations that regulated our social scene—a tacit code of conduct that almost had the formality of an employee manual. Each club, promoter, or publicist who offered us free food or VIP tables was entitled to a certain number of appearances from us. The promoters were a transient lot, shifting places as rapidly and bewilderingly as a game of three-card monte, and part of our job was knowing where they were and supporting them in their new endeavors. Michael Tronn, for example, had left Liquid and was now with Big Time Productions. He had been replaced briefly by Gerry Kelly of Shadow Lounge, but then Gerry left Liquid to become a part-owner of Level, which had just opened to hysterical fanfare in the old Glam Slam space. Alan Roth promoted parties at Chaos for Tommy Pooch and also threw a Friday night party at the Albion pool called Magic Garden. Mykel Stevens was still promoting Back Door Bamby, which he'd moved to Groove Jet. Tony Guerra alone was merciful to us, having remained at Bash for as long as I could remember.

When out at parties, we were always to have a cocktail in our hand and to create a general aura of fun—but not the kind of drunken, "Girls Gone Wild" fun that looked tacky or might get police and outside press involved. Dancing on tables was occasionally permissible; dancing *naked* on tables was not. Doing drugs or having sex in the privacy of a bathroom stall was generally tolerated; doing either in a public space or in an alley within, say, twenty feet of the club or party was verboten (except at circuit parties). The rules for private parties at people's homes were more flexible, largely governed by the preferences of the host and his or her relationship with local law enforcement.

Any repeat transgressors were dealt with swiftly and firmly. The court of good reputation never passed any public judgments, and you certainly never read about it in the gossip columns. It would simply happen that a certain mailbox, which used to overflow with invitations, was suddenly empty, or a particular name that had once carried weight with the doormen was no longer recognized.

This all sounds very dramatic—the truth is, things almost never came to such measures. All of us understood what was expected so intuitively, it never once had to be explained.

Christmas approached and Ricky, Kojo, Mike, and I pooled our resources to buy each other gifts. Mike got a gift certificate to his favorite comic-book store in South Miami and a couple of tickets to an upcoming Star Trek convention. We bought Kojo a life-sized standee of Dr. Evil from *Austin Powers*, which would say things like "Riiiiiiight" in a prerecorded Dr. Evil voice whenever you pressed a button on its belly. Ricky was crazy for James Bond movies, so we bought him a boxed set of Bond films starring Roger Moore—the definitive Bond, in Ricky's opinion. I received a set of leopard-print martini glasses from Moondance (I was, in those days, passionately fond of all things leopard print) and a copy of *Valley of the Dolls*.

"It's a theme gift," Ricky told me. "You'll lounge by your pool in sunglasses and a big hat with the book and a martini—it'll be very glamorous."

The holidays also brought the arrival of Lara, who made her yearly trek to Boca, and she and I went out for lunch and caught up. I started out talking about parties and nightclub exploits, but the conversation quickly turned to my financial affairs.

"You need to get out of this place," she told me. "Move to New York or somewhere where you can find a real job and make a life for yourself." Lara herself was planning a transfer to Sony's New York office within the next year, and her boyfriend was already making arrangements to follow her and attend law school. I found it impossible to think about my own life in terms of what I might be doing a year from now.

"But I love it here," I demurred. "Whose life is more fun than mine?"

Mike went to visit his parents in Nebraska, and Kojo was spending New Year's Eve with his on-again, off-again boyfriend, Sebastian. Ricky and I had decided to remain alone in our respective homes; New Year's Eve was for people with boyfriends, we'd agreed, or people who didn't party much the rest of the year.

I was comfortably settled in bed with a box of Mallomars at eleven thirty on New Year's Eve, when Ricky called with the news that Isabella was on the guest list for Susanne Bartsch's party at the Delano. Since Finn was in Ireland with his family, Isabella had invited us to join her.

"It's eleven thirty," I said. "There's no way I can get dressed and be anywhere before midnight."

"Come in your pajamas," Ricky responded. "That's what Isabella and I are doing."

I threw on a pale pink silk-and-lace nightgown that I'd bought in the optimistic days of Andrew, then donned a silver, man-tailored silk robe made by

Sulka in the '70s, and slid into a pair of silver mules adorned with pink ostrich feathers that I'd acquired at Fly Boutique. Some dark plum lipstick and a hint of light blush completed the ensemble. I alighted from a cab in front of the Delano twenty minutes later and spotted Ricky, in a red and black smoking jacket, and Isabella, wearing a negligee and boa. The three of us slid easily through the crowd outside.

We spotted Chris Paciello, but he was too busy canoodling with Jennifer Lopez to pay us much attention. Everyone else we knew, however—and quite a few people we didn't—laughed in conspiratorial delight at our audacity in showing up at the Delano in our intimate apparel.

The lobby and pool area had been transformed into a shimmering fairyland, swelling with a sea of faces so beautiful, it was impossible to reconcile any thoughts of disappointment or hardship with the sight of it. I thought wistfully of a line from a story by F. Scott Fitzgerald: *All these beautiful faces . . . must be absolutely happy.*

A full moon glowed over the ocean. Its light caught stray moisture in the air and formed a perfect, circular rainbow. "Look," I said to Ricky, pointing at the sky. "I bet it's a good omen."

The clock struck midnight and Ricky and I kissed lightly, toasting each other with champagne. "Here's to 1999, darling." His glass chimed against mine. "It's going to be our year."

TWENTY

I chose my outfit with more than usual care one Friday night in mid-February, selecting a gown made of a shining gold raw silk. It was strapless, tight in the bodice, and slit all the way up the front of my left leg. In the dim strobes of the club it would, I thought, look like a column of candlelight.

The occasion was a party called Celebrity Club, promoted on Friday nights at the Living Room by Kevin Crawford and his partner Desiree Reyes. Celebrity Club so perfectly distilled the essence of what made South Beach . . . well, South Beach . . . that it was a stroke of sheer genius.

The Living Room at the Strand was a two-part establishment—a nightclub that was also renowned as one of the best (and most expensive) restaurants on the Beach. Celebrity Club took full advantage of both components. Each week, a different SoBe "celebrity" was selected as the party's honoree. He or she was invited to bring a small group of friends to a comped dinner in the Living Room's restaurant. After dinner there was a full-blown party in the Living Room's private back room. Partiers in the know would access the room, not through the club's main entrance on Washington Avenue, but through the back-alley service entrance located in the rear of the establishment. The girl who worked this door on Friday nights was simply called L. She was tall and lanky and speckled with a constellation of tattoos, and she had the ruthlessly appraising eye of a horse trader when it came to sizing up candidates for entry into the inner sanctum. If L had done her job, and if everything was timed just right, the party would already be going full force by the time dinner was over and the guest of honor made it to the back.

Tonight was Ricky's Celebrity Club. Isabella was in New York covering Fashion Week for the *Miami Journal* and so, with a profusion of regrets, was forced to decline Ricky's invitation to dinner. Mike always had to work past eleven thirty on *The Times* at WAMI, and Kojo had retreated even further from the social scene after White Party. He'd felt slighted by the White Party Week committee in ways he was unwilling to specify and, despite still being active with the Winter Party committee, was out at night less frequently than ever.

Nevertheless, Ricky was more than able to fill the table. Kevin and Desiree were there, of course. Kevin was reed thin, with skin that was the rich, creamy brown of café au lait. His large amber eyes and taut, high-cheekboned face were so full of dynamic motion that he often reminded me of Japanese anime. He'd been a well-known promoter in New York before moving to South Beach, and moved in social circles that had brought him into close contact with the likes of Madonna and Kate Moss.

Desiree was Puerto Rican, but her tall, sleek good looks could just as easily have been Italian or Greek. Her perfectly straight, gleaming black hair fell to her collarbone, and almond-shaped black eyes provided a startling contrast to dreamily soft, Kewpie-doll features. Tonight she wore an elegant, ankle-length dress made from a black jersey material, which plunged from her neck almost to her navel. She and Kevin sat at opposite sides of the table like a pair of glossy, flawlessly balanced bookends.

Filling in the middle were Merle and Danny Weiss, Lydia Birdsong, and Christina Getty. I'd been all set to hate Christina—who was blond and beautiful and a *Getty*, for chrissakes—but she had proven so genuinely sweet that disliking her was impossible. Adrina and Adam had also been invited, but Adam was called out of town suddenly and Adrina made a last-minute substitution with her friend Paul. Paul was clearly gay, painfully skinny, and even more painfully timid. He was also quite obviously overawed by Adrina.

Ice buckets of champagne and dishes of caviar made their way cere-monially to and from our table. I listened to the conversations ebb and flow around me.

". . . picture of me in the *Wire* this week was absolutely *wretched*! And they used the same one two days later in *Ego Trip*. . . ."

". . . snowing on South Beach, people here are so flaky. . . ."

". . . kept throwing shoes at me from her closet while I was helping her get ready—but look how gorgeous . . ."

". . . and I told him: *You might be a baron but if I marry anyone for a title, it'll be someone who can make me a princess. . . .*"

". . . funded to make a documentary on thirteen island communities all over the world—Bora Bora, Majorca. You should come—I'll need to hire production assistants."

This last bit was addressed to me by Lydia. "I would definitely be interested," I replied enthusiastically. I pictured myself snorkeling in Tahiti, or drinking at a local dive bar with fishermen off the coast of Spain. "It sounds like an incredible opportunity."

Ricky was in his element. He bore the compliments he received in a manner that indicated gracious indifference to praise, even though I knew he couldn't have been more thrilled. "I'm very proud to be here with you," I whispered to him during a lull in the conversation. We squeezed hands under the table and shared a fond smile.

After dinner we all traipsed into the back VIP room, which looked like a cross between a harem and a Cirque du Soleil tent. Upon entry, you would get a general sense of reds and golds and peacock blues, but it was hard to discern much more because it was always so crowded. Ricky and I were given a reserved table and a bottle of Veuve, but it took us a while to fight through the drag queens, club kids, and local glitterati who spilled into every inch of available space and were even, in some cases, forced to dance on banquettes and tables. I warmly greeted and kissed people I had no recollection of ever meeting, simply because they approached me and said my name as if we knew each other.

Among the first people we ran into were Anastasia Monster of Art and her live-in manager, Roy Hansen. Anastasia was dramatically tall, slender, and black-haired. A former fashion model, she'd moved to South Beach and taken up a career as an artist—and what was possibly the art world's most attention-grabbing moniker. Born in Milan and raised (as SoBe legend claimed) in a Russian monastery, Anastasia was believed to be fluent in eight or nine languages. She was always out with Roy, a six-foot-six Norwegian native. With his long blond hair and full mustache and beard, he resembled nothing so much as iconic portraits of Jesus Christ—a coincidence that always prompted Ricky and me to ask each other, "Have you accepted Roy Hansen as your Lord and personal Savior?"

Anastasia gasped loudly as we passed, and we paused to stand on our tiptoes and kiss her and Roy hello. "I am just thinking of you!" she exclaimed to Ricky in her heavy Russian accent. "You are putting me in the next column, yes?"

Ricky assured her that she would see her name in *Palm* print, and the two of us continued the slow push to our table. A lissome waitress with a curtain of yellow hair was already there, arranging our champagne service.

"To Mr. Nightclub," I toasted when she'd filled our flutes. "The original South Beach Celebrity."

By three o'clock in the morning, Ricky and I and the various friends rotating in and out of our banquette had finished four complimentary bottles of champagne. I realized that we had arrived at the Living Room at ten o'clock for Ricky's dinner, and that we'd subsequently spent five hours in the same club—a rare occurrence at the height of Season. My throat was raw from cigarettes and from shouting small talk over thunderous music, and I was heartily sick of the sound of my own voice.

We were sitting with José Antonio, a freelance photographer who sometimes snapped pictures for Ricky's column. I yawned elaborately, stretching my arms languorously above my head. Ricky knew this routine and immediately said, "Don't go yet, sweetie!"

"I think I have to," I replied. *"Estoy muy cansada."*

"I didn't know you speak Spanish," José Antonio piped up.

"¡Por supuesto!" I exclaimed, in the accent I'd perfected while living with Eduard. *"Cuando estoy borracha, puedo hablar en español fluentemente."* ["When I'm drunk, I can speak Spanish fluently."]

They were laughing as Adrina joined us. She'd been dancing and her cheeks were moist and flushed. "Are you leaving?" she asked in a disappointed tone. She wrapped her arms around me and rested her head on my shoulder. "Stay! We'll get some more champagne."

"I'm *so* bushed, you guys." I dropped a kiss on Adrina's forehead. "Would it be horrible if I left?"

"Don't let Kevin see you," Ricky advised. "You know how he feels about people leaving early."

"I'll sneak out," I said. "Don't tell him I'm gone."

The party was packed, with hardly an inch of wiggle room to be found; I held my breath to squeeze through the crowd as I headed for the back-alley entrance. I'd almost made it to the door when I felt a hand on my arm. It was Adrina's friend Paul.

"I just wanted to tell you how great it was to meet you," he said. "You have such an amazing energy." He leaned in to kiss me on the cheek and pressed a small, hard object into my hand.

"It was great meeting you, too," I replied. I tilted my head slightly, indicating my fist. "What's this for?"

Paul awkwardly attempted a nonchalant smile. "I just thought you might like it."

"But . . ." I trailed off, perplexed. "Did you want me to *pay* you for it, or . . . ?" I'd been offered a bump or a line many times from somebody else's stash, but I'd never had a new acquaintance offer me an entire gram for no apparent reason.

"No, no," he protested. "It's a gift." He hesitated, then added in a tone that tried to be casual, "Maybe you and Ricky and Adrina and I could all have dinner sometime."

I felt something dart through my chest like pain, heard echoes of my own voice in high school eagerly offering, *I can write that paper for you.* A sudden image of the quiet, lamp-lit bedroom waiting for me at home floated before my eyes like a mirage. "I'd love to," I said, gently. I kissed him on the cheek and squeezed his arm. "I'll call Adrina tomorrow and set something up. But you know you don't have to give me anything, right?"

"Keep it," he said happily. "I have lots." Then he returned to the party, and I headed out the door with a good-bye wave to L.

I had made it through the alley and onto Washington Avenue, and had my hand on a cab door handle, when a voice behind me said, "Ex*cuse* me, Miss Thing!" I turned and saw Kevin Crawford approaching swiftly. "Where do you think you're going?"

I immediately felt guilty. "I'm sorry I didn't say good-bye, sweetie—I couldn't find you," I lied. "I was just headed home."

Kevin briskly tapped the roof of the cab, indicating that it should drive on. "No, you're not." He took my arm firmly. "Let's go back inside. I'll send you another bottle of champagne."

I sighed inwardly as we returned to the club—although I was flattered by the affection implied in all the fuss. Ricky appeared astonished when Kevin once again deposited me at our table. "You ratted me out, didn't you?" I tried to look stern. "You fully ratted me out."

Ricky's face was a picture of innocence wrongly accused. "Well, darling, Kevin came by and asked where you were and I *had* to tell him—how was I supposed to know he'd chase you through the alley like a lunatic?"

"You're a tough nut to crack, Pascal," I sighed, as the waitress returned to our table with another bottle of champagne. "I'm the only person I know," I added, "who gets kicked *into* clubs." We looked at each other and burst out laughing.

It was clear at this point that I was in for the duration, and I knew I'd need additional fortification to get through. "I'm going to powder my nose," I said to Ricky. "Could you pour me a glass of champagne?"

"I'll come with you," Adrina announced. Once we were a couple of feet away, she lowered her voice and confided, "I've got party favors in my bag."

"Me too," I whispered back.

Adrina and I emerged from our shared bathroom stall newly energized and fairly bursting with a general love of all mankind. We held hands so we wouldn't lose each other as we squeezed through the throngs separating us from our table. Music rolled over our heads insistently, almost a tactile presence in the room. "What's the story, morning glory?" said a voice startlingly close to my ear, and I looked up into John Hood's face.

"What's shakin', Daddy-O?" I responded merrily. I tried to slow the spread of perma-grin I felt coming on.

"Johnny Hood!" Adrina crowed, and Hood looked past me. "Hey, kitty-cat," he said. They kissed affectionately, the brim of Hood's hat brushing her temple. I looked at her suddenly the way a man would see her—her blond hair temptingly disheveled from dancing; her pliant form, clad in a tight pink dress, an invitation to riot. I saw green for a second (hating myself for it, yet unable to control my response) but recovered as Hood put his hand on my waist and said to Adrina, "Why don't you run along and tell Mr. Nightstick that his dame's dawdling on the wrong side of the tracks for a while."

I swatted his arm playfully. "Don't be a jerk, Hood," I said. But I pressed Adrina's hand and signaled that it was okay for her to head off without me.

"I want to introduce you to some people." He indicated a corner banquette where two other men were seated. They weren't old and they weren't young, and their conservative button-downs marked them as nonlocals. "They write for *Time*," Hood informed me.

I had clearly come in mid-conversation and I didn't even try to follow its threads after Hood and I were seated. I could tell that I'd been immediately sized up and categorized by these friends of Hood's. In my cleavage-baring dress, I had been relegated to a compartment labeled *Superfluous South Beach Eye Candy*. The talk zipped and looped briskly, from other writers they all knew to Hood's take on the glory days of early South Beach. I was silent for the most part, contentedly focused on nursing a cocktail and ducking the elbows and downward-tilted cigarettes that occasionally threatened the top of my head. I watched Hood—the way his hands moved, the changing nuance of his expression as he talked excitedly. He was sitting so close that I could feel his breath on my bare shoulder. I pulled out cigarettes occasionally and Hood lit them for me automatically, without breaking his conversational stride.

Time passed, I wasn't sure how much. I was eventually aware of the need for another bump and realized I should also check in with Ricky. "I'll be right back," I whispered to Hood, sliding out from the banquette.

Hood rose too. "Wait a second." He put his hand on my forearm to detain me, seeming to wait for something. Finally he said, "Gentlemen." His voice was quiet, yet he immediately had their attention. "The lady is standing."

They considered him for a moment, nonplussed. Their eyes flickered over to my face and back to his, and then they jumped hastily to their feet, bowing their heads slightly in my direction and murmuring vague apologies. My blood drummed staccato in my ears and I felt slightly flustered. "Excuse me, please," I said, returning their nods as I walked away.

I ran into Ricky as I was coming out of the bathroom. "There you are!" he exclaimed. "Don't tell me you've been with that juvenile delinquent this whole time."

"Okay, I won't tell you," I replied cheerfully.

"Well, it's almost four thirty; I think we should get going." I didn't respond, and Ricky regarded me narrowly. "You're not staying here with him, are you?"

"Yes." I paused, then added more decisively, "Yes, I am."

"Are you *leaving* with him?"

I sighed heavily and snarked, "Would you find this easier to follow if I acted it out with sock puppets?"

"All right, all right—do what you want." Every contour of his face radiated disapproval. "You don't have to be so high and mean."

I felt my own face soften. "I think the word you're looking for is 'defensive,'" I replied. "Your lips say, *Do what you want,* but your eyes say, *J'accuse!*"

He chuckled. "I just worry about you, honey." He hugged me tightly. "Call me whenever you get home—no matter how late it is," he admonished. "And you better not call me from jail!"

"Nobody's going to jail tonight," I assured him.

Hood stood up when I returned to the table. The other men also stood (without being prompted this time), taking their seats again once I was seated. "I stayed at the Chelsea Hotel for a while," Hood was saying, and I knew he was discussing the time he'd spent in New York. "It seemed like the right place for a wide-eyed young literary thug to hole up."

"New York is a place with history," one of the writers agreed. He cast his eye around the room, and I knew that the unspoken second half of his sentence was a dig at the brand-spanking-newness of South Beach. *All flash, no substance,* his eyes telegraphed with mild distaste. "But all anybody cares about now are celebrities, tabloids, and awards shows."

"People like awards shows because America is a uniquely achievement-oriented society," I remarked. "It could be argued that our most authentic cultural narrative is the rags-to-riches, pull-yourself-up-by-your-bootstraps story."

I had undoubtedly spoken with the goal of putting down these friends of Hood, who clearly lacked the social graces that would customarily keep one from disparaging a place whose hospitality one was accepting. But I also hoped that, if I could silence them, Hood and I might make our escape sooner. So I was unable to look at Hood directly, afraid my face would turn as red as the sunrise if I did. I locked my gaze instead on his two companions. They appeared momentarily surprised at having heard from me, then smiled appreciatively.

"And you haven't said two words all night," one of them observed.

I arched my back almost imperceptibly—in a way that could have passed as a light stretch, but that I knew would push my breasts more tightly against the top of my dress. "Well," I said demurely, "I'm quite shy." Hood stifled a cough, and I could tell he was trying not to laugh.

The conversation never regained its momentum after that. I fiddled absently with the straw in my empty cocktail glass and cast a sidelong glance at Hood. He rested his arm against the top of the banquette behind me, the sleeve of his coat brushing the back of my neck.

"Let's get out of here," he leaned in to murmur, and I nodded a wordless assent.

We got into the cab without any fixed destination. I think Hood may have said something, once we were settled, about wanting to show me some new books he had, and I probably pretended to agree that looking at books at five thirty a.m. was a fine reason to go back to his place. Five minutes later the cab pulled up to a tiny, two-story apartment building near Flamingo Park. Hood paid the driver and led me up to the unit on the second floor.

The front door opened into a white-walled living room. Hood pressed the base of a small lamp near the entrance and a wan, yellowish light stretched itself out. From the low ceiling, wide slatted windows, and ancient tile, I guessed that the apartment had been built in the '40s or '50s. I noted a round, battered valise in one corner, surrounded by cluttered stacks of books and papers. "This is my friend Will's place," Hood said. "I'm staying here for a while." As a seemingly unconnected afterthought he added, "He's out of town for a couple of weeks."

Hood busied himself pouring lines from a vial in his coat pocket onto a beaten-up wooden table. In the silence of the room, the *tap-tap-tap* of glass against wood was vaguely jarring. After we'd partaken, he took my hand and said, "Come on, I wanna show you the roof."

I followed him up a narrow staircase along the outside of the building, holding up the hem of my dress with one hand as my high heels skittered along the metal stairs. One of Hood's neighbors had planted jasmine, and the smell was almost overwhelming. I inhaled deeply as I looked out over the roof onto low-slung golden and pastel buildings, crowned with red clay and interspersed with soaring palm trees. The view was dotted, like an incomplete pointillist painting, with lamps from windows and trees lined with twinkle lights.

The other side of the roof overlooked Flamingo Park, a spacious expanse of land in the center of South Beach. In the mornings and afternoons, children utilized its playgrounds, public pool, and tree-lined walks. By night, it was a refuge for drug dealers and anonymous sexual acts never meant to see the light of day.

I leaned against the low wall that lined the roof's perimeter, and Hood's arms encircled me from behind. I felt his lips on the back of my neck. *Turn around,* he said, and I did.

There was nothing gentle or affectionate about the way we kissed, or how our bodies moved against each other—but, then, there had never been any of that between Hood and me. It was pure greed—fingers and tongues that groped and took as if what they wanted might be taken from them. I pushed Hood's hat from the top of his head, realizing that I'd literally never seen him without it. He seemed infinitely younger and smaller. *There you are,* I gloated softly. I cupped Hood's face in my hands and his mouth covered mine with such violence, I tasted blood on the inside of my lips.

The top of the wall pressed into my back; I heard a zipper and abruptly realized that my dress had fallen open to my waist. *Hood,* I said urgently. *Somebody might see us.*

Hood's voice was low and close against my ear; it thrilled along my nerve endings, following his hands from the small of my back to the base of my skull. *I want people to see us,* he said. *I want people to see me fucking you.*

The smell of skin overpowered the smell of jasmine and I didn't care anymore who saw or heard us. I wanted what he wanted; the wanting of it blocked out everything else.

Please, I think I whispered. The sun began its slow ascent, and the air around us purpled into morning.

TWENTY-ONE

Whatever there was of glamour in that night had completely dissipated by the next morning. Actually, it had dissipated three hours later that same morning—which is when I woke up next to Hood in the tousled bed in Will's extra bedroom. The veins in my forehead pounded a tarantella, the inside of my nose was a fiery, sand-coated desert, and I wished to the very bottom of my soul that I could somehow teleport to my own home.

I considered my options as I lay there. The first was to continue to lie there until Hood also woke up. I looked over at him, modestly covered by the blanket, sprawled out on his back with his face turned away. His chest was smooth and hairless as a boy's. There was no jaunty suit, no rakish fedora, no continuous string of cigarettes and clever match-lighting tricks—there was simply the irrefutable fact of his naked skin and steady, sleep-heavy breathing. What would his face show, I wondered, in that unguarded moment when he first opened his eyes and saw me in bed with him?

The idea of being next to him—equally naked and painfully sober—was suddenly unbearable.

This narrowed the scope of my options to leaving before he woke up. I got out of bed and padded softly around the room, reassembling my dress, underwear, and shoes. Then I gathered my purse and let myself quietly out the front door.

I'd been hoping for an overcast morning—something there's a fifty-fifty chance of on any given Miami day—but, as I stepped outside, white sunlight landed on my face like a resounding slap. I flinched and pulled out my cell phone to call a cab. My lips were puffy and bruised, moving unnaturally as I spoke.

It was nine thirty when I reached my apartment. I decided to call Ricky—who had, I reminded myself, instructed me to call whenever I got home, no

231

matter what time it was. "I'm home," I announced in response to Ricky's groggy hello. My own voice was raspy and about two octaves lower than usual.

"What time is it?" I heard him fumble around and then, sounding much more awake, he groaned, "Did you . . . ? Oh *God*, you didn't! Tell me you didn't."

"Wish I could," I replied. "But, you know, people go to hell for lying."

"Aw, *jeez!* Don't tell me anything else—I don't want to know *anything* else." He paused, momentarily in the throes of an early-morning coughing fit. Then he lowered his voice and asked almost grudgingly, "So how was it?"

"Well," I said thoughtfully, "sometimes, as a woman, what you want is a man who treats you delicately and tenderly, as if you were a priceless objet d'art."

"Yeah . . ." His voice was slow and unwilling, as if he dreaded what was coming next.

"And other times," I continued, "as a woman, you want a man to throw you up against the wall, rip your clothes off with his teeth, and treat you like the bad, bad girl you always knew you were."

Ricky now took to loudly clearing his throat, and it sounded as if he might be trying to restrain laughter. "I thought you were such a feminist," he finally managed, and I knew he must be desperate if he was playing the feminism card. Ricky hated it when I referred to myself as a feminist, firm in the belief that a woman couldn't be a feminist and still care about grooming or dresses. I think he half expected me to show up at a party one day, hairy-legged and clad in overalls.

"I *am* a feminist," I replied. "Sometimes even a feminist likes to be manhandled."

Ricky laughed outright at this, and I joined in. "That's enough out of you, missy. Just tell me you used condoms."

"Of course we used condoms," I replied seriously. "And I'd appreciate it if you didn't tell anyone. I don't know what's going on and I don't want it to be a whole *thing* that people talk about."

"How was it when you left?"

"Perfectly fine." My voice was breezily unconcerned. "He was asleep at the time."

Ricky's response was a concise and knowing "Ah." We said our good-byes and retired to the sanctuary of our respective beds.

I slept fitfully for the next few hours, half expecting the phone to ring with a call from Hood. None had come, however, by the time I got up at one thirty and took a shower. I had just crawled into clean sweats when the doorbell rang, and my heart beat slightly faster as I walked into the living room.

I looked through the peephole and saw Mike, carting a pizza from Pucci's. "Let me in," he called through the door. "I heard you tricked with Hood last night."

"Please announce that to my *entire* building." I sighed, unfastening the lock. I momentarily wondered if it was worth murdering Ricky for having so obviously spilled the beans.

There was a minor flurry in the kitchen as the two of us hunted for drinks, plates, and napkins. "So let me ask you," I said as I sectioned out slices onto paper plates, "how do you know if what you had was a trick or a relationship-type situation?"

"A relationship calls the next day," Mike told me. He poured a glass of soda. "A trick calls the next time he's horny."

As if on cue, the phone rang. We looked at each other for a moment before I went to see who it was.

"Hey, baby doll," said the sleepy voice on the other end. I smiled into the phone. "What's with the disappearing act?"

The next few days come back to me now more as a series of vignettes than as a linear sequence of events. Hood and I were almost always high, and in the time before we were too high to function there was sex. The sex and the drugs became a sort of continuum, so that I can't recall distinctly which preceded the other or which times they happened simultaneously.

The feeling of it—with all the violent surprise of a snatch-and-grab, something that left no room for anything beyond the immediate and physical—never changed much from that first night. I remember doing a couple of lines one afternoon and, in that first flush of heat, going into the bathroom to splash cold water over my face. When I looked up into the mirror, Hood was there behind me, and then suddenly my hands were pressed against the cold tile of the bathroom wall. *Tell me,* Hood said insistently, his lips somewhere between my ear and neck. *Tell me you want me to fuck you right here.* And I responded in a voice like somebody who'd had the wind knocked out of her, saying, *I need you to fuck me.* His hands were under my clothes and there was a feeling of excitement so sharp and inward pulling, it was almost painful. Then I guess it must have been later, because the next thing I clearly remember is being naked with Hood on the couch, near the coffee table where the lines were set up, and the room had darkened from afternoon into twilight. The slatted windows were open, casting horizontal shadows over Hood's face, and the room smelled like wet trees.

My car clocked a lot of mileage as Hood and I drove around and around the Beach, dropping in on the places where he scored drugs. The money flew out of my wallet faster than I could keep track of it. *I'll pay you back* was Hood's mantra, and I knew it was a lie even as I believed it.

We visited large houses on Pine Tree Drive and cramped apartments off Alton Road. The people who owned them were mostly men and mostly straight, and their homes—no matter what time of day or night we stopped by—were always full of the strung-out, draped carelessly against disheveled furniture and windows that had their hurricane shutters resolutely closed. It was as if their circadian rhythms were dictated by the rise and fall of their need rather than the rise and fall of the sun—and such, I reflected, was probably the case.

Although the people who purveyed, purchased, and provided the drugs were almost exclusively men, there were usually a few women at these gatherings. I came to understand that I would be expected to make nice with them while Hood conducted business. "I'm going on a diet," one of them confided to me one day, shouting slightly over the combined background blare of the CD player and the TV. No more than twenty, she had the long, sinuous torso of a snake charmer. "I'm going to stay up for two days straight doing crystal and not eat anything; I lose ten pounds every time."

"But you're so beautiful," I told her. I was glowing in that earliest and best part of my high, when everyone around me was gorgeous and wonderful and there to be loved, and I wanted more than anything to make each one of them understand—in a sincere and meaningful way—how astounding I thought they were.

But the girl's glittering eyes were inwardly focused, concentrating almost entirely on something that was happening inside her own head. Insofar as they included me at all, it was only as a co-conspirator in our group effort to kill time as pointlessly—and self-indulgently—as possible. She'd probably already forgotten that she'd even spoken to me.

I don't remember any of these people's names, because I rarely bothered to pay attention when Hood made introductions. There was always the guise of pretending we had merely dropped by for a social call, that the drugs were almost an afterthought. But that, of course, was a polite fiction, and I didn't see the point in socializing, or pretending more interest than I felt.

Hood, however, liked the socializing—not for its own sake, I realized, but because he saw himself as a man of action, and men of action *do* things. It was a ritual—almost an aesthetic—this going out and obtaining of drugs. Having them delivered, as Amy and I had done, would have violated some basic tenet in Hood's constitution that demanded constant motion.

There was always something restless in Hood—and this, I thought, was the reason he used drugs as heavily as he did. The speed with which his mind worked and his mouth motored was astounding; he talked to me endlessly about everything except the personal. He never told me (and I never asked) stories about embarrassing high school moments, or siblings (did he even have any?) or other women he'd been involved with once upon a time. But he would show me things he had written—magazine articles or beginnings of novels and screenplays—and explain the nuance of his writing faster than I could read it. Then he'd pull four or five books at a time from his teetering pile in the corner of Will's apartment, discoursing on the writers who'd influenced his own work at a rate that left me feeling like the slow reader in English class, who prays the teacher won't call on her and subject her plodding mispronunciations to the sneers of fellow students.

Hood explained to me once that he actually used cocaine to slow down, to bring everything to a more even keel and tamp down the relentless drumming of ideas—which made the thought of Hood *off* drugs almost frightening to contemplate. "The inside of your head must be a scary place to live," I told him.

I soon learned that coke wasn't Hood's only drug of choice, or even his primary one. We were in somebody's living room one night—one of Hood's innumerable drug connections—and I saw Hood balancing a piece of foil in one hand with a small rock in its center. He held a lighter flame beneath it with the other. In his mouth was a rolled up dollar bill that concentrated and inhaled the resulting smoke.

"Are you—" It was the first time I had ever asked the question literally. "Are you *smoking crack*?"

"Of course not." Hood's voice was disdainful. "This is heroin."

I'd never been in the presence of heroin before. I idly picked up a small foil package that lay on a nearby table, turning it curiously in my fingers.

"No." Hood's hand covered mine. His tone was gentle, but, when I looked up into his face, his expression left no room for argument. "Put it down."

With Will out of town those first couple of weeks we had the full run of his apartment, and I was happy to keep things that way. I sensed, even early on, that my relationship with Hood would be about damage control, about containing the effect he might have on other areas of my life. I had an idea that if I drew certain arbitrary boundaries around our relationship, I could control the fallout. So I decided to limit the amount of time and number of instances when Hood would be allowed into my apartment. I made a lot of decisions, actually, but those didn't become important until later on.

I knew with absolute certainty that allowing myself to fall in love with John Hood would be deeply self-destructive. To love an addict is to give up control of your life—and to give it up to someone who will never love you, or anything, more than his own need. It's akin to riding an accelerating train without an engineer and hoping, through sheer dumb luck, that it won't crash into a brick wall. I wanted the ride and the rush and the speed, but also to know where the quick exits were in case I saw any brick walls looming.

I say that now. Yet there's one night I remember so clearly, when I think I came as close to loving Hood as I ever would. It was one of those moments that are insignificant in and of themselves, but that later stand out in your memory with more clarity than the important things.

We were in Will's apartment, which was completely dark except for a pallid glow from the antiquated overhead in his '40s-style kitchen. I was waiting on the couch in the living room while Hood rooted around in a kitchen drawer for a fresh book of matches. He was partially undressed, wearing only his suit pants, a sleeveless white undershirt, and his fedora. As he was leaving the kitchen he stood briefly in the doorway that separated it from the living room and fired up a cigarette. His face was obscured except for the orange glow of the flame. The backlight from the kitchen was a penumbra around him.

I looked at him—and he was so perfectly noir, so precisely the embodiment of certain daydreams I'd always had, that it was almost as if he stood there in that moment because I had created him. I wanted to say something, something real that wouldn't be about drugs or sex or the sparring banter we usually engaged in. I opened my mouth to speak.

Then Hood reached over to snap the light in the kitchen off, and the moment passed.

Hood had turned up unexpectedly at Will's door one day, asking for a few nights of temporary shelter until one fallback plan or another came through. The few nights had turned into a month and counting, with no projected end in sight. Hood wasn't paying rent as far as I knew, yet Will had never once asked him to leave.

Hood and Will had struck up a friendship at the *Miami Sentinel* offices, where Will was a full-time staff writer. Will produced hard-hitting, hard-edged articles about the seamier underside of South Beach fabulosity—articles exposing various sex-and-drugs debacles and shady business deals. I often thought that Hood must be worth a year's free rent to a writer like Will—full of Chandleresque tales of bruiser bad luck, or the misdeeds perpetrated by SoBe's more sanctimonious and impenetrable scenemakers.

When I finally met Will, I was somewhat surprised to encounter a soft-spoken man in his late twenties. He was very tall and very thin, and conveyed an impression of amiable shyness that reminded me of Eduard in the early days of our relationship. I liked him for that. He had framed facsimiles of rough drafts by some of my favorite poets—Sylvia Plath, T. S. Eliot, Elizabeth

Bishop—hanging on the walls of his apartment, and I liked him for that, too.

A mutual sympathy sprang up between us. It was based in part on our shared love of books and poetry, but mainly I think it came from the way we felt about Hood. We both regarded him as a sort of freak accident that had befallen us, one we couldn't shake off and wouldn't if we could—even though we knew we'd probably pay for it in the end.

Will wasn't a party guy and he wasn't into drugs, and it must have been more than a little disruptive, the way Hood and I carried on in his apartment even after he'd returned to town. If he came home late enough at the end of his workday, we'd already be jazzed up and dressed to the nines; if he came home early, we might still be partially undressed, lines laid out on the coffee table and the unctuous residue of just-smoked heroin lingering in the air.

"Will needs a dame," Hood said more than once. I thought about Will—with his writing and his sincerity—and replied, "He should look for one over the causeway."

We did the Three Musketeers bit for a while, hanging out in Will's apartment in a convivial fashion as we discussed books or articles Will was writing before Hood and I would leave to make our first appearance of the night. Then one night I came over to pick Hood up, dressed in a long, slinky red gown that stopped just barely on the right side of indecency. Will was sitting on the couch as I entered. "Wow," he said. "You look sexy tonight."

I had started to smile and thank him for the compliment when Hood, who was standing next to me, demanded sharply, "What did you say?"

Will and I thought he was joking and we laughed. After all, I thought, Hood—who could talk such a dirty blue streak during sex—couldn't possibly be Puritan enough to object to Will's using the word "sexy" in reference to me.

Hood didn't laugh. A quick look at his face silenced me completely. I suddenly found myself remembering that Hood had served time in prison for beating up two men because he'd found them in his then-girlfriend's apartment.

"I invite a dame over," Hood said now, "and this is how you talk to her?"

Will was still trying to laugh the incident off. "C'mon, Hood," he said, with an effort at playful levity. He couldn't let himself take it seriously—not because it couldn't *be* serious, but because if it *was* serious, he'd have to decide what he was going to do about it. Then Will looked directly into Hood's eyes. His face froze, midlaugh, into an open-mouthed rictus.

I couldn't look at him. I turned instead to Hood and interjected in the lightest manner I could muster, "Hey—I think any rational person would agree that I'm *dead* sexy in this dress."

There were children playing outside, hide-and-seek in the gathering dusk. Their shrieks circled and drifted up through Will's open window into the silence of the room. *"You're* it! *You're* it!"

Hood ignored me as completely as if I hadn't spoken. "Apologize to her."

The half smiling, half panicked expression was still on Will's face. "Hood," I finally murmured impatiently. I put a hand on his arm. "Hood, for God's sake, leave it alone already."

Hood pulled a cigarette from his pocket and lit it casually. "Let's head to the Marlin," he said to me. His tone was abruptly normal, and, even though his face was expressionless, I could have sworn he was laughing. "I want to check out their new DJ before we hit Level." He didn't say anything to Will, who'd finally allowed his face to relax.

We turned toward the front door and Will came up behind me. "I'm sorry if I offended you," he said in an undertone.

"Please don't apologize." My voice was equally low. "You did absolutely nothing wrong." We smiled briefly at each other before I followed Hood down the stairs.

Hood and I snorted everything we could get our hands on that night, and what we couldn't inhale, we drank. Will was long-since asleep when we got back at five thirty, and the weight of Hood's body on top of mine in bed crushed any other thoughts I might have had. By the time I woke up the next afternoon, I hardly remembered that anything had happened.

In mid-March I got a job referral through Josh at the Agnew Group. It was at a nonprofit called the Family Assistance Organization, which provided emergency shelter to abused children. Family Assistance's fundraising manager had quit suddenly, leaving them high and dry vis-à-vis their annual fundraising gala, the revenues of which accounted for a healthy portion of their annual budget. The gala was scheduled for May, and Family Assistance was way behind the eight ball in terms of pulling it together.

I didn't want to accept a full-time position (*Every time I think I'm out of nonprofit,* I told Ricky, *they pull me back in*), but I agreed to get them through their gala. I also continued to work with Brent Carrigan and Cindy on Broadway Nights and with Ricky on the radio show, and my days were suddenly very full.

I think work was my safety valve, in a way. It would have been so easy, otherwise, for Hood's lifestyle to become my lifestyle—where the only thing distinguishing day from night was the location and quantity of our drug use.

I worked all day and Hood worked all night. I was somewhat vague as to what, exactly, Hood's work consisted of. Various establishments on the Beach wanted his services, hoping for the elusive hip factor that could spell the difference between riches and ruin. There was an Italian restaurant on Collins and 21st that took up much of his time, and this was where most of Hood's nights started. He was also working with Crobar—a Chicago club that was opening a much-talked-about SoBe extension in the Cameo Theater space sometime in December.

Drugs were the invariable alpha and omega of our nights; we'd usually meet up after I left work, driving around to make our initial score during the early part of the evening. Then I'd drop Hood off at his first stop of the night and hook up with him later at a club or bar, or—if his work kept him out late enough—back at my apartment. Needless to say, it was no longer feasible for us to spend all of our time together at Will's.

"You should give me keys," Hood said once. "Then you wouldn't have to wake up to let me in, and I wouldn't have to wake up early when you leave in the morning."

"I can't," I replied hastily. I had a vision of Hood's valise taking up an indefinite residence in the corner of my apartment—or, even worse, of coming home one day to find my apartment stripped and emptied. "I need to get special permission from my building to get copies made." I held up the keys and pointed to the big bold letters that said DO NOT DUPLICATE.

Hood arched an eyebrow at this, but didn't say anything else.

One of the ground rules I set for myself early on was that Hood and I would not be an official "couple." I would never, for example, refer to him as my boyfriend. There would be no exchanging of keys. People (other than my close friends) would never know the two of us were involved. There was a tremendous difference, I thought, between somebody who you were just fooling around with and somebody who was your boyfriend—and as long as Hood was the one and not the other, I felt reasonably confident that he could never hurt me, that whatever trouble he might get into wouldn't be my eventual problem.

I impressed upon my friends the importance of remaining mum on the subject, something I reminded Ricky of one night at a club called Jimmy'z. Jimmy'z was owned by Shareef Malnik and adjoined The Forge; their frontperson was infamous nightlife diva Regine. Regine had an illustrious career in nightclubs that spanned several decades, at least three continents, and over a dozen cities—having run clubs in places including Paris, Saint-Tropez, Rio, Cairo, Monte Carlo, and New York. People said that she'd entertained everybody from Dominick Dunne and Andy Warhol to Brigitte Bardot and Jackie Kennedy, and that it was Regine herself who had taught the Twist to the Duke of Windsor.

Ricky and I were seated in a banquette in Jimmy'z and had been briefly joined and recently left by Isabella and Finn. "Look," I said, "I know this goes without saying, but please don't say anything to Isabella about Hood and me."

Ricky looked a little shamefaced. "I already told Isabella."

"Oh, that's fine." I lit a cigarette. "Who could Isabella possibly tell? She only writes the most widely read gossip column *in all of South Florida*!"

"Isabella's column is *not* a gossip column," Ricky corrected me. "It's a *nightlife* column. And, anyway, I *had* to tell her, because she wanted to fix you up with a friend of Finn's and I had to give her a reason why she couldn't. And I know she won't tell anybody because she doesn't approve of this thing with you and Hood."

"Don't make Isabella your mouthpiece," I retorted hotly. "If you don't think I should be with Hood, have the balls to come out and say it yourself."

"What have I *been* saying for the past year and a half? *I don't think you should be with him!*"

"Clearly we're at an impasse." My tone was perfectly level. "Perhaps we should agree to disagree and change the subject."

We were temporarily spared further discussion by the arrival of Regine herself. She bussed us each on the cheek with a sweeping, "Hello, my darling ones," before seating herself next to Ricky. The strobe lights danced mischievously in her lacquered, flame-red hair.

"You just missed the Queen of the Night," I offered, referring to Isabella's recent departure.

Regine's green eyes flashed. "*I* am the Queen of the Night," she coldly informed me, and I was immediately mortified. I knew I had heard somewhere that one of the New York papers had so dubbed her back in the '80s—a fact I'd inconveniently forgotten.

I could see Ricky casting about for a way to rescue me from this faux pas, when Regine said, in a more conciliatory tone, "This is a beautiful gown you're wearing. It's Pucci?"

I was, in fact, wearing a wild Pucci print in swirling shades of hot pink, neon yellow, and electric blue and green. I'd rescued it from the Salvation Army, of all places, and happily confirmed Regine's guess.

She allowed us a small smile and briefly brushed her hand against our faces. "You are beautiful children," she said. And, with that, she was gone.

"Yikes," I said to Ricky. "I really stepped in it, huh?"

Ricky was quiet for a moment. "I'm not going to remind you," he started, clearly unwilling to have the subject changed, "that you're sleeping with a convicted felon and junkie whose real last name you don't know." He paused, his expression uncharacteristically serious. "But I will remind you that you live in a small town, and there's only so long you can keep a secret here."

I finished off my champagne in one long swallow and set the glass on the table with a hard click. "I'm going to powder my nose," I said. I mashed my cigarette into the ashtray. "When I get back, let's be talking about something else."

Ricky couldn't have been more wrong: As far as I knew then, or even know now, nobody guessed what was going on. At least, nobody other than my core group of friends ever asked any questions, or dropped any hints, or even referred to the matter in any way. It was actually a bit disconcerting at first; when your name and picture appear in print on a weekly basis, you can't help assuming the public at large has at least a passing interest in your private life.

But I realized that South Beach wasn't a town that pried into who you were sleeping with, or any of the details of your personal life that weren't directly related to the party scene. The only circumstance that would open the subject to gossip was if the relationship melted down in some messy, spectacular way—involving public fights, theft of money or property, or the involvement of law enforcement. One of our friends, for example, had recently left town over a scandal that involved his stealing money and checkbooks from men he was sleeping with. It was a sordid tale that certainly never made the papers, but was thoroughly hashed over in hushed whispers by all those in the know.

So it was perfectly possible for two people situated as Hood and I were—not prone to public displays of affection and generally circumspect on the subject of our private lives—to fly under the radar, almost completely unnoticed.

If anybody had really thought about it, they probably could've put two and two together. Hood and I were certainly out often enough. Much to Kojo's chagrin, we sidestepped Winter Party—an annual circuit party held in March—completely. We were, however, all over the Beach during Winter Music Conference, one of the largest club music conferences in the country. Hood knew as much about music as he did books—he'd had, he told me, a brief recording contract with Warner Music, and had hung out at CBGB back in the day with post-punk/no-wave bands like the Swans and Bush Tetras before moving into music journalism. He took me to the Cameo Theater, where we listened to Fatboy Slim spin while Hood described the extensive changes to the Cameo that the Crobar people were envisioning. We went to a Sony party at Warsaw and to hear Paul van Dyk at Groove Jet; everywhere we went, Hood gave me detailed backstories on the performers and the inner-industry workings that created their rises and falls.

Hood also accompanied me to Adrina's going-away dinner at Pacific Time one late March evening. Adrina was moving to New York with a boyfriend none of us had met—an occurrence that left me sadder than I would have thought. "She'll come back," Ricky assured me. "They always come back."

We were a small group, maybe ten or so, and Hood and I were seated

across from Adrina and Paul. Ricky sat on my other side. Ricky and I'd had
Adrina on our radio show for a going-away interview the day before, and the
conversation lingered first on the subject of that show and then on the show
Ricky and I had done the previous week, when we'd interviewed notorious drag
queen Shelley Novak.

It was at this point that Paul, who'd been looking for a way into the
conversation, made the unfortunate observation that I looked like Shelley
Novak. I was startled, and even Ricky—who always had something to say—was
surprised into momentary silence.

Thomas Strangie, the man who "played" Shelley Novak, was a black-
haired, black-eyed man of Italian descent who notoriously hated to shave.
Therefore, Shelley Novak resembled nothing so much as a very hairy-chested
man with five o'clock shadow who happened to be wearing a dress, giant fake
tits, and a sky-high blond wig. The contrast between dress and chest hair was a
Shelley Novak trademark, part of what made Shelley so hilarious, outrageous,
and all-around unforgettable.

But you can see where it wasn't exactly a compliment to be told that I
resembled her. Perhaps Paul was trying to say that, dark as I was, I looked
Italian in the same way as Thomas Strangie. People told me on a fairly regular
basis that I looked Italian (or Hispanic, or Lebanese, or Greek, or wherever
people gathered to be short and dark together). I was certain that Paul didn't
have the nerve to attempt cattiness with me—especially in a gathering where I
had so many more allies than he did.

Paul looked abashed and nervous as soon as the words left his mouth,
and my heart went out to him in his obvious discomfort. I was inclined to let
the whole thing pass unremarked.

Not Hood; the expression on his face was one of pure disbelief. He was
on his feet almost before I knew what was happening—ready to throw himself
on poor Paul, who cringed closer to Adrina. It took Ricky's and my strenuous
combined efforts to talk Hood down and back into his seat before any real
damage—physical or social—was done.

See? the look on Ricky's face told me plainly. *You can't take this man
anywhere.*

"People can't win for losing with you, can they?" I said to Hood later, when we were back at my apartment. I dropped my evening bag and Hood seated himself on the red velvet couch—two shades darker than the red I'd painted the walls—which I'd bought with my first Family Assistance paycheck. I was irritated and put on a Grateful Dead CD, something I knew Hood detested. "You're ready to kill them if they say I'm sexy and you're ready to kill them if they say I'm ugly."

Hood poured some coke onto my new wooden coffee table. I wanted to do a line, but had an indefinable sense that doing so would take the wind out of the sails of the argument I was trying to start.

Brown-eyed women and red grenadine, the Dead sang. *The bottle was dusty but the liquor was clean . . .*

"You're beautiful," Hood replied. He extinguished a match and dropped it in the ashtray. "Let them say you're beautiful if they need to sling words around."

Something inside me turned over. I walked over to the couch and crept into his lap, smiling as I pulled off his hat. "You're pretty hot-tempered for a WASP," I said softly.

"And you're pretty un-PC for a bleeding-heart-type liberal chick," he countered, also smiling.

We kissed. I thought to myself that whatever it was between us that needed to run its course hadn't done so yet—not when I still felt like water on a frying pan every time he kissed me.

I was leaving Family Assistance's offices the next evening, already planning my daily costume change from daytime worker bee to nightlife femme fatale. I wanted to wear something special for Hood, something that would make him proud to have me on his arm. My boss, Daniel, stopped me on the way out to ask if I had any big plans for the night. "I'm on my way to meet my boyfriend," I told him, a little shyly.

"Oh," he said teasingly. "So there's a *boyfriend* now—I didn't realize there was a *boyfriend.*" I laughed and turned my head away so he wouldn't see me blush.

I'd made a strict resolution never to use the B-word in reference to Hood. But, despite my resolution, I couldn't resist saying it to somebody—at least once.

"By the way," Daniel added, "the Bloodmobile is coming tomorrow." He handed me a brochure. "Most of us like to participate."

"Sure," I responded automatically, thinking, *Why do they always want my bodily fluids?* I took a look at the questionnaire in the brochure. It began with the usual stuff: height, weight, general health, HIV status, et cetera. My eyes scrolled down to the "Risk Factors" section.

Have you taken cocaine or any other street drug through your nose in the past 12 months? they wanted to know. *Have you had sexual intercourse with anyone who has taken cocaine or any other street drug in the past 12 months? Have you or anyone you've had recent sexual contact with been in a jail, prison, or detention center for more than 72 consecutive hours in the past 12 months?*

"I think I feel a cold coming on," I told Daniel. "It's probably not a good time for me to donate blood." I smiled ruefully and handed the brochure back, hastily retreating from the office.

TWENTY-TWO

Ambivalence is a hard state of affairs to maintain when it's the driving emotion holding a relationship together. No matter how much you consciously decide to push your uncertainties to the back of your mind, circumstances will eventually conspire to force your hand and make choices inevitable.

The first chinks in the armor of my denial appeared the Saturday afternoon after the blood drive. At Hood's suggestion we had gone to Kafka's, a secondhand bookstore on Washington Avenue. We were poking randomly through the shelves when Hood asked, "Hey, what are you doing tomorrow?"

"Brunch with my parents," I replied.

"Sounds cool," Hood said. "Mind if I come with?"

"Right." I didn't even look up from the well-worn copy of *The Love Machine* that I was flipping through. "We'll make a field trip to the burbs so you can have fun scaring the straights."

"I'm serious." Something in his tone made me look up. "I think it'd be swell to meet your folks."

"No," I said immediately—so immediately that I didn't have time to think of a tactful way to frame my response. The idea of introducing Hood to my parents was so patently preposterous, it could only be dismissed out of hand.

Hood's face darkened. "Are you saying you don't *want* me to meet them?"

"No . . ." I slowly reshelved *The Love Machine* and thought for a moment. What *was* I saying? I took the step of introducing a guy to my parents very seriously. I took *everything* that related to my parents very seriously. I never brought men home who I didn't think might, possibly, be around for the long haul.

On the other hand, Hood had introduced me to his mother. Briefly, and before we were "involved"—but still, I'd met her. If he wanted to meet my parents—and nobody was more surprised than I was that he'd taken up this idea—it seemed like a fair request. And Hood was brilliant; he was a published writer; he'd gone to Yale. I ticked off the good-on-paper justifications, one by one, in my mind.

I tried to picture John Hood in North Miami Beach, having brunch at the Bagel Bar with my parents of a Sunday afternoon—manic, chain-smoking John Hood, in some hepcat suit with his desperado's swagger. It would have been a hilarious thought, if it didn't make my stomach knot up.

My parents didn't even know I *smoked*. At the age of twenty-seven, I still scrupulously avoided so much as uttering a profane word in their presence. But they would take one look at John Hood and know every bad thing I'd done since I'd moved to South Beach. Hood's very brilliance—the speed and nature of it—would be damning evidence against me.

It was unthinkable.

"I'd love for you to meet my parents." The lie was so blatant, my face flamed incriminatingly as I spoke it. "But I haven't seen them in a couple of weeks and I think they want to do the 'quality time' thing."

"Gotcha." Hood put the copy of *The Naked Soul of Iceberg Slim* he'd been fingering back onto the shelf. "I'm going outside for a smoke."

The bell attached to the front door jangled in alarm as Hood loped outside. It had rained a few hours earlier, and there was a yellow, ambient quality to the late-afternoon air.

I had a passing, wistful thought as I watched Hood's retreating back—wondering what it would be like to be some other girl altogether; a girl with a steady job and a boyfriend who got along with her friends, and whose parents beamed complacently when she brought him home.

I had a smorgasbord of good reasons when, a few days later, I set up the dinner with Hood and Ricky. I was tired of fielding Ricky's disapproving remarks, I told myself, and also tired of being involved with someone who had to be cut off from every other aspect of my life. If Hood and Ricky could come to terms, things would be infinitely simpler.

But I also think it was my consolation prize—my attempt at offering something to Hood after having peremptorily refused him access to my parents. Ricky wasn't actually family, but, in my life on South Beach, he was the next best thing.

"You want me to play nice so the bouillon boy can stop stewing?" Hood asked with unnerving insight when I floated this idea. He sounded amused. "Ask his permission and tell him what my intentions are and all that jazz?"

"Oh, for God's sake," I replied, exasperated. "Does everything in our lives need to be a scene from *West Side Story*?"

"All right, all right," Hood said placatingly. "Set it up."

I invited Ricky to join us at Nemo's. "You be nice," I coached both Ricky and Hood—separately, of course—before we all converged. "Please."

Hood and I were waiting at our table when Ricky arrived. He kissed me on the cheek with a subdued "Hello, darling," then turned to Hood and said stiffly, "Hello, John." The elaborate cordiality of his tone was a gauntlet thrown down. Hood, of course, immediately took it up.

"Mr. Nightlight." He clamped his cigarette between his lips and rose to grasp Ricky's hand in both of his own. "Read any good pop-up books lately?"

"Well, I don't have the access to literature that *you* do, John." Ricky's voice was a sugarcoated acid bath. "I hear the prisons have *marvelous* libraries these days."

"Hey, kids," I said sternly. "If you boys can't behave, I'll turn this restaurant around and take everybody straight home."

Nobody laughed.

They say the two things that should never be discussed in polite company are politics and religion. But the only thing worse than the tense silence at that table were the strained attempts at conversation that sporadically burst out. I was desperate for a neutral subject we could all get behind, and I figured that, at the least, everybody at this table would be politically simpatico. So I steered the conversation to the upcoming presidential election. It was at this point that Hood made the rather startling revelation that he was a Republican.

I was flabbergasted. *"Really?"* I said. It was hard to reconcile what I knew of typical Republican conservatism with South Beach generally, or Hood specifically. I couldn't have been more surprised if he'd announced that he was joining the Peace Corps.

"Absolutely." Hood took a deep drag off his cigarette. "I'm a big believer in personal responsibility."

Ricky coughed loudly at this. I threw him a glare that should have burned a hole right through his head.

"I've never dated a Republican before," I remarked—and I knew, *knew*, that I was treading on the worst possible ground, but I was *that* desperate to turn the conversation. I tried to make my voice light and impersonal. "I never saw the point—I mean, if things worked out, what would our kids be?"

"Born addicted to heroin?" Ricky suggested.

I opened my mouth to jump down Ricky's throat, but Hood beat me to the punch. He was leaning back in his chair in a perfectly relaxed, casual way. His manner reflected nothing more than amused curiosity as he asked Ricky, "Got something you wanna say?"

Ricky looked Hood straight in the eye, and I knew he'd been waiting for this opening all night. "You're not good enough for her, Hood." He put slight emphasis on *Hood*. "You know it and I know it, and the only person at this table who doesn't know it is her."

Hood didn't make any of the usual or obvious protestations. He didn't say anything like, *That's for her to decide*, or *Stay out of our lives*, or *You don't know how I feel about her*. Hood didn't say anything at all. He calmly discarded his cigarette in the ashtray, folded his hands in front of him, and looked at me.

I tried to imagine what would happen if some guy, some friend of Hood's, had—in my presence—made a similar observation about me. Hood would've punched the guy's teeth into his throat. And it occurred to me that, perhaps, *I* wasn't good enough for *him*.

I gathered my purse and stood up. Hood stood also. "We have to go," I said quietly. I leaned down to press some money into Ricky's hand and kissed his cheek. "I love you," I told him, looking into his face and silently pleading with him to understand. "I'll call you tomorrow."

Ricky looked resigned. "I love you, too, darling."

The fundraising gala for Family Assistance was drawing ever closer, and the Broadway Nights series was also gearing up for its final show. My days were beyond full as I ran all over town, coordinating gala logistics and investing time at the Colony Theater with Brent and Cindy.

The margin of opportunity between when my workdays ended and Hood's began had narrowed until it was almost nonexistent, and our drug-intake schedules no longer synced up. There's a point, early on in a drug binge, where the drugs make everything sexier. As the high progresses, however, you eventually hit a point where sex is impossible. Or, at least, impossible for the man because he can't perform, and extremely distasteful for the woman—who probably, technically, *could* if she wanted to, but really, *really* doesn't want to. So it happened more frequently that Hood had started his high and was already out the door just as I was getting in from work; by the time he finished working, I was coming down and couldn't stand to be touched.

The weekends were when we made up for lost time. One Saturday in early April, Hood and I were driving around to make our usual score. He directed me over the causeway and I thought, with no small sense of excitement, that we were revisiting our Overtown coke bar. Instead, we ended up in Liberty City (Miami's answer to South Central), in front of a condemned-looking shack in the middle of a lot overgrown with waist-high weeds. A couple of people wandered out, skeletal and bright eyed.

"This is a crack house," I said to Hood. "You're not seriously going in there."

"*We're* going in there." Hood got out of the car and—always unfailingly polite—walked around to open my door. I immediately locked it. I handed him a few twenties, then rolled up the window.

"I'll wait here," I told him.

I waited nervously in the car with the engine running in reverse—so that I could bolt at a moment's notice if the need arose. My nerves were stretched to wire-tautness, and I didn't know if I was more afraid that the cops would show up or that they wouldn't. I had felt safe in the Overtown dive, but this was a different scene altogether.

Hood came out periodically to give me updates, cutting an unlikely figure in that setting. The money had been exchanged, he told me, but somebody had been dispatched to go someplace else to formally collect the goods. I greeted each of these status reports with a curt nod of my head. It was a half-hour before our stash was finally delivered, and I peeled out so fast that I left skid marks as I headed straight for the causeway.

In my peripheral vision, I saw Hood go through the familiar ritual of balancing a small rock in the middle of a piece of foil, using his other hand to center a lighter under it as he held a rolled up bill in his mouth. The sun shone brightly over the causeway; I knew that the goings-on in my car would be plainly visible to any police officer who happened to drive past. I pulled over and parked on the shoulder. Then I killed the engine and turned to face Hood.

"Perhaps it's my fault," I began calmly, "because I never really established any formal ground rules." I paused for breath. "But, just so you know, there is actually NO FREEBASING ALLOWED *IN MY CAR!*"

Hood dutifully put his paraphernalia away. "It's your fault," he informed me. "You were in such a hurry to leave, I didn't get to smoke any there."

"Jesus Christ," I muttered under my breath. I turned the keys in the ignition, put the car in gear, and drove in silence back to the Beach.

"My car has officially become the crack taxi," I told Mike and Kojo the next day. "It's the craxi." Then, in a voice like a PSA announcer, I intoned, *"The craxi: Because friends don't let friends drive drunk—to buy crack."*

"I thought you said he smoked heroin," Mike said.

I gestured helplessly. "Does it even matter anymore?"

We laughed about the incident, but it rankled. What did it mean that Hood had taken me to that place? What could he possibly think of me? I was spoiling for a fight.

I turned up at Will's apartment a few nights later at around eight o'clock. Will was nowhere to be found and Hood was on the couch. From the smell of the room, I could tell he had just smoked a portion of his stash.

I sat down next to him and did a couple of lines on the coffee table. High and happy from my workday, I slid closer and nibbled his ear suggestively.

He pushed me away—gently, but I thought I detected a certain amount of annoyance in the gesture. "I don't feel like making love now."

My hands shook slightly, and I pulled a cigarette from the pack on the table to cover. I lit it and inhaled deeply. "*Making love?*" I mocked. "Is that what you think we do?"

Hood's eyes focused on me more sharply. "What?"

"I thought we were *fucking*." I laughed pityingly and stroked the side of his face. "Poor Hood—I had no idea you were such a fragile flower."

Hood's face flickered. I felt a wild, triumphant thrill in the knowledge that I had, possibly for the first time, provoked an uncontrolled reaction in him. Then Hood rose slowly to his feet. There was a quick, nervous leap in my chest and, instinctively, I turned to avoid his gaze.

"The cats at Crobar are waiting," he finally said. He smoothed out his coat, pocketing his cigarettes and keys. "I'll walk you down."

"I can give you a ride if you want," I offered quickly.

"No, thanks," Hood replied, just as quickly.

We walked downstairs and he put me in my car, kissing me lightly on the cheek. "I'll call you later," he said, and closed the car door behind me.

I drove over to Kojo's. "Rachel Baum," he said through the speaker on the downstairs gate, sounding surprised. I walked up the stairs and hugged him. He was buttoning up a shirt and looked like he was dressing to go out.

"Did I catch you at a bad time?" I asked. "I can go if you're headed out."

"It's never a bad time for those boobs," he said. "Let me just go finish getting dressed."

I put down my purse and keys, and spotted some lines laid out on the kitchen counter. *Why not?* I thought. I bent my head over the counter, then recoiled at the burning sensation in my nostril. "Dammit!" I exclaimed. "What the hell is wrong with your coke?"

Kojo walked back into the living room, looking amused. "That's not coke," he informed me. "That's crystal."

"Uch!" I rubbed my nose vengefully. I suddenly felt very, very jittery. "Now I *know* you're going out." I paused. "Actually, now that I think about it, where are you going and how come I didn't know you were going there?"

Kojo rolled his eyes and I grinned impishly. He went into the kitchen and made us each a screwdriver. "So, really, what's with the drive-by? Are you okay?"

"I'm fine." I took a long swallow from my glass. "It's just that Hood's not going to call later and I don't want to be home for it."

Hood still hadn't called by Friday, which was the night of Cindy and Brent's final show at the Colony Theater. Brent had arrived in town earlier in the week to prepare for the event, and had fallen into the habit of treating Ricky and me to cocktails at Pacific Time or dinner at Joe Allen at the end of our workday. Brent Carrigan was proving to be a bad influence—one cocktail would inevitably turn into four or five, until I was practically staggering home at the end of the excursion.

The night before the show, Brent brought us to a small barbecue hosted by Lee Schrager on a rooftop deck at the InterContinental. The sky was darkening with clouds, and there was a threat of rain in the light gust that blew up from Biscayne Bay as we sat at a small table and chatted. "So what do you think about Evan Graham?" Brent said. "He's cute, huh?"

Evan Graham was the scheduled star of Broadway Nights' closing show, and we'd been hanging posters bearing his image and sending out his publicity photos for days. Having spent the past week knee-deep in Evan Graham promotion, I was by now very familiar with all things Evan Graham-related. Evan was Australian but he lived in New York, where he had just come off a starring turn in Les Miz. Evan was heralded by the New York press as one of the brightest young talents to come along in years. And, yes, Evan was cute. In fact, the word "cute" didn't do him justice: He was glossy-haired, blue-eyed, chiseled-cheekbones perfection.

"He's *beautiful*," Ricky said. I nodded an enthusiastic agreement.

"And he's straight." Brent's eyes gleamed mischievously in my direction.

"That's disappointing," I glummed. "I was totally hoping he could be my new gay BFF who was also a big gorgeous Broadway star."

"You can still be *friends* with him," Ricky said.

"Please." My nose wrinkled distastefully. "Any straight guy who's *that* talented and *that* good-looking has to be insufferable." I smiled at Brent. "No offense," I added. "I'm sure he's a dream to work with."

"Well," Brent said, "I told him all about you, and he's *dying* to meet you."

"What'd you tell him?" My voice was wary.

"I told him you were beautiful and fun and everybody on the Beach loves you." Brent sipped his martini as I rolled my eyes and colored slightly. *Definitely not everybody*, I thought. "And that you were single."

Ricky glanced over at me, but I remained silent. Brent, of course, knew nothing about Hood and undoubtedly thought he was stirring up all kinds of fun trouble by throwing me together with Evan Graham.

"I was hoping you guys could take him out tomorrow night after the show," Brent said now.

I groaned inwardly; I'd meant what I'd said about being positive that Evan would prove unbearably obnoxious. But Brent had been very good to Ricky and me; the least I could do was spend one night entertaining the star of his closing show.

"We'd be happy to." I turned to Ricky. "What do we have tomorrow night?"

"We're supposed to go to that party at Portofino," Ricky replied.

"Looks like Evan Graham couldn't have picked a better night to be in town," I said sunnily.

Evan was even better-looking in person than in his publicity photo, and his show had been phenomenal. In between numbers, he'd made warm and humorous commentary—and talked extensively about Julie, his fiancée back in New York. This, at least, had relieved any pressure I'd felt in thinking that our post-show outing was a setup.

But, rather than being the unbearable bore offstage I'd been anticipating, Evan had turned out to be attentive, charming, and possibly one of the funniest men I'd ever met. We were also joined by Jonathan, his pianist, who was gay, cute, and seemed exceedingly polite. I had high hopes that he and Ricky would hit it off.

"So tell me about your fiancée," I'd said, as the four of us hustled into a waiting cab. "I could use a good love story."

"Yes," he'd answered very seriously, "I do love her." Then he'd shifted his manner of speaking entirely, to the rushed and quiet tone of an announcer voicing-over nasty side effects in a drug commercial. *"Warning: Speaker is emotionally manipulative; may not refer to actual 'love'; please consult your therapist for details."*

That had gotten the first laugh. When I'd calmed down, I said, "Ah, I think I know that type; I dated a rabbi who should've come with a warning label."

His gaze took in the form-hugging, scoop-necked, black and gold gown I was wearing. "*You* dated a rabbi?"

"Well, he was also a psychologist," I replied, "which was actually very convenient. That way, he could totally judge and condemn my entire lifestyle, and then we could talk about how that made me feel."

Now I had him laughing. "What did he say during sex?" He affected an aggressive, grunting tone. *"Who's your rabbi, baby? Who's your rabbi?!"*

The two of us were off and running, and within a half-hour we were laughing and chatting as comfortably as if we'd been the best of friends for years. "So tell me," he whispered in the cab, "about this party we're going to tonight."

"I'm afraid I can't tell you anything about the guy who's throwing it. What's his name again, Ricky?"

"Oh, I don't know, darling." Ricky brushed some lint from his jacket, his careless tone clearly informing us that nothing was more pedestrian than knowing the man whose party you were attending. "He's some dot-com gazillionaire who just bought a place down here. He wants to get to know people and he had Susan Brustman put together a guest list for him." Susan Brustman was a local PR whiz.

I was unable to give Evan specifics about our host, but the legend behind the location and the man who'd built it was among the best on South Beach. Portofino Tower was a forty-four-story luxury high-rise at the very tip of the island, and had been the source of one of the most bitter real-estate battles in South Beach history. The brainchild of commodities-broker-turned-real-estate-kingpin Thomas Kramer, it had been protested loudly by the then-residents, who feared that such a tall tower in that location would block the majestic views of the ocean that lent the Beach much of its charm.

Thomas Kramer was a German real-estate developer in his early forties, a large, blond specimen of a man, and he had a personal history that made John Hood look like a kindergarten teacher. He'd spent fifty million dollars on a large chunk of the land south of 5th Street back in the early '90s, and he had entered the social scene as the proverbial wolf in wolf's clothing with his infamous nightclub Hell, which had opened in 1992. Over the course of the next few years, Thomas Kramer had run-ins with the police throughout Europe and Miami, on allegations ranging from bar brawls and various sexual assaults to the alleged beating of the owner of a quiet South Miami trattoria (where Kramer had been asked to extinguish his cigar), and one memorable instance at a South Beach restaurant, when he was accused of throwing a glass of wine in the face of a homeless man panhandling near his table.

But the best story about Thomas Kramer was the bitterly contested battle for the right to build Portofino Tower. A political firestorm had convulsed the Beach, resulting in protests and referendums and newly formed PACs that sprang up for the specific purpose of blocking his request.

As it happened, many of those on the city council most strongly opposed to him were Jewish—a fact that would be irrelevant to this story, except that when Thomas Kramer had finally, *finally* won permission to build his beloved Portofino, he hadn't been content to be a gracious winner. Four smaller towers had been erected high on top of the structure—so prominent and so high that you couldn't miss them from any vantage point on the Beach—and people said they had been specifically designed to look like the guard towers at Auschwitz.

I, of course, could neither personally confirm nor deny this rumor—except to say that, to my own untrained eyes, the towers atop Portofino did bear a suspicious resemblance to the guard towers in question.

Tonight was the first time I'd ever entered Portofino Tower, and I had to admit to being curious as to what the penthouse of this überexpensive monolith would look like. At close to 7,500 square feet, it was a breathtaking marvel of marble, floor-to-ceiling glass windows, wraparound terraces, sunken Jacuzzi bathtubs, and a magnificent pool. Assorted beautiful people occupied the space, sprawling with studied disaffection on white suede couches or posing with sultry detachment before the dramatic windows and their even more dramatic views of the ocean, Biscayne Bay, and Downtown Miami.

"You and I are in the wrong business," I told Ricky, looking around. "This guy is *our* age?"

"He's twenty-nine, I think," Ricky replied. I made a *geesh!* face.

The four of us helped ourselves to the champagne and canapés distributed by the passing waiters, then made our way out to one of the terraces. A breeze wove through my dress, although the air was starting to turn infinitesimally warmer—a signal to all of us SoBe old-timers that spring would soon be melting into summer.

The setting was elegant and the liquor flowed, but something about the party never quite gelled. It is, perhaps, inevitable that a party thrown by a man who doesn't know any of his guests will feel a little dry and restrained. People formed small clumps comprised of those they'd come with, speaking in tones somewhat more subdued than was the wont at South Beach parties.

Evan and I struck up a lively conversation, interrupted only by the constant non-sequiturs regarding Julie that Evan's pianist Jonathan felt obliged to interject. "Julie laughed so hard the first time you told that story," he would say, or, "Julie loves that shirt on you."

"I love that scent you're wearing," Evan said to me at one point. "Is that jasmine?"

Before I could reply in the affirmative, Jonathan jumped in with, "Doesn't Julie wear jasmine oil?"

It took me every ounce of social training to keep from rolling my eyes. "Would you excuse me for a minute?" I said instead. I walked over to where Ricky was talking with David Hart Lynch, the latest nightlife columnist for the *Wire*, who obligingly took our picture. But my head wasn't in the conversation. I drifted a couple of feet away and leaned over the balcony railing. A soft, cocktail-party samba played inside. *Dime ingrato . . . por que me abandonaste . . . y sola me dejaste . . .*

The unmistakable scent of saltwater wafted upward. *The air is redolent of salt*, I thought, remembering that long-ago night in my car with Hood. Looking down, I could almost make out the tiny speck that used to be the parking lot we'd inhabited that night.

Ricky kissed David Lynch good-bye and came up to put his hand on my back. "How are you feeling?"

"Very upwardly mobile." I smiled brightly. "I've made it from a crack house to the penthouse in the span of a week."

"*This* is where you belong," Ricky said firmly. "Not running around the ghetto with that hoodlum."

I looked out over the ocean. There was a ship on the horizon, a tiny smudge of light separating the dark sky from the darker water. I wondered if it was a freighter, or maybe a cruise ship full of travelers on their way to the tropics. The beauty of travel, I thought, was that as long as you were in motion, you would never have to think about if or where you belonged. "I don't know where I belong anymore," I said aloud. "I feel like I have all these different lives that don't mesh."

"Maybe something could mesh with Evan?" It was a question, and he glanced meaningfully over at Evan, still talking with Jonathan, as he asked it.

"Maybe." I sighed. "If Captain Cock-Block over there would shut his yaphole." As if he knew we were talking about him, Jonathan looked over. I smiled sweetly and waved at him before turning back to Ricky. The two of us laughed.

"He's just a jealous queen," Ricky said. "I can try to distract him if you want."

"Thanks, Mata Hari," I replied, "but that's not necessary. I don't want to fall into bed with some guy passing through town as a way of resolving things with Hood."

It wasn't what Ricky wanted to hear, but he was gracious enough not to contradict me. Instead, he declared, "This party's boring. Let's grab those guys and go someplace else."

We rounded up Evan and Jonathan, and the four of us cabbed over to 821. The cool-kid set was out in full force, reveling in the last throes of Season. The crowd at the bar was three deep, and, once Crispy had given us our cocktails, there wasn't a single square inch of available real estate. So we went upstairs to the tiny loft where the DJ booth was set up and had our drinks with DJ Shannon. We called Mike and Kojo, and they walked up Lincoln Road to join

us. With the uncanny perspicacity of men who like men, they immediately
sized up the situation and joined with Ricky in triple-teaming Jonathan in a
silent conspiracy to give me a clear shot at Evan.

The two of us leaned, side by side, over the low wall of the loft that opened
onto the space below, half shouting to be heard over the music. "So what's your
story?" he asked. "Do you have a boyfriend? You must have a boyfriend."

I lit a cigarette and watched the smoke undulate over the heads of the
partiers below us. "There's a guy, but . . . I don't know." I dropped the matches
into my handbag. "It wasn't really working out, I guess, and we had a fight a few
days ago and haven't spoken since."

Evan nodded understandingly. "Sounds like you should be seeing other
people."

I cocked my head to one side and allowed my mouth to bend into a half
smile. "Are you making me an offer?"

We looked at each other a beat longer than necessary. Then we both
laughed, and Evan playfully shoved his shoulder against mine.

There was a part of me that regretted the missed opportunity. The bigger
truth, though, was that I suddenly understood how much I missed Hood. Evan
was handsome and talented and funny, to boot . . . but he wasn't John Hood.

The evening ended chastely with a good-night peck on the cheek. Two
days later I received a package in the mail containing an ornately stunning
silver necklace from Brent Carrigan. It held nine or ten semiprecious stones
the size of golf balls, in various colors, and came with a matching set of
earrings.

Thanks for all your hard work on Broadway Nights, the card read. *I bought
this in Istanbul and can't think of anybody it would look better on. xoxo, BC.*

The Family Assistance Organization fundraising gala was held at the Miami
Beach Botanical Garden—a lush and lovely spot not far from the convention
center. It also wasn't far from Will's apartment. It had been nearly two
weeks since I'd spoken with Hood; I'd thought of calling him many times,
of apologizing, but something had always held me back. *Let him call me*, I
would think.

As I was in my car headed home after the event, however, I passed the turnoff to Will's apartment and had an abrupt change of heart. It was early, not even midnight yet. Hood might still be home before heading out for the evening. *I could swing by and say hello*, I thought. Somebody, after all, had to make the first move. And the breach between us was undoubtedly more my fault than his.

There was an odd feeling of both familiarity and strangeness as I parked my car and trekked up the staircase to Will's apartment. I rang the bell and heard footsteps echoing inside. Will was barefooted when he answered the door, wearing a T-shirt and shorts. His air was one of surprise.

"Hey!" I said cheerfully. I winced a little at my overeager tone. "Is Hood around?"

A week later, when he got his bank statement, Will would learn that Hood had forged a couple of his checks to the tune of about two hundred dollars. But Will didn't know that yet—he only knew that I was the last person he'd expected to find on his doorstep, and his face showed his confusion. "No, he's in Chicago."

Chicago . . . The unexpected word echoed in my head. My voice caught a little as I asked, "Do you know when he's coming back?"

Will's eyes softened into an expression of understanding and pity. The absolute certainty of what he was about to say struck me with the swift pain of an electric shock.

I hated Hood in that moment—hated him with such vicious, stabbing intensity that I hoped, wherever he was, he would fall down dead.

"He's not coming back. The guys from Crobar moved him out there."

That Saturday, Ricky, Kojo, Mike, and I went to a memorial for our friend Justin. Justin had been a regular on the party scene and had died of AIDS a week earlier. In addition to the formal funeral, Justin had requested a sunrise memorial on the beach. Six fifteen a.m. saw the four of us standing with a host of other mourners, sunglasses donned against the glare of the sun rising over the pale blue water.

The group around us was large and eclectic. Justin had been a drag queen, and there were a legion of drag queens in attendance—some in full drag and others who it was almost impossible to recognize in their ordinary street clothes. Justin's mother stood in the center of a small knot of family and close friends, and the rest of us stretched out from this axis at irregular intervals, the way a flock of seagulls arranges itself seemingly at random along a pier.

Small memorial booklets were passed our way. There were photos of Justin in and out of drag, a few nicely turned-out essays written by his closer friends, and some poetry that Justin himself had written before he died. On the last page was the Twenty-third Psalm. The familiar words had the smoothness of polished stones in my mouth: *The Lord is my shepherd, I shall not want . . .*

A few people spoke and then the group quietly dispersed, like strangers who gather together at an amusement park and drive home in separate cars at the end of the day.

"At my funeral," I said, "I want them to play 'I'm Every Woman.'" I took off my sunglasses and cleaned them against my black silk tank top. "The Chaka Khan version, not the Whitney Houston version." I pointed at Ricky and added, "I'm putting you in charge."

We all laughed, but the laughter was uneasy. *Any one of us*, we were thinking. *It could be any one of us. . . .*

"Let's get some breakfast," Kojo said. "How about the Diner?"

We all subtly recoiled from the idea. The 11th Street Diner, with its usual sunrise crowd of coming-down club kids and revelers, felt wrong.

"How about Denny's?" Ricky suggested. "I could go for the Moons Over My Hammy."

I rolled my eyes affectionately. "Ah, the siren song of the Moons Over My Hammy—seductive enough to lure even Mr. Nightclub into the plebeian recesses of Denny's."

The sun was shining in earnest now, with a hard, hot intensity. I put my sunglasses back on as the four of us walked through the bright sand toward Kojo's car.

TWENTY-THREE

South Beach summers are always rainy, but the rains came down especially hard that summer. Standing on my balcony, I'd watch the thunderstorms over the ocean while they were still miles away—thinking that the height of my building gave me a fortune-teller's advantage in knowing when and for how long the skies overhead would finally darken.

But the rain offered little respite from the stagnant heat that covered South Beach like an electric blanket missing an off button. Those of the locals who were in a position to do so left on short or extended vacations. Greg and Nicole Brier asked Ricky and me to spend part of the summer with them in the Hamptons, saying, "We'd love to have Mr. and Mrs. Nightclub at Jet East." Christina Getty invited us to her family's estate in South Africa. Ricky and I never felt our poverty more strongly than when we had to turn down these invitations—we were working stiffs, after all, no matter how wealthy some of our friends might be. For us, there was still work to pursue and money to chase after, and we couldn't afford to "summer" anywhere except right where we were.

People drifted in and out of town, in what I had come to realize was the perpetual life cycle of South Beach. There was a party at Liquid—either a going-away or a welcome-back, I couldn't keep track of which—for famed doorman Gilbert Stafford. Kevin Crawford moved to New York and Adrina moved back from New York, and we knew better than to ask what had become of the boyfriend she'd gone up there with. Adam also returned from his extended sojourn to God-knew-where; when I ran into him by chance one day at Score on Lincoln Road, I hugged him with the enthusiasm one usually reserves for a long-lost brother.

The South Beach Bistro closed, replaced by a bar-cum-nightclub called Squeeze. A new addition to the scenester circuit called Lola mushroomed up on

23rd Street, not far from Groove Jet. Lola was a dark, candlelit cavern, which pulled off the enviable feat of being simultaneously chill and chic. It featured a stylishly sleek bar, ubiquitous black candelabras, and large, comfy white beds scattered throughout the space. It was reminiscent of the semibohemian days before the megaclubs straddled the Beach.

Tuesday and Thursday nights usually saw us at Lola. We spent Friday nights poolside at the Albion for Alan Roth's Magic Garden party. A sultry, sexy little spot called Nikki Beach Club had opened in the Penrod's complex way on the tip of the island, finally giving the locals a reason to spend quality time south of 5th Street. Another tucked-away nook called Laundry Bar had opened behind Lincoln Road on Lincoln Lane—the relative obscurity of the location ensuring that the locals would always be able to find each other, far from the madding crowds of tourists who populated our shores during Season.

A Regal Cinemas multiplex also opened on Lincoln Road that summer. There was an undoubted convenience to having a mainstream theater on the Beach—before this, we'd had to trek out to the Byron Carlisle, way up on 71st Street, whenever we wanted to see a major studio release. Yet I couldn't help sensing that the nature of the Beach was changing. The Loews Hotel Corporation had opened the first convention hotel on South Beach—complete with conference facilities and several gigantic ballrooms—on a level of gorgeous grandeur evocative of the Fontainebleau and Eden Roc heyday. Huge high-rise apartment towers were suddenly springing up all over town, as if by the hand of a hyperactive child with too many Erector sets. Hot on the heels of the Regal multiplex came the Gap and a Pottery Barn on Lincoln Road. Some of the longtime mom-and-pop shops were being squeezed out—it was even rumored that 821 wouldn't be able to afford their rent much longer, and the idea of a Lincoln Road without an 821 was unimaginable.

At Mike's insistence, I ended up seeing the *South Park* movie four times in the Regal multiplex over the summer. I wondered, sometimes, if I oughtn't limit my patronage on principle, offering at least token resistance to the changes that threatened to turn Lincoln Road into any other mall in the country. But it was so easy to be seduced on those long, hot days by the clean, soft stadium seats, and the voluptuous chill of air-conditioning on sunburned skin.

My favorite Lincoln Road tradition by far was the antique fair, held every other Sunday afternoon, and I shopped it religiously. There was a real pleasure to be found in haggling over random odds and ends with the vendors, whose desperation always mounted as the heat of the day and the threat of thunderstorms progressed. I bought inexpensive lamps and tchotchkes and a couple of end tables—and slowly my apartment took on the "grown-up" character that Lara had referred to once.

I would frequently invite my mother on these jaunts, and we finally found something we could genuinely bond over. "Your Aunt Elaine used to have a lamp just like that one," she would tell me, or, "These look like the candlesticks your grandparents gave your father and me when we were first married." She would point out landmarks and businesses that had existed on the Beach since at least her own childhood, and I picked up tidbits of family and South Beach history as I pawed through the secondhand jewelry and handbags that I intended to incorporate into my look during the upcoming Season.

We ran into Brent Carrigan, who usually spent a couple of weeks during the summer in his South Beach home, on one of these expeditions. Introducing my mother to the man who had directed Barbra Streisand was one of my great South Beach moments. "I'm a big fan of your daughter's," Brent said, as the two of them shook hands. My mother didn't pay any particular attention to this compliment (of course he was a big fan of mine—who was anybody *not* to be a fan of her daughter's?). But as soon as Brent departed, I turned to her with my eyes as wide as saucers and exclaimed, "Do you know who he *is*?"

After leaving the antique market, I would usually meet up with Mike at WAMI's studios and head over to Kojo's apartment with him—that is, on the nights when we could find Kojo. Lately, he'd started going off on solitary forays, the nature of which he didn't care to share. Mike darkly mentioned the words "crystal" and "bathhouses" a few times but declined to say anything more.

Mike was working constantly, even on Sundays, struggling to keep *The Times* afloat. WAMI had, by now, pulled the plug on all of their original programming except for *The Times*. The rest of their schedule was filled in with basketball games, or marathon sessions of *M*A*S*H* and *Charlie's Angels* reruns.

The Times seemed safe for the moment, but Mike couldn't help wondering if and when they'd pull the plug on that, too.

As for me, I was still putting in a few hours a week with Family Assistance, laying the groundwork for their upcoming season of fundraisers while I tried to figure out my next move. I was driving home from their offices one day in June when I got a call from Lydia Birdsong on my cell.

"Hello, swee-tie." Her Australian accent made *sweetie* sound like two separate and emphatic words. I assumed she was calling to offer me work on that island culture movie she'd mentioned at Celebrity Club, which we'd discussed intermittently ever since. Instead she said, "I'm in a bit of a jam and I'm hoping you can help."

"Of course," I said automatically. "What's up?"

"I need to borrow a thousand dollars," she replied. "I'm about to be evicted from my apartment."

Lydia had invited me to a dinner party in her apartment only a month earlier, a small one-bedroom in one of the authentic Deco buildings. The kitchen had checkered black-and-white tiles, the furnishings were a rich mélange of items she'd collected all over the world, and her ceiling featured a mural painted by a local artist named Aaron. Aaron himself had been at the dinner. He'd played the role of impromptu cohost, and Lydia had served huge platters of smoked hors d'oeuvres and spicy South American dishes. Hearing now that she was about to lose the apartment was like hearing that the friend you'd seen yesterday had just died.

"I wish I could," I said ruefully. "I really do. But I don't have that kind of money." I was silent for a moment. "I'm trying to think who else you could ask."

She rattled off a few names of other people she had made her request to. Ricky's name was among them, and I knew then how doomed her quest would be—Ricky had hired an attorney to begin bankruptcy proceedings on his behalf only a week earlier. Even with his column, his steady day job, and all the freebies we received, the expense of his condo had finally become too much for him. He was giving it up and moving into a small studio in the Grand Flamingo—a two-tower megacomplex (nicknamed "the Death Star" by Kojo on account of its enormity) only three blocks from my own building.

Lydia eventually lost her apartment, moving in with a friend and getting a job at Moondance through Kojo. The next time Ricky and I saw her was the night of Enrique Colon's runway show at the school he attended, South Pointe Middle. The Beach was half-full at best in the last weeks of summer, but the audience was studded with the familiar faces of SoBe's year-round glitterati. We greeted Lydia, and also Isabella and Finn, who were saving seats for us, and posed for pictures shot by Glenn Albin and Iran Issa-Kahn. The front rows held Enrique's family, as well as Niki Taylor and fashion press from places like *Vogue* and *Marie Claire*. I doubted that South Pointe Middle had ever seen a more glamorous crowd.

Multicolored spotlights had been set up next to rows of metal folding chairs beneath the canopy of an ancient oak tree, which was speckled with twinkle lights. The chairs faced the catwalk that had sprung up for the models to strut down.

It was fun to watch the spectacle of it all—the "models," preteen class-mates of Enrique's, clearly loved the attention. They put their hands on their hips, pausing and thrusting their sharp little hipbones out with a rehearsed self-consciousness as the DJ played "The Rockafeller Skank" and the audience tittered affectionately. The clothes were wild and colorful, and when Enrique walked out with the models at the end of the show, bowing and beaming, his young face was flushed with pride.

We stayed around afterward and made the obligatory small talk—indeed, South Beach fashion shows were generally only a pretext for the socializing that inevitably followed. But the humidity lay on our skins like damp fur, and even the most artfully made-up faces wilted. There was a reason, Ricky and I sagely agreed, why these outdoor events were almost never held during the summer.

We couldn't leave before we'd kissed and congratulated Enrique. "This was all so beautiful," I said sincerely as I hugged him. I was rewarded with the brightest smile I'd seen in ages.

I was starting to wonder, though, what I was supposed to make of a town where a thirteen-year-old could have a high-profile fashion career, while people like Ricky and Lydia couldn't keep roofs over their heads.

Not that I was in much better shape. My stint with Family Assistance was nearing its close, and I was approaching the now familiar wall of unemployment. Standing there among the flash and flashbulbs, I thought, *What's going to happen to me?*

It was Ricky who, in mid-July, told me about BeachLife.com, one of a handful of dot-coms that were, at long last, springing up around South Beach. The only surprising thing was that it had taken so long for an industry based largely on hype, speculation, and fast cash to lay claim to South Beach—or "Silicon Beach," as we came to style ourselves.

BeachLife.com had taken up office space at the western end of Lincoln Road, requisitioning the old MTV Latino offices. Having just received a fresh round of funding, they were rapidly expanding, and their marketing department was short one director of event marketing.

I wanted that job as soon as I walked in for the interview. The office was a workplace wonderland of walls painted in primary-colored zigzags and bright, Kodachrome-colored furniture. Employees bustled around in jeans or funky little sundresses, and there wasn't a single face that appeared to be over thirty years old. I wanted the job even before I heard how high the salary would be (it was high), or about the stock options—which would vest in some incomprehensible formula explained in the literature I was given to take home. I was made to understand that when the company announced its IPO (another perplexing term), these options would make me rich—or, at least, permanently solvent—overnight.

They took a look at the final report that I'd put together on the FACTS Train, detailing all the work I'd done for the launch, and they wanted me, too. When they called to offer me the job two days later, I floated along in a cloud of bliss that carried me for weeks. Dot-com, as everybody knew, was the best business to be in these days. Even my parents, finally and for once, had nothing but praise when I gave them the news.

The job at BeachLife.com marked the beginning of a new era for me. For the first time in years, I was in a position to speak about my job in terms of its being a career. I was a "young professional" again, associating with other young professionals. I formed workplace friendships with some of the other women in the office, heading out with them into Miami's more corporate bars—places in Coral Gables or along Brickell Avenue—where I had gone with Eduard and the Leadership Miami crowd in my pre-South Beach days.

I saw Eduard himself in one of these bars, one day in August. The shock I felt upon spotting him wasn't the shock of feeling, but rather the shock of feeling so much less than I'd expected when I'd pictured the moment in my mind.

He walked over and we exchanged pleasantries. "I almost didn't recognize you," he said with a smile. "You look so different."

I smiled back. "And you look exactly the same."

We chatted aimlessly for a couple of minutes—my parents' new car, his sister's new baby—before he rejoined his friends and left. I had shared every day of my life with this man for almost four years, I was thinking; now we were hardly more to each other than strangers in a bar. It didn't make me sad, exactly, but it did make me wonder how much I'd changed since I'd left his house—or how much, as Amy had prophesied long ago, I'd simply become more of what I always had been.

I wasn't sure how well I fit in anymore with this professional crowd that Eduard and I had once been a part of. I felt morbidly self-conscious in the tighter clothes I'd become accustomed to wearing; none of the men on South Beach, gay or straight, ogled the chest I'd come to think of as a prop with as much persistence, or serious intent, as the men I met on the other side of the causeway. And, in casual conversations over cocktails or on first dates, I found myself stymied by such simple questions as *What do you do for fun?* or *What was your last boyfriend like?*

"I can tell you have a good soul, just by your eyes," a would-be suitor observed on one occasion.

"Oh, *that* pesky old thing?" I'd responded, with a quick, dismissive wave of my hand. "I traded that *years* ago for these fabulous breasts!" When he remained momentarily nonplussed, I'd added, "I'm sorry—it's just that whenever men talk about my eyes, I naturally assume they're referring to my breasts."

Mike and Kojo laughed long and loud at this story when I repeated it at Ricky's late-August birthday party, which was hosted by Alan Roth at Magic Garden. There had been a Mr. Nightclub birthday party committee this year and—when I understood that my responsibilities as a committee member would consist of nothing more than allowing my name to be printed on the invitations—I'd happily agreed to be a part of it. We watched as Ricky and Alan attended to the receiving line that had formed, the stack of gifts next to them growing larger and larger.

"See, *you* guys laughed," I said in frustration. "It's like I don't even know how to talk to regular straight guys anymore. I feel like Dian Fossey in *Gorillas in the Mist*—like maybe if I sit very quietly and don't make any sudden movements, they'll accept me as one of their own."

"You're too much for them, darling," Kojo said.

"I wish you guys would stop telling me that," I replied, even more frustrated. "Didn't we all assume that I'd eventually find a guy who wasn't part of the club scene and move on from all this?" They were silent. "Well, didn't we?"

"You mean, move on from us," Mike said flatly. He looked hurt.

"No!" I was genuinely shocked. "Of *course* not. That's not what I meant at all." I took Mike's hand. "It's just that . . ."

It's just that I don't want to end up with another John Hood, was what I wanted to say. But I hadn't spoken his name to anybody since the day he'd left.

I decided to change the subject. "So, tell me about this party tomorrow night that I'm not allowed to come to." I was referring to Ricky's second birthday party—a "boys only" party to be held in Kojo's loft. "I bet it's an orgy, isn't it?"

"God, I hope not." Kojo's voice sounded resigned. "I don't want to get stuck cleaning fag out of the upholstery for the next two weeks."

My tone was dry as I observed, "You can feel free *not* to say that to the next straight man I bring around."

It was early October when I went to New York for my first big Internet conference. I found myself falling in love that week—as so many had before me—with New York's size and pulse and casual frenzy. Brent Carrigan got me house seats to a Broadway show, Michael Tronn hooked me up with VIP access to a West Village hotspot called Life, and, in between work commitments and money's-no-object industry parties, I visited museums and bookstores and trendy boutiques in SoHo.

I also got to spend some quality time with Lara, who met me for cocktails after a hard day of conventioneering. Lara was navigating her own romantic difficulties, having abruptly split with her boyfriend of nearly three years. Almost nothing that anybody did surprised me anymore, but if there was one thing I'd always counted on, it was the sunny solidity of Lara's life.

"What *happened*?" I asked, when she broke the news. I was so shocked that I almost forgot to be sympathetic.

"We were talking about getting married," she replied, "and he said he wasn't sure. I told him that not being sure after three years wasn't good enough." There was only the faintest quaver in Lara's voice—and you'd have to know her pretty well to hear it—when she continued, "So I left."

"Wow." I marveled at the strength of her resolve, suspecting that I wouldn't be able to demonstrate that kind of fortitude under similar circumstances.

"You should think about moving to New York," Lara said, in what was now an official leitmotif in our conversations. "There are way more career options, and we could be single together in the same city for the first time since college."

There was something undeniably tempting in the idea. To be single with Lara, the two of us running around a city as big and exciting as New York, was a notion that played enticingly in my imagination.

But I knew in my heart that I had unfinished business in South Beach. Besides, I was a Miami girl. Miami Beach had been my family's home for almost as long as there had been a Miami Beach. *Whatever it is, I am too,* I would think. And I never stopped to analyze what that meant.

TWENTY-FOUR

It was Ricky who decreed that my twenty-eighth birthday couldn't be allowed to pass in the low-key fashion with which I typically celebrated my birthdays. "You should have a party this year," he told me. "Something with invitations and presents and the whole works."

"I don't know," I replied. "I don't feel right about asking a club to do something for me—especially since I'm not doing the radio show with you anymore." I kept my other concern to myself, since it was hard to articulate exactly, but it went something like: *I don't want to make myself that big of a target.*

We finally compromised on a mellow cocktail reception at a bar called Blue on Española Way, one of our favorite new hangouts. As the name would imply, the entirety of the smallish space was resplendent in deep, cool blues, and they drew a mostly local crowd. Since DJ Shannon spun at Blue on Thursdays, we decided to hold the party the Thursday right before my birthday. I bribed one of the graphic designers in my office to lay out a simple invitation and dropped it off with a printer on Washington Avenue.

Later that same day, I got a call at my office from Alan Roth. I couldn't tell if he was genuinely angry or just playing the bit for humor when he demanded, "Why are you having a birthday party on a Thursday night—and I had to hear about it *from my printer?*"

Alan had, by this time, migrated from the Tommy Pooch fold at Chaos and joined the Chris-and-Ingrid contingency at Bar Room, their latest enterprise on Lincoln Road. The space had been star-studded from the outset, drawing the likes of Samuel L. Jackson, Gwyneth Paltrow, and even—on one memorable occasion—Robert De Niro. Jennifer Lopez had been spied there one night, dancing with such reckless frenzy that her tube top had fallen down. Alan promoted a party in Bar Room's VIP on Thursday nights that Ricky and I usually made a point of attending, at least briefly.

"I—" I hesitated. Was he really upset? "I didn't want to impose on you," I concluded uncertainly.

Alan sounded mollified as he said, "You'll have it at Bar Room. I'll give you the VIP area in the back, five bottles of champagne, and a few bottles of vodka. And I'll take care of printing and mailing the invites."

"That's very sweet of you, Alan," I said, "but it truly isn't necessary."

"It's done," Alan replied firmly. "I already had the printer change the invitations."

I used my outrageous new salary to buy an extravagant new dress for my first big birthday party, a wildly expensive and wispy concoction—made of black sequins and netting—that was practically only half a dress. My friend Keith, a hairstylist and makeup artist, came to my apartment as soon as I left work to do my hair and makeup, his birthday gift to me. I looked every inch the after-dark diva as I stepped into a cab at eleven o'clock and headed to Bar Room, where Kojo, Mike, and Ricky were waiting outside.

It was still early, but the line in front of Bar Room was already around the block. *Fabrizio! Fabrizio!* people cried anxiously, trying to get the attention of doorman Fabrizio Brienza. Their eyes shot daggers at the four of us as we were warmly hugged and kissed by Fabrizio, who pulled back the velvet rope to let us pass.

Bar Room was a large cube, with a good-sized dance floor in the middle flanked by bars on either side. The decor was a palette of warm and elegant neutrals, highlighted by recessed lighting and two enormous crystal chandeliers that dangled over the room. We headed straight for VIP in the back where there was a separate velvet rope, along with a stoic bouncer in attendance.

The night was something of a blur. Mike presented me with a bumper of coke early on, saying, "Happy birthday, Mrs. Jones" (the name he'd started calling me when I was with Hood—as in "jonesing for a fix"). I tossed back glasses of champagne and vodka with heedless abandon, as I affectionately greeted all those who made an appearance. There were a few people whose absence surprised me—Adam and Adrina, for example, and Lydia. But Merle and Danny were there and presented me with a boa made from red-dyed ostrich feathers, which I immediately donned. Christina Getty gave me a beautiful silk nightgown, and Isabella and Finn brought me a bottle of perfume called, appropriately enough, Diva. A small gift pile accumulated as the crowd grew, and I promptly lost track of it; it was Ricky who made sure that everything was loaded into my cab when I finally left at the end of the night.

I had long since grown accustomed to being greeted by people who I wasn't sure I recognized. So when, as I returned from one of many bathroom trips, a handsome young Italian man who barely spoke English hugged and kissed me, I immediately returned the gesture and whisked him up into VIP with the rest of the party. It was only after I'd plied him with champagne and made out with him for about half an hour that I checked with Ricky and discovered that nobody knew who he was—he was simply a tourist who had stumbled into some remarkably good luck.

"Disco Inferno" came on, and Mike—who wasn't much of a dancer—made an awkward, valiant attempt to spin me around the low tables in the VIP section. He finally threw in the towel, saying, "Let's make out!"

"Okay!" I agreed happily. The two of us fell in a heap onto a banquette in a corner nook. Ricky walked by a few minutes later and did an actual spit-take, nearly dropping his martini glass.

"Oh my *God*!" he shrieked. "What are you *doing*?"

"Getting to second base," I replied, drunkenly unfazed.

"Oh, for crying out loud!" Ricky was clearly exasperated and started tugging on Mike's arm. "Would you please get *off* her?"

"What?" Mike was all innocence. "What did I do wrong?"

When the last bottle of champagne arrived at around four a.m., the crowd had thinned considerably; Ricky, Mike, Kojo, and I were almost the only ones left. "We haven't made a toast yet," Ricky said, pouring champagne into each of our flutes. "What should we toast to?"

Kojo raised his flute high. "To Rachel," he proclaimed. "Champagne for all her real friends, and real pain for all her sham friends."

"Happy birthday!" Ricky and Mike chimed in, and the four of us clinked our raised glasses together.

I woke up the next morning with a horrible sore throat, the kind that felt more like a cold than a hangover. My voice was hoarse and husky, with the beginnings of what I realized would probably be full-blown laryngitis. I even called in sick to work—something I'd sworn I would never do after a night of partying.

Unfortunately, I was also out of commission for the Make-A-Wish Ball, which Ricky and I were supposed to attend that night. Brent Carrigan was bringing in Broadway star Sam Harris to perform this year, and he'd invited Ricky and me to the private after-party he traditionally held in the Inter-Continental's Presidential Suite. I sent Ricky without me, telling him to give Brent my love and apologize for my absence.

I downed some NyQuil and was sound asleep when the phone rang at a quarter of midnight. "What are you *doing*?" said Brent's voice on the other end. I could hear music and people talking in the background. "We're having a *party*—get down here!"

"I can't, Brent," I croaked groggily. "Listen to me—I'm sick."

"How often am I in town?" Brent insisted. "Throw something on and be here in ten minutes." He hung up.

I sighed wearily; my very bones were achy. I had, however, never been good at turning down people who insisted on my presence—a quality, I reflected, that had probably determined the path my life had taken on South Beach as much as anything else.

My face in the mirror was ghostly pale as I began the painful process of applying makeup, and I decided to work with it rather than against it. I was generally so olive-skinned that there was something almost exotic about how white my face now looked against my black hair. I dabbed on a foundation that was lighter than my customary shade and applied very minimal eye makeup to my cold-hooded eyes. Then I selected a red lip liner, drawing the shape of my mouth about a size larger than I usually did, covering my lips in the deepest, reddest lipstick I owned. I threw on a long black dress, grabbed a handbag, and went out to hail a cab.

The sounds of music and clinking glasses drifted out into the hallway as I rang the doorbell to the InterContinental's Presidential Suite. Brent Carrigan was laughing as he opened the door. "Look at you!" he exclaimed as he shepherded me in. "Oh my God, I *love* the Elvira skin and I *love* the voice." I kissed Ricky hello, but Brent monopolized my side for the most part, bringing me from group to group and insistently repeating the story of: "Look at this girl—ten minutes ago she was on her deathbed, and here she is ready to party!"

Sometime around one thirty, everybody gathered around the piano to listen to Sam Harris and his pianist perform a couple of songs from Sam's upcoming CD.

"You know," I said wistfully to Brent, "if I could have any life other than my own, I'd love to be a chanteuse singing standards in a smoky bar somewhere."

"Why not do it now?" Brent said. "Climb on top of the piano and give us your best Michelle Pfeiffer."

"Oh, no." I was alarmed. "I can't sing. I sing like a bullfrog—really."

"You don't even know what your voice can do," Brent insisted, absolutely tugging me in the direction of the piano as I tried to pull backward. We were inching closer. "It's so *sultry* right now."

I was panicking and looking around for Ricky. "Please don't make me embarrass myself in front of all these people," I pleaded. Ricky had heard something of what was going on and joined his voice with Brent's.

"You should do it, darling!" he said. "We're all friends here."

I was standing in front of the piano. The pianist was smiling, and people were starting to look over. Brent chimed a cocktail glass with a spoon and said, "Listen up, everybody. Rachel's going to sing . . . what are you going to sing for us?"

There didn't seem to be much I could do at this point without making a bigger deal of the whole thing than was warranted. I turned to the pianist and asked, "Do you know 'How Long Has This Been Going On'?"

"Of course," he responded. "What key?"

"Oh God, I don't know." I looked helplessly at Brent. He had me sing a couple of notes to him, sotto voce, then conferred with the pianist.

There are things you end up doing in life that, at the time, seem perfectly natural—and it isn't until you look back years later that you shake your head in a kind of wonder and think, *Was that really me? Did I really do that?* That night at Liquid had been one of those instances—the night when I'd stood high on a swing on the club's ceiling and tossed erotic poetry, like so many gold coins, onto the heads of the partiers below.

This wasn't one of those moments; I knew this one for what it was as it was happening. There was something positively surreal about me—*me*—standing at a party in a penthouse, being pressed by a Broadway director to sing publicly. As much as I knew that I didn't have the voice for it—and as much as I typically loathed doing anything that I couldn't do well—I also knew that whatever embarrassment I might suffer would be temporary. I'd have the story to tell for the rest of my life.

Besides, the question in the song was one I'd been asking myself more and more as the days went by.

> *I could cry salty tears*
> *Where have I been all these years?*
> *Little wow, tell me now*
> *How long has this been going on . . .*

· · ·

The two biggest buzz items on the Beach that Season were the millennium New Year and the much-anticipated opening of Crobar, which was finally scheduled to take place in December. Even White Party Week, which had come and gone much as the previous year's, didn't overshadow them.

The hottest New Year's Eve party would be thrown in Chris and Ingrid's new space, called Ice Palace—a fourteen-thousand-square-foot monster of a venue in the Design District. Ricky and I had been at its unveiling party, somewhat breathless at the sheer size of it. The New Year's Eve fete would be the creation of Susanne Bartsch, and the tickets—prohibitively expensive though they were—were the hottest tickets in town.

But everything changed on the first day of December, when Chris Paciello was arrested—charged with racketeering, robbery, and murder. It was said that he would be extradited to New York and prosecuted under the RICO statutes, the same statutes they used to prosecute the Mafia and organized crime.

Had the government chosen to test a nuclear bomb in the middle of Lincoln Road, we couldn't have been more astonished—or more outraged.

Not Our Chris became our common refrain as the news reports spread like brush fire. Not *our* Chris, who contributed so generously to the Make-A-Wish

Foundation and the Health Crisis Network. Not *our* Chris, always polite and soft-spoken, who treated us all so well. It was the mantra we maintained, even as increasingly lurid tales leaked out: a housewife in Staten Island who'd been murdered in a botched-up robbery; instances of alleged police graft and attempted bribes; and—most shocking of all—an alleged plot to take out a contract on the life of Gerry Kelly, after he'd left Liquid to open his own club, Level.

That was when we knew for sure it couldn't be true. South Beach was about fun, not violence—anybody who knew anything knew that. Even the Versace murder had been an aberration, a one-off spree waged by an outsider. They (and we were a trifle vague as to who "they" were) had been looking for a way to shut down our party for years; this was merely the latest, and most absurd, attempt.

The town became a media circus in the following days, and garish headlines like "Chris Paciello's Double Life" and "Goon Over Miami" blared forth in papers all over Miami and New York. A loyal crowd of scenesters, including Ricky, trekked to the Miami federal courthouse in a show of support on the day of Chris's bond hearing, loudly proclaiming his innocence to the press.

For the first time in forever, my parents were interested in the details of my life on South Beach. "Do you *know* him?" my mother asked one night over a family dinner.

"Marginally," I answered, hastily adding, "But I don't believe he's guilty."

My father, a lawyer of some thirty-five years' standing, chuckled. "Kid," he told me, "innocent people don't get prosecuted under RICO."

In the face of this, all my arguments to the contrary deflated like a pricked balloon.

Against the backdrop of this turmoil, Crobar finally opened its doors. It was hard to say if the wild fanfare surrounding Crobar was a reaction to the Chris Paciello news or existed despite it. Most people on the Beach still remained firmly in the *Not Our Chris* camp—but I think we all knew that Liquid's days were numbered. Maybe it was time to start thinking about what would come next.

Carpenters, lighting technicians, and craftsmen had been gutting the interior of the Cameo Theater for months, and the papers were full of speculation as to what Kenny and Cal, Crobar's owners, had in store. For me, it was impossible to think about Crobar and not think about Hood. I couldn't help wondering if he was still working for them in Chicago, if he would come back to participate in their South Beach opening.

Ricky and I had learned valuable lessons about much-hyped club openings at Level's debut back in January. We'd arrived fashionably late, as per the unwritten laws of South Beach social etiquette, and discovered that we couldn't get anywhere near the front door. Eventually, a service entrance in the back had been opened and Level staffers had discreetly wrangled the red-carpet regulars in that direction. Still, it had taken us nearly half an hour to get inside, and we intended not to repeat the experience.

Lara was down once again visiting her parents, and Ricky and I had invited her to join us at Crobar, along with her new boyfriend, Ross—a coworker she'd started dating in late October, only three weeks after her breakup with her last boyfriend.

I was inclined to be skeptical about this new relationship, falling as it did into both the "office romance" and "rebound" categories. But I had to reassess everything when I met Ross. He and Lara arrived at Cameron Diaz's restaurant Bambu to meet Ricky and me for dinner before we all headed to Crobar. Ross was all the things I would have expected from a boyfriend of Lara's—great-looking, smart, funny, Jewish. I didn't know how ready she could be to dive into a new relationship, but I couldn't blame her for thinking that this one might be worth the plunge.

Ricky and Lara, who'd heard so much about each other, got along instantly. "Look at how handsome you are," Lara said admiringly when I introduced them. "You must have guys all over you constantly."

"Ooh, we love her!" Ricky exclaimed, and I laughed. It was so exactly like Lara to intuitively suss out the right thing to say—and so like Ricky to love the attention. Good impressions were further cemented when Lara grabbed up the check at the end of the meal and announced, "Dinner's on Sony Music."

We lucked into a cab right outside of Bambu and headed for Crobar. But our cab was unable to deposit us in front of the club—the hordes of people clamoring to get in stretched for a full two blocks in all directions. There was, we realized, no physical way for us to get close enough to the door for the doorman to spot us. Even the cops on hand, sweating profusely in the reasonably cool December night, were unable to manage the chaos.

"What are we going to do?" I murmured to Ricky. I had promised Lara, who had never come to visit me on South Beach before, a fun club night. While I knew she didn't really care what we did, I'd wanted to show her something of what my life on the Beach was like.

Then, to our far right, we saw a beacon of hope—a placard bearing the inscription MERLE & DANNY rose high above the throngs. Ricky and I looked at each other, our eyes suddenly gleeful. We grabbed Lara and Ross's hands with an imperative, "Come on!" and wrestled through the crowd. A small cluster of our friends had gathered behind the MERLE & DANNY sign, stopping to laugh with Merle and Danny Weiss and congratulate them on their foresight.

"How does this help us?" Lara asked. "We're farther away than we were before."

"Just watch," I replied.

Gilbert Stafford himself was working the door for Crobar's opening night. His six-foot-five frame left its post and bore down on the frenzied masses, his deep voice booming, "Clear a path! *Clear a path!*" He came and took Merle and Danny's hands and led our group into the club as the crowd parted before us—a giant black Moses leading the Israelites across the Red Sea and into the Promised Land.

As it turned out, most of the thrill of the experience was in getting through the front doors. It was so jam-packed that my chin was practically in Lara's cocktail when we spoke, and all four of us were constantly jostled and stepped on by our fellow revelers.

"Take me to the Deuce!" Lara shouted into my ear above the music and the din. "I'm dying to see that place." I caught Ricky's eye and nodded my head toward the front door, and the four of us fought our way out.

Walking into the Deuce felt like walking into my own past. With everything that had changed on the Beach over the years, the Deuce remained exactly the same—down to the life-sized photo of Humphrey Bogart hanging on the wall. I almost expected to find Amy in her usual corner, projecting her typical air of sultry detachment, or turn around and see Hood there with a lighter at the ready, saying, *Hey hey, baby doll* . . .

"Are Mike and Kojo around?" Lara asked.

"Mike's in Nebraska with his parents," I replied. "And Kojo's . . . not available." Nobody had heard from Kojo in four days. Mike called from Nebraska every day in a panic to inform me that Kojo still hadn't checked in—which, obviously, I already knew. I also knew by now that Kojo would turn up when, and only when, he was ready.

Most SoBe locals were still at Crobar, so the four of us had the Deuce almost all to ourselves. There hadn't been room to dance at the club, but there was plenty of room to dance here, and we went about it energetically. Ross was a great dancer—a well-matched partner for Lara, who loved to dance almost more than anything. The two of them took turns feeding the jukebox, selecting tracks by the Rolling Stones and Three Dog Night. *Everyone is lucky, everyone is so kind, On the road to Shambala* . . .

"Oh, I love this song!" Lara exclaimed softly to Ross. She beamed at him. "Did you pick it because you know I love it?"

"How could I *not* know you love it—you've been playing it every day for the last two weeks." The corners of his mouth curved upward as he looked into her face.

I knew then—knew in the indefinable way that you know things about the woman you've been best friends with for ten years.

"She's going to marry him," I whispered to Ricky. "I'm going on the record."

Lara and Ross headed back to New York to celebrate the millennium *à deux*. Ricky had made contact with a small camera crew from the BBC that was planning to spend the millennium New Year's on South Beach, shooting film for a documentary series they were producing. The original plan had been for them to follow Ricky and me around for a few days, culminating at the New Year's Eve party at Ice Palace. Since Chris's arrest, however, we'd had to recalibrate, and took them instead to a house party in a penthouse apartment in South Pointe Towers.

We became something of a traveling circus over the next few days, with the cameras following us in and out of bars, clubs, and friends' homes. It was odd to have them with us wherever we went—the light shining in our faces made us reflect more self-consciously upon everything we said and did. Ricky's and my normally effortless banter became more of a put-on; we caught ourselves actively setting each other up for punchlines, or for Ricky's ruminations on the ebb and flow of clubland fads and fashions. But he became increasingly quiet as the days progressed—until, by New Year's Eve, he was hardly talking at all.

Most of my attention, however, was focused on Matthew, one of the BBC producers. Matthew was a semi-starving novelist living in London when he wasn't producing documentaries. When the cameras were off or away, we discussed our favorite books and writers. I told him about the Hannah Kahn Poetry Foundation, which I'd recently rejoined, and what it was like to turn my attention back to writing after so much time away from it. He talked to me about the life of a freelancer, struggling to support himself while he wrote his novel. It was a John Hood level of discourse, without any John Hood drama. So it seemed inevitable when, after the New Year's Eve party at South Pointe, the two of us ended up back in his hotel room. The tragedy of the whole thing was that he was returning to England on New Year's Day.

We said our good-byes and exchanged e-mail addresses bright and early that first morning of 2000. I called Ricky as soon as I got home, as I always did after a particularly successful hookup, ready to give him the blow-by-blow.

His voice was unusually subdued when he answered the phone, and his responses to my story were markedly listless. "What's wrong?" I finally asked.

There was a long pause. "I think maybe we've been spending too much time together," he said. "I think we should see less of each other."

My breath caught in my throat; my face felt as tingly and red as if somebody had put their hands around my neck and squeezed hard. "What are you saying?" I demanded hoarsely. "Are you saying you don't want to be friends anymore?"

"Maybe not for a little while." His voice was reluctant—and I couldn't tell if it was because he was unsure of what he was saying, or because he was trying not to hurt me more than necessary.

"Fine." My own voice was deliberately hard. "Whatever. Do what you want." I hung up before another word was said.

I got into my car and drove for a while, an old habit of mine in moments of crisis. I felt like somebody who'd received a mortal injury and only gradually begins to feel the pain and finality of it. My mind was racing, unable to settle on any one fixed thought. An agonized *What did I do?* was followed by, *How could he?*

I drove around the deserted streets and highways of early-morning Miami for nearly two hours, trying to sort it all out. The one thing I'd always prided myself on was that I'd never forced myself on anybody, never begged anyone to remain a part of my life. When somebody told me to leave, I left without an argument. When a guy stopped calling, I didn't call him. I had made one exception to this rule in the case of John Hood—and look where it had gotten me.

But it occurred to me now, almost as a new thought, that some things in life were bigger than pride—were worth fighting for. After everything—*everything*—Ricky and I had been to each other, who was he to treat me this way?

My initial hurt turned to anger. *Fuck this*, I thought. I punched the accelerator and the car lurched forward, keeping pace with my swelling sense of outrage. I raced back over the causeway and straight to Ricky's apartment building. I parked in the guest parking lot, slamming the car door as hard as if I thought he'd be able to hear it. Then I rode up the elevator and stalked down the familiar long corridor on the second floor, pounding on the door to Ricky's apartment at the very end.

I didn't even realize I was crying until Ricky opened the door and I saw his alarmed expression. With all the ups and downs the two of us had seen each other through in the past few years, he had never once seen me cry.

"How could you say that to me?" My voice sounded like something broken. "How could you just throw me out of your life and not even tell me *why*?"

Ricky had never seen me cry, but I had seen him cry a handful of times. So I knew by the tautness of his face that he, too, was struggling with tears. "I'm sorry," he said, turning away. He wiped at his eyes. "But you were spending so much time talking to those BBC people when the cameras were off." He took a deep breath. "I felt like this was my shot—like you were stealing my shot."

My anger evaporated and I laughed, even as the tears continued to stream down my face. "What are you, new here?" I exclaimed. "I was trying to sleep with the producer! I swear to you, that's the only thing—the *only* thing—I was even thinking about."

Ricky was laughing now too. "I should have remembered that it's always about your hormones." He hugged me. "I'm sorry. I'm so sorry for saying those things."

I hugged him back, tightly. "Don't you know," my voice cracked again, "that almost everything I have that's good in my life, I have because of you? That if it weren't for you, I would've crawled back into my parents' house after I moved out of Amy's and never left it?"

"And you've done so much for me," he replied huskily. "I couldn't do what I do if it wasn't for you supporting and encouraging me."

"Well, then, that's that." I ran my hands through my hair. "We're two codependents who can't live without each other, so we should clearly never fight again."

Ricky laughed a second time. "How about we order a pizza?" he said. "And then you can tell me about your night—I thought you had a policy against sleeping with transients."

"Generally, I do." I grinned ruefully. "But the great thing about the holidays is that you can always justify empty calories."

TWENTY-FIVE

By the middle of January, BeachLife.com had yet to launch the "product" (i.e., the BeachLife website). As the director of event marketing, however, the product wasn't my responsibility—only the hype was.

To this purpose, I was responsible for creating exhibits and demonstrations at trade shows and conventions all over the country. I spent much of Season crisscrossing the map for these events, and when I wasn't traveling to places like New York, L.A., San Francisco, or New Orleans, I was preparing for the next round of travel. I limited myself to one or two parties per night instead of the usual four or five when I was in town, but my picture was in the papers and my mailbox was as full of invitations as ever. I almost had the feeling that I could put my scenester standing on autopilot, that I had reached a point where it would run itself with little or no effort on my part.

Hotels and restaurants opened that Season, and other hotels and restaurants closed or changed hands. A place called B.E.D. was the hot club *du moment*. Kevin Crawford was back in town, promoting at some new venue. A weekly party called Beige, transplanted from New York, popped up on the scene. Beige was held at the Raleigh Hotel's pool, which was lush with waterfalls and private cabanas. The inaugural night was especially chichi, and I broke out the yellow boa for the first time since Gerry Kelly's birthday party. The boa was the big hit it had been before; I was interviewed for *Deco Drive*, danced a wild salsa with Perry Farrell, and even had my picture taken for Brazilian *Vogue*. "*Darling!*" the photographer gushed, to my deep amusement. "Who is your *stylist*?"

In February, when the *Sunpost* did its annual send-up of the Academy Awards, Cubby named me "Best Supporting Actress in a Supporting Garment." It was his usual brand of left-handed compliment, but the clipping nonetheless occupied a place of honor in my scrapbook. A promoter named Maxwell Blandford hosted elegant soirees at the Delano's Rose Bar. Michael Tronn promoted a weekly event called The Fights at Amnesia. The Fights was a party planned around actual boxing matches, held in a regulation-sized ring in the center of Amnesia's vast, open-air courtyard.

I have a picture taken of the two of us on one of those nights, sitting together ringside. I'm wearing an orange and black silk handkerchief top, which tied at the neck and waist and left my back completely bare. My head is resting affectionately—if somewhat wearily—on Michael's shoulder, and the two of us look quite happy together.

Nevertheless, it had all started to feel the same. "It's like there's only one party," I would say to Ricky, "and it just keeps changing locations." I sometimes felt like a pinball in a machine, zipping around wildly but ultimately bouncing off the same bumpers again and again. I had worked to achieve a level of immediate recognition, and all the advantages that came with it; now that I finally had it, I found myself slightly, and surprisingly, bored.

My big thrill had once been to walk into a South Beach party and know almost everybody in the room. But now, inexplicably, I found it thrilling to walk into a party and not know anybody at all. I once again enlisted with Miami's professional organizations and cocktail parties—this time joining ones with a technology bent: WITI (Women in Technology International), for example, or the Miami Internet Alliance. My favorites, though, were the enormous free-for-alls held out of town at dot-com conventions. Parties of over two thousand guests would eventually break into smaller gatherings of forty or fifty, continued in the lavish hotel suites of . . . well, we never really knew who. But the liquor and coke were always dispensed with a free hand, and the anonymity of it all meant you could be as reckless as you wanted without giving a single thought to who you might end up exchanging guilty glances with the next day.

I had rejoined the Hannah Kahn Poetry Foundation, and by March I had taken up a relationship with Ethan, another member of the group. He was an unlikely choice in many ways; recently divorced at forty-eight, he was on the somewhat short and distinctly potbellied side, and was chronically underemployed.

My friends met Ethan only once, when the Hannah Kahn group invited me to give my own reading one night at the Books & Books in Coral Gables.

The next night, the three of them turned up in my apartment as a group, their expressions somewhere between amused and genuinely concerned.

"We're staging an intervention," Mike announced. "We want to make sure you know what you're doing."

"He's a genius of a poet," I told them matter-of-factly. "And he's a Viking in the sack."

Which was, when all was said and done, the one-two assessment that summed it up best. Ethan was an unbelievably gifted poet—sometimes I would read things he had written and marvel, *I actually know this guy personally*. And, after years in a bad and apparently sexless marriage, Ethan had a lot of (ahem) energy pent up and went about the work of releasing it with marked enthusiasm. While he wasn't the long-awaited boyfriend/soulmate who would integrate seamlessly into the rest of my social life, I had long since given up hope of finding that relationship anyway.

At least I never had to sanitize my nightlife adventures for Ethan's sake; I would tell him about clubs, drugs, and party exploits, and to him—so far removed from the scene, both geographically and philosophically—it sounded young and sexy. "A brunette bombshell," was how he said he'd described me to his friends. Looking at my life through his eyes reminded me that there was something glamorous in the outrageous getups that had, by this time, become little more than uniforms hanging in my closet.

Ethan lived about an hour's drive north of South Beach, and he would head down to my apartment every Saturday night, staying until Sunday night. We would lock the doors, turn off the phone, and order in huge meals ("going into lockdown," was how Kojo described it). There was no question of its being serious—Ethan was recovering from his divorce, and I couldn't even imagine settling down with him—but it was an entirely agreeable arrangement. It was the kind of relationship that begins for no particular reason, and can carry on indefinitely because there's no particular reason to end it.

So my personal life was full, if not entirely fulfilling. Work was good, and the stock market continued its dizzying upward climb. My own company, although spending rapaciously, wasn't actually generating any money yet—but then, nobody seemed to expect us to.

I threw a party at Level the first Thursday in April. BeachLife.com was finally scheduled to launch officially within the month, and I had been instructed to put together an event for our investors and selected "friends and family." Level—at 44,000 square feet and with its enormous stage that hosted many of the wilder shows on the Beach—seemed like the perfect choice. We invited around three hundred people, a small gathering as such things go, and hired Santana to perform for us. Santana was hot that year, Carlos Santana having collected eight Grammys a month earlier for his album *Supernatural*; there was something agreeably decadent about going to the trouble and expense of bringing him in to perform to so small a group.

I had been busy all day managing on-site logistics, so I hadn't been tuned in to news of the outside world. But people wandered into my party that night looking a little shell-shocked. They spoke in whispers—the way that people talk behind their hands or in hushed tones about a friend's terminal illness.

The NASDAQ, the technology stock market, had taken a precipitous plunge that day. For any number of unfortunate people, rich only yesterday, their stock options were suddenly worth no more than the paper they were printed on. Some of the guests said that it was simply an inevitable, and foreseeable, "correction." Others dismally insisted that it was the beginning of the end of the glorious tech bubble.

We had all thought of ourselves as being part of something that would change the world. But standing there and listening to the conversations, I thought to myself that the world had just changed us.

Things were looking bleak for BeachLife.com by early May. The website that was supposed to have launched in April still hadn't gone live. Our investors were growing impatient and anxious, and we heard through the office grapevine that no additional funds would be forthcoming. People were murmuring nervously about pink slips and sending résumés to other companies on the sly. I freely admit that I was one of them; I had, as I'd thought years earlier, long since become an expert in downward trajectories.

It took me only two weeks to find a new position with another start-up dot-com that sold winter-sport garb online. It seemed like a bit of a disconnect (selling snowboarding gear from South Beach), but the salary they offered was even higher than my current one, and I was bumped up to the proud title of director of marketing. I gave my two weeks' at BeachLife.com and left—as it turned out, only one week ahead of a general bloodletting that left most of my former coworkers unemployed.

Not all technology and dot-com wealth had been decimated, however. There were those who had made their fortunes early on and whose resources were still incalculably huge. Predictably, many of the flashier ones found their way down to South Beach.

Perhaps the most noteworthy member of this cash-saturated tribe was Shawn Lewis, a thirty-one-year-old technology mogul who had arrived from somewhere up north with—if reports were to be believed—a fortune of close to three hundred million dollars. Like many a wealthy playboy before him, he'd become infatuated with the nightlife scene. He decided to buy-in in a big way, purchasing property all over town and opening club after club.

Some press types were calling Shawn "the new Chris"; I don't think the locals wanted a new Chris Paciello any more than a child wants a new puppy on the same day his beloved dog dies. There was something about it that felt queasily similar to a vulture picking the bones of a corpse—especially when Shawn bought Liquid and announced plans to open yet another new club in the same space. And unlike Chris, with his laid-back charm, Shawn seemed to be courting our approval a little too blatantly. South Beach wasn't like other towns, we said; you couldn't just come here and expect, for no more than the price of a shiny new venue, to have the in-crowd at your beck and call. And so the in-crowd, coldly and firmly, turned their backs on all of Shawn's enterprises. For our own part, Ricky and I never once set foot in any of Shawn Lewis's various clubs.

It might seem surprising, then, that we all received invitations to Shawn's wedding when he engaged himself to marry a Miami Dolphins cheerleader. Even more surprisingly, we all eagerly accepted. Word had it that a million dollars had been spent on the wedding, and South Beach loved a gaudy spectacle like a hooker loves payday. And when we heard, two weeks before the big day, that the wedding had been called off but the reception would proceed anyway, we were even more excited. This development lent the entire thing a decided theater-of-the-absurd quality.

Air-conditioned buses were hired to transport us from Shawn's North Bay Road mansion to the rented mansion on Star Island where the party itself would be held. There were actual circus performers—midgets, contortionists, women dressed as mermaids—cavorting about the manicured grounds. An enormous tent, which seemed to stretch up and out for miles, sheltered flower-laden tables. Ice sculptures dripped ponderously beside titanic mounds of Beluga caviar, oysters, and sushi. Fountains spewed forth champagne in cold, rushing streams. In the center of the tent was the mansion's swimming pool, which had been covered with Plexiglas to form a dance floor.

"It's very Gatsbyesque, isn't it?" I commented to Ricky.

According to the engraved cards bearing our names, Ricky's and my table was adjacent to the bandstand and dance floor. From this vantage point, we had a prime view of the reporters and camera crews milling about. They'd been invited by Shawn's publicist to capture a wedding, and were equally content— like the rest of us—with the flotsam and jetsam left in its wake.

Ricky and I spent most of the afternoon alternating between the champagne fountains and crowded dance floor. I stumbled a bit during one particularly adventurous maneuver, bumping into somebody, and was suddenly face-to-face with Amy Saragosi.

In a sense, the only real surprise was that I hadn't run into her sooner. "I can't believe, in a town this small, that I never see her," I would frequently observe to Ricky.

Ricky, who was more plugged in to local gossip than I was, would generally reply that Amy was traveling all the time. Still, on some level, I'd been mentally preparing for a confrontation ever since the night of the Groove Jet anniversary party, the last time I'd laid eyes on her.

And here she was. All the things I'd planned over the years to say when I saw her again dwindled down to nothing more than a subdued, "Hey."

"Hey," she answered, in a tone of studied disinterest.

"You look beautiful," I said, meaning it. She was wearing an elegant, peacock-blue silk dress that circled gracefully around her feet. After all this time, I was struck by the simple fact of Amy's beauty—a beauty composed of fine features, shining hair, and the hints of a life lived beyond even my own feverish dreams.

I thought of the girl I'd been when I met Amy—the girl who'd believed she could never live a life that measured up to her daydreams. I felt a sudden, poignant nostalgia for the feeling of discovery I'd had in those first months of our friendship, of thinking that the things I'd always imagined were not only possible, but about to happen to me. I'd spent so many years making so many plans, I reflected, and a casual conversation struck up one day over cigarettes had changed my life more than any plans I'd made.

"Thanks." Amy conspicuously didn't return the compliment. But it couldn't really be the same for her; Amy had changed my life, but I hadn't changed hers. Her eyes turned in the direction of her date, who promptly spun her away.

"Are you okay?" Ricky asked.

"I'm fine," I replied, and shrugged.

I *was* fine. But I drank a bit more heavily after that than I should have. I went to the bar to refresh my cocktail, and O. J. Simpson—who had lately bought a home in our neck of the woods—cut in front of me in line, monopolizing the attention of the bartender.

"*Who*," I demanded of nobody in particular, "does a girl have to brutally stab to death to get a drink around here?"

Ricky, standing next to me, hissed, "Shhhh! He'll hear you!"

"Whatever," I said in disgust. "What kind of a person invites *O. J. Simpson* to their wedding?"

Season was essentially over after that. For us, the crash was made even rockier by the death of Kojo's younger brother from an overdose in early June. Kojo's older brother had also died of an overdose several years earlier, and so the blow was especially harsh.

Kojo ended up inheriting his brother's trust fund and, freed from the necessity of earning a paycheck, quit his job. "Kojo doesn't do well without a job," Mike observed presciently. I knew Mike was right—the one thing that had given us comfort where Kojo was concerned was that he was responsible about his job and would always pull himself together to show up for it. Without the structure of regular working hours, however, the sole structure in Kojo's life became his bathhouse-and-crystal routine. Mike would try to tell me stories of things Kojo did or that happened to him there—irresponsible sex, robberies. Some of the rougher scenarios he described were more than I could stand hearing.

"You're exaggerating," I would say shortly. "Kojo doesn't tell *me* any of this."

"That's because he doesn't want you to know," Mike would answer. "I think he thinks of you as 'Mommy' or something."

"Well, there's a disturbing thought." I sighed.

The four of us had always made jokes, a fair percentage of which had always been self-deprecating. But Kojo's jokes now focused almost exclusively on the social rejection he'd felt at the hands of the South Beach party crowd, or on the sexual rejection he claimed he received in the bathhouses (the only sense in which he would touch on the subject in my presence). The jokes were meant to be funny, but, in listening to them, we always had the feeling that we were looking directly through an open window into Kojo's private pain, the ferocity of which we'd clearly underestimated.

"He complains that people reject him because of his appearance," Mike said. "But then he goes to those bathhouses where people judge you on nothing *but* what you look like."

We didn't know how to deal with this subject. We certainly thought Kojo was good-looking. More than that, though, we loved Kojo's brilliant wit, his good heart. Anybody would love that about him. People already *did* love that about him. *Ocean Drive* had just published its list of "The 100 People You Need to Know on South Beach," and Kojo was the only one of us whose name was on it. The rest of us had had to work at popularity, at least a little; all Kojo ever had to do was show up. Why couldn't he see it in himself?

We wondered if Kojo felt guilty, having lost his father and both of his brothers in recent years and inheriting the money from all three that had, intermittently, financed his South Beach lifestyle. Or maybe the insecurities came from a deeper place—something that lacked the easy analysis of armchair psychology, some self-destructive urge the rest of us would never really understand.

I said that I was respecting his privacy in not pressing him for information about what he was doing—or that, as I'd learned from John Hood, an addict would be an addict until he decided to change on his own. Nothing I did would make a difference.

The real truth, though, was that I was just as happy not knowing the details. What I had always loved most about Kojo was his sensitivity; for all the cutting humor or biting wit that he was capable of, he never wounded—because you always knew that Kojo could never stand to hurt anybody. So the thought of Kojo hurting himself, or letting other people hurt him, was excruciating; and I found myself subtly, but with deliberate purpose, turning away from him.

I did attempt, on one occasion, to talk to Kojo about his sudden weight loss, and the persistent rash that had developed on his arms and seemed to spread daily. I played dumb, acting as if I didn't know what was causing it, trying to probe gently around the boundaries.

"Allergies," Kojo told me.

"Ah," I responded sympathetically. "I get skin allergies too sometimes." And the subject was dropped.

Ricky and Mike were also in the throes of relationship issues. Everybody Ricky dated either ended up giving him the "let's be friends" speech after only a few weeks or was, he was convinced, attaching himself to Mr. Nightclub in an effort to get a leg up on the social ladder. Mike was recovering from the latest in a string of boyfriends who would enter his life, move into his apartment, and eventually leave him high and dry with significant dents in his bank account.

"I'm going to stop helping people," he bitterly announced one day.

"I think, maybe, you need to set up better boundaries," I replied carefully, "so you don't get taken advantage of. But I don't think you want to be the person who doesn't help anybody at all."

"Why not?" Mike replied. "I never get anything back."

I was silent for a moment. "I worked in nonprofit for a long time," I finally answered, "with volunteers. And when you volunteer, you know you'll never get back what you put into it. That's kind of the point, actually; it's not about getting something back, it's about being the kind of person you want to be—the kind of person who helps people."

Mike laughed—with humor, I noted, and not scorn. "I always thought you were such a cynic."

"I may talk like a cynic," I responded, pulling a comical face. "But I break like a little girl."

All I could offer either of them were a sympathetic ear and the occasional attempts I made to fix Ricky up. There was a coworker of mine, for example, funny and cute as a button—and with no interest whatsoever in the SoBe scene—who I told Ricky about in June.

"Is he a top or a bottom?" Ricky wanted to know.

"I assure you," I replied, "I have no intention of asking."

It's this town, the two of them would say to me. *It's impossible to have a quality relationship in this town.*

It was a statement that I longed to contradict, but I hardly had the track record to back up any assertions to the contrary. The closest I'd come to a long-standing relationship since moving to South Beach was Ethan—a relationship that hadn't gone downhill yet only because it wasn't going anywhere at all.

Living in a small town is like living in a fishbowl—not only because everybody always sees you and knows what you're doing, but also because the smallest stone dropped into its waters sends the entire thing rippling and roiling. You can feel what's coming long before you ever see it.

So it came as no surprise, really, when I answered the phone one afternoon in July and the voice on the other end said, "Hey, it's Hood."

Hood was back in town. I hadn't seen him—but then, I didn't need to. A man like John Hood didn't reappear in a town like South Beach without being noticed.

"Hi." My voice was neutral and stilted.

It was a Sunday afternoon and Ethan was over. He looked up curiously when he heard my odd tone, but didn't comment. "I'll go in the other room," he whispered, "so you can talk." He went into the bedroom and shut the door.

"What, do you have someone there?" Hood's voice sounded suspicious. Then he tried for playful good humor. "Do I have to come over there and patrol your hallway to stop other cats from tomcatting around?"

Is he completely delusional? I wondered. *Does he honestly think he can come back a year later and pick up where we left off?*

The one thing I could have said to end things once and for all was that there *was* someone there. Another man, in fact. *My boyfriend is here right now,* I might say. Any other obstacle I presented could, in Hood's mind, eventually be worn down through persistence or even disregarded altogether. But, in accordance with his own particular code of honor, Hood would respect another man's territory the same way he would expect others to respect his.

I remained mute, listening to the whir of the air-conditioning fill the silence of the room. The plants on my windowsill bent beneath its currents, and I watched them as disconnectedly as if they belonged to somebody else.

"Is this not a good time?" Hood asked.

"No," I replied, finally finding my voice. "It'll never be a good time."

I hung up the phone.

TWENTY-SIX

Hood didn't call again after that. I deleted his number from my caller ID almost immediately, afraid I'd be tempted to call him back.

I heard through the grapevine that he was working with the owner of Lola. I was inclined to start avoiding the place at first, even though Ricky and I were, by this time, habitual attendees. But then, with the sort of self-righteous indignation that only masks a deeper desire to do something you know you shouldn't, I thought, *Why should I change my routines just because Hood decided to show up again?*

I made a scrupulous point of going to Lola exactly as frequently as I had before, only deviating from this schedule at Ricky's suggestion. I never got high before I went, never drank too much or stayed too late while I was there, and never admitted to myself upon leaving at the end of the night that I was at all disappointed at not having seen Hood.

It seemed that I was doomed to play out the same issues again and again, in more ways than one. My company had been doing well, I'd thought—at least, we were doing a good job of doing better than other Internet companies. But then, one payday, the direct deposits for our paychecks didn't post to our bank accounts. *Just an accounting error,* we were reassured by the president of our company, and the money made its appearance two days later.

But we knew. Not one employee was fooled into thinking that the company had no financial problems beyond a slightly inattentive accountant. And, indeed, it was only a few weeks later when I arrived at work one morning and found that there was no work. The office was empty and locked, our last round of paychecks still hadn't cleared, and the question of whether or not anybody would receive severance pay was clearly laughable.

"Is it so much to ask," I asked Ricky and Mike, "that I get one decent, stable, long-term job? Is that really such an unrealistic goal?"

Mike was, by this time, dealing with his own unemployment—WAMI having

296

finally succumbed to low ratings and disorganized management. He used connections he'd made through the local NLGJA (National Lesbian and Gay Journalists Association) chapter to line up freelance production work for some of the local stations, but there wasn't much here for him in terms of full-time employment.

The logical thing to do, of course, was to begin looking for another job. And so I did. But the burst of the dot-com bubble was taking its toll on everything, most especially the marketing agencies that had flourished under the lavish budgets of the tech boom. I thought about going back to my freelance work, but I was starting to feel that this would be the inevitable cycle of my career in South Beach. I had a sudden vision of myself, someday making a list of people who I could call to borrow rent money from.

It took Kojo two days to surface after I left him a panicky message about having lost my job. When he did finally check in, however, he sounded completely sober and sympathetic. "I'm not worried about you," he said firmly. "I bought stock in Rachel Baum a long time ago."

The only one who declined to be sympathetic was Ethan. It's true that I spent my first two weeks of unemployment agonizing over possible poverty and homelessness. But it was hard for me to feel that I'd been imposing on him, when I'd spent the better part of the past six months listening to him discuss the ins and outs of his divorce.

Things came to a head during a phone conversation. "I'm going through a lot of my own stuff with the divorce," he told me. "I don't think I have it in me to be a *friend* right now."

"Huh." I considered this. "I think we should just be friends."

"But—" He sounded confused. "I just said that—"

"Exactly!" I said cheerfully. "You take good care now."

"The Terminator," Ricky said, shaking his head fondly, when I told him this story the next day.

With everything that was going on, my love life should have been the least of my concerns. So there was no good reason, I told myself while sitting at the bar at Lola one September night, for my heart to knock so bruisingly against my rib cage when I felt a familiar hand on my shoulder.

I spun around and there Hood was. I was holding a cigarette and he presented a lit match. I bent my head to it, relieved to have an excuse for turning my eyes from his. Then I was angry with myself, sensing that, in accepting the light, I'd also tacitly accepted an invitation to conversation.

Ricky was sitting next to me. The two of them acknowledged each other with brief nods, but Hood's eyes didn't leave my face.

"Come to the office for a second," he said, as if we had last seen each other only yesterday. 'I want to talk to you."

I forced myself not to look at Ricky. "I just got this." I indicated the full martini glass in front of me.

Hood impatiently pulled a twenty-dollar bill from his pocket and tossed it onto the bar. "Now you can get two more." He held out his hand to me.

The only way to get out of it now would be to have a minor confrontation with him—here in the middle of the bar and in front of Ricky—and that wasn't something I was willing to face. Besides, no matter what I told myself, I knew that I had to hear whatever Hood wanted to say, simply because I wouldn't be able to live with not hearing it. So, still not looking at Ricky, I silently put my hand in Hood's and allowed him to help me from the bar stool.

We crossed the room and entered the miniature maze of Lola's hidden office space. Instead of going into one of the offices, however, Hood pushed open a side exit and we were in the alley.

"Hood," I said, "I thought you wanted to talk to me in the office."

"I do want to talk to you," he replied. "But not here. Let's go back to my place."

I stopped in my tracks, pulling my hand from his grip. Then I laughed a short, mirthless laugh. "You really think I'm that easy, don't you?" I marveled.

"You?" Hood's tone carried a hint of amusement, his lips tightened in the smallest of grins. But there was something of sincerity in his eyes as he said, "You're the only dame I know who makes me nervous."

I laughed again—this time a full, genuine laugh that reverberated off the walls of the alley. I didn't laugh only because it struck me as ridiculous whenever Hood said I made him nervous. I laughed because I had to admire the sheer virtuosity of his ability to play me, and his unabashed nerve in executing his game. And it was a testament to his skill that I knew I was being manipulated, yet went along anyway—I found the effort flattering, in fact; I always had.

"Let's go." I sighed, resigned. "But you better sit on your hands in the cab—I mean it."

Hood's hands flew into the air. "When have I ever been less than a perfect gentleman?"

I raised an eyebrow. "How do you want that list, alphabetically or chronologically?"

The cab deposited us in front of a small apartment building on Collins Avenue. I followed Hood through the entrance and down a dilapidated, paint-peeling hallway into a harshly lit stairwell. The top of the stairs opened into another crumbling hallway. We stopped in front of a wooden door in the middle of the hall, and Hood turned a key in the lock, stepping aside to allow me to enter first.

He flicked a switch next to the door and a naked overhead bulb sprang to life, illuminating a smallish, square living room. The dusty, hardwood floors were completely bare—in fact, the entire room was completely bare, except for one wall lined with stacks of books and papers, and a futon mattress occupying a corner.

A small kitchen adjoined the living room and opened into it via a tiny, marble-covered breakfast bar. Hood laid out a few lines of coke there, saying, "A cat I know had to split town suddenly, so he gave me this place for a couple of months."

I crossed over to the bar and took a rolled-up bill from Hood's hand. The room was full of laughter and music from the street below as, with the ease of long practice, I bent my head over the lines and brought it back. I stood with one hand resting on the bar while the other rubbed my nose.

Hood did the same. We were standing very close to each other, so close that I could see my face reflected in his pupils. I waited for him to say whatever it was he'd brought me here to say. Would there be an explanation for having left without a word? An apology, perhaps? The outright declaration of feeling that I'd been waiting for since we'd first met three years ago? *I can't stay away from you; you mean more to me than the other women have; leaving you was the biggest mistake I ever made. . . .*

Hood brought his hand up to the side of my face, and my eyes closed as he lowered his lips to mine.

There had always been a particular intensity in kissing Hood, especially right after doing a line. It felt like mainlining uncut thrill. But this time it also felt wrong, like something that should have been happening to someone else. I broke off and took a step backward. "Hood—" I paused and looked around the room.

There was a time when I would have been enthralled with this room—would have seen glamour in the noir-ish, transient grittiness of it. It represented everything that Hood was and everything that had, once upon a time, been beyond what girls like me were supposed to experience.

Now Hood's apartment just looked empty and seedy—depressing, really—and like nothing so much as exactly the kind of place where people who "had to split town suddenly" would live. Hood would always live in such places. He was a nomad by nature and I, despite my fantasies to the contrary, was not. Waiting for the explanation as to why he had left or showed up again when he did, or why he sometimes called and sometimes didn't, would be like waiting for a man to explain why his eyes were brown. It was part of what had drawn me to him in the first place; I had wanted to try on the freedom and unpredictability in his life that were so completely the opposite of everything I'd hated about my own life before moving to South Beach.

Sometimes the opposite of what you hate isn't what you love. The knowledge came to me as an absolute truth: This wasn't where I belonged anymore.

I remembered the night I met Hood, the riddle he'd posed to cap off an evening of witty repartee. Two villages on opposite sides of a river without a bridge, he'd told me—a river so deep, so wide, so swift, that it was impossible to swim, sail, or wade across it. So how did the people from one village get to the other?

The punchline, of course, was that it was supposed to be a riddle without an answer. *I don't know either,* he'd said. *But it's been nice holding your hand.*

But I knew now what the answer was—it was that they didn't. They never could.

There was still so much in Hood—so much!—that I wanted. And yet, almost before I knew I'd made a decision, I heard myself saying, "I can't spend the rest of my life playing Bonnie and Clyde with you."

Hood lit a cigarette. The smoke streamed from his mouth to take shape in the room, giving form and texture to unspoken things. The noise from the street seemed unbearably loud in the silence that ticked by.

I cleared my throat, and Hood looked at me. "It's getting late," I said softly.

He extinguished his cigarette in an ashtray. "I'll walk you to a cab."

We walked wordlessly downstairs and onto the street. Hood hailed a cab and opened the door, saying, "I'll see you." He kissed my cheek, his hand resting lightly on the small of my back, and I briefly closed my eyes again as I pressed my cheek to his. My chest felt tight as I watched his reflection recede in the cab's rearview mirror, the feet and then yards the car put between us already becoming months and years. A line from a Robert Hass poem trailed through my head: *Longing, we say, because desire is full / of endless distances . . .*

It was the last time I ever saw John Hood on South Beach.

"I'm thinking about moving to New York," I said the next time I called Lara, very much in the tone of a person who's testing an idea. "It's not just about work, though—I mean, I'm not just thinking about moving because I lost this job."

"I know," Lara replied.

I'd been turning the idea over in my mind ever since that night with Hood, when I'd had my epiphany that some people are nomads in life and that I wasn't one of them. Stability, though, didn't necessarily mean living in one town your whole life; there was nothing stable about going from job to job, or relationship to relationship, every few months.

But it wasn't only about stability versus chaos. There'd always been sides of my personality that I'd been afraid to act on—things that were sexy and daring and wild. What had held me back for years wasn't a fear that people might not approve; I'd been afraid they might not see those things in me if I tried to show them. And if nobody else saw them, maybe I'd have to admit that they'd never really been there. Maybe, instead of being everything I wanted to be, I could only be the one thing that everybody else had always expected.

Amy and Hood had been the first ones to see those other sides—to accept and encourage. And when they weren't around, South Beach itself had stepped in to receive me, without question, as whoever and whatever I presented myself as. But was that just a function of the environment we were in, or was it because I'd actually achieved something? I felt like I needed to take the person I'd grown into someplace bigger and see if the changes stuck.

Besides, I'd been sending out résumés in Miami for weeks now, without getting a single request for an interview. My savings were dwindling, and something needed to be done.

I started scanning online job boards for positions in New York, not going to bed at night until I'd e-mailed at least fifteen résumés. Within a month I had enough interview requests to justify investing in a plane ticket and asking Lara if I could camp out on her couch for two weeks. The night that I got my first official offer—as national director of marketing for an IT consulting firm—Ross and Lara treated me to dinner at Nobu in Tribeca to celebrate.

The next step was to find housing. Looking for an apartment in New York was a demoralizing experience—so demoralizing that there were moments when I almost reconsidered the whole thing. My deus ex machina materialized when Brent Carrigan—the only other person besides Lara and my parents who knew that the move was official—called to hear how my apartment hunt was going. "Where's your office going to be?" he asked.

"Maiden Lane," I answered.

"I live a block from there!" he exclaimed. "You should look in my building."

"Right," I said. "Like I can afford anything in *your* building."

"I think the studios start at two thousand a month," he said. "That's not so far out of your range. Plus you won't have to pay a broker's fee if I refer you."

Brent's building was a luxury high-rise located within easy walking distance of my new employer. The plush elegance of the lobby with its uniformed doormen, recessed lighting, and buttery leather sofas almost intimidated me after the railroad flats and dusty walk-ups I'd been looking at in outer Brooklyn.

The apartment itself was beautiful—an airy corner unit filled with marble and granite, windows and light. From its thirty-second-floor view, all of Manhattan lay spread before me. The view to the right was of the Brooklyn Bridge and the East River, and I liked the idea that, even though I was leaving South Beach, I'd still be able to see water every day. Two days later I brought my various checks over to the building and signed the lease.

"Who's more glamorous than I am?" I observed to Lara as I was leaving for the airport. "I have an apartment in South Beach and an apartment in Manhattan."

She laughed and hugged me. "I'll see you in a month," she said.

One month. In only one month, I was moving to New York.

TWENTY-SEVEN

My friends, naturally, knew that I had gone to New York to interview for jobs. I'd even called them between interviews to hash over details before heading for the next round. But I'd saved for my return the news that an offer had been made and accepted; I wanted to tell them in person.

I left a message for Kojo first, saying that I had something important to tell everybody as a group—something that I didn't want to have to repeat a bunch of times—and so I wasn't telling anybody until I got them all together. And, to give Kojo credit, he did call back within two hours. I asked him, and then Ricky and Mike in turn, to be at my apartment that night at around six o'clock, when Ricky got off work.

I made cocktails for everybody, and we took them into the living room, seating ourselves on the floor. Even after I'd filled my apartment with furniture, I noted, we'd never gotten out of the habit of sitting cross-legged in a circle on the floor. In anybody else's apartment, we sat on the sofa or in chairs—but coming to my place had always meant camping out.

There was a general pause after I broke the news, then an outburst of congratulations and hugs and questions. "Did you end up getting an offer at the place you told me about?" Kojo wanted to know. "The one where you thought the HR guy was gay?"

"That's the one," I admitted, as I sipped my vodka cranberry.

"How'd you know he was gay?" Mike asked.

"Because after the 'official' part of the interview, during the 'hey, let's chitchat like regular people' part, we were talking about South Beach and he made some passing reference to tricks." I grinned. "Straight guys don't 'trick,' you know."

"I knew they'd offer you the job," Kojo asserted. "You have fag-hag superpowers."

"Like Aquaman," Mike interjected. He scrunched his eyes shut, put his hands to his temples, and exclaimed, *"Fags, heed my call!"*

I laughed until my stomach hurt and my eyes were damp. "What am I going to do without you guys?" I asked, a little mournfully, although I'd told myself beforehand that this wasn't the time for tearful speeches—not yet.

"You won't have to live without us forever," Ricky said. "You'll be back— they always come back."

I leaned across to put my hand over his.

"No, sweetie," I said gently. "Not me."

Life began to move very quickly after that. There were so many arrangements to make, so many loose ends to tie up. I had to visit my leasing office to formally break my lease, call the utility companies, take out classified ads so my parents could sell my car after I'd left. That was my first truly wrenching moment of loss—when I realized I'd have to bid a final farewell to the craxi. Who would drive her after I was gone? And what would I do in those moments when it was all too much for me, if I didn't have a car to drive around in until I felt better?

I spent more time with my parents over those next few weeks, trying to have dinner with them almost every night. My mother planned to cook up a storm for the going-away party she'd insisted on throwing, and she had endless questions about my own food preferences and those of my friends.

"You're the best cook I know," I told her. "I'm sure whatever you make will be fine." I smiled mischievously, adding, "And in excessive quantities."

Kojo and Mike were always in and out of my apartment, dropping in randomly at odd hours. Mike came more frequently than Kojo, of course, but they were both old hands at the moving game and offered invaluable advice about how to pack and what to discard. "Just promise me you'll get Kojo to my parents' house on time Friday night," I pleaded with Mike. "It can't be that whole South Beach 'seven o'clock means eight thirty' rigmarole."

Ricky took it upon himself to plan my South Beach going-away party. I knew his heart was in the right place, but for the first few days after my announcement he didn't call me nearly as often as usual. I understood—I couldn't even imagine how I would feel if I were in his place. But going through all the scrapbooks and photo albums I'd accumulated over the years—where practically every photo or newspaper clipping included him as well—I wasn't about to let him go that easily. So I called constantly, with questions about everything from which of my mountainous archives of papers to discard, to random questions about New York (Ricky's old stomping grounds). We both knew what the subtext was to these conversations: *Just checking in; just making sure you're still with me.*

But that was only the first few days. By the time we were down to two weeks and counting before my departure, Ricky was at my apartment and we were looking through stacks of photos. I found an early one of the two of us, taken at the Chaka Khan show at Glam Slam.

"I know I should say something about how young we look," I said. "But I think we still look just as young, and even more fabulous."

"Well, you had that awful eighties hair back then," he replied, and we laughed.

"I know I've said it before," I said softly, "but I can't even picture what my life would have been like these last few years without you."

"I couldn't have asked for a better sidekick," he replied, and smiled playfully as I smacked him for calling me a *sidekick*. Then he hugged me. "I couldn't have gotten as far as I have if it weren't for you—I knew it the minute I saw you walking across that room in KGB."

I squeezed him back hard. "I guess some things are meant to be," I said, pressing my cheek against his shoulder.

I arrived at my parents' house early on the night of my going-away party. The house smelled like my mother's cooking, like family dinners and childhood birthday parties and the horrible fights I'd occasionally had with my parents as a teenager over our shared meals. I'd felt so alienated from them for so many years. Maybe, I reflected, it was because you could end up resenting people in direct proportion to how badly you want to make them happy.

My mother had invited all of my cousins and aunts and uncles. I watched as she tried to make sense of a somewhat subdued version of Mike and Kojo's usual antics, while my father bemusedly tried to find common ground with Ricky. I took the three of them through the house, showing them my old bedroom and framed photos from my childhood. "I love that Kojo," my mother said at one point, and I sighed—because Kojo, typically, had pulled me aside not five minutes earlier to confide anxiously that he thought my mother hated him.

I stacked the gifts I'd received in the room with my bags and changed into the dress I planned to wear to the going-away party at Ricky's, which would later move to Opium Garden in the old Amnesia space. The dress was a long, skintight, leopard-printed sheath.

My mother raised an eyebrow when I re-emerged but didn't comment. Instead she hugged me tightly. "I can't believe you're moving away," she said with tears in her eyes—and I had to give her credit for having made it dry-eyed through the last month. "I want you to know how proud your father and I are of you."

I was surprised at the tears that sprang into my own eyes. "Thank you," I murmured.

"Go." She smiled as she pushed me away to dab at her face. "Just make sure you're here by seven thirty tomorrow to leave for the airport—we should leave early in case there's a problem with the car or an accident on the highway, or—"

"Oy, mom, I *know*," I interrupted, and we both laughed. "I'll be here in plenty of time," I told her. "Don't worry about me."

The party at Ricky's apartment was small. He'd invested in lots of liquor and a few trays of hors d'oeuvres and crudités, and invited a select group—mostly closer friends and some people from the WOMB. Isabella and Finn came, arriving shortly after Merle and Danny. Mike, who'd disappeared after leaving my parents' house, entered dramatically and poured a Baggie full of white powder into a mound on Ricky's coffee table.

"For Mrs. Jones," he announced, obviously quite pleased with himself.

I glanced over at Kojo; surprisingly, though, he didn't go near the coffee table all night. I was encouraged briefly—until I realized that coke wasn't Kojo's drug of choice, and, even if it were, Kojo now only wanted to do his drugs alone, or with strangers in a bathhouse. Mike, of course, had understood that.

A lot of thought had gone into the songs that were selected to play on Ricky's stereo. I smiled warmly when Odyssey's "Native New Yorker" came on. *You're no tramp, but you're no lady . . . ,* Ricky sang.

"Fuck you," I objected. "I'm a delicate fucking flower."

Ricky shook his head sadly. "You already sound like a New York City girl," he observed, and I kissed his cheek noisily.

Kojo's contribution was "Champagne Supernova" by Oasis, and he insisted on dancing with me. "With all the dancing and meaningful songs," I observed, "it feels like prom."

"I didn't go to my prom," Kojo said. "I couldn't find a beard."

"I didn't either." I laughed. "I couldn't find a date."

I was good and high by the time the party moved over to Opium at midnight. Tony Guerra was promoting there these days, and it was a total scene—which was exactly what I'd been hoping for. Adrina and Adam were there in all their beautiful blond glory. Michael Tronn and Kevin Crawford showed up, and the owners of Lola. David Hart Lynch came to represent the *Wire*, Manny was there for the *Journal*, and Cubby took my picture for the write-up in his column for the *Sunpost*. "Don't take any digs at me," I warned him mock-sternly. "I won't be here to defend myself."

Even Genghis appeared briefly, startlingly handsome as ever in a white crewneck tee and perfectly fitted, dark-olive pants. "I can't believe you're leaving." He kissed me on the cheek. "You've come such a long way."

"You should know," I replied. "You were the first person on South Beach who told me I was sexy." Then I laughed and blushed as he said suggestively, "I wasn't the last, though—right?"

I drank hard and danced even harder, whirling from one pair of arms to another until I couldn't keep track anymore of who was who. I wanted everything around me to meld into a haze of light and music and warm faces, something I could remember as a single snapshot of what South Beach—at its best—had been for me. A song by Celia Cruz came on and Ricky spun me onto the dance floor.

Ella tiene fuego
Cuando mueve las caderas

"I'll always be the person who taught you how to dance salsa," Ricky said proudly.

"Don't give yourself too much credit," I responded drily. "I *did* live with a Cuban man for nearly four years, you know."

"He didn't know how to dance." Ricky expertly twirled me out, then pulled me back in. "I can tell by what you called 'dancing' when I found you."

"My Pygmalion," I said with a sigh, and threw my arms affectionately around his neck.

People started trickling out sometime around three o'clock, but Ricky, Kojo, Mike, and I closed the place. Then we piled into separate cars—the three of them in Kojo's and me in mine—and drove to the beach to watch the sunrise.

The four of us were silent as we sat together on the sand. We knew that we would keep in touch and talk on the phone and still be each other's best friends, but it would never really be the same. We'd been a family, and none of us would ever have a group—a small community within the island of a small community—quite like this again. I rested my head on Ricky's shoulder. The rising sun turned the water into a cauldron of dancing gold coins, which eventually settled into a deep, placid blue.

Finally I stood up, dusting the sand from my dress. "I should head home," I said. "I still have to change before I go to the airport."

"Go like that," Ricky suggested, tossing his head theatrically. "Let New York know who you are."

Kojo handed me a gift-wrapped CD, and I unwrapped it to find the soundtrack from *Working Girl*. "The first day of your new job," Kojo instructed, "as soon as you get settled in, call Mike and me and put us on speaker—and play the song 'New Jerusalem' from your desk."

I nodded as I placed it in my handbag, not trusting myself to speak for a moment. Then I hugged Mike. "I'm going to miss you guys so much." My throat felt strained, and I heard Mike sniffle. "I don't know how I'll get through my everyday life without you in it."

"You won't have to," Mike answered. "I'll call you every five minutes." And I laughed because I knew he would.

Then it was Kojo's turn. "I love you," I said, as I embraced him.

"And I love your boobs." We both chuckled, but I pulled him closer and said in a quiet voice, "Take care of yourself."

Kojo's only answer was to hug me tighter.

Saying good-bye to Ricky was the hardest part. My eyes threatened to overflow as he said, "Here, darling, to remember it all by," and gave me a small photo album filled with pictures we'd taken over the years—a montage of beads and boas, of garish getups and ragtag revelries where we'd danced until dawn (or decorum) had sent us home. He'd even included a shot of John Hood and me—the two of us together at some long-ago party, held in some long-ago club that no longer existed. I remembered so well that wide, giddy grin I'd always felt in Hood's presence, but I'd never seen a picture of it until now. *Ah,* I thought, *so this is what it looked like to feel that way.*

I was touched by Ricky's thoughtfulness. The water and sand sparkled blurrily before my eyes as I clung to him.

"Scarecrow," I murmured huskily, "I think I'll miss you most of all."

The sun had climbed high enough to take on the sweet, amber tint of autumn in South Beach. I hugged each of them again, and they piled into Kojo's car. Then I put on my sunglasses and got into my own car, turning it in the direction of the causeway.

EPILOGUE
New York City Girl

They say you have to live in New York for at least five years before you can consider yourself a New Yorker. It's April now, and this November will mark my official five-year anniversary. As always, the beginning of springtime in New York knocks me out. One day the trees are stunted and barren from the cold of winter, and the next there's the thinnest possible haze of green all over the city—and, one day after that, everything bursts into such a riotous explosion of leaves and flowers, you wonder how it's possible that it was all so bleak only a day before.

New York gears up in the spring, at just about the same time that South Beach is winding down for the end of Season. But I won't be spending today in either New York or South Beach. Today I'm driving to Pennsylvania.

"Do you have everything you need?" Gregory asks, as I head out the door. "Cell phone, map, credit cards—everything?"

My family and all of my closer friends have met Gregory by now. But New York can be a difficult town to bring everybody together in, and there are a handful of coworkers and acquaintances who haven't yet received an introduction. *What's he like?* they ask me.

There's probably nothing more difficult than describing the man you love, because nothing sounds more banal to others than the gushing descriptions of a lover. *The bluest eyes . . . such a good heart . . . always remembers . . . laugh every day . . .*

"The first thing he does every morning is smile," I told one work friend, a little shyly, feeling on the one hand that I was revealing something silly or nondescriptive, and on the other that I had gotten to the real substance of things. Because it's true—the first thing Gregory does every morning is smile. I usually wake up before he does, and I'll rub his shoulder or kiss his forehead lightly. As soon as he feels my hand, before his eyes are even open or he's fully

311

conscious, he smiles—a sleepy, happy grin. Every single morning. And it breaks my heart every time.

"I have everything," I tell Gregory, and kiss him good-bye. "I'll call you when I'm driving back."

The forward crawl of life pushes us irrevocably from the past into the future. But some memories linger more stubbornly than others, insisting on being laid to rest. So today I'm driving into Pennsylvania, to visit John Hood.

My first year in New York was unquestionably the hardest. I'd lost my job in the wake of September 11—my company had primarily serviced the large financial institutions in Manhattan's financial district and, with so many of them departing, staff cuts had to be made.

Fortunately, I'd learned the hard way on South Beach how to make something from nothing. I knew how to hunt down freelance work—where to find it, how to pitch it, and how to scrounge out some kind of existence from it. One especially rough month, Kojo even loaned me money to cover my rent. He had moved to L.A. by then, having acknowledged that his problem with drugs was, indeed, a problem—one that could best be remedied by moving away from the South Beach party scene. Mike was skeptical about the efficacy of this decision. "It's not like there aren't drugs and bathhouses in L.A.," he noted. Mike was himself planning a move to L.A. in search of work, nothing having panned out for him on South Beach. Kojo was so far gone by this time, though, that Mike didn't have high hopes of seeing much of him.

Ricky was the only one of us who remained on the Beach. He was of the opinion that I should move back.

"I told you I'm not coming back," I replied impatiently. "At least, I'm not coming back with my tail between my legs because I couldn't make it here."

Besides, I didn't know what there was to go back to. The entire country was in full-on recession mode, and Miami's few industries were hit hard. Tourism was South Beach's bread and butter, but now people were nervous about terrorism and thus flying less frequently. And, in the aftermath of Chris

Paciello, the celebrities visiting South Beach were of the B-and-C-list variety. While I didn't believe the predictions of those who said South Beach was dead (they'd been predicting the death of the Beach since at least my grandmother's day), I couldn't see how my options there would be better than they'd been when I moved.

It was in the midst of my unemployment phase that Lara and Ross got married. I brought Ricky as my date, having just broken up with a boyfriend who had "accidentally" impregnated his ex-girlfriend while living with me rent-free in my apartment (truly, my life was like a country-western song in those days).

Gregory was one of Ross's groomsmen, a best friend from college. I had met him on a handful of occasions, always struck by his intelligence and humor. We had talked for hours at the engagement party, about Peggy Lee and black-and-white movies and a million other things. He was one of the funniest people I'd ever met—funny in a way that was loud and boyish and unabashed, but dead-on wicked at the same time.

"You look staggeringly beautiful tonight," he told me, as I hovered around Lara in my crimson bridesmaid dress.

I laughed and blushed, saying, "You did see the bride, right?" Then the band struck up "Lady Marmalade," and Ricky tugged me onto the dance floor.

Gregory called a month later with the suggestion that we get together sometime for drinks or a movie. Sitting with him in a Moroccan-themed lounge on the Lower East Side, I decided that he reminded me of Kojo, in a way, with his razor-sharp humor that nevertheless never offended, and of Mike, with his generosity and general air of boyishness. He reminded me of Brent Carrigan, with his encyclopedic knowledge of all things theater and film. He even reminded me of Ricky, with his love of the dramatic and outrageous.

I think I wanted him to be my entire group of friends rolled up into one person, and I was very determined that we would be good friends. I needed an available-every-day best friend in New York. Lara was newly married and, although Brent and I spent a great deal of time in and out of each other's apartments, he was on the road half the time with plays and projects.

Soon Gregory and I were talking on the phone four or five times a day. It was Gregory who got the first phone call when I finally found a job at *Rolling Stone*, with the title of senior event marketing manager—responsible for producing *Rolling Stone*'s concerts and throwing its parties.

We saw each other at least once or twice a week, and I soon became as comfortable in his apartment as I was in my own. We spent long hours talking about our past and present exploits. Gregory was an editor at a high-profile entertainment industry magazine, but he had his own colorful past. He'd spent a year in his twenties touring Europe with a funk band—scoring them everything from hookers to heroin in his capacity as roadie. He'd been writing a screenplay on and off for years, and I told him about the poetry and short stories I wrote in my own free time.

There were the occasional club nights that he accompanied me to. I had intended to put the club scene behind me once I moved to New York, but there were a surprising number of South Beach/New York overlaps that connected me to it, at least marginally. Kevin Crawford, for example, was once again living in New York, and Michael Tronn was also up here for a time. There were New York promoters who were friends of South Beach promoters, and I found—with no particular intention on my part—that I was once again coming home to party invitations in the mail.

Gregory wasn't really a club guy, but his personality was such that he was equally comfortable in any setting—from quiet dinners with the bookish types I'd befriended to four a.m. revelries in the VIP rooms of Chelsea or meatpacking district clubs. I still talked to Ricky and Mike almost every day, and to Kojo every couple of weeks when he resurfaced after a bender, but Gregory had become my daily confidant. I remember the night when I told him the whole, long story of John Hood—one of those nights at his apartment when we killed a bottle of wine and talked until the wee hours. The funny thing was that, by the time I got halfway through the story, I wasn't thinking much about Hood anymore; I was thinking that I'd never in my life seen anything as compassionate as Gregory's eyes. Nobody had ever been compassionate to me on the subject of Hood. Everybody had always treated my relationship with him as some sort of affliction that needed to be overcome. Nobody had ever looked at me like Gregory did, with eyes that said, *I know; I understand.*

Beneath that, his eyes also held a twinkle. *There are very few real tragedies in life*, the twinkle said. *There will always be things for us to laugh about.*

And it was Gregory who I went to on that day, that awful day, when Kojo called to say he had good news and bad news. The good news was that he was, finally, in a recovery program. He'd stuck with it for a month so far and believed that he was in for good.

I was just breathing a sigh of relief after years of worrying about Kojo when he gave me the bad news: he was HIV positive.

I don't remember exactly what I said—although Kojo assures me now that it was something appropriately sensitive and supportive—because all I could think was, *Not Kojo; please not Kojo. Kojo can't die.*

"I'm healthy," Kojo said, as if reading my mind. "I've already started on meds and my T-cell count is high, and there's no reason why I can't live a long and healthy life." He paused. "It probably *saved* my life, in a way."

I was silent for a long moment. "I always turned a blind eye," I finally said, "because I didn't want to know. But if you ever do anything again that jeopardizes your health, you and I are done." My voice shook. "I *mean* it, Kojo. I can't watch you hurt yourself anymore."

"You won't have to," Kojo promised. And, from that day to this, Kojo has been as good as his word.

It was around this time that I decided to write to John Hood. I had run into Will several months earlier at the Deuce during a brief trip back home, and he'd filled me in on the major events in Hood's life since I'd left the Beach. Hood had actually departed soon after I had, pursued by troubles that had made it imperative for him to get lost for a while—quick. He'd spun through New York and then into Pennsylvania. One day, hungry for a fix and down to almost no money, he'd walked into a bank in Pennsylvania hill country and stuck a gun in the teller's face. He'd been caught almost immediately and was sentenced to three and a half to ten years in prison.

Will told me that Hood had written to him often, asking for my address or a way of getting in touch with me. "I know it would mean a lot to him if you wrote."

I hesitated. "I'm trying to make a new life for myself in New York," I finally said. "It's one thing to be the girl who has an ex-boyfriend in prison. It's another thing to be the girl who has an ex-boyfriend in prison—*who she writes to*."

Will had laughed, saying, "I'll e-mail you his address. You do whatever you think is right."

It took me months to get anything on paper. But, in the aftermath of Kojo's diagnosis, I couldn't help feeling that there were some people who—in whatever capacity—you don't want to lose altogether. *Dear Hood*, I wrote tentatively one day. By this time, I hadn't seen or spoken to him in almost three years. *This will probably seem inappropriately out-of-the-blue, but Will recently told me . . .*

I got a reply only a week later. *Great, great day in the mailbag*, it began. *Two smiling postcards from Prince Edward Island, a charming little watercolor card from Miami, and—be still my crooked heart—a dispatch from a dame I thought forever left back over a burned bridge. I pinch myself. Spectacular.*

And so our correspondence began. The letters were generally light and amusing; Hood read the *New Yorker* and the *New York Times* avidly in prison, and was always full of questions about whether I'd read this or that book, or gone to see a particular art exhibit or concert. "Hood's letters make me feel like I'm not getting enough out of New York," I told Ricky over the phone once—who of course sighed in dismay that, even now, Hood wasn't out of our lives.

It became easy enough, as the months went on, to convince myself that Hood was as cheerful and productive with his writing in prison as could be expected; that any thorny questions about *us*, at least in my own mind, had been rendered irrelevant by time and circumstances, and I consciously avoided the potential pitfalls inherent in any topic that might become too personal. Then one day, in a missive full of references to Central Park and a New York club called KGB, Hood dropped in one additional line: *Apropos of something, check out the article in this week's* New Yorker *about the poet John Clare—then tell me if I've completely sapped out.*

I purchased the *New Yorker* the next day, bringing it home and flipping to the article in question. There was an excerpt on the facing page from a poem titled "I am!":

I am! yet what I am none cares or knows,
My friends forsake me like a memory lost;
I am the self-consumer of my woes,
They rise and vanish in oblivious host,
Like shades in love and death's oblivion lost;
And yet I am! and live with shadows tost

Into the nothingness of scorn and noise,
Into the living sea of waking dreams,
Where there is neither sense of life nor joys,
But the vast shipwreck of my life's esteems,
And e'en the dearest—that I loved the best—
Are strange—nay, rather stranger than the rest.

I'd always taken pride in the fact that I had never shed a single tear over John Hood. But, reading that poem, I buried my face in a sofa cushion and cried—cried for Hood, for all of us.

It was only a few weeks later that Gregory and I were at Chelsea Piers having cocktails one Sunday afternoon, and he told me about a date he'd gone on the previous night. The date had gone well, he'd said—and the word "serious" even made it into the conversation.

Gregory and I dated other people, of course, and I always recounted for him my adventures and misadventures on the New York singles scene with great aplomb. He, however, was more reticent with the details of his own love life, so to hear him discuss somebody in this way was something of a shock.

I dismissed my initial reaction as the obvious response to what I'd secretly dreaded for the past three years—the inevitable day when Gregory would find a girlfriend, who would undoubtedly put a quick end to our friendship. I think my shock must have shown, because I remember Gregory treating me very gently for the rest of the afternoon, kissing me more solicitously on the cheek than usual when he put me in a cab home.

We didn't talk much over the next few weeks. I didn't know who this girl was, but I didn't want to hear any more about her. I developed insomnia, and although I was tired all day at work and couldn't concentrate, my extreme exhaustion did nothing to help me sleep at night. I agonized over the knowledge that I was such a bad person, I couldn't bring myself to be happy about my friend's possible happiness.

The tension finally broke one Friday night nearly a month later, when I called Lara and announced tearfully, "I love Gregory; I love him like you love Ross. I don't know what to do."

Lara laughed. "Well, the first part is the smartest thing you've ever said," she told me, "and the second part is the dumbest." When I was silent, she added, "Go tell him!"

"But what if it's too late?" I asked. "There's this other girl now who he thinks he might be 'serious' about."

"Trust me," Lara responded. "It's not too late."

I spent the rest of that night pacing my apartment and smoking, and called Gregory as early the next morning as was decent. I couldn't bring myself to go over to his apartment and confront him, afraid to look him in the face if his answer wasn't the one I wanted to hear. "I have to talk to you," I began awkwardly. "I . . . I think that I have . . . feelings for you . . . that are—" I paused. "That are more than friendship. And it's okay," I rushed on, "if you don't feel the same way, because—"

"Yes," Gregory interrupted me. "I do. I always have."

"Really?" I laughed, giddy with the sudden release of a month's worth of anxiety.

Gregory laughed too. "Would you get over here?"

I grabbed a cab over to his apartment, and the first thing he did when he opened the door was kiss me. I was thinking what a great kiss it was, one of the best ever—not for any particular thing that it was or wasn't, but because it was Gregory, and I loved him.

We sat on his couch and talked and laughed, not quite sure what to do with ourselves in our new condition. And there were suddenly so many things to talk about—about *this* and about us, and what our friends would say.

"It could be awkward," I observed, "if things don't work out—because of the whole Lara and Ross connection."

"I've thought about that," Gregory replied, with happy mock gravity. "There's only one solution."

"What's that?"

"We'll have to be madly in love with each other for the rest of our lives."

I beamed even as I rolled my eyes. "Oy," I said. "Who's writing your dialogue these days—Hallmark?"

We understood each other so well. He knew I was really saying, *I'm so happy right now, it's almost embarrassing; I can only deal with it through humor.* And when he gave me a good-natured shove as a reward for my sarcasm before kissing me again, I knew that he was saying, *Yeah, it's a line—but I meant it.*

It's April now, as I head out of New York in my rental car. It's been a long time since I've had the feel of a car in my hands—window rolled down, tunes cranked up, lit cigarette dangling casually out the side. A song by ELO comes on and I sing along with the radio. *You'll be the way you were before . . . when you don't want me anymore . . .*

I had promised Hood a visit a long time ago, but there never seemed to be a right time. The one thing I've learned living on islands—whether the island of South Beach or the island of Manhattan—is that any voyage that takes you over a bridge starts to feel as remote and improbable as scouring the Himalayas in search of Shangri-la.

But Hood just got turned down for parole. He's understandably despondent, and when he renewed the request for a visit, it seemed wrong to turn him down. Besides, if I'm honest with myself, I have to admit that I want to see him, too.

So I follow New York's highways into New Jersey's, and then down into Pennsylvania. I know that I'm getting close as the landscape shifts subtly. Prisons are always built in ugly places—the places where nobody would live voluntarily. The scenery is flat in some spots and hilly in others, but bleary and brown in all directions. I think of the opening lines of T. S. Eliot's poem "The Wasteland": *April is the cruellest month, breeding / lilacs out of the dead land, mixing / memory and desire . . .*

Eventually, I pull up to a huge parking lot enclosed by bars and monitored by prison guards and cameras. I cross the street and am buzzed through bulletproof glass doors into a newish-looking gray industrial building. I find myself in a large, bone white waiting area, where I'm instructed to stow my purse in a row of lockers off to the side. Then I'm further instructed to remove my shoes, and a guard comes to scan me and pat me down.

After that I'm shown to a metal detector, which I pass through into a small vestibule where the palms of my hands are scanned and I'm patted down again. I officially sign in, and I look through more bulletproof glass to where I finally see Hood, in the visitors' room, signing in as well.

A steel door buzzes open and Hood and I are standing in front of each other for the first time in almost five years. *He looks so much the same*, I think, surprised at the rush of emotion I feel as I hug him. The cheap synthetics he's wearing feel alien in my arms, but my body remembers the height and warmth of his body. My hand reflexively finds the hair at the nape of his neck, where I used to bury my fingers when we kissed. I pull away, suddenly self-conscious.

Hood smiles—that familiar, small tightening of his lips meant to indicate a grin. It's odd to see him without a hat. He's clad in a brown prison uniform and burgundy slip-on shoes of some kind. Hood always knew how to wear his clothes; even in the prison uniform, there's something about the way he has it arranged just so that almost succeeds in making it look like a real outfit.

We seat ourselves in facing chairs from among the rows of pleather-and-wood chairs bolted to the floor, angling away from the vending machines and wall-mounted television sets that have attracted most of the crowds. The din in the room is loud, as children and wives reunite with the men they've come to visit. It reminds me a bit of our old nightclub days, when we had to shout over the music and the masses to be heard. But our seats are no longer plush velvet banquettes; these seats are like nothing so much as the rows of seats in a bus station or airport terminal. Hood and I face each other like two acquaintances meeting by chance, our tickets marked for different destinations.

The conversation is hard at first, with awkward starts and stops. Our letters flow so naturally—two writers playing out ideas on a page. Nothing about this meeting feels natural, though, and I find myself at a loss for words.

"Your hair is longer," Hood finally says. It is—it's much longer than it was in the South Beach days. I've let it grow halfway down my back in untamed curls. It's an innocuous observation, in a way, but a world of subtext belies it: It takes time to grow hair this long; a person's whole life could change in that much time.

I tell Hood that I work for a rock 'n' roll magazine now, and so I have rock 'n' roll hair. He smiles again. "You like shilling for Jann Wenner?" he asks, referring to the founder and publisher of *Rolling Stone*. I reply with a vague, "It's a gig," not wanting to tell him how much I love my life, how wild and interesting of a place I'm finding the outside world to be.

But the ice is broken and Hood is off. The manic speed of his conversation is different from what it used to be. Before, it was fueled by drug binges and the nonstop stimulation of clubs. Now, I can tell, he's just desperate for someone to talk to—someone, anyone, who isn't a part of here.

Hood tells me about a screenplay he's working on, called *Fat Black*, and a novel entitled *A Beach Called South*. There's also a collection of short stories named *Scumbag*. I laugh at that one. "I'm assuming it's autobiographical?"

Hood laughs too. "Of course!"

It's hard for me to pay attention at times while Hood speaks. I keep thinking about all the improbable places where my relationship with this man has led me. I had been reluctant, long ago, to let Hood too far into my life, afraid that doing so would eventually lead me someplace like here. Yet here I am anyway. I'm searching for something to say when Hood offers, in an uncertain tone I've never heard from him, "I worry sometimes that prison has taken something from me. I wonder if I'll still have a place where conversation and cool and art and knowing are at a premium when I get sprung."

On some level, I've always thought of Hood and South Beach as a single entity. I think about all the times people have predicted the death of the Beach over the decades: in the '20s, after an unnamed hurricane wiped out most of Miami Beach and led to the construction of the Art Deco buildings in the '30s, which are still the Beach's pride and joy; in the '60s, when the studio stars like Elizabeth Taylor left and in the '80s, when *Miami Vice* left; in the '90s, when

Versace was shot and Chris Paciello was arrested; and, most recently, in the aftermath of 9/11.

Yet South Beach, like the best of its denizens, always reinvents itself. There are things that no economic vagaries or the waning of trends can take from it—the alchemy of white sands, turquoise waters, and dazzling tropical flowers. I remember something I once heard a film critic say to explain Audrey Hepburn's imperishable charm: *God came down and kissed her on the cheek.*

"You're the most talented person I've ever known," I tell Hood truthfully. "Nothing can take that from you. And anybody who doesn't get that—fuck 'em." I stick my tongue out slightly, conscious as ever how much Hood hates to hear me swear.

"So this cat makes you happy?" he asks, shifting the subject away from himself, and I'm momentarily caught off guard. I've written to him about Gregory, of course, but wasn't sure if or how he would bring it up. I can't find the right words at first, but I know I'm smiling because Hood says, "Ah—the dame is wearing a Mona Lisa smile."

My grin widens and I look down at the floor. "He makes me very happy," I say.

"He'd better." Hood manages a scowl—a caricature of the old South Beach Hood, who was himself a caricature of some long-ago, black-and-white-movie antihero. "He doesn't want to have to answer to the Hood."

"I think you'd like him, actually," I respond, for lack of anything better to say.

"I'm sure we'd get along famously," Hood replies. I can't help blushing when he adds, "After all, we do have one significantly uncommon thing in common."

Technically, I can stay today almost as long as I want. But I've fixed two hours for the visit, knowing how long the drive back will be. In only a few minutes my two hours will be up. I'm anxious, suddenly, with the awareness of time rushing away from me.

There are things I still want to say—things that, I realize now, I came here to tell Hood. I wonder if he's also struggling with the might-haves and could-haves that seem to make up more of our relationship than the things that actually happened, if there are things he, too, had finally planned to tell me. I find myself, after all these years, knowing as little about what Hood thinks or feels as I ever did.

I loved you, I think about telling him. *I see you everywhere in the streets of New York. Sometimes I think about what we could have been to each other.* . . .

My throat is heavy as I press him into a hug. "Take care of yourself," I whisper into his shoulder, giving him the one good-bye kiss the prison rules allow. I release him, my hand remaining in his for a moment.

"Come back sometime." His eyes smile into mine as he squeezes my hand.

"Sometime," I echo, also smiling. I return the pressure of his hand before letting go.

I cross the room and the guard buzzes me through the door, which slams shut behind me with a loud, steely clang. I pause on the other side of it, breathing the outside air. Then I claim my purse and keys and walk to the parking lot, my eyes searching the twilight for the unfamiliar shape of the rental car that will drive me home.

ACKNOWLEDGMENTS

It is with enormous gratitude that I thank the following people for all of their contributions and efforts on behalf of this novel.

Agent extraordinaire, Alan Nevins of The Firm, who firmly believed in this book while it was still only half a manuscript. I also thank Kevin and Julie Yorn for having made the introduction.

My editor, Patrick Price. It was my modest hope while writing this to someday have an editor. To have ended up with the best of all possible editors—one whose genius improved the final version so greatly that I can't believe it's the same book—was a stroke of luck I could never have foreseen. I also thank Assistant Editor Emily Westlake, whose insights, enthusiasm, and endless patience carried me through some of my worst moments of self-doubt.

Bruce Mason, the freelance literary publicist who defies all stereotypes of freelance publicists with his dedication, cheerful hard work, exceptional talent, and general humanity. Most important, Bruce has always been a friend first and a publicist second, which makes him worth a price above rubies.

Andrea and Steve Kline, the best and truest of friends, who pulled off the extraordinary double feat of bringing my agent and my fiancé into my life—and that's just the tip of the friendship iceberg. I'm still working out mathematically exactly how long I'll have to live to have a shot at repaying you.

Richard Jay-Alexander, who read every page of the manuscript as it was being written, did me the incredible honor of loving it almost more than I did, and helped me find my voice, my characters, and my courage over more angst-ridden midnight conversations than I'm sure either of us can remember.

Without the many years of unswerving friendship and support of Tony Miros, there wouldn't have been a book to write in the first place. Tony also proved an inexhaustible trove of names, dates, and descriptions, and it was to him that I turned whenever my own memory was in doubt. And I certainly never could have gotten through the writing process with my sanity intact without the great wisdom and understanding of Digby Leibovitz, the most good-hearted soul I know.

To the first and best of my writing mentors, Sam Faith, I am indebted for more than I can express here—particularly the single best piece of advice on writing I've ever received: "Go back and wring out the extra words like water from a sponge."

Since unpublished writers would starve without "real" jobs, I am enormously fortunate to have received early in my marketing career the mentoring of Kristen Routh Silberman, one of the savviest marketing gurus I've ever known. Kristen's brought her general brilliance to bear on this book more than a few times, and I couldn't have gotten even close to here without her. I also thank my other favorite marketing genius, Claudia Strauss, who has contributed more good book advice and gainful employment than I would have dared ask for. And much appreciation goes to Jill Rudnick, who has gone above and beyond to keep me in paychecks since my move to New York.

I am grateful to David Hauslib, of Jossip.com, who was an early and enthusiastic supporter of this book, and without whose support I might still be toiling in obscurity. I am also deeply grateful to the following friends—the book's untiring cheering section—without whom I definitely wouldn't have kept going: Kevin Crawford, Claudia DiRomualdo, Kim Falconer, Jerry Farrell, Lee Floersch, Michael Gitter, Keli Goff, Steve Greco, Greg Hill, Janet Jorgulesco, David Juskow, Jim Kiick, Alan Klein, Andrew Kole, Anise Labrum, Lea Melone, Tom Nolan, Matt Olivas, Eugene Patron,

Kate Rockland, Gina Schramm, Peri Stedman, and Michael Tronn.

Finally, I thank South Beach—the places and people who formed the richest source material a writer was ever blessed with. I can truly say that I was so inspired by South Beach that I wanted to write a book, and not the other way around.

ABOUT THE AUTHOR

A fourth-generation Miami Beach native (rare in a town where people occasionally die, but nobody seems to be born), Gwen moved to South Beach in 1997 and contributed feature articles to *Miamigo* magazine and the *South Beach News*. She also coproduced and cohosted South Beach's *Live With Mr. Nightlife* radio show on WOMB from 1998 to 1999. Gwen currently lives and works in Manhattan, most recently working as special projects manager at Wenner Media, publisher of *Rolling Stone* and *Us Weekly*. *Diary of a South Beach Party Girl* is her first novel.